Christmas is a time for giving, but once the tree is trimmed and the presents are wrapped, take time to give yourself the gift of these magical romances in

All I Want For
Christmas...

Roses for Christmas by Betty Neels

Once Burned by Margaret Way

A Suitable Husband by Jessica Steele

D0784539

Betty Neels spent her childhood and youth in Devonshire before training as a nurse and midwife. She was an army nursing sister during the war, married a Dutchman, and subsequently lived in Holland for fourteen years. Betty started to write on retirement from nursing, incited by a lady in a library bemoaning the lack of romantic novels. Betty Neels has sold over 35 million copies of her books, worldwide.

Margaret Way takes great pleasure in her work and works hard at her pleasure. She enjoys tearing off to the beach with her family at weekends, loves haunting galleries and auctions and is completely given over to champagne 'for every possible joyous occasion'. She was born and educated in the river city of Brisbane, Australia, and now lives within sight and sound of beautiful Moreton Bay.

Jessica Steele lives in a friendly Worcestershire village with her super husband, Peter. They are owned by a gorgeous Staffordshire bull terrier called Florence, who is boisterous and manic, but also adorable. It was Peter who first prompted Jessica to try writing, and after the first rejection, encouraged her to keep on trying. Her thanks go to Peter for his help and encouragement.

BETTY NEELS

MARGARET WAY

JESSICA STEELE

All I Want For
Christmas...

MILLS & BOON®

DID YOU PURCHASE THIS BOOK WITHOUT A COVER?
If you did, you should be aware it is **stolen property** as it was
reported *unsold and destroyed* by a retailer. Neither the author nor
the publisher has received any payment for this book.

*All the characters in this book have no existence outside the imagination
of the author, and have no relation whatsoever to anyone bearing the
same name or names. They are not even distantly inspired by any
individual known or unknown to the author, and all the incidents are
pure invention.*

*All Rights Reserved including the right of reproduction in whole or in part
in any form. This edition is published by arrangement with Harlequin
Enterprises II B.V. The text of this publication or any part thereof may not
be reproduced or transmitted in any form or by any means, electronic or
mechanical, including photocopying, recording, storage in an
information retrieval system, or otherwise, without the written
permission of the publisher.*

*This book is sold subject to the condition that it shall not, by way of trade
or otherwise, be lent, resold, hired out or otherwise circulated without the
prior consent of the publisher in any form of binding or cover other than
that in which it is published and without a similar condition including this
condition being imposed on the subsequent purchaser.*

*MILLS & BOON and MILLS & BOON with the Rose Device
are registered trademarks of the publisher.*

*First published in Great Britain 2005
Harlequin Mills & Boon Limited,
Eton House, 18-24 Paradise Road, Richmond, Surrey, TW9 1SR*

ALL I WANT FOR CHRISTMAS…
© Harlequin Enterprises II B.V., 2005

Roses for Christmas, Once Burned and *A Suitable Husband*
were first published in Great Britain by
Harlequin Mills & Boon Limited in separate, single volumes.

Roses for Christmas © Betty Neels 1975
Once Burned © Margaret Way 1995
A Suitable Husband © Jessica Steele 2001

ISBN 0 263 84946 5

059-1005

*Printed and bound in Spain
by Litografia Rosés S.A., Barcelona*

ROSES FOR CHRISTMAS

by

Betty Neels

by La ...   Barcelona

CHAPTER ONE

THE LOFT WAS warm, dusty and redolent of apples; the autumn sunshine peeping through its one dusty window tinted the odds and ends hanging on the walls with golden light, so that the strings of onions, cast-off skates, old raincoats, lengths of rope, worn-out leather straps and an old hat or two had acquired a gilded patina. Most of the bare floor was taken up with orderly rows of apples, arranged according to their kind, but there was still space enough left for the girl sitting in the centre, a half-eaten apple in one hand, the other buried in the old hat box beside her. She was a pretty girl, with light brown hair and large hazel eyes, extravagantly lashed and heavily browed, and with a straight nose above a generous, nicely curved mouth. She was wearing slacks and a thick, shabby sweater, and her hair, tied back none too tidily, hung down her back almost to her waist.

She bit into her apple and then bent over the box, and its occupant, a cat of plebeian appearance, paused in her round-the-clock washing of four kittens to lick the hand instead. The girl smiled and took another bite of apple, then turned to look behind her, to where a ladder led down to the disused stable below. She knew the footsteps climbing it and sighed to herself; holidays were lovely after the bustle and orderly precision of the ward in the big Edinburgh hospital where she was a Sister; the cosy homeliness of the manse where her parents and five brothers and sisters lived in the tiny village on the north-ernmost coast of Scotland, was bliss, it was only a pity that on this particular week's holiday, both her elder brothers, James and Donald, should be away from home, leaving Henry, the youngest and only eight years old, recovering from chickenpox, with no one to amuse him but herself. She doted on him, but they had been fishing all the morning, and after lunch had been cleared away she had gone to the loft for an hour's peace before getting the tea, and now here he was again, no doubt with some boyish scheme or other which would probably entail climbing trees or walking miles looking for seashells.

His untidy head appeared at the top of the ladder. 'I knew you'd be here, Eleanor,' he said in a satisfied voice. 'There's something I must tell you—it's most exciting.'

'Margaret's home early from school?'

He gave her a scornful look, still standing some way down the ladder so that only his head was visible. 'That's not exciting—she comes home from school every day—besides, she's only my sister.'

Eleanor trimmed the core of her apple with her nice white teeth. 'I'm your sister, Henry.'

'But you're old…'

She nodded cheerfully. 'Indeed I am, getting on for twenty-five, my dear. Tell me the exciting news.'

'Someone's come—Mother's invited him to tea.'

Eleanor's eyebrows rose protestingly. 'Old Mr MacKenzie? Not again?'

Her small brother drew a deep breath. 'You'll never guess.'

She reached over for another apple. 'Not in a thousand years—you'd better tell me before I die of curiosity.'

'It's Fulk van Hensum.'

'Fulk? Him? What's he here for? It's twenty years…' She turned her back on her brother, took a bite of apple and said with her mouth full: 'Tell Mother that I can't possibly come—I don't want to waste time talking to him; he was a horrid boy and I daresay he's grown into a horrid man. He pulled my hair…nasty arrogant type, I've never forgotten him.'

'I've never forgotten you, either, Eleanor.' The voice made her spin round. In place of Henry's head was the top half of a very large man; the rest of him came into view as she stared, so tall and broad that he was forced to bend his elegantly clad person to avoid bumping his head. He was very dark, with almost black hair and brown eyes under splendid eyebrows; his nose was long and beaky with winged nostrils, and his mouth was very firm.

Eleanor swallowed her apple. 'Well, I never!' she declared. 'Haven't you grown?'

He sat down on a convenient sack of potatoes and surveyed her lazily. 'One does, you know, and you, if I might say so, have become quite a big girl, Eleanor.'

He somehow managed to convey the impression that she was outsized, and she flushed a little; her father always described her as a fine figure of a woman, an old-fashioned phrase which she had accepted as a compliment, but to be called quite a big girl in that nasty drawling voice was decidedly annoying. She frowned at him and he remarked lightly: 'Otherwise you haven't changed, dear girl—still the heavy frown, I see—and the biting comment. Should I be flattered that you still remember me?'

'No.'

'Could we let bygones be bygones after—let me see, twenty years?'

She didn't answer that, but: 'You've been a great success, haven't you? We hear about you, you know; Father holds you up as a shining example to Donald.'

'Donald? Ah, the medical student. I'm flattered. What's in the box?'

'Mrs Trot and her four kittens.'

He got up and came to sit beside her with the box between them, and when he offered a large, gentle hand, the little cat licked it too.

'Nice little beast. Don't you want to know why I'm here?' He chose an apple with care and began to eat it. 'How peaceful it is,' he observed. 'What are you doing now, Eleanor? Still a nurse?'

She nodded. 'In Edinburgh, but I'm on a week's holiday.'

'Not married yet?' And when she shook her head: 'Engaged?'

'No—are you?'

'Married? No. Engaged, yes.'

For some reason she felt upset, which was ridiculous, because for all these years she had remembered him as someone she didn't like—true, she had been barely five years old at their first meeting and tastes as well as people change; all the same, there was no need for her to feel so put out at his news. She asked the inevitable female question: 'Is she pretty?'

The dark eyes looked at her thoughtfully. 'Yes, ethereal—very small, slim, fair hair, blue eyes—she dresses with exquisite taste.'

Eleanor didn't look at him. She tucked Mrs Trot up in her old blanket and got to her feet, feeling, for some reason, a much bigger girl than she actually was and most regrettably shabby and untidy. Not that it mattered, she told herself crossly; if people came calling without warning they could take her as they found her. She said haughtily: 'Tea will be ready, I expect,' and went down the ladder with the expertise of long practice. She waited politely for him at the bottom and then walked beside him out of the stable and across the cobbled yard towards the house. She walked well, her head well up and with a complete lack of self-consciousness, for she was a graceful girl despite her splendid proportions and tall, although now her head barely reached her companion's shoulder.

'It hasn't changed,' her companion observed, looking around him. 'I'm glad my father came just once again before he died; he loved this place. It was a kind of annual pilgrimage with him, wasn't it?'

Eleanor glanced up briefly. 'Yes—we were all sorry when he died, we all knew him so well, and coming every year as he did...' She paused and then went on: 'You never came, and now after all these years you have. Why?'

They had stopped in the open back porch and he answered her casually: 'Oh, one reason and another, you know.' He was eyeing her in a leisurely fashion which she found annoying. 'Do you always dress like this?'

She tossed back her mane of hair. 'You haven't changed at all,' she told him tartly. 'You're just as hateful as you were as a boy.'

He smiled. 'You have a long memory.' His dark eyes snapped with amusement. 'But then so have I, Eleanor.'

She led the way down the flagstoned passage and opened a door, while vivid memory came flooding back—all those years ago, when he had picked her up and held her gently while she howled and sobbed into his shoulder and even while she had hated him then, just for those few minutes she had felt secure and content and very happy despite the fact that moments earlier she had been kicking his shins—she had lost her balance and fallen over and he had laughed, but gently, and picked her up…it was silly to remember such a trivial episode from her childhood.

The sitting room they entered wasn't large, but its heterogeneous mixture of unassuming antiques and comfortable, shabby armchairs, handmade rugs and bookshelves rendered it pleasant enough. It had two occupants: Eleanor's mother, a small, pretty woman, very neatly dressed, and her father, a good deal older than his wife, with thick white hair and bright blue eyes in a rugged face. He was in elderly grey tweeds and only his dog collar proclaimed his profession.

'There you are,' exclaimed Mrs MacFarlane. 'So you found each other.' She beamed at them both. 'Isn't it nice to meet again after all these years? Fulk, come and sit here by me and tell me all your news,' and when he had done so: 'Did you recognise Eleanor? She was such a little girl when you last saw her.'

Eleanor was handing plates and teacups and saucers. 'Of course he didn't recognise me, Mother,' she explained in a brisk no-nonsense voice. 'I was only five then, and that's twenty years ago.'

'A nice plump little thing you were, too,' said her father fondly, and smiled at their guest, who remarked blandly: 'Little girls so often are,' and Eleanor, although she wasn't looking at him, knew that he was secretly laughing. It was perhaps fortunate that at that moment Henry joined them, to sit himself down as close to him as possible.

'Are you going to stay here?' he enquired eagerly. 'I mean, for a day or two? And must I call you Doctor van Hensum, and will you…?'

'Call me Fulk, Henry, and yes, your mother has very kindly asked me to stay for a short visit.'

'Oh, good—you can come fishing with us, Eleanor and me, you know, and there's an apple tree she climbs, I daresay she'll let you climb it too if you like.'

'Eat your bread and butter, Henry,' said Eleanor in the same brisk voice. 'I'm sure Doctor van Hensum doesn't climb trees at his age, and probably he's not in the least interested in fishing.' She cast the doctor a smouldering glance. 'He may want to rest…'

She caught the quick gleam in his eyes although his voice was meek enough. 'As to that, I'm only thirty-six, you know, and reasonably active.'

'Of course you are,' declared Mrs MacFarlane comfortably, and passed him the cake. 'I can remember you fishing, too—and climbing trees—Eleanor used to shriek at you because you wouldn't let her climb trees too.' She laughed at the memory and her daughter ground her splendid teeth. 'So long ago,' sighed her mother, 'and I remember it all so vividly.'

And that was the trouble, Eleanor told herself, although why the memory was so vivid was a mystery beyond her.

'And now,' interpolated her father, 'you are a famous physician; of course your dear father was a brilliant man—you were bound to follow in his footsteps, and your mother was a clever woman too, and an uncommonly pretty one. I'm afraid that we none of us can hold a candle to your splendid career, although Eleanor has done very well for herself, you know; in her own small sphere she has specialized in medicine and is very highly thought of at her hospital, so I'm told.' He added with a touch of pride: 'She's a Ward Sister—one of the youngest there.'

'I can hardly believe it,' observed Fulk, and only she realized that he was referring to her careless appearance; no one, seeing her at that moment would have believed that she was one and the same person as the immaculately uniformed, highly professional young woman who ruled her ward so precisely. A pity he can't see me on duty, she thought peevishly, and said aloud: 'Donald—he's younger than I—is at Aberdeen and doing very well. He's going in for surgery.'

She encountered the doctor's gaze again and fidgeted under it. 'He was in his pram when you were here.'

He said smoothly: 'Ah, yes, I remember. Father always kept me up to date with any news about you; there's Mary—she's married, isn't she?—and Margaret?'

'Here she is now,' said Mrs MacFarlane, 'back from school—and don't forget James, he's still at boarding school.' She cast a fond look at her last-born, gobbling cake. 'Henry's only home because he's had chickenpox.'

There was a small stir as Margaret came in. She was already pretty and at twelve years old bade fair to outshine Eleanor later on. She embraced her mother, declaring she was famished, assured Eleanor that she would need help with her homework and went to kiss her father. She saw the doctor then and said instantly: 'Is that your car in the lane? It's absolutely wizard!'

Her father's voice was mildly rebuking. 'This is Fulk van Hensum, Margaret, he used to come and stay with us a long time ago—you remember his father? He is to stay with us for a day or so.'

She shook hands, smiling widely. 'Oh, yes—I remember your father and I know about you too.' She eyed him with some curiosity. 'You're very large, aren't you?'

He smiled slowly. 'I suppose I am. Yes, that's my car outside—it's a Panther de Ville.'

It was Henry who answered him. 'I say, is it really? May I look at it after tea? There are only a few built, aren't there—it's rather like an XJ12, isn't it? With a Jag engine…'

The big man gave him a kindly look. 'A motorcar enthusiast?' he wanted to know, and when Henry nodded, 'We'll go over it presently if you would like that—it has some rather nice points…' He smiled at the little boy and then addressed Eleanor with unexpected suddenness. 'When do you go back to Edinburgh?'

She looked up from filling second cups. 'In a few days, Friday.'

'Good, I'll drive you down, I've an appointment in that part of the world on Saturday.'

She said stiffly: 'That's kind of you, but I can go very easily by train.'

Her mother looked at her in some astonishment. 'Darling, you've said a dozen times how tedious it is going to Edinburgh by train, and then there's the bus to Lairg first…'

'I drive tolerably well,' murmured the doctor. 'We could go to Lairg and on to Inverness. It would save you a good deal of time, but of course, if you are nervous…'

'I am not nervous,' said Eleanor coldly. 'I merely do not want to interfere with your holiday.'

'Oh, but you're not,' he told her cheerfully. 'I have to go to Edinburgh—I've just said so. I came here first because I had some books my father wanted your father to have.'

Which led the conversation into quite different channels.

It was a crisp, bright October morning when Eleanor woke the next day—too good to stay in bed, she decided. She got up, moving quietly round her pretty little bedroom, pulling on slacks and a sweater again, brushing and plaiting her hair. She went down to the kitchen without making a sound and put on the kettle; a cup of tea, she decided, then a quick peep at Mrs Trot and the kittens before taking tea up to her parents; and there would still be time to take Punch, the dog, for a short walk before helping to get breakfast.

She was warming the pot when Fulk said from the door: 'Good morning, Eleanor—coming out for a walk? It's a marvellous morning.'

She spooned tea carefully. 'Hullo, have you been out already?'

'Yes, but I'm more than willing to go again. Who's the tea for?'

'Me—and you, now you're here.'

He said softly: 'I wonder why you don't like me, Eleanor?'

She poured tea into two mugs and handed him one, and said seriously: 'I think it's because you arrived unexpectedly—quite out of the blue—you see, I never thought I'd see you again and I didn't like you when I was a little girl. It's funny how one remembers...'

He smiled. 'You were such a little girl, but I daresay you were right, I was a horrid boy—most boys are from time to time and you were bad for me; you made me feel like the lord of creation, following me around on those fat legs of yours, staring at me with those eyes, listening to every word I said—your eyes haven't changed at all, Eleanor.'

Her voice was cool. 'How very complimentary you are all of a sudden. You weren't so polite yesterday.'

He strolled over and held out his mug for more tea. 'One sometimes says the wrong thing when one is taken by surprise.'

She didn't bother to think about that; she was pursuing her own train of thought. 'I know I'm big,' she said crossly, 'but I don't need to be reminded of it.'

He looked momentarily surprised and there was a small spark of laughter in his eyes, but all he said was: 'I won't remind you again, I promise. Shall we cry truce and take the dog for a walk? After all, we shall probably not meet again for another twenty years or even longer than that.'

She was aware of disappointment at the very thought. 'All right, but I must just go up to Mother and Father with this tray.'

He was waiting at the kitchen door when she got down again, and Punch was beside him. 'I must take Mrs Trot's breakfast over first,' she warned him.

They crossed the back yard together and rather to her surprise he took the bowl of milk she was carrying from her and mounted the ladder behind her while Punch, wary of Mrs Trot's maternal claws, stayed prudently in the stable. The little cat received them with pleasure, accepted the milk and fish and allowed them to admire her kittens before they left, going down the short lane which separated the manse and the small church from the village. The huddle of houses and cottages was built precariously between the mountains at their back and the sea, tucked almost apologetically into a corner of the rock-encircled sandy bay. As they reached the beach they were met by a chilly wind from the north, dispelling any illusion that the blue sky and sunshine were an aftertaste of summer, so that they were forced to step out briskly, with Punch tearing down to the edge of the sea and then retreating from the cold waves.

Eleanor was surprised to find that she was enjoying Fulk's company; it was obvious, she told herself, that he had grown into an arrogant man, very sure of himself, probably selfish too, even though she had to admit to his charm. All the same, he was proving himself a delightful companion now, talking about everything under the sun in a friendly manner which held no arrogance at all, and when they got back to the house he surprised her still further by laying the breakfast table while she cooked for Margaret before she left for school. Half way through their activities, Henry came down, rather indignant that he had missed the treat of an early morning walk, but more than reconciled to his loss when Fulk offered to take him for a drive in the Panther. The pair of them went away directly after breakfast and weren't seen again until a few minutes before lunch, when they appeared in the kitchen, on excellent terms with each other, and burdened with a large quantity of flowers for Mrs MacFarlane, whisky for the pastor and chocolates for Margaret. And for Eleanor there was a little pink quartz cat, a few inches high and most beautifully carved, sitting very straight and reserved, reminding her very much of Mrs Trot.

'We had the greatest fun,' Henry informed his waiting family, 'and I had an ice cream. We went to the hotel in Tongue—one of those with nuts on top, and the Panther is just super. When I'm grown up I shall have one, too.'

Eleanor, the little cat cradled in her hand, smiled at him lovingly. 'And so you shall, my dear, but now you're going straight up to the bathroom to wash your hands—dinner's ready.'

The rest of the day passed pleasantly enough, and if she had subconsciously hoped that Fulk would suggest another walk, she had no intention of admitting it to herself. As it was, he spent most of the afternoon with his host and after supper they all played cards until the children's bedtime.

She wakened at first light the next morning, to hear her brother's excited whispering under her window, and when she got out of bed to have a look, it was to see him trotting along beside the doctor, laden with fishing paraphernalia—Punch was with them, too; all three of them looked very happy, even from the back.

They came in late for breakfast with a splendid catch of fish, which provided the main topic of conversation throughout the meal, and when they had finished Mrs MacFarlane said brightly: 'Well, my dears, fish for dinner, provided of course someone will clean it.' A task which Fulk undertook without fuss before driving Mr MacFarlane into Durness to browse over an interesting collection of books an old friend had offered to sell him.

So that Eleanor saw little of their guest until the late afternoon and even then Henry made a cheerful talkative third when they went over to visit Mrs Trot. It was while they were there, sitting on the floor eating apples, that Fulk asked her: 'What time do you leave tomorrow, Eleanor?'

'Well, I don't want to leave at all,' she replied promptly. 'The very thought of hospital nauseates me— I'd like to stay here for ever and ever...' She sighed and went on briskly: 'Well, any time after lunch, I suppose. Would two o'clock suit you?'

'Admirably. It's roughly two hundred and fifty miles, isn't it? We should arrive in Edinburgh in good time for dinner—you don't have to be in at any special time, do you?'

'No—no, of course not, but there's no need...really I didn't expect...that is...'

'There's no need to get worked up,' he assured her

kindly. 'I shouldn't have asked you if I hadn't wanted to.' He sounded almost brotherly, which made her pleasure at this remark all the more remarkable, although it was quickly squashed when he went on to say blandly: 'I've had no chance to talk to you about Imogen.'

'Oh, well—yes, of course I shall be delighted to hear about her.'

'Who's Imogen?' Henry enquired.

'The lady Fulk is going to marry,' his big sister told him woodenly.

He looked at her with round eyes. 'Then why didn't she come too?'

Fulk answered him good-naturedly, 'She's in the south of France.'

'Why aren't you with her?'

The doctor smiled. 'We seem to have started something, don't we? You see, Henry, Imogen doesn't like this part of Scotland.'

'Why not?' Eleanor beat her brother by a short head with the question.

'She considers it rather remote.'

Eleanor nodded understandingly. 'Well, it is—no shops for sixty miles, no theatres, almost no cinemas and they're miles away too, and high tea instead of dinner in the hotels.'

Fulk turned his head to look at her. 'Exactly so,' he agreed. 'And do you feel like that about it, too, Eleanor?'

She said with instant indignation: 'No, I do not—I love it; I like peace and quiet and nothing in sight but the mountains and the sea and a cottage or two—anyone who feels differently must be very stupid...' She opened her eyes wide and put a hand to her mouth. 'Oh, I do beg your pardon—I didn't mean your Imogen.'

'Still the same hasty tongue,' Fulk said mockingly, 'and she isn't my Imogen yet.'

It was fortunate that Henry created a welcome diversion at that moment; wanting to climb a tree or two before teatime, so that the rest of the afternoon was spent doing just that. Fulk, Eleanor discovered, climbed trees very well.

They played cards again until supper time and after their meal, when the two gentlemen retired to the pastor's study, Eleanor declared that she was tired and would go to bed, but once in her room she made no effort to undress but sat on her bed making up her mind what she would wear the next day—Fulk had only seen her in slacks and a sweater with her hair hanging anyhow. She would surprise him.

It was a pity, but he didn't seem in the least surprised. She went down to breakfast looking much as usual, but before lunchtime she changed into a well cut tweed suit of a pleasing russet colour, put on her brogue shoes, made up her pretty face with care, did her hair in a neat, smooth coil on the top of her head, and joined the family at the table. And he didn't say a word, glancing up at her as she entered the room and then looking away again with the careless speed of someone who had seen the same thing a dozen times before. Her excellent appetite was completely destroyed.

It served her right, she told herself severely, for allowing herself to think about him too much; she had no reason to do so, he was of no importance in her life and after today she wasn't likely to see him again. She made light conversation all the way to Tomintoul, a village high in the Highlands, where they stopped for tea. It was a small place, but the hotel overlooked the square and there was plenty to comment upon, something for which she was thankful, for she was becoming somewhat weary of providing almost all the conversation. Indeed, when they were on their way once more and after another hour of commenting upon the scenery, she observed tartly: 'I'm sure you will understand if I don't talk any more; I can't think of anything else to say, and even if I could, I feel I should save it for this evening, otherwise we shall sit at dinner like an old married couple.'

His shoulders shook. 'My dear girl, I had no idea... I was enjoying just sitting here and listening to you rambling on—you have a pretty voice, you know.' He paused. 'Imogen doesn't talk much when we drive together; it makes a nice change. But I promise you we won't sit like an old married couple; however old we become, we shall never take each other for granted.'

She allowed this remark to pass without comment, for she wasn't sure what he meant. 'You were going to tell me about Imogen,' she prompted, and was disappointed when he said abruptly: 'I've changed my mind—tell me about Henry instead. What a delightful child he is, but not, I fancy, over-strong.'

The subject of Henry lasted until they reached Edinburgh, where he drove her to the North British Hotel in Princes Street, and after Eleanor had tidied herself, gave her a memorable dinner, managing to convey, without actually saying so, that she was not only a pleasant companion but someone whom he had wanted to take out to dinner all his life. It made her glow very nicely, and the glow was kept at its best by the hock which he offered her. They sat for a long time over their meal and when he at last took her to the hospital it was almost midnight.

She got out of the car at the Nurses' Home entrance and he got out with her and walked to the door to open it. She wished him goodbye quietly, thanked him for a

delightful evening and was quite taken by surprise when
he pulled her to him, kissed her hard and then, without
another word, popped her through the door and closed it
behind her. She stood in the dimly lit hall, trying to sort
out her feelings. She supposed that they were outraged,
but this was tempered by the thought that she wasn't
going to see him again. She told herself firmly that it
didn't matter in the least, trying to drown the persistent
little voice in the back of her head telling her that even
if she didn't like him—and she had told herself enough
times that she didn't—it mattered quite a bit. She went
slowly up to her room, warning herself that just because
he had given her a good dinner and been an amusing
companion there was no reason to allow her thoughts to
dwell upon him.

CHAPTER TWO

THE MORNING WAS dark and dreary and suited Eleanor's mood very well as she got into her uniform and, looking the very epitome of neatness and calm efficiency, went down to breakfast, a meal eaten in a hurry by reason of the amount of conversation crammed in by herself and friends while they drank tea and bolted toast and marmalade.

She climbed the stairs to Women's Medical, trying to get used to being back on the ward once more, while her pretty nose registered the fact that the patients had had fish for breakfast and that someone had been too lavish with the floor polish—the two smells didn't go well together. Someone, too, would have to repair the window ledge outside the ward door, and it was obvious that no one had bothered to water the dreadful potted plant which lived on it. Eleanor pushed the swing doors open and went straight to her little office, where Staff Nurse Jill Pitts would be waiting with the two night nurses.

The report took longer than usual; it always did on her first day back, even if she had been away for a short time; new patients, new treatments, Path Lab reports, news of old patients—it was all of fifteen minutes before she sent the night nurses to their breakfast, left Jill to see that the nurses were starting on their various jobs, and set off on her round. She spent some time with her first three patients, for they were elderly and ill, and for some weeks now they had all been battling to keep them alive; she assured herself that they were holding their own and passed on to the fourth bed; Mrs McFinn, a large, comfortable lady with a beaming smile and a regrettable shortness of breath due to asthma, a condition which didn't prevent her wheezing out a little chat with Eleanor, and her neighbour, puffing and panting her way through emphysema with unending courage and good humour, wanted to chat too. She indulged them both; they were such dears, but so for that matter were almost all the patients in the ward.

She spent a few minutes with each of them in turn, summing up their condition while she lent a friendly ear and a smile; only as she reached the top of the ward did she allow a small sigh to escape her. Miss Tremble, next in line, was a cross the entire staff, medical and nursing, bore with fortitude, even if a good deal of grumbling went on about her in private. She was a thin, acidulated woman in her sixties, a diabetic which it seemed impossible to stabilize however the doctors tried. Painstakingly dieted and injected until the required balance had been reached, she would be sent home, only to be borne back in again sooner or later in yet another diabetic coma, a condition which she never ceased to blame upon the hospital staff. She had been in again for two weeks now, and on the one occasion during that period when it had been considered safe to send her home again to her downtrodden sister, she had gone into a coma again as she was actually on the point of departure, and it was all very well for Sir Arthur Minch, the consultant physician in charge of her case, to carry on about it; as Eleanor had pointed out to him in a reasonable manner, one simply didn't turn one's back on hyperglycaemia, even when it was about to leave the ward; she had put the patient back to bed again and allowed the great man to natter on about wanting the bed for an urgent case. He had frowned and tutted and in the end had agreed with her; she had known that he would, anyway.

She took up her position now at the side of Miss Tremble's bed and prepared to listen to its occupant's long list of complaints; she had heard them many times before, and would most likely hear them many more times in the future. She put on her listening face and thought about Fulk, wondering where he was and why he had come to Edinburgh. She would have liked to have asked him, only she had hesitated; he had a nasty caustic tongue, she remembered it vividly when he had stayed with them all those years ago, and she had no doubt that he still possessed it. She could only guess—he could of course be visiting friends, or perhaps he had come over to consult with a colleague; he might even have a patient... She frowned and Miss Tremble said irritably: 'I'm glad to see that you are annoyed, Sister—it is disgraceful that I had to have Bovril on two successive evenings when my appetite needs tempting.'

Eleanor made a soothing reply, extolled the virtues of the despised beverage, assured Miss Tremble that something different would be offered her for her supper that evening, and moved on to the next bed, but even when she had completed her round and was back in her office, immersed in forms, charts and the answering of the constantly ringing telephone she was still wondering about Fulk.

But presently she gave herself a mental shake; she would never know anyway. Thinking about him was a complete waste of time, especially with Sir Arthur due to do his round at ten o'clock. She pushed the papers to one side with a touch of impatience; they would have to wait until she had checked the ward and made sure that everything was exactly as it should be for one of the major events in the ward's week.

She ran the ward well; the patients were ready with five minutes to spare and the nurses were going, two by two, to their coffee break. Eleanor, longing for a cup herself, but having to wait for it until Sir Arthur should be finished, was in the ward, with the faithful Jill beside her and Mrs MacDonnell, the part-time staff nurse, hovering discreetly with a student nurse close by to fetch and carry. She knew Sir Arthur's ways well by now; he would walk into the ward at ten o'clock precisely with his registrar, his house doctor and such students as had the honour of accompanying him that morning. Eleanor, with brothers of her own, felt a sisterly concern for the shy ones, whose wits invariably deserted them the moment they entered the ward, and she had formed the habit of stationing herself where she might prompt those rendered dumb by apprehension when their chief chose to fire a question at them. She had become something of an expert at mouthing clues helpful enough to start the hapless recipient of Sir Arthur's attention on the path of a right answer. Perhaps one day she would be caught red-handed, but in the meantime she continued to pass on vital snippets to any number of grateful young gentlemen.

The clock across the square had begun its sonorous rendering of the hour when the ward doors swung open just as usual and the senior Medical Consultant, his posse of attendants hard on his heels, came in—only it wasn't quite as usual; Fulk van Hensum was walking beside him, not the Fulk of the last day or so, going fishing with Henry in an outsize sweater and rubber boots, or playing Canasta with the family after supper or goodnaturedly helping Margaret with her decimals. This was a side of him which she hadn't seen before; he looked older for a start, and if anything, handsomer in a distinguished way, and his face wore the expression she had seen so often on a doctor's face; calm and kind and totally unflappable—and a little remote. He was also impeccably turned out, his grey suit tailored to perfection, his tie an elegant understatement. She advanced to meet them, very composed, acknowledging Sir Arthur's stately greeting with just the right degree of warmth and turning a frosty eye on Fulk, who met it blandly with the faintest of smiles and an equally bland: 'Good morning, Eleanor, how nice to be able to surprise you twice in only a few days.'

She looked down her nose at him. 'Good morning, Doctor van Hensum,' she greeted him repressively, and didn't smile. He might have told her; there had been no reason at all why he shouldn't have done so. She almost choked when he went on coolly: 'Yes, I could have told you, couldn't I? But you never asked me.'

Sir Arthur glanced at Eleanor. 'Know each other, do you?' he wanted to know genially.

Before she could answer, Fulk observed pleasantly: 'Oh, yes—for many years. Eleanor was almost five when we first met.' He had the gall to smile at her in what she considered to be a patronising manner.

'Five, eh?' chuckled Sir Arthur. 'Well, you've grown since then, Sister.' The chuckle became a laugh at his little joke and she managed to smile too, but with an effort for Fulk said: 'She had a quantity of long hair and she was very plump.' He stared at her and she frowned fiercely. 'Little girls are rather sweet,' his voice was silky, 'but they tend to change as they grow up.'

She all but ground her teeth at him; it was a relief when Sir Arthur said cheerfully: 'Well, well, I suppose we should get started, Sister. Doctor van Hensum is particularly interested in that case of agranulocytosis—Mrs Lee, isn't it? She experienced the first symptoms while she was on holiday in Holland and came under his care. Most fortunately for her, he diagnosed it at once—a difficult thing to do.' His eye swept round the little group of students, who looked suitably impressed.

'Not so very difficult in this case, if I might say so,' interpolated Fulk quietly. 'There was the typical sore throat and oedema, and the patient answered my questions with great intelligence...'

'But no doubt the questions were intelligent,' remarked Sir Arthur dryly, and the students murmured their admiration, half of them not having the least idea what their superiors were talking about, anyway.

They were moving towards the first bed now, and Eleanor, casting a quick look at Fulk, saw that he had become the consultant again; indeed, as the round progressed, his manner towards her was faultless; politely friendly, faintly impersonal—they could have just met for the first time. It vexed her to find that this annoyed her more than his half-teasing attitude towards her when he had entered the ward. He was a tiresome man, she decided, leading the way to Mrs Lee's bed.

That lady was making good progress now that she was responding to the massive doses of penicillin, and although her temperature was still high and she remained lethargic, she was certainly on the mend. Sir Arthur held forth at some length, occasionally pausing to verify some point with the Dutch doctor and then firing questions at random at whichever unfortunate student happened to catch his eye. Most of them did very well, but one or two of them were tongue-tied by the occasion. Eleanor, unobtrusively helping out one such, and standing slightly behind Sir Arthur, had just finished miming the bare bones of the required information when she realized that Fulk had moved and was standing where he could watch her. She threw him a frowning glance which he appeared not to see, for the smile he gave her was so charming that she only just prevented herself from smiling back at him.

Perhaps he wasn't so bad after all, she conceded, only to have this opinion reversed when, the round over, she was bidding Sir Arthur and his party goodbye at the ward door, for when she bade Fulk goodbye too, he said at once: 'You'll lunch with me, Eleanor,' and it wasn't even a question, let alone a request, delivered in a silky voice loud enough for everyone to hear.

'I'm afraid that's impossible,' she began coldly, and Sir Arthur, quite mistaking her hesitation, interrupted her to say heartily: 'Nonsense, of course you can go, Sister— I've seen you dozens of times at the Blue Bird Café'— an establishment much favoured by the hospital staff because it was only just down the road and they were allowed to go there in uniform—'Why, only a couple of weeks ago you were having a meal there with young Maddox, although how he managed that when he was on call for the Accident Room I cannot imagine.'

He turned his attention to Fulk. 'The Blue Bird isn't exactly Cordon Bleu, but they do a nice plate of fish and chips, and there is the great advantage of being served quickly.' He looked at Eleanor once more. 'You intended going to your dinner, I suppose? When do you go?'

She didn't want to answer, but she had to say something. 'One o'clock,' she told him woodenly and heard his pleased: 'Excellent—what could be better? Van Hensum, we shall have time to talk over that case we were discussing.' He beamed in a fatherly fashion at Eleanor, fuming silently, and led the way down the corridor with all the appearance of a man who had done someone a good turn and felt pleased about it. Fulk went with him, without saying another word.

Eleanor snorted, muttered rudely under her breath and went to serve the patients' dinners, and as she dished out boiled fish, nourishing stew, fat-free diets, high-calorie diets and diabetic diets, she pondered how she could get out of having lunch with Fulk. She wasn't quite sure why it was so important that she should escape going with him, because actually she liked the idea very much, and even when, as usual, she was battling with Miss Tremble about the amount of ham on her plate, a small part of her brain was still hard at work trying to discover the reason. All the same, she told herself that her determination not to go was strong enough to enable her to make some excuse.

She was trying to think of one as she went back to her office with Jill, to give her a brief run-down of jobs to be done during the next hour—a waste of time, as it turned out, for Fulk was there, standing idly looking out of the window. He had assumed his consultant's manner once more, too, so that Eleanor found it difficult to utter the refusal she had determined upon. Besides, Jill was there, taking it for granted that she was going, even at that very moment urging her not to hurry back. 'There's nothing much on this afternoon,' she pointed out, 'not until three o'clock at any rate, and you never get your full hour for dinner, Sister.' She made a face. 'It's braised heart, too.'

Fulk's handsome features expressed extreme distaste. 'How revolting,' he observed strongly. 'Eleanor, put on your bonnet at once and we will investigate the fish and chips. They sound infinitely more appetizing.'

Eleanor dabbed with unusually clumsy fingers at the

muslin trifle perched on her great knot of shining hair. 'Thanks, Jill, I'll see.' She sounded so reluctant that her right hand looked at her in amazement while Fulk's eyes gleamed with amusement, although all he said was: 'Shall we go?'

The café was almost full, a number of hospital staff, either on the point of going on duty or just off, were treating themselves to egg and chips, spaghetti on toast or the fish and chips for which the café was justly famous. Fulk led the way to a table in the centre of the little place, and Eleanor, casting off her cloak and looking around, nodded and smiled at two physiotherapists, an X-ray technician, and the senior Accident Room Sister with the Casualty Officer. There were two of the students who had been in Sir Arthur's round that morning sitting at the next table and they smiled widely at her, glanced at Fulk and gave her the thumbs-up sign, which she pointedly ignored, hoping that her companion hadn't seen it too. He had; he said: 'Lord, sometimes I feel middle-aged.'

'Well,' her voice was astringent, 'you're not—you're not even married yet.'

His mouth twitched. 'You imply that being married induces middle age, and that's nonsense.' He added slowly: 'I imagine that any man who married you would tend to regain his youth, not lose it.'

She gaped at him across the little table. 'For heaven's sake, whatever makes you say that?' But she wasn't to know, for the proprietor of the Blue Bird had made his way towards them and was offering a menu card. He was a short, fat man and rather surprisingly, a Cockney; the soul of kindness and not above allowing second helpings for free to anyone who was a bit short until pay day. He stood looking at them both now and then said: ''Ullo, Sister, 'aven't met yer friend before, 'ave I?'

'No, Steve—he's a Dutch consultant, a friend of Sir Arthur Minch. Doctor van Hensum, this is Steve who runs the café.'

The doctor held out a hand and Steve shook it with faint surprise. 'Pleased ter meet yer,' he pronounced in gratified tones. 'I got a nice bit of 'ake out the back. 'Ow'd yer like it, the pair of yer? Chips and peas and a good cuppa while yer waiting.'

A cheerful girl brought the tea almost at once and Eleanor poured the rich brew into the thick cups and handed one to Fulk. 'Aren't you sorry you asked me out now?' she wanted to know. 'I don't suppose you've ever had your lunch in a place like this before.'

He gave her a thoughtful look. 'You're determined to make me out a very unpleasant fellow, aren't you? I wonder why?' He passed her the sugar bowl and then helped himself. 'No, I've never been in a place quite like this one before, but I've been in far worse, and let me tell you, my girl, that your low opinion of me is completely mistaken.'

'I never...' began Eleanor, and was interrupted by the arrival of the hake, mouthwatering in its thick rich batter coat and surrounded by chips and peas; by the time they had assured Steve that it looked delicious, passed each other the salt, refused the vinegar and refilled their cups, there seemed no point in arguing. They fell to and what conversation there was was casual and good-humoured. Presently, nicely mellowed by the food, Eleanor remarked: 'You were going to tell me about Imogen.'

He selected a chip with deliberation and ate it slowly. 'Not here,' he told her.

'You keep saying that—you said it in the car yesterday. Do you have to have soft music and stained glass windows or something before she can be talked about?'

He put his head on one side and studied her face. 'You're a very rude girl—I suppose that's what comes of being a bossy elder sister. No, perhaps that's too sweeping a statement,' he continued blandly, 'for Henry assured me that you were the grooviest—I'm a little vague as to the exact meaning of the word, but presumably it is a compliment of the highest order.'

'Bless the boy, it is.' She hesitated. 'I'd like to thank you for being so kind to him—he's a poppet, at least we all think so, and far too clever for his age, though he's a great one for adventure; he's for ever falling out of trees and going on long solitary walks with Punch and tumbling off rocks into the sea when he goes fishing. We all long to tell him not to do these things, but he's a boy…having you for a companion was bliss for him.'

'And would it have been bliss for you, Eleanor?' Fulk asked in an interested voice, and then: 'No, don't answer, I can see the words blistering your lips. We'll go on talking about Henry—he's not quite as strong as you would like, your father tells me.'

She had decided to overlook the first part of his remark. 'He's tough, it's just that he catches everything that's going; measles, whooping cough, mumps, chickenpox—you name it, he's had it.'

He passed his cup for more tea, eyed its rich brown strength, sugared it lavishly and took a sip with an expressionless face. 'I shudder to think what this tea is doing to our insides,' he remarked lightly. 'Have you a good doctor?'

'Doctor MacClew. He's quite old now, but he's been our doctor all our lives. He's a dear and so kind, although I daresay he's old-fashioned by your standards.'

'My standards?' He looked quite shocked. 'My dear Eleanor, you're at it again, turning me into someone I'm not. Why should you suppose that I would set myself up above another doctor, probably twice my age and with at least twice my experience, and who has had to improvise, make decisions, take risks, diagnose without X-rays and be his own Path Lab in an emergency? I, remember, have the whole range of modern equipment and science behind me—I need not open my mouth until all the answers have been given me.'

She said indignantly: 'Don't exaggerate. That's not true; a good physician doesn't need any of those things—they only confirm his opinion. You know as well as I do that you could manage very well without them.'

He lifted his thick brows in mock surprise. 'Why, Eleanor, those are the first kind words you have uttered since we met.' He grinned so disarmingly that she smiled back at him. 'Well, you know it's true.'

He said slowly, watching her: 'Do you know I believe that's the first time you've smiled at me? Oh, you've gone through the motions, but they didn't register. You should smile more often.' He heaved a sigh. 'How delightful it is not to be quarrelling with you.'

She eyed him with disfavour. 'What a beastly thing to say! I've not quarrelled with you, I've been very polite.'

'I know, I'd rather quarrel, but not now—let's call a truce.'

She seized her opportunity. 'Tell me about Imogen.'

He leaned back on the hard wooden chair. 'What do you want to know?'

Eleanor was so surprised at his meek acceptance of her question that she didn't speak for a moment. 'Well, what does she do and where does she live and where will you live when you're married, and is she very pretty?' She added wistfully: 'You said she was small…'

'Half your size and very, very pretty—you forgot to ask how old she is, by the way. Twenty-six, and she doesn't do anything—at least, she doesn't have a job. She doesn't need to work, you see. But she fills her days very nicely with tennis and swimming and riding and driving—and she dances beautifully. She lives in den Haag and I live near Groningen, about a hundred and fifty miles apart—an easy run on the motorway.'

'But that's an awful long way to go each weekend,' observed Eleanor.

'Every weekend? Oh, not as often as that, my dear. Besides, Imogen stays with friends a good deal—I did tell you that she's in the south of France now and later on she will be going to Switzerland for the winter sports.' His voice was very level. 'We decided when we became engaged that we would make no claims on each other's time and leisure.'

'Oh,' said Eleanor blankly, 'how very strange. I don't think I'd like that at all.'

'If you were engaged to me? But you're not.' He smiled thinly. 'A fine state of affairs that would be! You would probably expect me to sit in your pocket and we should quarrel without pause.'

'Probably.' Her voice was colourless. 'I think I'd better go back to the ward, if you don't mind…' She was interrupted by the cheerful booming voice of Doctor Blake, Sir Arthur's right-hand man, who clapped a hand on her shoulder, greeted her with the easy friendliness of a long-standing acquaintance and asked: 'May I sit down? It's Doctor van Hensum, isn't it? I've just been with Sir Arthur and he mentioned that you might be here still—I'm not interrupting anything, am I?'

'I'm just on my way back to the ward,' said Eleanor, and wished she wasn't. 'I'm a bit late already.' She smiled a general sort of smile and got to her feet. 'Thanks for the lunch,' she said quickly and hardly looking at Fulk. He had got to his feet too, and his 'Goodbye, Eleanor,' was very quiet.

She had no time to think about him after that, for Miss Tremble had seen fit to go into a coma and it took most of the afternoon to get her out of it again. Eleanor missed her tea and the pleasant half hour of gossip she usually enjoyed with the other Sisters and went off duty a little late, to change rapidly and catch a bus to the other side of the city where an aunt, elderly, crotchety but nevertheless one of the family, would be waiting to give her supper. It had become a custom for Eleanor to visit her on her return from any holidays so that she might supply her with any titbits of news, and although it was sometimes a little tiresome, the old lady had got to depend upon her visits. She spent a dull evening, answering questions and listening to her companion's various ailments, and when she at last escaped and returned to the hospital, she was too tired to do more than climb into bed as quickly as possible.

It was two more days before she discovered, quite by chance, that Fulk had gone back to Holland only a few hours after they had shared their meal together in the Blue Bird Café, and for some reason the news annoyed her; she had been wondering about him, it was true, but somehow she had taken it for granted that he would come and say goodbye before he left, although there was no reason why he should have done so, but one would have thought, she told herself peevishly, that after making such a thing about taking her to lunch, he could at least have mentioned that he was on the point of leaving;

he hadn't even said goodbye. She paused in her reflections: he had, even though he hadn't told her he was leaving; probably thinking it was none of her business, anyway—nor was it.

She glared at her nice face in the silly little mirror on the office wall and went back to her work once more, and while she chatted with her patients and listened to their complaints and worries, she decided that Fulk wasn't worth thinking about, quite forgetting that she had told herself that already. She would most probably not see him again; she could forget him, and the beautiful Imogen with him. She finished her round and went back down the ward, the very picture of calm efficiency, and went into her office, where she sat at her desk, staring at the papers she was supposed to be dealing with while she speculated about Imogen; it was strange that although she had never met the girl and was never likely to, she should have such strong feelings of dislike for her.

CHAPTER THREE

THE DAYS SLID BY, October became November and the bright weather showed no sign of giving way to the sleet and gales of early winter. The ward filled up; acute bronchitis, pneumonia, flu in a variety of forms, followed each other with an almost monotonous regularity. Eleanor, brimming over with good health and vitality herself, had her kind heart wrung by every fresh case. They got well again, of course, at least the vast majority did, what with antibiotics and skilled nursing and Sir Arthur and his assistants keeping a constant eye upon them all, but Eleanor, wrapping some elderly lady in a shabby winter coat, preparatory to her going home, wished with all her heart that they might stay in the ward, eating the plain wholesome food they never cooked for themselves, enjoying the warmth and the company of other elderly ladies; instead of which, going home so often meant nothing more than a chilly, lonely bed-sitter.

They weren't all elderly, though. There was the teenager, who should have been pretty and lively and nicely curved, but who had succumbed to the craze for slimming and had been so unwise about it that now she was a victim of anorexia nervosa; the very sight of food had become repugnant to her, and although she was nothing but skin and bone, she still wanted to become even slimmer. Eleanor had a hard time with her, but it was rewarding after a week or two to know that she had won and once again her patient could be persuaded to eat. And the diabetics, of course, nothing as dramatic as Miss Tremble, but short-stay patients who came in to be stabilized, and lastly, the heart patients; the dramatic coronaries who came in with such urgency and needed so much care, and the less spectacular forms of heart disease, who nonetheless received just as much attention. Eleanor didn't grudge her time or her energy on her patients; off-duty didn't matter, and when Jill remonstrated with her she said carelessly that she could give herself a few extra days later on, when the ward was slack.

And towards the end of November things did calm down a bit, and Eleanor, a little tired despite her denials, decided that she might have a long weekend at home. She left the hospital after lunch on Friday and took the long train journey to Lairg and then the bus to Tongue, warmly wrapped against the weather in her tweed coat and little fur hat her mother had given her for the previous Christmas, and armed with a good book, and because it was a long journey, she took a thermos of tea and some sandwiches as well. All the same, despite these precautions, she was tired and hungry by the time she reached the manse, but her welcome was warm and the supper her mother had waiting was warm and filling as well. She ate and talked at the same time and then went up to bed. It was heavenly to be home again; the peace and quiet of it were a delight after the busy hospital life. She curled up in her narrow little bed and went instantly to sleep.

She was up early, though, ready to help with the breakfast and see Margaret and Henry off to school, and then go and visit Mrs Trot and her fast-growing family.

'We'll have to find homes for them,' she declared as she helped with the washing up.

'Yes, dear.' Mrs MacFarlane emptied her bowl and dried her hands. 'We have—for two of them, and we thought we'd keep one—company for Mrs Trot, she's such a good mother—that leaves one.'

'Oh, good.' Eleanor was stacking plates on the old-fashioned wooden dresser. 'What's all this about Henry going climbing?'

'His class is going this afternoon, up to that cairn—you know the one? It's about two miles away, isn't it? Mr MacDow is going with them, of course, and it's splendid weather with a good forecast. He's promised that they'll explore those caves nearby.'

'The whole class? That'll be a dozen or more, I don't envy him.'

Mrs MacFarlane laughed. 'He's very competent, you know, and a first-class climber—the boys adore him.' She looked a little anxious. 'Do you suppose that Henry shouldn't have gone?'

'Oh, Mother, no. Can you imagine how he would feel if he were left behind? Besides, he's pretty good on his own, remember, and he knows the country almost as well as I do.'

Her mother looked relieved. 'Yes, that's true,' she smiled. 'I've always said that if I got lost on the mountains I wouldn't be at all frightened if I knew you were searching for me.'

Eleanor gave her mother a daughterly hug. 'Let's get on with the dinner, then at least Henry can start out on a full stomach. Are they to be back for tea? It gets dark early...'

'Five o'clock at the latest, Mr MacDow said—they'll

have torches with them...I thought we'd have treacle scones and I baked a cake yesterday—he'll be hungry.'

Henry, well fed, suitably clothed, and admonished by his three elder relations to mind what the teacher said and not to go off by himself, was seen off just after one o'clock. The afternoon was fine, with the sky still blue and the cold sunshine lighting up the mountains he was so eager to climb. Not that there was anything hazardous about the expedition; they would follow the road, a narrow one full of hairpin bends, until they reached the cairn in the dip between the mountains encircling it, and then, if there was time, they would explore the caves.

'I shall probably find something very exciting,' said Henry importantly as he set off on his short walk back to the village school where they were to foregather.

Eleanor stood at the door and watched them set out, waving cheerfully to Mr MacDow, striding behind the boys like a competent shepherd with a flock of sheep. She said out loud: 'I'd better make some chocolate buns as well,' and sniffed the air as she turned to go indoors again; it had become a good deal colder.

She didn't notice at first that it was becoming dark far too early; her mother was having a nap in the sitting room, her father would be writing his sermon in his study and she had been fully occupied in the kitchen, but now she went to the window and looked out. The blue sky had become grey, and looking towards the sea she saw that it had become a menacing grey, lighted by a pale yellowish veil hanging above it. 'Snow,' she said, and her voice sounded urgent in the quiet kitchen and even as she spoke the window rattled with violence of a sudden gust of wind. It was coming fast too; the sea, grey and turbulent, was already partly blotted out. She hurried out of the kitchen and into the sitting room and found her mother still sleeping, and when she went into the study it was to find her father dozing too. She took another look out of the window and saw the first slow snowflakes falling; a blizzard was on the way, coming at them without warning. She prayed that Mr MacDow had seen it too and was already on the way down the mountain with the boys. She remembered then that if they had already reached the cairn, there would be no view of the sea from it, the mountains around them would cut off everything but the sky above them. She went back to her father and roused him gently. 'There's a blizzard on the way,' she told him urgently. 'What ought we to do? The boys...'

The pastor was instantly alert. 'The time,' he said at once. 'What is the time, my dear?'

She glanced at the clock on the old-fashioned mantelpiece. 'Just after three o'clock.'

'MacDow gave me some sort of timetable—he usually does, you know, so that we have some idea...if I remember rightly, they were to have reached the cairn by half past two. He intended to give them a short talk there; interesting geographical features and so on, and between a quarter to three and the hour they would enter the caves and remain there until half past three. They're simple caves, nothing dangerous, and it's possible they're still inside them, unaware of the weather conditions. He's sensible enough to remain in them until the weather clears—it's probably only a brief storm.'

He got up and went to look from the window in his turn. The snow was coming down in good earnest now and the wind had risen, howling eerily round the little house. 'I'm afraid,' said the pastor, 'that this is no brief storm. With this wind there'll be drifts and the road will be blocked and there's no visibility... We'd better get a search party organised.' He looked worried. 'It's a pity that almost all the men are at work...'

'I'll wake Mother,' Eleanor told him, 'while you ring Mr Wallace.' She sped back into the sitting room, roused her mother, and went back into the hall to get her boots and anorak; she would be going with Mr Wallace, the owner of the only garage within miles, and any other man available, she hadn't been boasting when she had said that she knew the surrounding country like the back of her hand, even in the worst weather she had a natural instinct for direction. She was tugging on her boots when someone rang the front door bell and she called: 'Come in, the door's open.' It would be someone from the village come to consult the pastor about the dangers of the weather.

It wasn't anyone from the village; it was Fulk, standing there, shaking the snow from his shoulders. 'Hullo, everyone,' he said cheerfully, just as though he had seen them only an hour or so previously, 'what filthy weather,' and then: 'What's wrong?'

They were all in the hall now and it was Mrs Mac-Farlane who explained: 'The children—Henry's class at school—they went up the mountain for a geographical climb—more than a dozen of them with Mr MacDow, their teacher. They're all properly clothed and equipped, but this weather—there was no warning—it's a freak blizzard; it could last for hours and it's not very safe up there in bad weather.' Her voice faltered a little.

His voice was very calm. 'A dozen or more boys—is Henry with them?'

The pastor nodded. 'We were just deciding what's the

best thing to do—there are very few men in the village at this time of day…'

He paused and Mrs MacFarlane said suddenly: 'It's wonderful to see you, Fulk.'

Eleanor hadn't said a word. Relief at the sight of Fulk had given way to the certainty that now everything would be all right; he looked dependable, sure of himself and quite unworried, whatever his hidden feelings might be; probably it was his very bulk which engendered such a strong feeling of confidence in him, but it was a pleasant sensation, like handing someone else a heavy parcel to carry.

'How far up?' he asked, and looked at her.

'There's a cleft in the mountains about two miles up—it's on the right of the road and there's a cairn…it's sheltered on all sides and there are caves quite close by. They were going to explore them.'

She looked out of the window again. The howling gale and the snow were, if anything, rather worse.

'The road?'

'Narrow—about one in six, perhaps more in some places, and there are three hairpin bends.'

He said nothing for a moment and then grinned suddenly, reminding her very much of Henry when he was plotting something. 'Is there a bus in the village?'

She understood at once. 'Yes, Mr Wallace has one, a fourteen-seater, old but reliable—he's got chains too.'

'Good. We'll want rope, torches, blankets—you know all that better than I do—whisky too, shovels and some sacks.'

'How many men will you take?' asked the pastor. 'There aren't many to choose from, I'm afraid: old MacNab and Mr Wallace, and myself, of course.'

'One with me—if we make a mess of it, a search party can start out on foot. Give us an hour.'

'I'm coming with you,' Eleanor said quietly.

Fulk didn't seem surprised. 'I thought you might. I'm going to see about borrowing that bus—could you get some tea in flasks to take with us?'

Eleanor was already on the way to the kitchen. 'I'll see to it. How did you come?'

'With the Panther. I drove straight into the stable—I hope that's all right?' He nodded cheerfully to all three of them as he opened the door, letting in a flurry of snow and a powerful gust of wind before shutting it behind him.

He was back in a surprisingly short time, the lights of the bus lightening the snowy gloom as he came to a slithering halt before the door. He got out, leaving the engine running, and came indoors bringing Mr Wallace with him.

'Ye'll need a man who kens the road,' remarked that gentleman once they were inside. They stamped the snow off their boots and shook their shoulders, making havoc in Mrs MacFarlane's neat hall.

'Well,' said Fulk, 'Eleanor said she would come—she knows the way.' He smiled at Mr Wallace with great charm. 'I should value your advice on this—it seems a fairly sensible idea, for if we make a mess of things you would be here to organize a search party on foot, something I wouldn't know a thing about. I understand the men are away from home until the evening.'

Mr Wallace nodded. 'Building an extension on the hotel in Tongue, though they'll not get far in this, neither will they get home all that easy.' He gave a not unfriendly grunt. 'Ye're a good driver? My bus isn't any of your fancy cars, ye ken.'

'I've taken part in a number of rallies,' murmured Fulk, and left it at that, and Mr Wallace grunted again. 'We'll need to clear the school house—aye, and get blankets too.'

Fulk nodded. 'Are there enough men to mount a search if necessary?'

'Aye,' said Mr Wallace again, 'we'll manage. Ye'd best be off.'

Fulk turned to look at Eleanor standing patiently, muffled in her hooded anorak, slacks stuffed into boots, a woollen scarf tugged tight round her throat and a pair of woollen mitts on her hands. 'OK?' he asked, and didn't wait for her answer. 'We'll be back as soon as possible,' he assured her parents. 'Give us a couple of hours, won't you?'

He bent to kiss Mrs MacFarlane on the cheek, swept Eleanor before him out of the house and opened the bus door for her. 'Thank God you're a great strapping girl,' he observed as he climbed into the driver's seat beside her, 'for I fancy we shall have to do a good deal of shovelling on the way.'

Eleanor said 'Probably,' in a cold voice; until that moment she had been more than glad to see him, now she wasn't so sure. Even in the most awkward of situations no girl likes to be described as strapping.

They didn't speak again for a little while; Fulk was occupied in keeping the bus on the road down to the village and then out on the other side, away from the sea towards the mountains. The snow was falling fast now, tossed in all directions by the violence of the wind. The road had disappeared too, although the telegraph wires were a guide until they reached the side road which would take them up between the mountains.

Fulk braked gently. 'Up here?' and Eleanor, staring ahead at the little she could see, said: 'Yes—we must be mad.'

Her companion laughed. 'Though this be madness, yet there is method in't—and that's your Shakespeare, and a very sensible remark too.' He changed gear and started up the narrow road.

They were soon in trouble; the first bend came after a hundred yards or so, and although it wasn't a sharp one and it was still possible to see its curve, the bus skidded on the bank of snow which had already built up along its edge. Fulk prepared to get out. 'Keep the engine going, whatever you do,' he cautioned her, and disappeared into the swirling snow, armed with sacks and shovel. It seemed an age before he climbed in again, the snow thick on him. Eleanor slid back into her own seat and brushed him down as best she could, then sat tensely while he hauled the bus round the bend. It went with reluctance, sliding and slipping, but the sacks held the back wheels and they were round at last.

'I don't dare to stop now,' said Fulk. 'The sacks will have to stay—is it straight ahead?'

'Yes—there's a spiky rock on the left before the next bend, it's a sharp one and there's bound to be a drift— I should think we'll both have to dig.'

He spared a brief, smiling glance. 'OK, if you say so—it'll mean leaving the bus, though.' He began to whistle, and she realized that he was enjoying himself, and upon reflection she was bound to admit that so was she, in a scary kind of way.

It took them ten minutes' hard digging to clear the

angle of the road when they reached it. Eleanor had got out when she saw the rock, and floundered ahead in the appalling weather, looking for landmarks—a stunted tree, the vague outline of the railing which guarded the angle of the road. Once she was sure of them she waved to Fulk, who joined her with the shovels, leaving the bus reluctantly ticking over. They worked together until they had made some sort of track, so that Fulk, with a great deal of skill and muttered bad language, was able to go on again, toiling up the road, narrower and steeper now but happily sheltered a little on one side from the gale, so that although there were great drifts piling up on the opposite bank, their side of the road was still fairly clear.

Eleanor blew on her cold fingers. 'We're nearly half way—there's a left-hand bend in about fifty yards—very exposed, I'm afraid.'

Fulk chuckled. 'Eleanor, if ever I should need to go to the North Pole, remind me to take you with me; you seem to have an instinctive sense of direction.' He had raised his voice to a shout, for the wind, now that they were higher, was howling round the bus, beating on its windows, driving the snow in thick, crazily spiralling flurries.

Eleanor wiped the windscreen uselessly. 'It's some-where here,' she cried, and as the windscreen wipers cleared the view for a few seconds: 'You can just see the beginning of the curve—there's a stone…it's blocked further on,' she added rather unnecessarily.

'Work to do, girl,' said Fulk cheerfully, 'and for heaven's sake don't go wandering off; I'd never find you again. Out you get, I'll fetch the shovels.'

It was hard work, even clearing a rough path just wide enough for the bus was an agonisingly laborious business. Eleanor, shovelling away with her young strong arms, found herself wondering how her companion's Imogen would have fared. Would she have shovelled? Would she have come on the crazy trip in the first place? Decidedly not; she would have stayed behind by the fire, and when Fulk returned she would have greeted him with girlish charm, deliciously scented and gowned, and with not a hair out of place, and he would have called her his precious darling, or something equally silly. Eleanor, her spleen nicely stirred, shovelled even harder.

It was heaven to get back into the bus at last. She sat, huffing and puffing in its warm haven, looking like a snowman. Fulk, getting in beside her, looked her over carefully. 'Cold but cuddly,' he pronounced, and leaned over to kiss her surprised mouth. Heaven knew what she might have said to that, but he gave her no chance to speak, starting at once on the slow business of coaxing the bus along the road once more, an operation fraught with such difficulties that she was kept fully occupied peering ahead, ready to warn him should he get too near to the low stone wall, just visible, guarding the outer edge of the road. The other side was shut in now by towering rocks, which, while forbidding, at least served as a guide.

'The cairn's on the right,' declared Eleanor, 'where the rock stops, and for heaven's sake be careful, there's a kind of canyon, fairly level once you get into it. If they're sheltering anywhere near, they must surely see our lights.'

Fulk didn't answer. He was fully occupied in keeping the bus steady; it took several attempts to get round the rocks and into the canyon, for the bus danced and skidded as though its wheels were legs, but once they were between the walls of rock, it was comparatively peaceful—true, the wind howled like a banshee and the snow was as thick as ever, but there was a semblance of shelter. Fulk skidded to a slow halt, leaving the engine running. 'Journey's end,' he declared. 'Now to find everyone and stow them away before we die of exposure.'

They got out and stood, holding hands for safety's sake, striving to pierce the gloom around them. 'Someone's shouting,' cried Eleanor, 'and there's a torch—look, over there, to our right,' and when she would have started off, found herself held firmly against Fulk.

'No, wait—stay just where you are while I get the rope.'

She hadn't thought of that in the excitement and relief of knowing that the boys were safe and found; she waited patiently while he secured the rope to the bus and paid out a length of it, slinging the coils over one arm. 'Now we can all get back,' he pointed out, and took her by the arm. 'Switch on your torch, the more light the better.'

The boys were all together, close against an overhanging rock which afforded them some shelter, and when they would have plunged forward to meet them, Fulk shouted: 'Stay where you are—where's Mr MacDow?'

It was Henry who shouted back. 'He's here, behind us, Fulk—he's hurt his leg. He fell down outside the cave and now he doesn't answer us any more.'

Eleanor heard Fulk mutter something, then shout: 'Is there anyone in the caves still?'

There was a chorus of 'No's' and a babble of voices explaining that when they had wanted to leave the caves the entrance had been almost completely blocked with snow. 'We had to dig with our hands,' explained Henry, and then: 'Can we go home now—it's cold.'

Fulk was tying the rope round himself. 'This minute,' he bellowed hearteningly. 'Eleanor, I'll stay here and have a look at MacDow, get this lot collected up and hustle them into the bus and make sure that every one of them has a hand on the rope— Understood?'

She heard herself say in a meek voice, 'Yes, Fulk,' and blundered away, going to and fro through the knee-deep snow, organising the little group of boys, making sure that they understood that they were to use the rope as a guide and never let go. She had them lined up and ready to start when Fulk loomed up beside her. 'Could you manage to bring back a couple of splints—luckily Mr Wallace put a couple in the bus. MacDow has a fractured tib and fib.'

She nodded and urged the boys to get started. It wasn't far, but the snow was deep and the rope awkward to hold, but they made it at last and she opened the bus door in almost tearful relief and helped the boys on board. They were cold and frightened too and she would have liked to have given them the hot tea, but she must get the splints to Fulk first; she set them rubbing their arms and legs and taking off wet boots, dragged out the splints, and as an afterthought, the folded stretcher she found beside them, and made her unwieldy way back to where Fulk was waiting.

He hailed her with a 'Splendid girl!' when he saw the stretcher, and proceeded to splint the broken leg, using Mr MacDow's scarf as well as his own to tie it on, and when Eleanor would have helped get the schoolmaster on to the stretcher, he waved her on one side, lifting the man gently himself. When he was ready he shouted: 'I hate to ask you, but can you manage the foot end? He's a small man, thank the Lord; I'll have to wind the rope as we go—do you think you can do it?'

She nodded sturdily and they set off slowly because of winding the rope, which somehow he managed to do without putting the stretcher down, a mercy, actually, for she was quite sure that if she had had to put her end down she would never have been able to pick it up again. She was speechless with exhaustion when they arrived at the bus, and when she would have helped Fulk drag the stretcher on board and into the aisle between the boys, he shook his head and told her in a no-nonsense voice to get in first. She scrambled through the door, leaving it open and subsiding on to the nearest seat, feeling peculiar, vaguely aware that two of the boys were hauling on one end of the stretcher, helping Fulk, and that she was going to faint unless she did something about it. But it was Fulk who did that; she felt a great arm steady her while he held a brandy flask to her lips and poured the stuff relentlessly down her throat. She choked, said 'Ugh!' and felt almost at once much better.

'How silly of me,' she declared stoutly, and met his dark concerned gaze firmly. 'I'm fine,' she told him, feeling dreadful. 'I'll get some hot tea into these boys before we start back.'

Just for a moment she thought that he was going to kiss her again, but he only smiled briefly, took the brandy from her and said: 'I'll follow behind with this, but MacDow first, I think, though I daresay he will prefer whisky.'

She managed a smile at that and fetched the tea, doling it out into the plastic beakers her mother had thoughtfully provided. The boys were being very good, even laughing a little as they struggled out of their wet coats and boots. She went up and down the bus, pouring the drinks down their willing throats, handing out biscuits, climbing carefully over poor Mr MacDow, lying on the floor in everyone's way; he was feeling easier now; he had come to nicely and the whisky had put fresh heart into him so that he took the biscuit she offered him and nibbled at it.

The bus seemed quite crowded, what with a dozen small boys, recovering their spirits fast, the stretcher, herself and Fulk; there was a lot of melting snow too, and Eleanor, feeling an icy trickle in her neck, wondered which was worse, to be numb with cold or horribly damp. She forgot the unpleasantness of both these sensations in the sheer fright of the return journey. The boys more or less settled and Mr MacDow as comfortable as he could be made, she took her seat by Fulk once more, sitting speechless while he manoeuvred the bus backwards on to the road again, an undertaking which took some considerable time, and on their way at length, staring out at the white waste around her through the curtain of snow, she felt a strong urge to beg him not to go another inch, to stop just where he was and let someone come and rescue them; an absurd idea, bred from cowardice, she chided herself silently, and closed her eyes to shut out the awful possibilities waiting in store for them on the way down. She opened them almost immediately; if he could sit there driving so calmly, then she could at least do her part. 'You need to keep a bit to the left,' she warned him. 'I'll tell you when we reach the corner—shall we have to get out and dig again?'

'Probably, but not you this time—I'll take a couple of the bigger boys with me.'

Which he did, and after that the journey became rather less of a nightmare; true, they skidded and bumped around and once shot across the road in an alarming manner, but the road was easier to make out as they descended it, so that she was able to leave her seat from time to time to see how the boys were faring, wrapping them more closely in blankets and taking round more biscuits. It was a relief to find that Mr MacDow had gone to sleep.

She could hardly believe it when the bus rocked to an uneasy halt and Fulk shouted: 'Everybody out—one at a time and no shoving!'

Every house in the village had its lights on and the school house doors were standing wide; willing helpers helped the children out of the bus and hustled them inside where anxious mothers claimed their offspring and began the task of getting them into dry clothes, feeding them hot milk and massaging cold arms and legs. There were no men back yet, Mr Wallace told them, but he had done them proud, with a roaring stove and hot drinks and offers of help to get the children to their homes. They lifted Mr MacDow out last of all and carried him to the warmth of the stove and Eleanor, getting awkwardly out of her anorak and kicking off her boots, paused only long enough to call a brief 'Hullo,' to her father before going to help Fulk. The leg was set as well as it could be done with what they had at their disposal, and Mr MacDow, very white, was given another generous dose of whisky before Fulk asked: 'Is there a telephone working?'

Mr MacFarlane shook his head. 'I'm afraid not. The most I can promise is that the moment it's possible

they'll get it mended—they're very quick about it.
Should MacDow be in hospital?'

'It would be better for him, though it's possible to
manage as we are. Shall I just take a quick look at the
boys? Those who live near enough could go home, the
rest will have to be given a bed for the night. I've my
case in the car, I'll give MacDow something to ease the
pain and get him home too. Is there someone to look
after him?'

'His wife—she's expecting a baby, though.' Eleanor
sounded doubtful.

'In that case, if she would be so kind as to put me up
for the night I could keep an eye on him.' He glanced
round. 'If I could have a hand, we could get him home—
but we had better check the boys first.'

A job which was quickly done. The boys seemed little
the worse for their adventure, in fact, now that it was all
over, they were beginning to enjoy themselves. They
went, one by one, escorted by mothers, grannies and big
sisters, until there was only Henry left.

Fulk collected Mr Wallace and old Mr MacNab, who
had stayed to help with the schoolmaster. 'We'll go now.
Eleanor, stay here with your father and Henry, I'll be
back in ten minutes.'

'Why?' She was a little impatient; she wanted to get
home and eat a huge meal and then go to bed and sleep
the clock round.

He didn't answer her directly, only said: 'Ten
minutes,' and went away, leaving the three of them by
the stove. Eleanor fell asleep at once and only roused
when Fulk's voice wakened her with: 'Come on, home.'

She looked at him owl-eyed, said 'Oh,' in a lost voice
and got herself to her feet, dragging on her anorak and

boots once more and hunting for her torch, and then following the others out into the cold night. The snow had slowed its mad pace and the wind, although strong, was no longer a gale. It was dark too, for the electricity had failed while she slept. It was a miracle that it had survived so long, but they had their torches and with Fulk leading the way, battled their way in single file until the dim light from the oil lamp in the manse hall told them that they were home.

Mrs MacFarlane had the door open before they could reach it, and whatever worry she had felt she effectively concealed now. 'Into the sitting room,' she greeted them. 'There's hot coffee ready and while you're drinking it I'll get Henry into a hot bath—he can have his supper in bed.' She smiled at them all, although her eyes anxiously sought Fulk's face. 'He's all right, Fulk?'

He smiled reassuringly. 'Cold and hungry, that's all. Bed and bath are just the thing. He behaved splendidly—they all did.'

Henry puffed out his chest. 'I wasn't really frightened,' he declared, 'though it was very cold.'

His mother put a hand on his shoulder. 'You shall tell me all about it, dear, but we mustn't be too long; Eleanor will want a bath too—and Fulk.' She glanced round as they were leaving the room. 'You'll spend the night, Fulk?'

He explained about spending the night at Mr MacDow's house. 'But I would love a bath, if I may…'

Mrs MacFarlane nodded briskly. 'Of course, and you'll stay for supper too—they won't expect you back for a little while, will they? I'm on edge to hear all about it, but first things first.' With which words she led Henry upstairs.

They had their supper round the fire. Eleanor, warm at last from her bath, her hair plaited tidily and wrapped in a thick dressing gown, could have slept sitting there. She spooned her soup slowly, content to be back home and safe with Fulk sitting unconcernedly opposite her. She frowned a little, her tired mind grappling with the fact that it was possible to like someone very much even when one didn't like him at all. It didn't make sense, and she gave up presently, thinking that it was absurd to suppose that she had ever not liked him. After all, she had been a very little girl when she had vowed to hate him for ever—and a girl had a right to change her mind. She smiled sleepily at him and was strangely disturbed at his intent, unsmiling look. He said good night very shortly afterwards, and Eleanor went upstairs to bed, to wake in the night and wonder about that look. She turned over and curled herself into a ball under the bedclothes; probably they would bicker just as they always did when next they met. It would be nice if they didn't, she thought sleepily as she closed her eyes again.

CHAPTER FOUR

THE BRIGHT SUNSHINE and complete lack of wind just didn't seem true the next morning. Eleanor took an astonished look out of the window, dressed quickly in an elderly kilt and thick jersey, and went downstairs to breakfast. Her mother looked up as she went into the kitchen. 'There you are, darling,' she said happily. 'How lovely to have yesterday over and done with. Breakfast's ready—don't forget it's church at ten o'clock.'

Eleanor nodded. 'I hadn't forgotten, Mother, but there'll be time to clear the path before I need to dress.' She carried the plates to the table and went to call Henry. 'When's Margaret coming back?' she asked as they sat down at the table.

'As soon as the snow plough clears the road, and I imagine they will be out already—that was a freak blizzard, it didn't get far. The men were telling me that the telephone was still working between Durness and the west coast, although the lines were down to the south of us, and beyond Lairg the roads are pretty clear. I wonder how Fulk got on at the MacDows'.' He glanced at his son. 'Henry, are you not hungry?'

Three pairs of eyes stared at the youngest member of the family. Usually he ate as much as the three of them together, but now, this morning he was pecking at his food in a manner totally unlike him.

'Do you feel ill, darling?' his mother asked anxiously.

'I'm just not hungry—I expect I'll eat an enormous dinner to make up for it.'

Eleanor studied him unobtrusively; he looked all right, a little pale perhaps, and certainly listless; could be that he hadn't got over his chickenpox as well as they thought he had. Doctor MacClew might go over him again—she hoped worriedly that the boy hadn't caught a chill; it would be a miracle if they all escaped with nothing at all.

She had intended asking Henry to help her with the snow on the path between the manse and the little church, but instead she helped her mother wash up, made the beds and went outside on her own. There was still an hour before church and the exercise would do her good. She was almost ready when a large hand came down on hers, so that she was forced to stop shovelling.

'Good morning,' said Fulk. 'None the worse for our little adventure, I see. Here, give me that and go and make yourself decent for church.'

'No, I won't,' said Eleanor immediately. 'For one thing, I'm dressed for it and you're not.'

He still had her hand fast. 'And for the other thing?' he prompted her softly.

'Well, I don't much like being told what to do.' She looked up at him and the question tripped off her tongue before she could stop it. 'Does Imogen do exactly as you say?'

He didn't look in the least put out, only a little surprised. 'It's hard to say; I don't remember any occasion when it was necessary for me to ask her to do anything.'

She blinked. 'How funny!'

The dark eyes became cold, he said silkily: 'Funny? Perhaps you would explain…'

She said hastily: 'I didn't mean funny funny—just strange. Don't you see much of each other?' She went on staring at him, asking for trouble and not much caring.

'I hardly feel that it is any of your business, Eleanor, and if you're trying to cast doubts into my head, I can assure you that it's a waste of time.' His voice was as cold as his eyes; he wasn't bothering to conceal his anger. But she was angry too now, with him and with herself for starting the whole miserable conversation in the first place.

'You're awful,' she said, making it even worse, 'just as bad as you used to be; I might have known…I thought just once or twice that I'd been mistaken, that you'd changed, but you haven't.' She tossed her head. 'Here, take the beastly shovel!' Her glance swept over his undoubtedly expensive tweeds and well-tailored camel hair topcoat. 'You'll look very silly shovelling snow in Savile Row suiting, but that's your affair!'

She flounced back indoors, muttering at his roar of laughter.

When she came downstairs twenty minutes later, in her tweed coat and little fur hat, it was to find him in the sitting room, talking to the rest of the family, and he looked as though he had never seen a snow shovel in his life. He got to his feet as she went in and said gravely: 'I like that hat,' and added to the room at large: 'It's surprising what clothes do for a woman.'

Her father turned round to look at her. 'Indeed, yes. Fulk is quite right, my dear, that is a pretty hat, though I thought you looked very nice yesterday in that hooded thing.'

'Father, my oldest anorak!'

'Your father's got something there—you did look nice. You looked sensible and trustworthy too, exactly the kind of companion a man wants when he's on a ticklish job.'

She gasped. 'Well, I never…after all the things you said!'

He grinned. 'Coals of fire, Eleanor.'

'A whole scuttle of them—what's come over you?'

He answered lightly, 'Oh, a change of heart,' and got to his feet again. 'Ought we to be on our way?'

The church was very full. Even those who usually attended only upon special occasions had turned up, deeming yesterday's occurrence well worth a few prayers of thanks. The small building, bursting at the seams, rocked to the thankful voices, and Eleanor, who sang quite well in an amateurish way, sang too, a little off-key on the top notes but making up for that by her enthusiasm. Fulk, standing beside her, glanced at her several times, and Mrs MacFarlane, watching him, wondered if her daughter's slightly off-key rendering of the hymns nettled him at all, then changed her mind when she saw the little smile tugging the corners of his mouth.

Fulk went back to the MacDows' house after church, casually taking Eleanor with him. 'And before you fly into a temper because you don't want to come,' he informed her as soon as they were out of earshot of the rest of the family, 'I want to ask you something. Does Henry strike you as being his usual self?'

'Oh, you've noticed it, too,' she exclaimed, quite forgetting that she had intended to be coolly polite and nothing more. 'You don't think he's sickening for something?'

'I can't tell, but I had an idea in church. Would your mother and father allow him to come and stay with me for a few weeks?' He saw her sudden look of alarm. 'No, don't instantly suspect that he's dying of some obscure disease—he's a tough little boy and healthy enough, but he has a good brain, much above average, I should imagine, and he tends to work it too hard. A holiday wouldn't do him any harm, away from lessons and even the remote chance of going to school. I'll keep a fatherly eye on him and he'll be free to roam where he likes. I live in the country, you know, and there's plenty for him to do. I'll see that if he must read, it will be nothing to tease that brain of his…'

They were almost at the MacDow croft. 'Why are you doing it?' asked Eleanor, then wished she hadn't spoken, for it sounded rude and for the moment at any rate, they were friends. But Fulk only answered placidly: 'I like the boy.'

'It's a marvellous idea,' she ruminated, half aloud, and then choosing her words carefully: 'Will there be anyone else? I mean, does anyone else live in your house?'

His smile held a tinge of mockery. 'Still determined to think the worst of me, Eleanor?' And when she said sharply: 'No, of course not,' he went on smoothly: 'I've a housekeeper, a good sort who will feed Henry like a fighting cock—there are a couple of other people around too, but Imogen won't be there; that's what you really wanted to know, wasn't it? And if you credit me with entertaining young women while she's away then I must disappoint you—my household would do credit to a monk.'

'I can't think why you should suppose me to be interested in your private life,' declared Eleanor haughtily. She tossed her head rather grandly, tripped up on a hidden lump of snow and fell flat on her face. Fulk scooped her up, stood her on her feet, brushed her down, kissed her swiftly and said gently: 'There's no need to get uppity.' A remark she didn't have time to answer because

they were on the doorstep and Mrs MacDow was opening the door.

The schoolmaster was sitting in a chair drawn up to
the fire, a pair of very out-of-date crutches by his side.
He greeted them cheerfully and when Eleanor expressed
surprise at seeing him there in his dressing gown, smok-
ing his pipe and looking almost normal, he laughed and
assured her that it was all the doctor's doing.

'Not ideal,' murmured Fulk. 'The crutches are heir-
looms from some bygone age, but they'll do until we
can get you into Durness. They'll do an X-ray and put
the leg in plaster and a walking iron—all you'll need
then is a good stout stick.'

They stayed talking for a few minutes, lighthearted
argument as to the ill-fated climbing expedition. 'We
should have been in a pretty bad way if you hadn't come
along,' said Mr MacDow. 'We knew a search party
would come out after us sooner or later, but if they'd
waited until there were enough men, the boys would
have been in poor shape to tackle the scramble down.
That was a brilliant idea bringing the bus, though how
you managed to get it up there beats me.'

'We had our difficult moments,' Fulk acknowledged.
'Luckily Eleanor proved to be a sort of pocket compass.'

They looked at her and she went a faint pink, so that
she looked quite eye-catching, what with flushed cheeks
and the fur hat crowning her brown hair. 'I couldn't have
driven the bus,' she pointed out, 'and if the men had
been here they would have found the way just as well—
better, perhaps.'

'They wouldn't have fancied taking that bus,' declared
the schoolmaster. 'We'll be indebted to you, Doctor—I
doubt if we'll ever be able to do the same for you, but
you've made a great many friends in the village.'

'Thank you—and that reminds me, I wanted a word with you about young Henry. I've spoken to Eleanor already, but I should appreciate your advice before I say anything to Mr MacFarlane.'

Eleanor had to admit that he put his case very well; Mr MacDow agreed wholeheartedly that Henry was far too clever for his age. 'A real boy, make no mistake about that,' he observed, 'but the laddie tires himself out, reading beyond his years; working away at problems, wanting to know this, that and the other. He could miss a few weeks at school and never know the difference. If you say it would do the boy some good then I'll not say nay, Doctor, provided his father hasn't any objection.'

The pastor had no objection at all and his wife was openly delighted. 'What a dear man you are, Fulk,' she exclaimed. 'It's just what will do him the most good; his head is stuffed with algebra and science and learning to play chess, and there's no stopping him.' She looked so happy and relieved that Eleanor bent to kiss her swiftly in understanding. 'He's over in the loft,' said Mrs MacFarlane, 'feeding Mrs Trot and the kittens, do go and tell him yourself.' She added in an offhand way, 'Go with Fulk, will you, Eleanor? Henry forgot to take the milk with him, and Mrs Trot will need it before the evening.'

Henry was sitting where his big sister usually sat, on the floor with the kittens playing round him, while Mrs Trot ate her dinner. He had heard them on the ladder and turned his head to watch them. 'I thought it was you,' he remarked. 'It isn't our dinnertime yet, is it?'

'Almost.' Eleanor chose an apple and offered it to Fulk before taking one for herself; they shared the sack of potatoes and munched contentedly for a minute or two until Fulk asked: 'Henry, how do you feel about spending a week or two with me in Holland?'

The little boy's face became one large grin. 'Me? Honour bright? Just me? Oh, Fulk, how absolutely smashing!' The grin faded. 'I have to have a passport. I was reading about that the other day—I haven't got one.'

'That's OK, that can be arranged, but we'll need to go to Glasgow for it. I tell you what, if I take Eleanor back tomorrow, you could come with us and we could see about it on the way—that's provided the roads are clear. We can get your photo taken and go to the Passport Office and see what they can do for us. If it's OK, we'll come back here and pack your bags.'

'Oh, golly!' Henry was on his feet, capering round the bare boards, only to stop abruptly. 'I'll have to leave the kittens.' His face fell as he picked up the smallest and ugliest of them, the one no one wanted. 'No one's offered for Moggy.'

Eleanor felt a glow of warmth as Fulk exclaimed instantly: 'I will—I've a dog and my housekeeper has a cat of her own, but we could do with a kitten. We'll take him with us.'

'I say—really? You mean that, Fulk?'

'I mean it—I'm partial to kittens around the house.'

Eleanor's tongue was too quick for her once more. 'Supposing your Imogen doesn't like him?'

Fulk turned a bland face to hers. 'My dear girl, don't you know that people in love are prepared to do anything for the loved one's sake?'

An observation which depressed her very much; quite possibly Imogen was a very nice girl, prepared to sacrifice her own likes and dislikes just to please Fulk; which was a pity, because it was hard to dislike a nice girl, and she had made up her mind to dislike Imogen.

She contented herself by saying: 'Well, I wouldn't know about that. I say, there's really no need to take me back tomorrow—Edinburgh will be right out of your way, and the roads...'

'Nervous? Surely not after yesterday's little trip. We can go via Glasgow and if there's any hitch or waiting about to be done, we can take you to the hospital and then go back there.'

He made it all sound so easy—convenient, almost. She found herself agreeing with him as Henry tidied the kittens back into their box, planted Mrs Trot beside them and announced that he was quite ready for his dinner.

The meal was an animated one, with everyone talking at once, and Eleanor was the only one, so she thought, to notice that Henry ate hardly anything at all. But she wasn't; she looked up and caught Fulk's eyes upon her and knew that he had seen it too and wasn't going to say anything. Obedient to that dark glance, she didn't say anything either.

The snow ploughs and the weather had done their work by morning; the roads were clear, the telephone and the electricity were once more functioning and although there was a good deal of snow still lying around it wasn't likely to hinder them much. Fulk was at the manse by half past ten, having got up early and driven Mr MacDow, wedged on to the back seat, into Durness, where they had X-rayed the limb, clapped it in plaster and a walking iron and handed him back to Fulk, who had in turn handed him over to his own doctor's care. He brought the news that the road to Lairg was more or less clear and beyond that there should be no difficulties, and they left at once, stopping to lunch in Inverness at the Station Hotel, where even the magnificence of the restaurant and the remarkable choice of food did little to increase Henry's appetite. Of course, he was excited, thought Eleanor worriedly as she joined in the cheerful talk of her companions. Whatever was wrong with the boy's appetite hadn't affected his spirits.

The Panther made light work of the hundred and seventy miles remaining of their journey, so that they reached the Passport Office with half an hour to spare before it closed for the day and they would have been there sooner, only they had stopped on the way for some instant passport photos of Henry. Eleanor stayed in the little outer office while Fulk and Henry went to see what could be done. It was a dull little room, with nothing to read but pamphlets about emigrating and a stern warning of the dire punishment awaiting anyone who tampered with their passport. She read these interesting titbits of information several times, and then for lack of anything else to do, found paper and pen in her handbag and amused herself making a list of things she would like to buy; it was a long list and imaginative and she headed it boldly 'Things I would like to have,' and underlined it twice. She was on the point of crossing out the more frivolous items when Fulk and Henry came back, looking pleased with themselves; obviously they had been successful. She stood up, dropped her handbag, her gloves and the paper and asked: 'Is it OK?' to the two bent forms scrabbling round on the floor picking up her possessions.

Henry lifted his head. 'Rather. Fulk talked—they were super. We're to call and fetch it when we go.'

'And when's that?'

'The day after tomorrow.' Fulk spoke absentmindedly, Eleanor's piece of paper in one hand. 'What's this—don't tell me I shouldn't read it for it's not a letter. Besides, you shouldn't drop things all over the place so carelessly.'

'I was surprised,' she excused herself. 'It's only a list.'

She put out a hand which he instantly took hold of and held. 'Sable coat,' he read in an interested voice, 'Gina Fratini dress, Givenchy scarf, Marks and Spencer sweater, toothpaste,' he chuckled and went on slowly, 'surgical scissors, every paperback I want, roses for Christmas. Seems a pretty sensible list to me, but why roses for Christmas, Eleanor?'

She tugged at her hand to no good purpose. 'Oh, it's just something silly, you know…I mean, if anyone bothered to give me roses, masses of them, I mean, not just six in cellophane—when everyone else was having potted hyacinths and chrysanthemums, I'd know that I meant something to—to someone…' She paused because he was looking at her rather strangely. 'Like the sables,' she went on chattily, 'and the Givenchy scarf…'

'But not the toothpaste,' he suggested, half laughing.

'No.' She took the odds and ends Henry was holding out to her and stuffed them away and said brightly: 'How nice that everything went off without a hitch. Aren't you wildly excited, Henry?'

Henry said that yes, he was, and began to explain exactly how a passport was issued and the conditions imposed. 'And wasn't it clever of Fulk to know that he had to have a letter from Father to show them?' he demanded. 'I shall be glad when I'm grown up and can do those sort of things.' He cast a disparaging look at his surroundings. 'May we go soon?'

Fulk took them to tea; to the Central Hotel, large and impressive with its draperies and its mirrors and chandeliers. Henry looked round, his eyes wide. He had never been in such a place before for his tea, and it was an experience which he was enjoying. Eleanor blessed Fulk for his understanding of a small boy's idea of a treat, and tried not to worry at the small meal her brother was making.

They took her back to Edinburgh when they had finished, going with her to the Nurses' Home door, after a protracted walk across the forecourt because Henry wanted to know exactly where everything was and how many people worked in the hospital for how many hours and how much money. 'I shall be a famous doctor,' he told them, 'a physician, like Fulk. Perhaps I might be your partner—you'll probably be needing one by the time I'm grown up, Fulk.'

'Very probably,' Fulk agreed gravely. 'Now let us say goodbye to Eleanor and make for home, shall we? It's a long drive; you can sit in the back and go to sleep, if you wish.'

'Go to sleep? Of course I shall sit with you in front and watch the dashboard and you can explain...'

'You're sure you want him?' asked Eleanor, giving her brother a hug and looking anxiously at Fulk over his small shoulder.

'Quite sure.' He smiled and held out his hand. 'Don't work too hard,' he advised her, and didn't say goodbye, only put her case inside the door for her and then cast an arm round Henry's bony frame and turned away. She was tempted to delay them with some question or other; she didn't want to be left, but she remembered that he had a journey of many hours before him. She went through the door and closed it quietly without looking back.

She felt bad-tempered in the morning, due, she told herself, to the long car journey the day before and all the excitement during the blizzard. That it might also be due to the fact that Fulk hadn't bothered to say goodbye to her was something she had no intention of admitting, not even to herself. Despite her best efforts, she was snappy with the nurses and found the patients tiresome too, and making the excuse that she had to wash her hair and make a telephone call home, she didn't go, as she usually did, to the Sisters' sitting room when she got off duty, but retired to her room, where she sat on her bed and brooded.

Hunger drove her down to supper, and in the babble of talk round the table, her unusual quietness was hardly noticed, although several of her closer friends wondered if she were starting a cold or merely feeling unsettled after her weekend. Probably the latter, they decided, and bore her off to drink tea with them, carefully not asking questions. Someone had asked her at breakfast that morning if she had found the blizzard very awful and she had answered so briefly that they had concluded that for some reason or other she didn't want to talk about it.

She felt a little better the next morning, though; she was a girl with plenty of common sense, to let herself be put out by something which wasn't important to her was plain foolish; she went on duty determined to be nice to everyone and succeeded very well, plunging into the daily problems of the ward with zest, listening to Miss Tremble's everlasting grumbles and conducting a round with Sir Arthur and his retinue with her usual good humour and efficiency. It was at the end of this time-consuming exercise that he, sipping coffee in her office, remarked: 'You look washed out, Sister. Shovelling snow evidently doesn't agree with you.'

'Shovel…how did you know that, sir?' She put down her cup and eyed him in some surprise.

'Van Hensum told me—he must have worked you too hard.'

She rushed to Fulk's defence. 'No—indeed no, Sir Arthur, I did very little, he was the one who did everything.'

'H'm, well—he didn't mention his own activities.'

She told her companion at some length, sparing no details. 'So you see,' she concluded, 'he was pretty super.' She frowned; the whole family had got into the habit of using Henry's favourite word. 'He…' she began; there was no other word— 'He was super.'

Sir Arthur studied his nails and hid a smile. 'I have always found Doctor van Hensum—er—pretty super myself, purely from a professional point of view, of course.' He got up. 'Many thanks for the coffee, Sister.' He glanced at his watch. 'Dear me, is that the time?' He wandered to the door and she accompanied him down the short corridor which led to the swing doors, where he nodded affably, muttered something about being late as usual and hurried away.

Eleanor went back into the ward and plunged into her work once more. The temptation to sit down somewhere quiet and think about Fulk was tempting but pointless. Her mind edged away from the idea that it would be nice if he were to call with Henry on their way to Holland, but Fulk didn't do things to oblige people, only to please himself. This glaring untruth caused her to frown so heavily that Bob Wise, the Medical Officer on duty, walking down the ward to meet her, asked: 'I say, are you angry with me about something?'

She hastened to deny it with such friendliness that he was emboldened to ask her to go out with him that evening. A film, he suggested diffidently, and brightened visibly when she agreed. He was a pleasant young man, very English; he had paid her what she realized was a rare compliment when he had first come to the hospital, telling her that she spoke like an English girl, a remark which she rightly guessed had been born from homesickness and the girl he had left behind him. They had become casual friends since then and from time to time spent an evening together.

So she went to the cinema with him and afterwards sat over a cup of coffee with him in a nearby café, while he told her the latest news of his Maureen. They had known each other since childhood; he had told her that the first time they had met, and their plans had been settled long ago. Eleanor, listening to him discussing the wedding which was at least two years away, wondered what it would be like to have your future cut and dried; to know that you would never be tempted to fall in love with anyone else—it would be wonderful to be as sure as that. She had fancied herself in love on several occasions, of course, but never so deeply that she had felt that life would stop for her when she fell out of it again. Her mother had declared on more than one occasion that she was hard to please; perhaps she was. She sighed a little and begged Bob to describe, just once more, the engagement ring he had bestowed upon Maureen.

She was so busy the next morning that she had no time to think of anything at all but her work. She heaved a sigh when she had dished the dinners, sent most of the nurses to their own meal, and started on her second round of the day, this time accompanied by the most junior nurse on her staff. They tidied beds as they went, made the patients comfortable for their short afternoon nap, and under Eleanor's experienced eye the little nurse took temperatures, had a go at the blood pressures, and charted the diabetics. They had reached Miss Tremble's bed and were, as usual, arguing with that lady, this time about the freshness of the lettuce she had had on her dinner plate, when she broke off her diatribe to say: 'Here's that nice doctor again, Sister.'

Eleanor managed not to turn round and take a look, but the little nurse did. 'Ooh, isn't he groovy—I think he's in a hurry, Sister.'

She couldn't go on pretending that he wasn't there. She turned round and started to walk down the ward towards him with Miss Tremble's urgent: 'And don't forget that we haven't finished our discussion, Sister,' and the little nurse, uncertain as to what she should do, dogging her footsteps.

Fulk was businesslike. 'Forgive me for coming into the ward without asking you first, Sister,' he said, all politeness. 'I did mention it to Sir Arthur, but it seemed best not to telephone you.' He smiled: 'We are rather short of time.'

'We?'

'Henry is here too and dying to see you. I hope you won't mind, I left him in your office.' He glanced at the little nurse and gave her a nice smile. 'Could Nurse keep an eye on the ward for a couple of minutes while you say goodbye to him?'

'Yes, of course. Nurse Angus, you could take Miss Robertson's temp, and have a go at her BP too—I'll only be a moment.'

She walked down the ward beside Fulk without speaking, partly because he was behaving like a consultant again and partly because she couldn't think of anything to say, but once through the door and in the office with Henry prancing round her, Fulk became Fulk once more, his dark face alight with amusement. 'Well, Henry,' he asked, 'I'm right, aren't I? She doesn't look like Eleanor at all, does she?'

She stood while they looked her over slowly. 'No,' said her brother at last, 'she doesn't. I like you better with your hair hanging down your back, Eleanor, and up an apple tree or fishing, though you look very important in that funny cap.' He looked at Fulk. 'Don't you like her better when she's home?' he appealed.

'Oh, rather. She terrifies me like this, all no-nonsense and starch.' Fulk grinned at her. 'Looking at you now,' he declared thoughtfully, 'I can see that you have changed quite a bit since you were five—for the better. I am not of course discussing your character.'

He gave her no time to answer this, but: 'We have to go, we're on our way to Hull. Henry wants to know when he can telephone you once we get home.'

'I'm off until one o'clock tomorrow—will you have got there by then?'

'Lord, yes. Say goodbye, boy, or we shall miss the ferry.'

She bent to Henry's hug, slipped some money into his hand and begged him to send her a postcard or two, then gave him a sisterly pat on the back, for Fulk was already at the door. 'Have fun,' she said, and added a casual goodbye to Fulk who, although he had said nothing, she felt sure was impatient to be gone, but he came back from the door.

'Don't I get a kiss too?' he asked at his silkiest, and not waiting for her to speak her mind, bent his head.

When they had gone she stood looking at the closed door; Henry had kissed her with childish enthusiasm, but Fulk's technique had been perfect; moreover the enthusiasm hadn't been lacking, either.

CHAPTER FIVE

HENRY TELEPHONED the next day, his breathless voice gabbling excitedly over the wire into her interested ear. The journey had been super, so had the Panther, so was Fulk's house, and Moggy hadn't minded the dog at all and had settled down very well and wasn't that super too?

Eleanor agreed that everything was just as super as it could be; she wasn't going to get any interesting details from him, that was apparent, and she was disappointed when he rang off without any mention of Fulk other than a highly detailed account of his driving.

A series of postcards followed, inscribed in her brother's childish hand, and from the sparse information they conveyed, she concluded that life for him was just about as perfect as a small boy could wish for, although exactly what made it so wasn't clear, and when she telephoned her mother it was to hear that his letters home were almost as brief as the cards he sent and exasperatingly devoid of detail.

It was almost a week after Henry had gone that he mentioned, on a particularly colourful postcard, that his throat was a bit sore; the information had been sandwiched between the statement that he had been to a museum at Leeuwarden, and had eaten something called *poffertjes* for his supper, so that she had scarcely noted it. Mrs MacFarlane had written to say that Fulk had telephoned several times to say that Henry appeared to be enjoying himself, so much so that on the last occasion he had suggested that the boy might like to spend another week or so with him so that he could be in Holland for the feast of Sint Nikolaas. 'And of course your father and I said yes at once,' wrote her mother. 'How kind Fulk is.'

Very kind, Eleanor had to agree, feeling somehow deflated as she finished the letter and hurried off to change out of uniform. Perry Maddon, the Casualty Officer, was taking her to the theatre that evening and she was quite looking forward to it; he was another nice lad, she thought as she slid swiftly into a plain wool dress, but she would have to take care not to encourage him. At the moment they were good friends and that, as far as she was concerned, was how it was going to stay. He wasn't the man she could marry—she didn't give herself time to consider the matter further, but caught up her coat and made for the hospital entrance.

The evening was a success, the play had been amusing and afterwards they had coffee and sandwiches at the Blue Bird and walked down the road to the hospital, talking lightly about nothing in particular. It had been a pleasant evening, Eleanor decided as she tumbled into bed, so why had she this sudden feeling of impending disaster? So strong that it was keeping her awake. It couldn't be the ward; Miss Tremble, usually the root of any trouble, had been perfectly all right all day, and although there were several ill patients she didn't think that they would take a dramatic turn for the worse. She did a mental round of the ward in her sleepy head, trying to pinpoint the probable cause of her disquiet. 'My silly fancy,' she chided herself out loud, and went at last to sleep.

Only it wasn't fancy; Fulk van Hensum came the next day, walking into the ward as she served the patients' dinners from the heated trolley in the middle of the ward. She was facing away from the door so she didn't see him come in, but the little nurse, her hand outstretched to take the plate of steamed fish Eleanor was handing her, said happily: 'He's here again, Sister.'

'And who is here?' queried Eleanor, busy with the next plate. 'Sir Arthur? One of the porters? The Provost himself?'

The little nurse giggled. 'It's that great big man who came last time, Sister.' She smiled widely over Eleanor's shoulder, and Eleanor put down the plate and turned her head to have a look.

It was Fulk all right, standing very still just inside the ward door. He said at once: 'Good day to you all. Sister, might I have a word with you?'

His voice was calm, as was his face, but she went to him at once. 'Something's wrong,' she said, low-voiced. 'Will you tell me, please?' She lifted her lovely eyes to meet his dark steady gaze.

'It's Henry, isn't it?' she added, and took comfort from his reassuring little smile. When he spoke his voice held the considered, measured tones of a doctor and he took her hands in his and held them fast; their grip was very comforting. 'Yes, it's Henry. He has rheumatic fever.'

Her mouth felt dry. 'I remember now, he had a sore throat—he wrote that on one of those postcards… Is he—is he very ill?'

'You mean, is he going to die, don't you, my dear? No, he's not. He's very ill but not, I think, dangerously so.' His smile became very gentle. 'If that had been the case I shouldn't have left him, you know.'

'No, of course not. How silly of me, I'm sorry. Is he in hospital?'

Fulk's brows rose a little. 'Certainly not. He's at my home with two excellent nurses to look after him. The only thing is, he wants you, Eleanor.'

'Then I must go to him—may I come back with you?' She raced on, thinking out loud without giving him a chance to answer her. 'No, that won't do—I expect you're over here on business of your own, but I could go tonight. They probably won't give me leave, but I shall go just the same. I must telephone Mother first, though, and you'll have to tell me where you live—you wouldn't mind, would you?'

He had her hands still in his. 'Dear girl, how you do run on, and there's no need. I'm here to take you to Henry; I've already telephoned your parents and I've been to see your Principal Nursing Officer. You're free to go just as soon as you can hand over to your staff nurse. I'm on my way to Tongue now to fetch Margaret; she's coming too, for when Henry feels better he'll want to be up and about, and he mustn't do too much too soon, you know that as well as I—I thought she might help to amuse him during his enforced idleness. She will be ready and waiting for me; we'll be back to pick you up within a few hours.'

She looked at him in bewilderment. 'Fulk, Tongue's three hundred miles from here, even in that car of yours it would take you hours...'

'Of course it would, but I've a plane to fly me up to Wick, and as good luck would have it, James is at the manse and will drive Margaret to the airport to meet me; we should both arrive there at about the same time and be back here without much time lost.'

She smiled rather shakily at him. 'You've thought of everything. Thank you, Fulk. Tell me what time I'm to be ready and where I'm to meet you.'

'Good girl!' He looked at his watch. 'There'll be a taxi to take you to the airport—can you be ready by five o'clock? You may have to wait for a little while, for I'm not sure just how long we shall be. Bring enough luggage for a couple of weeks—and don't forget your passport, and when you get to the airport go to the booking hall and wait until we come. OK?'

Eleanor nodded. 'Yes. Oh, Fulk, how kind you are— I feel so mean…'

He didn't ask her why she felt mean, only smiled faintly and gave her back her hands. 'Go and finish those dinners,' he advised her. *'Tot ziens.'*

A little over four hours later, sitting quietly in the airport, her one piece of luggage at her feet, Eleanor had the leisure to look back over the afternoon. It had been all rush and bustle, of course, but there had been no difficulties; Fulk must have seen to those. She had merely done exactly as he had told her to do, trying not to think too much about Henry, keeping her mind on prosaic things, like what to wear and what to pack. She had taken the minimum of everything in the end, and worn her warm tweed coat over a green jersey dress, and because it was a cold evening and it might be even colder in Holland, she had put on the little fur hat and the fur-lined gloves she had bought herself only that week. She looked very nice, and several men turned to give her a second look, although she was quite unaware of this— indeed, she was unaware of Fulk standing a little way off, looking at her too, until she had a feeling that she was being watched, and when she saw who it was she stood up quickly, relief sending a faint colour into her pale face as he walked over to her and picked up her baggage.

'You haven't been waiting too long?' he asked. 'Margaret's waiting in the plane—if you're ready?'

Perhaps he was tired, she thought as she walked beside him; his voice had sounded austere and formal, as though her being there annoyed him. Perhaps it did, but it was no time to split hairs as to who liked whom or didn't. Henry was the only one who mattered. She followed him through the formalities, taken aback to find that he had chartered a plane to take them over to Holland; she had supposed that they were going on a normal flight, but perhaps there wasn't a direct flight to Groningen. It must be costing him the earth, she worried silently, but there wasn't time to think about that now; Margaret, waiting eagerly for them, was full of messages from her mother and father and questions about Henry, all jumbled up with excited talk about her journey. 'And wasn't it lucky that I had my passport for that school trip last summer,' she wanted to know, 'and that James was home. There's a letter from Mother in my pocket. She's very worried, but she says she knows Henry's going to be all right with you and Fulk there— Oh, look, we're moving!'

It was only when they were airborne and Margaret had become silent enough for Eleanor to gather her wits together that she realized what the journey had entailed for Fulk. He had been very efficient and it must have taken his precious time—consultants hadn't all that time to spare from their work—and the cost...her mind boggled at that. She turned round to where he was sitting behind them, wanting to tell him how grateful she was, and found him asleep. He looked different now, the faint arrogance which she detected from time to time in his face had gone. He bore the look of a tired man enjoying an untroubled nap, and for some reason it put her in mind of that time, so long ago, when he had picked her up and comforted her. He had been safe then, he was safe now; nothing could happen to her... Her face softened and she smiled faintly, then composed her face quickly, but not quickly enough.

'Now, why do you look at me like that?' demanded Fulk softly. 'I could almost delude myself into believing that you had changed your opinion of me.'

'You have been very kind,' she began primly, and he grinned.

'Ah, back to normal and that disapproving tone of yours.'

'That's unfair!' she cried. 'I was just going to thank you for being so absolutely marvellous, and now you mock at me and it's impossible for me to say it...'

'So don't, dear girl; my motives have been purely selfish, you know. If you're with Henry I shall feel free to come and go as I please.'

'That's not true—of all the silly tales! You know as well as I do...' She stopped and looked away for a moment and then back again at his smiling face. 'I'm truly grateful.'

He said, gently mocking: 'That I should live to see the day when Eleanor MacFarlane is grateful to me,' and then, before she could protest at that: 'What is in that cardboard box?'

'Crowdie—Henry loves it. I thought, when he gets better and begins to eat, he might like it on his bread and butter. There's a little Orkney cheese too. They'll keep in the fridge—you've got one, haven't you?'

There was a gleam at the back of his eyes. 'I believe so—if not, I'll get one the moment we arrive.'

She looked at him in astonishment. 'But surely you must know what you've got in your own house?'

'Well, I'm a busy man, you know—I tend to leave such things to my housekeeper.'

'The sooner you have a wife, the better,' declared Eleanor matter-of-factly. 'She'll see to your household. I expect your housekeeper will be glad to have someone to consult about such things.'

'Well, I shall have a wife soon, shan't I?' His voice was meek. 'Though I have a strong feeling that Imogen won't wish to be bothered with such things as fridges—she isn't very interested in the kitchen.'

'Oh, I'm sure she will be once you're married,' said Eleanor hearteningly.

'And you? Do you like the kitchen, Eleanor?'

She drew Margaret's sleeping head on to her shoulder. 'Yes, of course, but it wouldn't do if I didn't, living where we do—you've seen for yourself how far away it is; we have to be independent of shops, you know.'

'You don't hanker after the bright lights?' He asked the question half seriously.

'No—at least I don't think so; I don't know much about them.'

'So if some man living at the back of beyond wanted to marry you, you wouldn't hesitate to say yes?'

'If I loved him I wouldn't hesitate, but then it wouldn't matter where he lived.'

He gave a little nod, much in the manner of one who had solved himself a problem. 'Is Margaret asleep?' and when she said yes: 'You had better close your own eyes—it may be well past your bedtime by the time you get your sleep tonight.' His voice was cold and formal again, he closed his eyes as he spoke and she looked at him indignantly; he had a nasty way of making her feel, when it suited him, of no account.

Hours later, sitting by Henry's bed, holding his hot

hand in hers, she had all the time in the world to concede
that Fulk's advice had been good. She had dozed off,
still indignant, and had only wakened as they came in to
land at Eelde airport, a little to the south of Groningen,
where she and Margaret had been bustled out with ruth-
less efficiency by Fulk, guided through Customs and told
to get into the back seat of the waiting Panther, and when
Margaret had declared with sleepy peevishness that she
was hungry and wanted to go to bed, he had told her
with bracing kindness that she would be given her supper
in no time at all and be tucked up in bed before she
knew where she was; he gave Eleanor no such assurance,
though, and she bit back the yawn she longed to give
and tried to appear alert and wide awake. Not that that
had mattered at all, for he didn't look back at her once,
which didn't stop her asking the back of his head: 'Do
you live in Groningen? Is the city far from here?'

    He answered her over a shoulder as he took the car
away from the airport approach roads and turned into a
country road which seemed to her to be very dark. His
voice was a little impatient. 'Ten kilometres to the north,
but we only go through the outskirts. I live another eight
kilometres further on.' He turned away again, under the
impression, she decided crossly, that he had told her all
she needed to know of the geographical details. She sat
in silence then, Margaret once more asleep beside her,
and looked out of the window—not that she had been
able to see much, only the road ahead, spotlighted by
the car's powerful headlights, but presently the road had
woven itself into the city's edge and she gazed out upon
the lighted windows of the houses and stared up at the
rooftops. It was a pity that it was such a dark night, for
she could see so little, and very soon they had left the
streets behind them once more and were back in the

country. She tried again, being a dogged girl. 'What is the name of the village you live in?'

'I don't live in a village. The nearest one is called Ezingum.' He had sounded impatient still and she had lapsed into silence once more, straining her eyes to see what was outside the window. She was rewarded by a glimpse of water presently—a river, a canal perhaps, never the sea? She wanted to ask the silent man in front of her, but he would only grunt or at best answer her with that same impatience.

She sighed, much louder than she knew, and had been surprised when Fulk said quietly: 'We're almost home,' and turned the car into a narrow lane—but it wasn't a lane; she had caught a glimpse of towering gateposts on either side of the car. It was a drive, running between grass banks with the wintry outlines of larch trees above them. They rounded a bend and Eleanor saw Fulk's house for the first time. Henry had described it as a nice house and she had conjured up a rather vague picture in her mind of a pleasant villa in the residential part of Groningen, but from the number of lighted windows and the impressive porch before which they were stopping, it wasn't in the least like that. This house, even in the semi-dark, was large and solid—the manse would probably fit very nicely into its hall. She had wakened Margaret then, hushed her fretful voice demanding to know where they were, and got out of the car because Fulk had opened the door for her. As she stood beside him on the smooth gravel sweep, he had said briefly: 'Welcome to Huys Hensum, both of you,' then swept them up the steps to the front door, open now and with a little round dumpling of a woman waiting for them.

'Juffrouw Witsma,' he had introduced her, shaking her

hand and saying something to her in his own language, and they had all gone into the house...

Eleanor looked at the clock, took Henry's pulse, slipped the thermometer under his thin arm, and checked his breathing. His temperature was up a little since she had taken it last. She charted it and looked anxiously at his small white face. He was sleeping now, but he was restless too, although Fulk had expressed satisfaction at his condition. She settled back into her chair and allowed her thoughts to wander once more.

Her first glimpse of the house had taken her off balance; obviously her previous conception of Fulk as being a successful doctor, comfortably off, but no more than that, would have to be scrapped. His home, even at the first glance, had been revealed as old, magnificent and splendidly furnished. He had led them across the lofty square hall, with its polished floor strewn with rugs, its panelled walls and enormous chandelier hanging from an elaborate ceiling, into what she had supposed to be the sitting room, a room large enough to accommodate ten times their number, but somehow homelike with its enormous armchairs and sofas flanking the hooded fireplace, handsomely framed portraits on the walls and a variety of charming table lamps set on fragile tables. He had invited them to sit down, saying that he would go at once to Henry to see how he did. He was back within a short while, reassuring them at once that the boy was holding his own nicely. 'He wants to see you, Eleanor,' he had told her. 'I haven't told him that Margaret is here, time for that when he feels more himself. Juffrouw Witsma has supper ready for us—I suggest that we have it at once so that Margaret can go to bed.'

She had agreed at once, only begging that she might see Henry first, and he had raised no objection, merely remarking that if she didn't mind, he and Margaret would start their meal. 'And then if you are not back, I'll take Margaret up to her room and see her settled in,' he promised, 'but first I will show you where Henry is.'

The stairs were oak and uncarpeted, with a massive banister, and at their top she followed him across a wide landing and down two steps into a little passage, thickly carpeted. With his hand on one of the three doors in it, he turned to her. 'The day nurse is still here, I shall be taking her back to Groningen in the morning, but I arranged with the hospital that unless I telephoned, there would be no need for the night nurse.' He stared down at her, his eyes half hidden by their lids. 'Your room is next door and communicates with his, and he will be quite safe to leave while he is sleeping, but you will do just as you wish—you have only to ask for anything you require and if you would prefer the night nurse to come, I will see to it at once.'

She had thanked him sincerely. 'You are being so very kind and you have done so much already…there's no need of a nurse; if you don't mind, I'd like to be with Henry, just in case he wakes up during the night.'

He had nodded without comment and opened the door for her. She remembered how the beauty of the room had struck her and the feeling of gratitude towards Fulk for not dismissing Henry as just another little boy, prone to clumsiness and a little careless, but had considered him worthy of such handsome surroundings. But she had barely glanced at the blue and white tiled chimneypiece, the massive pillow cupboard, the tallboy and the little games table with the half-finished jigsaw puzzle on it, her eyes had flown to the narrow bed with its carved headboard and blue counterpane. Henry had looked very small and white lying there. She could hardly remember speaking to the nurse, who smiled and shook hands; she had gone at once to the chair drawn up to the bedside and sat down in it and taken her brother's hot little paw in her own hands. He had opened his eyes and said in a thread of a voice: 'Eleanor—Fulk said he'd fetch you. I'll go to sleep now.'

She had stayed quietly there while Fulk took the nurse down to her supper with Margaret and himself, promising that he would be back very shortly. 'I'm quite all right,' she had assured him, longing for a cup of tea.

He had smiled then. 'At least let me take your coat,' he suggested, 'and do be a sensible girl; you will be in and out of this room all night unless I am much mistaken, and if you don't eat you will be fit for nothing.'

He had been right, of course. He had come back surprisingly quickly and taken her place by the sleeping boy, urging her not to hurry: 'And if Henry wakes,' he had promised, 'I'll tell him you're at supper. Margaret is in her room—the second door facing the stairs—one of the maids is unpacking for her. I expect you would like to say goodnight to her.' He sat down and picked up a book and Eleanor, feeling herself dismissed, went out of the room.

Margaret, much refreshed by her supper, was disposed to be excited. 'Only imagine, a maid to unpack,' she told Eleanor, 'and there's a bathroom, all for me, and look at this room, isn't it sweet?'

It was indeed charming, pink and white and flowery with its white-painted furniture and chintz roses scattered over the curtains. Eleanor had admired it, kissed her sister goodnight and gone downstairs, where she found the housekeeper hovering in the hall, ready to lead her to her supper, a meal taken in another vast room, furnished with graceful mahogany pieces which could have been

Sheraton. She had eaten her way through soup, ham soufflé, light as air, and baked apples smothered in cream and had been happily surprised when Juffrouw Witsma, looking a little puzzled, brought in a tea tray and set it before her. She went back upstairs presently, feeling a good deal better both in self and in temper, and Fulk must have seen it, for he said at once: 'That's better. Did you get your tea?'

Eleanor had beamed widely at him. 'Oh, yes, thank you. Do you drink tea in the evening here—with your supper, I mean?'

His mouth had twitched, but she hadn't seen it. 'Well, no, but I thought that you might like it.'

She had told him that he was most thoughtful and he had said smoothly: 'Oh, there's a streak of good in every villain, you know,' and gone on to speak of Henry and his treatment. 'He's very slightly better, I fancy. It's a question of nursing and keeping him at rest while the antibiotics get to work.' He walked to the door. 'There's a bell by the bed, you have only to ring.' He had gone before she could utter a word.

Eleanor shook her head free of her thoughts and glanced at the clock again, a splendid cartel model in bronze. It was well after midnight and Fulk hadn't returned, although he had said that he would. She considered unpacking and getting ready for bed and then returning to her chair; she could doze well enough in it— she would give Fulk another half hour, she decided, just as he opened the door and came quietly towards her.

He studied the chart she offered him, cast an eye over the child and said reassuringly: 'Never mind the temperature, it should settle in a day or two. I've telephoned the manse to let them know we've arrived safely—they send you their love. Now go and have your bath and get ready for bed, I'll sit here in the meantime—I've some writing to do.'

There seemed no point in arguing; she went to her room and looked around her. Someone had unpacked her things; her nightie and dressing gown had been carefully arranged on a chair, her slippers beside it. The bed, a delicate rosewood affair canopied in pale pink silk, had been turned down and the pink-shaded lights on the bedside tables switched on. It was a lovely room, its dressing table and tallboy matching the rosewood of the bed, its gilded mirrors and chintz-covered chairs giving it an air of luxury. Eleanor kicked off her shoes and, her tired feet inches deep in carpet, went to investigate the various doors. A cupboard, a vast one, handsomely equipped with lights and drawers and shelves so that her own few bits and pieces looked quite lost in it; and then a bathroom, small and pink and gleaming, with an extravagant supply of towels and soaps and bath luxuries to make her eyes sparkle. She ran a bath, dithered blissfully between Christian Dior and Elizabeth Arden and rushed out of her clothes; she would allow herself ten minutes.

It was a little longer than that before she went back to Henry's room, swathed in her blue quilted dressing gown, her hair plaited carelessly. Fulk stood up as she went in, casting her the briefest of glances as he busied himself collecting his papers.

'My room is at the front of the house, in the centre of the gallery,' he told her. 'If you want help, don't hesitate to call me—in any case I shall look in early in the morning, and we can discuss things then. He still has two more days on antibiotics, it's a question of patience.'

Eleanor nodded, fighting down an urge to cast herself on to his shoulder and burst into tears, something she felt he would dislike very much. When she had been a little girl, he had frequently called her a watering pot and she had no intention of giving him the chance to do so again. So she wished him a calm goodnight and took up her position by Henry's bed once more.

He wakened several times during the next few hours, staring at her with round hollow eyes, obediently swallowing his medicine, taking the drink she offered, but about three o'clock he fell into a more natural sleep, and presently, despite her efforts not to do so, Eleanor fell asleep too. She wakened two hours later; Henry was still sleeping and Fulk, in a dressing gown of great magnificence, was standing on the other side of the bed, looking at her. She struggled to get rid of the sleep fogging her head and mumbled apologetically: 'I must have dropped off—it was three o'clock…'

'Go to bed,' Fulk urged her with an impersonal kindness which nonetheless brooked no refusal. 'I'll stay here for an hour or so.'

She yawned widely. Bed would be heaven and with Fulk here to look after Henry, she knew that she would sleep, but she said at once: 'No, I can't do that; you have to go to Groningen in the morning—you said so.'

'I can go later.' He dismissed the matter. 'Do as I say, Eleanor—you'll be of no use to anyone as you are.'

Not perhaps the kindest way of putting it, but true, nevertheless. She got to her feet and said uncertainly: 'Very well, but you will call me? If I could just sleep for a couple of hours…'

He hadn't moved from the bed, he didn't look at her either, only said softly: 'Of course you will be called,' and bent over Henry.

She trailed off into the bedroom, her anxious mind full of the possibility of Henry's heart being damaged by his illness, so tired that she couldn't think about it properly any more. Her thoughts became a jumble of ward jobs she might have left undone before she left, her mother's worried letter, the fact that she had forgotten to bring any handkerchiefs with her, Miss Tremble's diet, which really didn't matter anyway, Henry's small white face and Fulk, popping up over and over again. She was wondering about that when she fell asleep.

CHAPTER SIX

ELEANOR WAKENED to find a fresh-faced young girl by her bed, holding a tray. She smiled when Eleanor sat up, put the tray on her knees, went to open the long brocade curtains, saying something friendly in a soft voice as she did so, and went away.

Eleanor shook the last wisps of sleep from her head, registered that it was light and morning, even if a grey one, and saw that the little Sèvres clock on the table beside her showed the hour to be half past eight.

She bounced out of bed and, dressing gown askew, no slippers on her feet, tore silently into the next room. Fulk was exactly as she had left him, the sheets of closely written paper scattered round his chair bearing testimony to his industry. There was a tray of coffee on the small table drawn up beside him; fragrant steam rose from the cup he was about to pick up. Henry was asleep.

Fulk raised his head and looked at her; at any other time she would have been furious at the mocking tilt of his eyebrows, but now she had other things on her mind. 'Why didn't you call me?' she demanded in a whispered hiss.

The eyebrows expressed surprise as well as mockery. 'Did Tekla not bring you your breakfast? I asked her to do so.'

'Yes, she did.' She added a belated thank you. 'But it's half past eight.' She paused to survey him; he looked tired, but perhaps that was due to his unshaven chin and

93

all the writing he had done. 'You have to go to Groningen,' she reminded him.

'How tedious that remark is becoming, Eleanor.' His voice was tolerant but his eyes still mocked her. 'I'm quite capable of organising my own day without your help, you know, and in any case at the moment you are being nothing but a hindrance. Go and eat your breakfast and put some clothes on.' The glance he gave her left her in no doubt as to what he thought of her appearance. 'You can have half an hour.'

He began to write once more, pausing only to add: 'Henry has slept soundly. We will discuss his treatment before I leave the house.'

She looked at him blankly, realizing dimly at that moment that her childish opinion of him had undergone a change, which considering his arrogant manner towards her was a little bewildering. She bit her lip and drew in her breath like a hurt child, murmured incoherently and turned on her heel. Fulk reached the door a second or so before she did and caught her by the shoulders. 'Why do you have to look like that?' he asked her harshly, and when she asked: 'Like what?', he went on: 'Like you used to when I wouldn't let you climb trees.' He gave her a little shake. 'I never thought...' he began, then went on in quite a different voice: 'I'm sorry, Eleanor— I had no right to speak to you like that. You've been wonderful—I whisked you away with no warning and then allowed you to sit here all night.' He bent and kissed her cheek gently. 'Now go and dress and eat your breakfast—please, Eleanor.'

She smiled then. 'You must be tired too, and you've a day's work before you. You've been so kind, Fulk—I keep saying that, don't I?—but I can never thank you enough.' She added shyly: 'You've changed.'

'We have both changed—no, that's not right, you've not changed at all.'

Refreshed by a hasty breakfast, she bathed and dressed in a russet skirt and sweater, piled her hair neatly, and went back to Henry's room. Fulk was waiting for her. 'I'll be back within half an hour,' he told her from the door, and then: 'You haven't made up your face, it looks nice like that.'

She was left staring at the closing door, but only for a moment, for Henry opened his eyes at that moment and said in a wispy voice: 'Gosh, I'm thirsty.'

She gave him a drink, persuaded him to take his medicine, took his temperature and pulse, and washed his face and hands. 'And later on,' she told him firmly, 'after Fulk has been to see you, I shall give you a bedbath and change the sheets, and then you'll have another nice nap before lunch. Do you ache, my dear?'

Henry nodded. 'A bit, but I feel better, I think. When is Fulk coming?'

'Very soon—he's been sitting here for these last few hours while I had a sleep. He has to go to the hospital this morning.'

Henry closed his eyes, 'He's super,' he mumbled, 'I shall certainly be a doctor when I'm a man, I'm quite certain of that now—I shall be like Fulk; very clever and kind.'

'Yes, dear.' She smiled at him. 'Now stick out your tongue and I'll clean it for you. No, you can't do it; I'm sure Fulk has told you that you will get well much more quickly if you just lie still. I know it's a dead bore, but in a few days you'll be able to sit up. Shall I tell you a secret? Margaret came with us, she's coming to see you presently, and when you're better she'll be able to play cards with you.'

Henry smiled. 'Smashing—and will you read to me, too?'

'Certainly. Are there any English books here?'

'Dozens and dozens, they're in the library downstairs. Fulk lets me go there whenever I want, just so long as I put the books back again. He bought some in Groningen for me, too.'

'Splendid, we'll go through them together later. Now you're going to drink your milk, my dear.'

Fulk came back a few minutes later. Immaculately dressed, freshly shaved, he showed no sign of tiredness. His manner was friendly as he checked his small patient's pulse, gently examined him and pronounced himself satisfied. 'Two more days of antibiotics,' he stated, 'and by then you will be feeling much better, but that won't mean that you can get up, because you can't—it's important that you rest even if you think it a waste of time, so you will do exactly what Eleanor tells you—you understand that, old chap?'

He glanced at Eleanor, who murmured agreement; antibiotics might bring about a wonderful improvement in rheumatic fever; they also caused the patient to feel so well that there was a danger of him getting up too soon and doing far too much, and that would do his heart no good at all.

'Why?' asked Henry.

The big man eyed the small boy thoughtfully. 'Since you are going to be a doctor one day, you are quite entitled to know the reasons for lying still and having everything done for you. I will explain them to you, but not now, for it would take quite a long time and I haven't even five minutes—I'm due at the hospital.' He grinned cheerfully at the white face on the pillow, barely glancing at Eleanor as he wished them *tot ziens*. She supposed that she had been included in his farewell, even if with such unflattering casualness, and her own 'goodbye' was cool. She took care not to watch him as he left the room too, so that it was all the more vexing when he popped his handsome head round the door again and found her gaze fixed upon it.

'You'll need some time off,' he reminded her. 'If you agree, Margaret could sit with Henry for an hour and certainly while you have your meals—she's a sensible child, isn't she?' He smiled at her suddenly. 'Why were you looking like that?' he asked.

'Like what?'

'Disappointed—bewildered—wistful, I'm not sure which. Never mind, I'll find out some time.' He had gone, and this time he didn't come back.

The day passed slowly. There wasn't a great deal for Eleanor to do, but Henry, normally the best-tempered child in the world, was rendered querulous by his illness, so that she was constantly occupied with him. It was only after he had fallen into an uneasy sleep in the early afternoon that she felt free to ring the bell and ask for Margaret to take her place while she ate her lunch; there would be no question of her taking time off; it wouldn't be fair on Margaret to leave her for more than a short time with her brother. Eleanor whispered instructions to her young sister and slipped from the room, to make her way downstairs to where her belated lunch was to be served in a small room behind the dining room in which she had had her supper on the previous evening. It was a cheerful apartment, with an open fire, a circular table accommodating six chairs, a mahogany side-table, beautifully inlaid, and a bow-fronted cabinet with a fluted canopy, its panels delicately painted. There was a tapestry carpet on the polished floor and the white damask cloth and shining silver and glass made the table very inviting. She sat down, apologising in English for her lateness, an apology which Juffrouw Witsma waved aside with nods and smiles and a gentle flow of soothing words which, while making no sense at all to Eleanor, nevertheless conveyed the assurance that coming down late to lunch was a trifling matter which wasn't of the least consequence.

The fresh-faced girl, Tekla, served her with a thick, delicious soup and then bore the plate away to return with a tray laden with a covered dish, a nicely arranged assortment of breads, cheeses and cold meats and a pot of coffee. The covered dish, upon investigation, contained an omelette which Eleanor devoured with a healthy appetite before pouring her coffee from the beautiful old silver coffee pot, and while she sipped the delicious brew from a delicate porcelain cup, she couldn't help but reflect upon the splendid style in which Fulk lived. Imogen was a lucky girl—that was, Eleanor reminded herself hastily, if she could put up with his occasional arrogance and his nasty habit of ignoring other people's remarks when he wished, although it wasn't likely that he would ignore Imogen. She switched her thoughts rather hastily, because for some reason or other she found that she didn't want to think about her.

She finished her meal quickly, not wanting to be away too long from Henry, and besides, she still had to go to the library and find a book so that when the invalid wakened presently she could read aloud to him.

There were a number of doors and several passages leading from the hall. She ignored the sitting room and the archway beside the staircase because it obviously led to the kitchen, and tried the door across the hall—Fulk's study; she cast an interested eye over the heavy masculine furniture, the enormous desk with its high-backed chair, the equally large wing chair drawn up to the old-fashioned stove, and the one or two rather sombre portraits on the panelled walls, and then shut the door again, wishing very much to stay and examine the room inch by inch.

She tried the big arched double doors next, facing the sitting room. This, then, was the library; she sighed with pleasure at the sight of so many books ranged on the shelves, the gallery running round the upper walls, and the little spiral staircase leading to it. There were two solid tables too with well upholstered leather chairs drawn up to them and reading lamps conveniently placed. She wandered round, wanting to pull out a handful of books and sit there and browse through them, but that wouldn't do at all; she glanced at her watch and quickened her steps, examining the shelves as she went. Henry had been right, there were quite a few children's books; she selected two or three and hurried back upstairs.

Henry was still asleep. Eleanor went over to where Margaret was perched anxiously by the bed and thanked her warmly. 'Darling, what are you going to do now?' she asked. 'You're not bored?'

Her sister shook her head. 'My goodness, no! Fulk telephoned someone he knew who has a daughter as old as I am, and she's coming over to spend the afternoon. Her name's Hermina and she speaks a little English.' She added seriously: 'Will you be all right if we go into the gardens for a walk?'

Eleanor glanced outside. It was a grey afternoon, but dry. 'Yes, love, but let me know when you come back, won't you? Is Hermina staying for tea?'

'Yes. Fulk said he'd be home for tea, too—but he's got to go out this evening.'

Evidently he preferred to share his plans with Margaret, thought Eleanor huffily, and then felt ashamed of the thought because he had been so kind to them all. She kissed her sister gently and took her place by the bed, and when she had gone, whiled away the time until he woke up, hot and cross and in a good deal of pain, by leafing through the books she had brought from the library: *Moonfleet, Treasure Island* and *The Wind in the Willows*. On the front page of each Fulk had written his name in a neat, childish hand, very much at variance with the fearful scrawl in which he had written Henry's notes.

She bathed Henry's hot face and hands, gave him a cooling drink and coaxed him to take his medicine. His temperature was still far too high, she noted worriedly, but took comfort from the fact that the antibiotics still had two days to go. She sat down again, picked up *The Wind in the Willows* and began to read aloud, stopping after half an hour to turn on the lamp and glance at the clock. Henry was lying quietly, listening to her placid reading, feeling for the moment a little better. She read on, with short intervals for him to have a drink, aware of a longing for a cup of tea herself. She embarked on chapter three, telling herself that Margaret would be along at any moment now.

But when the door eventually opened it was Fulk, not Margaret, who came in. He said hullo in a quiet voice and went at once to Henry, and only when he had satisfied himself that the boy was no worse he said: 'There is tea for you in the sitting room, Eleanor. The little girls are just finishing theirs, but Juffrouw Witsma will make you a fresh pot.'

'What about you?'

'I? I shall sit here with Henry.'

'Your tea?'

His voice held faint impatience. 'I had tea at the hospital.' He went to the door and held it open for her, and she found herself going across the wide gallery and down the staircase without having said a single word.

Margaret jumped up as she went into the sitting room. 'I was just coming to you when Fulk came home,' she explained, 'and he said he was going to sit with Henry while you came down to tea—you don't mind, Eleanor?'

'Not a bit.' Eleanor glanced at the girl standing beside her sister and smiled. 'Is this Hermina?' she wanted to know as she shook hands. The girl was pretty, with pale hair and blue eyes and a wide smile; excellent company for Margaret, and how thoughtful of Fulk... She frowned, remembering how impatient he had been with her only a few minutes ago.

She poured herself a cup of tea from the little silver pot Juffrouw Witsma had set beside her and bit into a finger of toast. The two girls had wandered off to start a game of cards at the other end of the room, and she was left alone with her thoughts. But they were small comfort to her, what with Henry so poorly and Fulk treating her as though she were an evil necessity in his house—and yet upon occasion he had been rather nice... She poured herself another cup of tea, ate a piece of cake and went back upstairs.

'There wasn't all that hurry,' observed Fulk from his chair. He closed a folder full of notes as he spoke and got to his feet. 'Go and get your coat and take a brisk walk outside—the gardens are quite large.'

'I don't want...' began Eleanor, and caught his eye.

'Very well, but can you spare the time? Margaret could come...'

He sighed. 'I have the time,' he told her in a patient voice which made her grit her teeth. 'I wouldn't have suggested it otherwise. I have asked Juffrouw Witsma to sit here while you have dinner this evening, otherwise arrange things to suit yourself, but you must have exercise.' He picked up a book and sat down again. 'I shall be out.'

'Where?' asked Henry unexpectedly.

'That's rude, Henry,' Eleanor pointed out. 'You mustn't ask those sort of questions.'

Fulk cast down his book and strolled over to the bed. 'Hullo, boy—you're better—not well, but better. All the same, you will go on lying here doing nothing until I say otherwise.' He glanced quickly at Eleanor and addressed the boy. 'I'm going out to dine.'

'Who with?'

'Henry!' said Eleanor, mildly admonishing.

'Imogen's parents.'

'The lady you're going to marry?'

Fulk only smiled and the boy went on: 'Are they nice? As nice as Mummy and Daddy?'

Fulk thought for a moment. 'They're charming; their home is well ordered and they know all the right people.'

'Is it a big house? As big as this one?'

'Not quite as big.'

'I like your house,' his patient informed him seriously, 'but I like my home too, though I expect you find it rather small. Does the lady you're going to visit cook the dinner?'

The big man's mouth twitched as though he were enjoying a private joke. 'No, never. Now, your mother is a splendid cook, and even though your home is small it's one of the nicest houses I've been in.'

Henry beamed at him rather tiredly. 'Yes, isn't it—though I expect you'd rather live here.'

'Well, it is my home, isn't it?' He turned to Eleanor. 'Supposing you telephone your mother and father before you settle down for the evening? Tell them that this young man is picking up nicely and if he's as good tomorrow as he's been today, we'll bring the telephone up here and he can speak to them himself.'

'Oh, you really are super!' Henry declared, and fell instantly asleep.

Fulk went back to his chair. 'Well, run along, Eleanor.' He glanced at the slim gold watch on his wrist and smiled in casual, friendly dismissal, so that she went to her room without saying anything, put on her coat, snatched up her headscarf and mitts and went crossly downstairs. As soon as Henry was fit to be moved, she promised herself rashly, she would take him home, not bothering to go into the difficulties of such an undertaking. Not for the first time, she wondered why Fulk had bothered to bring her over to his home; Henry's persuasive powers, most likely, certainly not from his own wish.

It was cold and almost dark outside, with a starry, frosty sky and a cold moon which lighted her path for her. She walked briskly right round the house along the gravel drive which surrounded it and then down to the gates and back again. The house, now that she had the time to look at it properly in the moonlight, was even bigger than she had at first thought; she stood still, trying to imagine what it would be like to live in it and have it for a home, and while she stood there she heard a dog barking and remembered that she hadn't yet seen the dog

Henry had mentioned, nor for that matter had she seen Moggy. She went indoors and poked her head round the sitting room door, where the girls were still playing cards.

'Have you seen Fulk's dog?' she asked her sister.

'Oh, yes—he's an Irish wolfhound, his name's Patrick O'Flanelly, but Fulk calls him Flan. Henry's kitten is here too—he's over here in the corner.'

She led the way to the other end of the room where Moggy lay sleeping in an old shopping basket lined with a blanket. 'Flan goes everywhere with Fulk, you know, he's in the kitchen now, having his supper, do you want to see him?'

'Yes, I'd love to, but not now, I'm going back to sit with Henry.'

Margaret slid a hand into hers. 'Fulk says Henry's better and that in a few days he'll be able to sit up and play some games with me. Are you going to telephone home? The place you have to call is here by the telephone—Fulk left it for you.'

He might get impatient with her, but he wasn't to be faulted when it came to making things easy for her. She dialled the overseas exchange and a few minutes later heard her mother's voice.

'Henry's better,' she said at once because she knew that that was what her mother wanted to hear, and went on to reassure her before handing the telephone over to Margaret and hurrying back upstairs; it would never do for Fulk to be late for his dinner engagement.

It seemed very quiet after he had told her what to do for Henry, said a brief goodnight and gone away without a backward glance, indeed, she had the impression that he was glad to be going. Her brother was drowsing and she sat tiredly, hardly thinking, waiting for him to wake up so that she could do the variety of chores necessary for his quiet night, and if his temperature was down, she promised herself, and he seemed really better, she would get ready for bed and then sit with him until he fell asleep and then go to bed herself. She yawned widely at the very thought, then got up to study her brother's sleeping face; he did look better, and Fulk had said that he was, and she was quite sure that he would never have gone out for the evening unless he had felt easy in his mind about the boy.

It struck her all at once that she had no idea where Fulk had gone; she would have to go downstairs and find out, she was actually on her way to the door when her eye lighted on a fold of paper tucked into *The Wind in the Willows*. It was a note, brief and to the point, telling her that should she need Fulk, he could be reached at a Groningen number. 'The Atlanta Hotel,' he had scrawled. 'Don't hesitate to let me know if you are worried. If I have left the hotel, try this number.' He had printed it very clearly so that she could make no mistake. She read the businesslike missive through once more, wondering whose the second number was; not the hospital, she knew that already. She told herself sharply not to be nosey.

It was past midnight before Henry finally fell into a quiet sleep. Margaret had tiptoed in to say goodnight hours before; Eleanor decided to have her bath and get ready for bed, something which she did speedily, with the door open so that she might hear the slightest sound, but Henry slept on, with none of the restless mutterings and tossing and turning of the previous night. She glanced at the small enamel clock on the dressing table, decided that she would read until one o'clock and went back to her chair once more; she should have chosen a book for herself while she had been in the library; now she would have to content herself with *The Wind in the Willows,* a book she had read many times already. She settled down to enjoy Toad's activities.

The clock's silvery chimes recalled her to the time. She looked once more at Henry, sleeping peacefully, yawned widely and then gave a choking gasp as Fulk said from the door: 'Still up? There's no need tonight, you know—he's better.'

She peeped at him through the curtain of hair she hadn't bothered to plait. He was leaning against the door jamb, his hands in the pockets of his exquisitely tailored dinner jacket; elegant and self-assured and not over-friendly. She wondered why. Perhaps dining with Imogen's parents had filled his mind with thoughts of her, and coming back to herself, sitting untidily wrapped in a dressing gown and her hair anyhow, could be irritating to him. She said apologetically: 'I know—I'm going to bed now; I've been reading and I forgot the time.'

He came across the room and took the book from her knee. 'Well, well,' his eyebrows rose an inch, 'bedtime stories. A little old for Toad, aren't you, Eleanor?'

'I've been reading it to Henry,' she snapped, 'and I don't see what age has to do with it, anyway,' she said pointedly: 'It's your book.'

He was leafing through it. 'Yes, but I fancy I've outgrown it.'

'And that's a pity, though from what I remember of you, you probably didn't enjoy it when you were a little boy.'

He grinned at her. 'Meaning that even at an early age I had already formed my regrettable character?'

She remembered the trouble he had taken over Henry, and how he had gone to the rescue of the children on that snowy afternoon, and was filled with contrition. 'Oh, Fulk, I didn't mean that, really I didn't. I suppose I'm tired and my tongue's too sharp—and how could we possibly agree about anything?'

He put the book down. 'Now, why not?'

'Well, we don't lead the same kind of life, do we? All this…?' She waved a hand at the luxurious room. 'And me—I like sitting in the loft at home with Mrs Trot…' It sounded very silly when she had said it, and she wasn't looking at him, so she didn't see his smile.

'One can have the best of both worlds,' he observed blandly.

'Now what on earth do you mean by that?' she demanded in a whisper.

'Never mind now. Has Henry slept all the evening?'

'Yes, and so restfully too. Do you suppose he'll wake before morning?'

'Unlikely—the antibiotics have taken effect; he'll feel fighting fit in the morning and it will take our united efforts to keep him quiet in bed.'

She fetched a small sigh. 'It's such a load off my mind—we all love him very much, you see. I'll never be able to thank you enough for all you've done.'

'I may take you up on that one day.' He bent and kissed her cheek lightly. 'Now let us examine these charts.'

He studied her carefully kept records, took Henry's pulse, used his stethoscope on the small sleeping chest, expressed satisfaction at his findings, and went to the door. 'With care he'll do, and no after-effects, either.'

His smile was so kind that she found herself saying: 'What a dear you are! I do hope you had a pleasant evening; I don't suppose you get out much.'

'Er—no—not when Imogen is away. The evening was

pleasant enough. Imogen's mother was interested to hear about Henry and sends her good wishes for his speedy recovery.'

'How very kind of her.' She was laying the charts tidily on the table. 'You must miss Imogen very much.'

He didn't answer her, merely wished her goodnight and closed the door soundlessly. If she hadn't been so tired she might have wondered at that. As it was she took a final look at her small brother and went thankfully to her bed.

CHAPTER SEVEN

FULK HAD BEEN quite right; Henry wakened in the morning feeling so much more himself that he wanted to get up; Eleanor was arguing gently with him about it when Fulk walked in and said at once: 'Ah, good—I see that you are on the road to recovery, boy. Eleanor, go and have your breakfast while I explain to Henry just why he has to stay quietly in bed for a little longer.' He glanced at her. 'You slept? Good. I've had breakfast and I don't need to leave the house for an hour, so don't hurry back.' His smile dismissed her.

Margaret caught her up on the staircase and tucked a hand into hers. 'It's all so grand,' she confided, 'but Fulk doesn't seem to notice it, does he?'

'Well, I suppose when you've lived in a place like this all your life, it's as much home to him as the manse is to us, dear.'

'Fulk says Henry's better, he says that if I ask you nicely you might let me come and talk to Henry later on. May I?'

They had reached the small room where they had their breakfast and sat down at the table, essayed a *'Goeden morgen,'* to Tekla and made much of Flan who had joined them silently. Margaret offered him a piece of toast and said: 'I went to see Moggy just now, he's in the kitchen with Juffrouw Witsma—he likes her cat, you know, but he had his breakfast here with Fulk, he always does.'

Eleanor was conscious of surprise; Fulk was a busy

man and yet he hadn't just consigned Moggy to the care of his housekeeper, he had offered him companionship as well. She hadn't expected it. 'Does he?' she commented, 'how nice.' Fulk had qualities she hadn't suspected. 'He doesn't have much time...'

Margaret slipped Flan some more toast. 'No, he doesn't, does he? But when he comes home in the evening he always fetches Moggy to sit with him. Flan sits with him too, of course.'

They ate their breakfast without haste while they discussed various ways of amusing Henry during his convalescence. 'Cards,' declared Margaret emphatically, 'he loves playing cards.'

'As long as he doesn't get too excited. Draughts, too, and what about Ludo?'

Margaret curled her lip. 'Eleanor, that's a child's game!'

'But Henry's a child, dear.'

'Oh, I know that, but he's so bright for his age—why, he's been playing chess with Daddy ever since last winter.'

'Heavens! What about Monopoly? That's a good game, but he might get too excited. Anyway, I'll ask Fulk.'

But there was no opportunity to do that when she went back upstairs. Fulk had resumed his role of doctor again, and beyond giving her his precise instructions about her brother, he had nothing more to say, indeed, his very manner discouraged her from anything but a meek: 'Yes, Fulk, no, Fulk,' in answer.

The day passed without incident, and Henry was so much improved by the afternoon that Eleanor felt justified in allowing Margaret to sit with him for a brief while, so that she might take a brisk walk in the gardens.

They were larger than she had thought and in excellent order. She poked around, exploring paths and examining the variety of shrubs and trees bordering them, and it was quite half an hour before she returned to the house, to find a Mercedes outside the front door; it was a 450SE, and a new model, all gleaming coachwork and chromium. It looked a little vulgar. Perhaps it belonged to Hermina's father, although Eleanor couldn't remember Margaret saying that her new friend would be coming that afternoon. She mounted the steps, pausing in the vestibule to take off her boots, for she had got them muddy at the edge of the pond she had discovered behind the house, and it would never do to sully the shining floors. She tugged off her headscarf, pulling her hair askew as she did so, and with the boots dangling from one hand, opened the inner door and started for the stairs. She had a stockinged foot on the lowest tread when the drawing room door opened and a woman came out and stood looking at her.

She was of middle age, handsome in a large way and dressed with taste and, Eleanor guessed, great expense. Her voice, when she spoke, was commanding and her English, although fluent, was heavily accented.

'You are the nurse?' She sounded surprised too, which wasn't to be wondered at, thought Eleanor reasonably; the word hardly conjured up a windswept hairdo, stockinged feet and muddy boots dangling...

She said: 'Yes, I am. Did you want me?'

The lady advanced a foot or two. 'Do you know who I am?' she enquired.

'I'm afraid I don't—ought I to?' Eleanor hoped her voice didn't betray her growing dislike of her interrogator.

'Did the professor not tell you?'

'The professor? Who's he?…oh, you mean Fulk.' Eleanor smiled and met a stony stare.

'I,' said the lady weightily, 'am the professor's future mother-in-law.'

Eleanor stopped herself just in time from saying 'Poor Fulk', and murmured a polite how do you do instead. Surely Imogen wasn't like this dreadful woman—Fulk must love her very much to be able to put up with her mother. She said, still polite: 'It was kind of you to enquire about my brother—he's better today; we're all very relieved.'

Imogen's mother inclined her severely coiffured head graciously. 'I am glad to hear it. I must say that you are hardly what I imagined you to be.' Her cold eyes swept over Eleanor's somewhat tatty person, so that she felt constrained to say: 'Oh, I look better in uniform—and now if you will excuse me I must go back to my brother. I expect you're waiting for Fulk?'

'No, Nurse, I came to see you. As Imogen is not here, I felt it to be my duty…'

'To look me over and make sure that I wasn't getting my claws into Fulk?' asked Eleanor, quite forgetting her manners. 'Well, I daresay you feel better about it now— I'm not the glamorous type, you see—I just work for a living. Goodbye, Mevrouw…I don't know your name, I'm afraid.'

She started up the stairs and was brought to a halt by the commanding voice. 'Oss van Oss, Nurse, Baroness Oss van Oss—and you are quite correct. I can quite see now why Fulk is not in the least attracted to you—I am greatly reassured. I told him last night that I considered it a little irregular for you to be in his house, and I advised him to obtain one of the older nurses from his hospital in your place now that the little boy is no longer

dangerously ill. I would not wish to influence him un-
duly, but I have dear Imogen's feelings to consider.'

Eleanor had swung round to face the Baroness. 'Can't
she look after her own feelings?' she enquired pertly,
and then: 'What a horrid conversation this is, isn't it?
You might as well know that your daughter's feelings
are of no importance to me, but my brother's health is.
I shall stay here until he is better, and since, as you have
just told me, Fulk isn't in the least attracted to me, I
can't see what all the fuss is about. Goodbye, Baroness
Oss—no, Oss van Oss, isn't it?'

She went on her way unhurriedly, aware that she was
being stared at, and despite her deliberate step, she
seethed with rage. How dared the woman come to look
her over, and how dared Fulk allow it? She was just
beginning to like him despite his offhand manner, now
she found herself disliking him more than ever. She
would have something to say when she saw him!

Which wasn't until much later, although he came in
the early evening to see Henry; but he brought someone
with him, an elderly man, who called Henry little man
and herself dear lady, and muttered a good deal to himself. Fulk introduced him as Professor van Esbink, explaining that he had thought a second opinion of Henry's
condition might reassure them all. Eleanor hadn't answered him and had given him a stony stare when he
smiled at her, so that the smile turned into a mocking
one before he turned away to answer his learned colleague's questions. Any other man might have been dis-
concerted, but Fulk wasn't like other men. She became
very professional in her manner and when she saw the
two gentlemen to the door, her manner was not only
professional, it was glacial, at least towards Fulk.

'You've taken umbrage,' said Henry from his bed, and

when, an hour later, Fulk came back he pointed this interesting fact out to the doctor. 'Eleanor is in a temper,' he said, 'and I don't know why.'

Fulk glanced across the room to where Eleanor was standing, measuring medicine into a glass. 'She's plain ratty,' he declared cheerfully, 'and I think I know why.'

'Why?' asked Henry with interest.

'Since I have no intention of telling you, I shouldn't waste time asking, boy. Let us concentrate instead on what Professor van Esbink had to say about you. He agrees with me that you are doing very nicely, but just as I explained to you, you still have to remain quietly in bed, though I think that Margaret might come and play some quiet game with you for a couple of hours each day, and I daresay Moggy would be glad to visit you.'

'Oh. I say—may he really come? On to my bed?'

'Why not? And certainly he may stay here as long as he likes. I daresay that once he has been shown the way, he'll pop in and out as the fancy takes him.' He smiled down at the boy. 'I'll go and find Margaret and ask her to bring him up here for a little while, shall I?'

He was back very soon with Margaret, clutching Moggy. The kitten was settled under Henry's hand, and his sister ensconced in a chair by the bed. 'And no sitting up, Henry,' said Fulk firmly. 'Margaret, ring the bell if you should need us, I'm going to take Eleanor down to dinner.'

Eleanor cast him a look to freeze a man's bones, 'I am not hungry, thank you.'

He said nothing at all, merely crossed the room, took her by the arm and led her away, hurrying her down the staircase so fast that she had much ado not to trip up.

In the drawing room he shut the door behind them and invited her to sit down by the fire. 'And what would you like to drink?' he enquired solicitously. 'Not spirits, I think; they might only serve to inflame your temper even more. How about Madeira? Pleasantly alcoholic without clouding the mind.'

She accepted the glass he offered her, for there was really nothing else she could do about it. Besides, it gave her a few minutes in which to gather her thoughts; she had no wish to lose her temper; calm, cool, reasoning, with a slight hint of hurt feelings would fill the bill very well.

'I'm waiting for the outburst,' he prompted blandly, so that she was instantly possessed of a great desire to speak her mind. But she made a strong effort to keep her cool; her voice was mild as she said slowly: 'Your future mother-in-law came this afternoon, but I expect you know that already.'

'Juffrouw Witsma told me when I came in. I wondered if she would.'

Eleanor put her glass carefully down on the charming little lamp table at her elbow. 'You knew she was coming? To look me over? I cannot quite understand why you could not have reassured her sufficiently; it would have saved her a journey.' Her voice, despite her best efforts, became a little shrill. 'She was good enough to explain to me that as you were not in the least attracted to me she felt quite at ease about me, although she considered that I should be—removed...' She choked on rage. 'How dared you allow her...she's a detestable woman, and I have no intention of apologizing to you for saying so; it's to be hoped that your Imogen doesn't take after her.' Her wrathful voice petered out before the expression on Fulk's face, but it served to fan her temper at the same time. 'If I go, I shall take Henry too,' she told him flatly. 'I'll get an ambulance if it takes every penny I've got—and I hope I never, never see you again!'

She picked up her glass and was annoyed to find that her hand was trembling so that it was hard to hold it steady. Fulk must have seen it too, for he came over to her, took the glass from her and put it down again. 'A family heirloom,' he explained mildly. 'You know, Eleanor, it is a remarkable thing that you can stir up my deepest feelings with such ease; at one moment I am so angry with you that I could cheerfully wring your neck, and at the next I find abject apologies for my shocking behaviour tripping off my tongue. Of course I discussed you with Baroness Oss van Oss, but hardly in the manner which she implied—indeed, I imagined that she was joking when she said that she would like to meet you and see what you were like for herself, and when she persisted, I told her that I could see no reason why she shouldn't if she wished—I imagined that it would be a friendly visit, no more; I had no idea that she was going to upset you and I am deeply sorry for that. And as for all that nonsense about replacing you with another nurse, I have no intention of doing any such thing; you will remain until you are perfectly satisfied that Henry is well again.' He smiled wryly. 'You know, I have the strongest feeling that we should be laughing about the whole thing, enjoying the joke together. And here we are, quarrelling again.'

'People who don't like each other always quarrel,' said Eleanor, not bothering to look at him.

'Ah, yes—I was forgetting that you have a long-standing dislike of me; not even the common denominator of Henry's illness has altered that, has it?' He put her glass back into her hand. 'Drink up and we will go in to dinner. I'm hungry.'

It was disconcerting that, just when she was striving to reduce her rage to reasonable argument, he should dampen it down by wanting his dinner. She wasn't sure if she wanted to laugh about it or have a good cry.

She found herself in the dining room, facing him across the broad expanse of linen set with heavy old silver and delicate glass, and rather to her surprise she found that she was hungry too, and after a little while, enjoying herself. The food was delicious and Fulk's gentle flow of small talk was undemanding and mildly amusing. She studied his face as he bent to pull gently on one of Flan's ears—the dog was sitting like a statue beside his chair, watching him with adoring eyes. Fulk was smiling a little and she wondered if she had been mistaken at the expression on his face when she had mentioned Imogen. She still wasn't quite sure what it had been, only it had made her uncertain; perhaps she had been mistaken about him, too—perhaps all her ideas about him had been wrong. It was an ever-recurring thought which refused to be dispelled, and the memory of her strongly voiced wish never to see him again struck her so forcibly that she put down her spoon and stared at the contents of her plate, wondering what she should do about it.

'Don't you like caramel custard?' asked Fulk. 'I'll ring and get Juffrouw Witsma to bring something else.'

Eleanor transferred her gaze from her plate to his face. 'I like it very much, thank you.' She went on quite humbly: 'Fulk, I'm sorry I was so rude just now—about Baroness Oss van Oss, I mean. I had no right to speak like that and I'm sure your Imogen is the nicest and most beautiful girl in the world, and if you want to discuss me with anyone, I—I really don't mind; I'm only the nurse, after all, and I don't care about anything except getting Henry well again so that he'll grow up strong and healthy.'

He got up and came round the table to sit carelessly on it beside her so that he could look down into her face. 'My dear Eleanor,' he begged, 'for heaven's sake don't talk like that, it just isn't you—so meek and penitent. And you're not 'only the nurse,' he paused, his dark eyes looking over her head, 'you are a great many things...' His sombre expression was gone, he grinned at her. 'Shall we telephone your people before we go upstairs?'

Henry had a relapse the next day; not a severe one but sufficient to delay his convalescence. Eleanor, looking back on those few days when they were happily past, wondered how she would have got through them without Fulk's help. Henry had been querulous and difficult and the very mention of another nurse coming to relieve Eleanor caused him to toss and turn in such a frenzy of unrest that the idea was given up and Fulk took turns with Eleanor in nursing him, something which he did with no fuss at all, apparently being quite able to work at his consulting rooms and the hospital by day, and sit up for a good part of each night without any ill effects.

Happily the relapse had been a brief one; on the fourth day Henry had woken up with a temperature which was almost normal again, demanding tea and toast and Margaret to talk to. Eleanor, hearing voices in her brother's room at five o'clock in the morning, had gone at once to see what the matter was, and discovered Fulk sitting back in his chair, sharing a pot of tea with his patient. He had taken one look at her distraught countenance and said comfortably: 'Fetch a tooth mug, Eleanor, and join us in our early tea; Henry is debating the important question as to what he would like for his breakfast. I fancy that we are out of the wood.'

She had gone back into the bathroom and picked up the mug and then sat down on the edge of the bath. She had been wanting to have a good cry for some time now, but somehow the opportunity had never occurred, but now, opportunity or not, the tears poured down her cheeks, willy-nilly. She hardly noticed when Fulk took the mug from her, wiped her face with a towel and sat down beside her. 'Watering pot,' he said kindly, 'you weep as copiously as you used to when you were a little girl.'

She sniffed into the towel. 'So would you if you were me,' she declared in a muffled voice. 'I've been so afraid that Henry...do you suppose there will be any lasting damage?'

'Unlikely.' Fulk had put an arm round her and it felt very comforting. 'This setback only means that he has to take a little longer to get on to his feet again.'

Eleanor sniffed. 'You're sure?' And then because of the look of surprise on his face: 'Oh, I do beg your pardon, just for a moment I forgot who you were—of course you're sure. How happy Mother and Father will be...' She sat up and felt his arm slacken. 'I'll get dressed and get some breakfast for Henry—shall I get some for you too? You've been sitting there since twelve o'clock, you must be hungry. If you're very quick, you could get at least three hours' sleep before you need to leave.'

'So I could, but I won't, I'll have breakfast with Henry and you. Scrambled eggs for him and weak tea, and I'll have eggs and bacon—three eggs, and toast and marmalade and coffee—you have whatever you like for yourself. Don't dress; if Henry has a light meal now he will probably sleep again for several hours and that will do him good as well as keep him quiet.' He studied her face. 'You don't look too bad,' he remarked. 'Off with you and I'll come down and carry the tray up for you—fifteen minutes, OK?'

'OK,' she smiled rather mistily, and went down to the kitchen, a vast room with a vaulted ceiling, cupboards which would have housed a family, an imposing dresser which took up the whole of one wall, and enough labour-saving gadgets to gladden the heart of the most pernickety woman—no wonder Juffrouw Witsma always looked so contented! Eleanor peered around her with envy and opened the nearest cupboard door.

Fulk had been right again; Henry ate every morsel of his frugal breakfast, murmured 'Super,' and went at once to sleep, not to wake again until the morning was far advanced, demanding something else to eat. And that evening when Fulk came home they all played a sedate game of Ludo, careful not to get too excited about it, and when finally Henry had been tucked down for the night they went down to dinner, leaving Tekla on guard, because, as Fulk pointed out, she was a sensible girl with a string of small brothers and sisters of her own and knew how to handle children. Their meal was a cheerful one, for Margaret and Fulk were on excellent terms with each other and between them soon had Eleanor laughing with them.

The week passed quickly after that, with Henry improving rapidly—too rapidly, for he wanted to do everything at once. It was easier when at the end of the week, Fulk said that he might sit out for an hour or two each day, so that he and Margaret could amuse themselves at the small card table, and Eleanor seized these brief periods in which to take brisk walks, enjoying the wintry weather and the cold wind after so many days indoors. She ventured out of the grounds after the first day, exploring the narrow lanes running between the flat, frost-covered water meadows. There wasn't a great deal to see, but it was peaceful as well as invigorating. She told herself that she felt much better for these outings, while at the same time aware that there was a hard core of sadness somewhere deep inside her, which for some reason or other she was loath to probe.

She saw little of Fulk; he left early each morning and sometimes he wasn't back until after they had had their dinner in the evening. He saw Henry twice a day, of course, but his remarks were mostly limited to the boy's condition, and recommendations as to his further treatment. Walking briskly back to the house on the Friday afternoon, Eleanor found herself looking forward to the weekend; Fulk would be home.

He arrived after tea, driving the Daimler Sovereign he used for the short journey to and from the hospital and his consulting rooms. Eleanor, who happened to be in the hall when he came in, thought that he looked tired and bad-tempered with it; he must have had a tiresome day. She said 'Hullo,' in a conciliatory voice and asked: 'Shall I ask someone to bring you some tea?'

He had shrugged himself out of his topcoat and started across the hall towards his study, his briefcase in his hand. 'No time,' he told her briefly, and went inside, closing the door firmly behind him. Eleanor went upstairs to make sure that Henry wasn't getting above himself, cautioned him in a sisterly fashion, bade Margaret keep a sharp eye on her brother and went downstairs again to look for Moggy. She was returning from the kitchen, the kitten tucked under one arm, when she encountered Fulk once more, and urged on by a wish to see his tired face smile, asked: 'Did you have a bad day?'

He checked his stride to look at her. He was in a bad

temper all right, his dark face frowning, his mouth a straight line; it surprised her very much when he said: 'No,' but she waited a moment, thinking that he might want to say something else. When he did speak, she was even more surprised.

'I'm going away for the weekend,' he said in a bland, cold voice she didn't much care for. 'Henry's quite safe to leave; in any case, I've asked Professor van Esbink to keep an eye on him. I'm leaving in half an hour and when I return on Tuesday I shall go straight to my rooms, so if you wish to say anything, you had better say it now.'

Eleanor stood, her mouth a little open, quite unable to think of a single word to say. When he said, still in that hateful voice: 'You're not usually so short of words,' she snapped her mouth shut and then said: 'What am I supposed to say? I'll wish you a pleasant weekend if that's what you want, though in your present nasty temper I should be sorry for your companions, but perhaps you'll feel better by the time you get to wherever you're going.'

'Fishing!' he declared. 'You want to know where I'm going, don't you? Cannes—to see Imogen.'

Eleanor was conscious of a peculiar sensation which she didn't have time to ponder. She said with false cheerfulness: 'How nice for you both,' and then more urgently: 'You're never going to drive all that way and then back again by Tuesday?'

He raised his brows. 'Why ever not?'

'It's miles—you're tired already…'

His voice was silky now. 'Eleanor, I brought you here to look after your brother. And now, if you will excuse me.'

'It's too far,' declared Eleanor wildly.

'Roughly seven hundred and fifty miles—fifteen hours' driving on excellent roads.' He smiled thinly. 'If it makes you feel better, I shall only drive six or seven hours before I rack up for the night. I should be in Cannes some time during tomorrow afternoon.'

'But coming back?' she persisted, and then drew a sharp breath as he said blandly: 'I haven't been so fussed over since I had a nanny.'

She stood just where she was, watching him go, listening to the high-powered whine of the Panther. It sounded very loud in the quiet house.

'Fuss over him!' said Eleanor to no one in particular. 'Of course I fuss over him, and how fantastic it is that I've only just this minute discovered that I'm in love with the wretch.' The sad feeling could be explained now, as well as the eager looking forward to the weekend; perhaps she had known all the time without realizing it.

She kissed the top of Moggy's furry little head and started slowly up the staircase; the less she thought about it the better; by the time she saw Fulk again on Tuesday she would have forced herself to accept the idea and turn her back on it—because that was what she was going to have to do. She allowed herself a few moments of pure envy of Imogen, wondering what it would be like to know that a man loved you so much that he would make a round trip of fifteen hundred miles just to be with you for a day. She sighed so deeply that Moggy became dislodged and stuck a needlelike claw into her arm; she didn't feel it, her thoughts were with Fulk, driving through the dark winter evening and on into an even darker night, intent on reaching his Imogen as quickly as possible.

Eleanor paused at the top of the stairs; if she had been

Imogen she would have gone half way—no, the whole way, to meet Fulk. After all, the girl did nothing, while he was wearing himself to a shadow, what with his work at the hospital, his own practice, and staying up half the night with Henry. That there was something absurd in describing a large man of fifteen stone or thereabouts as being worn to a shadow didn't cross her mind. She could only imagine him going to sleep at the wheel of his powerful car and crashing somewhere remote and dying before anyone could reach him. She opened Henry's door, offered Moggy to her brother and allowed herself to be persuaded to enjoy a game of three-handed whist. She played very badly; understandable enough, considering that her head was full of Fulk and nothing else.

The weekend dragged by on leaden feet for Eleanor. Somehow she got through it, thankful that Henry was indeed well again and that Margaret was perfectly content to stay where she was. She telephoned her parents each evening because Fulk had told her to do so, giving them a racy account of Henry's progress and even venturing to speak of his return in the not too distant future. 'Perhaps for Christmas,' she essayed. 'I've not given a thought to presents yet, we're miles from the shops, you know, and I haven't been able to get out much—I'll have to rush round and buy them when we get back.' The thought of the ward and of Miss Tremble, who would certainly be there, and all the rush and bustle of Christmas in hospital gave her no joy at all, and her feelings must have sounded in her voice, for her mother asked: 'You're all right, dear? You sound…perhaps you're tired.'

Eleanor agreed that she was and handed the receiver to Margaret.

It was late on Tuesday evening before she saw Fulk.

It had been a cold day with a hint of snow. Probably it was this inclement weather as well as his long drive which had so lined and sharpened his handsome features. Henry had been asleep for some time and Margaret was flitting around in her dressing gown, putting off her own bedtime for as long as possible while Eleanor carried up the lemonade which Henry might want in the night before going downstairs once again to fetch Moggy to sleep on the end of the invalid's bed. She was on her way upstairs once more, the little beast under her arm, when the door behind her opened and shut, and when she turned round: 'How's Henry?' asked Fulk.

She saw his tired face. 'He's splendid. Professor van Esbink telephoned twice, but there was no need for him to come.'

Fulk threw his coat and gloves into a chair and crossed the hall to stand at the foot of the stairs. 'I know, he telephoned me this morning. He has a high opinion of you, Eleanor, did you know that? He would like you to work for him.'

She digested this flattering information in silence and jumped when he said sharply: 'Well, aren't you going to ask me if I had a pleasant weekend?'

'Well, I did want to,' she told him spiritedly, 'but I didn't feel like being snubbed.'

He moved very fast; he was beside her almost before she had finished speaking. She hadn't bargained for it and he was far too near for her peace of mind, and that peace was wholly shattered when he kissed her quite fiercely on her mouth, all without saying a word. He was back in the hall again while she was still blinking over it.

'I'm going to have something to eat,' he told her in a perfectly ordinary voice. 'I'll be up to see Henry later.'

CHAPTER EIGHT

FULK DIDN'T COME for almost an hour, which gave Eleanor time to find a number of good reasons for his behaviour. It had been a kind of reaction, she told herself; he had been with Imogen and probably he was missing her terribly, and because Eleanor had been the only girl around he had probably kissed her to relieve his unhappy feelings. It was a silly argument, but she couldn't think of a better one. The obvious thing to do was to ignore the whole incident, which wasn't very easy, but by the time he did appear, she had succeeded in acquiring a calm manner and a placid face, although beneath this exemplary façade her feelings were churning around inside her in a most disturbing manner.

But it had all been rather a waste of time, for he had barely looked at her and his manner, when he spoke, was very much that of the family doctor—affable, impersonal and just a little out of reach. He stayed only long enough to assure himself that all was well with Henry before wishing her a casual good night and going away again, and she went to bed shortly afterwards, quite bewildered and very unhappy.

Henry was allowed up the next day; dressed, he looked small and thin and far too pale, but his appetite was excellent and although his exercise was very limited, he was at least on his feet once more. The weather was still wintry, but Fulk, after the first couple of days, took him for short drives each day, fitting them in, Eleanor suspected, during his lunch hour, but when she had remonstrated about this, he had told her quite sharply that he had plenty of free time during the middle of the day and that he enjoyed the drives as much as his passenger did.

It would be Sint Nikolaas in a few days; Eleanor, who had heard all about it from Margaret, who had in her turn got it from Hermina, wondered if Fulk intended to do anything about it. She didn't like to bring the subject up in case he felt that she was expecting him to celebrate the occasion in some way, but on the other hand Margaret had told Henry about it and she had heard them speculating together as to whether they would be getting any presents; she would have to do something about it after all. Until this moment she hadn't needed any money; she had a little English money with her, but no Dutch, and it looked as though she would need some; she didn't like the idea, but she would have to talk to Fulk about it.

But there was no need; at breakfast the next morning, a meal at which she arrived a little late because of Henry's small demands, Margaret was already broaching the matter. Fulk, immersed in his mail, as he almost always was, got to his feet as she joined them, wished her good morning and went back to his letters. Eleanor didn't think that he looked over-friendly, but Margaret hadn't noticed his withdrawn expression, or if she had, she had decided to ignore it.

'Fulk,' she said cheerfully, 'I want to go to some shops and I expect Eleanor does too, only I don't know how to set about it. I haven't any money, though Eleanor has, but it's pounds. Could we leave Henry for just a little while, do you suppose?'

He put down the letter he was reading and gave her his full attention. 'My dear child, that can easily be arranged—how stupid of me not to have thought of it before.' He glanced at Eleanor, his eyebrows raised. 'Why did you not ask me sooner?'

'Well—I hadn't thought about it, not until yesterday, and I had no idea that Margaret was going to say anything to you—I'd made up my mind to ask you myself.'

'You should have asked sooner. I'm afraid that I can't spare the time to stay with Henry, but I will arrange for a nurse to come for the day and keep him company— would tomorrow suit you?'

He smiled nicely at her, although she had the impression that his mind was occupied by some other matter. She said diffidently: 'Well, if it's not being too much of a bother...'

He was reading his letter again. 'None whatever,' he assured her. He got up to go very shortly afterwards, pausing only to say: 'Let me have what money you wish to change, Eleanor, and I will give you guldens for it.'

When he had gone Eleanor turned to her sister. 'Darling,' she cried, 'whatever made you ask Fulk? I mean, he was so preoccupied. I'd thought about it too, but really this morning of all times, when you could see that he had all those letters.'

'Pooh,' said Margaret forcefully, 'he'd read them all ages ago. He wasn't busy at all, just staring at that letter he was holding—he'd read it at least six times—I watched him. Besides, I want to buy Henry something for Sint Nikolaas, he'll be frightfully disappointed if he doesn't get a present. How shall we go? I suppose Groningen is the nearest place?'

'I should think so—perhaps there's a bus. I wonder if a taxi would cost a lot?' Eleanor frowned. 'And when are we to go? In the morning or after lunch, and do you suppose there will be someone in the shops who'll speak English?'

She worried about it on and off during the rest of the day, which turned out to be a waste of time, for when Fulk came home he told them that he would return during the midday break and drive them into Groningen and pick them up again when he had finished his work in the afternoon. 'Better still,' he suggested, 'I'll show you where my consulting rooms are and you can come there. Eleanor, if you will come with me, I'll give you the money you require.'

She fetched her purse and followed him across the hall to his study. 'I'm not sure how much we need to spend,' she told him. 'It's just a present for Henry, and I want to buy something for Margaret, too…'

He had gone to his desk and opened a drawer. 'How much money can you spare?' he asked her bluntly.

'Well, would ten pounds be enough?' It sounded a lot of money and they hadn't much to buy.

He had his head bent so that she couldn't see his face, he said gently: 'I daresay—all the same, supposing I let you have more than that; you can repay me later. I should perhaps have warned you that it is customary to give everyone a small gift on Sint Nikolaas Eve; perhaps you should buy some small trifle for Juffrouw Witsma and Tekla and Bep—oh, and old Mevrouw Brom, too.'

'Oh, yes, of course, if that's the thing to do. I thought it was just for children.'

She watched him counting out the notes, loving every dark hair on his head and every line on his good-looking face, and there were lines, she could see that; perhaps he was working too hard, that long journey to Cannes must have tired him out. She cried soundlessly: 'Oh, Fulk, why did you have to fall in love with the wrong girl?'

and because he was holding the money out to her with thinly veiled impatience, took it from him, thanked him quietly and left him alone.

He had gone in the morning when she got down to breakfast. The nurse, a cheerful young girl, arrived just after ten o'clock, and Henry, happy enough now that he knew the shopping expedition was largely for his benefit, seemed content to stay with her. Eleanor and Margaret had an early lunch and when Fulk got back they were ready and waiting for him.

He had Margaret beside him on their short journey, apparently enjoying her cheerful chatter, but his manner was remote; although kind enough, when he had occasion to address Eleanor. 'We'll go to my rooms now and from there you can walk to the shops—they're close by and you can't possibly get lost. I shall be ready about four o'clock, so don't bother with tea, we'll have it together before we go home.'

They were in the city now, driving along a street with a wide canal running beside it, but presently Fulk turned into a narrow road which led to a square lined with old red brick houses, before one of which he stopped. 'I'm on the ground floor,' he explained. 'Ring and walk in when you come back.' He got out and opened the doors for them to get out too. 'Go straight across the square and down that passage you can see in that corner, it will bring you out into one of the shopping streets.' He nodded briefly. 'Enjoy yourselves. Forgive me, I'm late,' he told them, and went up the stone steps and in through the front door. As they walked away, Eleanor wondered if he had had any time for lunch; she thought it unlikely.

They had a lovely afternoon, first window-shopping, to gaze at the tempting displays of jewellery, leather-work, scarves and party clothes suitable for the festive season, but presently, aware that they were quite unable to buy the pink velvet dress Margaret coveted, or the crocodile handbag Eleanor had set her heart upon, they made their modest purchases, handkerchiefs and scarves for the staff at Huys Hensum, a game of Scrabble for Henry as well as a sketchbook and coloured pencils— over Fulk's present they pondered for some time; everything had cost a good deal more than Eleanor had anticipated and many of the things which they might have chosen were far too expensive, but finally they decided on a book. It was *The Ascent of Man* which, Margaret pointed out, he would read with pleasure. 'He's very clever,' she urged, 'and clever people read that kind of book.'

It was while Eleanor was paying for it—and a lot of money it was too—that she noticed her small sister's downcast face. 'What is it, love?' she asked. 'Have you changed your mind—we can easily find something else…'

Margaret shook her head. 'No—the book's fine, it's just that I wanted some money to buy something, but we haven't any left, have we?'

Eleanor peered into her purse. She had used up the ten pounds and almost all of the extra money Fulk had advanced her. 'Well, no,' she admitted, 'only a few of those little silver things—*dubbeltjes,* but I tell you what we'll do, we'll go back to Fulk's rooms—it's almost time, anyway, and I'll borrow some more money from him and we can come back quickly and get what you want before we meet him for tea. Will that do?'

They found their way back easily enough to the square, rang the old-fashioned brass bell, and walked in, just as Fulk had told them to do. There was a door on the left of the narrow hall with his name on it and they went in: the waiting room, richly carpeted, nicely furnished, too, with flowers and plenty of magazines—none of your upright chairs and last year's *Woman's Own* laid out like fish on a slab with a gas fire burning economically low. Here the chairs were comfortable, dignified, and upholstered in a pleasing damask in various shades of blue. There were plenty of tables to accommodate handbags, gloves and parcels, too. Eleanor thoroughly approved of it; she approved too of the nice, cosy-looking nurse sitting at her desk; a woman to inspire confidence in the most timid of patients and probably very competent as well. She smiled at them now and spoke in excellent English.

'Professor van Hensum is occupied with his last patient—if you would seat yourselves?'

But there was no need, for as she spoke the door at the other end of the room opened and a military-looking gentleman marched out with Fulk just behind him. He went across to the nurse and said something to her, exchanged some laughing remark with his departing patient and went to Eleanor and Margaret.

'Have you had a good shop?' he wanted to know. 'I'll be two minutes.' He turned away, but Margaret slid a hand into his to stop him. 'Fulk, please will you lend us some more money? Eleanor hasn't any left and there's something I want to buy.'

His hand was already in his pocket. 'How much do you need? Fifty gulden, a hundred?'

'For heaven's sake!' exclaimed Eleanor. 'That's far too much. Margaret, could you manage with ten gulden, or perhaps fifteen?'

'I tell you what we'll do,' said Fulk easily, 'we'll go along to the shops now and you can decide how much you want to spend when we get there. Eleanor, do you want to borrow any more for yourself?'

She was grateful to him for being so matter-of-fact about it. There was still some small thing to choose for Margaret. She did some hasty mental arithmetic; she had some more money at Huys Hensum, but not much, and she had no intention of being in his debt. 'Ten gulden would be nice if you could spare it,' she told him, and wondered why he smiled.

She was grateful when they reached the shops, too, for he suggested that she might like to go off on her own while he stayed with Margaret. It left her free to buy the headscarf Margaret had admired before rejoining them outside Vroom and Dreesman's main entrance. Eleanor had to wait a few minutes for them and whiled away the time watching the passers-by thronging the pavements, the women warmly clad with scarves pulled tight against the wind, the children encased in bright woollen outfits, their chubby faces, blue-eyed and pink-cheeked, peering out from under knitted caps, the men, large and solid in thick, short topcoats and a sprinkling of fur caps—and all of them laden with parcels.

Eleanor felt all at once lonely and far from home and her thoughts must have been reflected in her face, for Fulk said at her elbow: 'You're sad, and I wonder why?' He didn't wait for an answer, however, but took them to a nearby café; a cheerful, colourful place, warm and faintly Edwardian with its dark red carpet and panelled walls and little round tables. They drank their tea and ate rich cream cakes to the accompaniment of Margaret's happy chatter, lingering over the meal so that it was quite dark when they left the café at length and went back to Fulk's consulting rooms. During their drive home it was Margaret who did most of the talking, and although Fulk laughed and joked with her readily enough he was absent-minded, and as for Eleanor, she could think of nothing to say at all, for her head was full of Fulk.

At the house she went straight to Henry's room so that the nurse could be freed to return to Groningen with Fulk. Her brother greeted her happily, thanked the nurse nicely, expressed the opinion that he would like to meet her again, and watched silently while Eleanor added her own thanks to his together with a box of chocolates, gaily wrapped. When the nurse had gone, he asked: 'Why did you give her a present?'

'Well, it was kind of her to come at such short notice to keep you company.'

Henry thought this over. 'Yes. She was nice to Moggy and Flan too. Her name's Wabke and it's her day off, she told me, but Fulk asked her to come and sit with me and she did because she likes him very much, and he gave her fifty gulden...'

'Fifty? Good gracious, I wonder...' She had no chance to worry about whether she should pay him back fifty gulden or not, because Henry asked urgently: 'Did you have tea?'

'Yes, dear.' She had tossed off her hat and coat and gone to sit on the side of his bed.

'So did we. We had a very short walk, just round the house, and then Tekla brought our tea to the sitting room; sandwiches and cake and little biscuits with nuts on them and hot buttered toast. We ate quite a great deal. Wabke says this is a very grand house. Is it, Eleanor?'

'Well, yes, it is rather.' She was still doing sums, wondering if she had enough money to pay Fulk the fifty gulden as well as the money she had borrowed. Henry cut into her calculations with: 'What did you have for tea?'

'Oh, gorgeous cakes,' she brought her mind back with difficulty to their conversation, 'though I think your tea sounded lovely. My cake was chocolate and pineapple and whipped cream arranged on a piece of pastry.'

'What did Margaret have?'

Eleanor was saved from the details by Fulk's entrance. His 'Hullo, old chap, how's the day been?' was uttered in his usual kindly tones, but he didn't look at her at all.

Henry grinned tiredly. 'Super! I like Wabke. Gosh, it's smashing to feel like me again. We went for a walk, you know, ever such a short one, and then we played Ludo and cards, only Wabke isn't very good at games, but she laughs a lot and she liked Moggy and Flan. I hope I shall see her again before I go home.'

'I'll make a note of it,' Fulk assured him gravely, and took his pulse. 'You've done enough for today, though—supper in bed and go to sleep early—remember what I told you? I'll come and see you before I go in the morning.' He glanced at last at Eleanor. 'I shall be out this evening.'

She stopped him at the door. 'Oh—then could you spare a minute…?'

'Unless it's urgent, no. I'm late already.' He smiled faintly. 'Good night, Eleanor.'

Which left her feeling snubbed and still fretting about the fifty gulden. And where was he going? It was none of her business, of course, but she did want to know. Being in love, she decided as she got ready for bed some hours later, was no fun at all, and why couldn't she have fallen for someone like Perry Maddon, who liked her for a start, instead of Fulk, who didn't like her at all half the time, and he had far too much money too and led the kind of life she wouldn't enjoy. That wasn't true; she would enjoy it very much, living in this large, magnificently appointed house, with Juffrouw Witsma and Tekla and Bep to run it. Wearing beautiful clothes too, going out with Fulk to balls and parties, secure in the knowledge that he would come racing home each evening because he couldn't bear to be parted from her...the sad feeling inside her which she had managed until now to ignore, dissolved into silent tears.

She didn't go down to breakfast the next morning until she was sure that Fulk had gone, making the excuse to Margaret that Henry had slept late. Her sister gave her a disconcerting stare. 'You've been crying,' she stated. 'You never cry—what's the matter, Eleanor?'

'Nothing, love—I think I'm just a little tired, and I've been so worried about Henry.' Eleanor managed to smile. 'I'll have a cup of coffee and feel fine again. I thought we might write the labels for the presents— Henry could do Fulk's.'

It was a small task, quickly done. She helped Henry, now becoming very independent and inclined to do more than he ought, and then with Margaret, walked in the gardens. There was a nice little wild corner almost out of sight of the house, where there were squirrels and any number of birds. They stopped to feed them and then went on to the pond to feed the ducks. 'What a pity,' Eleanor observed, 'that Fulk has so little time to enjoy his own garden.'

'Oh, but he does,' protested Henry. 'Before I was ill, we used to come here every day after lunch before Fulk went back to his work. Flan came too; we went around looking at things. He must have a lot more patients now, for he doesn't come for lunch any more, does he? He's not often home for tea, either, is he?'

A remark which set Eleanor's unhappy thoughts on an even more unhappy course. It really seemed as though

Fulk didn't want to see more of her than he absolutely had to. Perhaps, despite what he had said, Imogen's mother had impressed him with the unwisdom of having her in the house and risking Imogen's feelings being hurt, but in that case, why didn't the girl come back and keep an eye on the situation herself? Not that there was a situation. Eleanor frowned, wondering how much longer it would be before Henry would be fit to travel home; Christmas wasn't far off now and that was a good arguing point. She had already made up her mind to talk to Fulk that evening; she would broach the subject at the same time.

She had no chance until after tea. She had sat on tenterhooks, playing cards with the children while she listened for the car, and when she had at last heard it, she threw in her hand in a manner to bring a flood of remonstrances from her companions, and heedless of their annoyed cries, ran downstairs. She reached the hall as he opened the house door and barely giving him time to get inside, said: 'Fulk, I'd like to speak to you, could it be now?'

He raised his eyebrows. 'If it's as urgent as all that, and presumably it is. You look ready to burst with your feelings, Eleanor. Come into the study.'

He shut the door behind her and waved her to a chair. 'Talk up, dear girl,' he begged her. 'I'll listen, but I've things to do at the same time, if you have no objection.'

It was awkward addressing his broad back while he bent over his desk opening and shutting drawers, taking things out and putting other things away. He looked at the clock too, which hardly encouraged her. Eleanor drew a deep breath. 'It's three things really,' she began ungrammatically. 'I want to know how much money I owe you, and that includes what you paid the nurse who came to look after Henry yesterday, and then I want to know how soon he can go home…' She saw him stiffen and hurried on: 'We can never thank you enough for all you've done, but we must be a perfect nuisance to you.' And when he didn't say anything: 'And if he isn't well enough to travel, I'll go if you want me to. I've been thinking, Baroness Oss van Oss was quite right—I mean, about me being here and Imogen not liking it. I wouldn't have liked it either, I'd have come…' She paused just in time and changed what she had nearly said to: 'I wouldn't want to—that is, I don't want to upset her even though there's no reason for it, but if I go home you could let her know and she wouldn't mind Henry being here, would she?' She was quite unaware of the pleading in her voice.

She thought she heard Fulk laugh, but of course she must have been mistaken; what was there to laugh about? She sighed a little and waited for him to answer.

He shut a final drawer and leaned against the corner of the desk, jingling his keys gently up and down in one large, well-kept hand.

'You were a tiresome little girl,' he remarked in a gentle voice, 'always wanting to know things, and now that you're grown up you are still tiresome, though perhaps not quite in the same way. I haven't the least idea how much you owe me; when I have the time I will see about it and let you know, since you will only nag me until I do. And no, Henry is not well enough to go home, and no, I do not wish you to leave my house, and may I add in passing that Baroness Oss van Oss never has and never will influence me in any way. There is only one person who can do that, but she hasn't yet realized that. And now you really must excuse me—I've a date.'

Eleanor stood up too quickly. 'Oh, I didn't know,' she

said blankly, and was rendered speechless by his bland: 'How should you? I didn't mention it before.'

She had had no intention of asking, but she heard herself enquiring: 'Are you going away again?'

'Yes. I'll go and see Henry before I leave and if there is anything I think you should know, I'll leave a note on the mantelpiece.'

She said fiercely: 'I don't understand you; you tell me I'm not to go home and yet you make a point of keeping out of my way—I suppose it's for Henry's sake.'

His face was in the shadows. 'Suppose what you like, Eleanor,' he offered calmly, and she turned on her heel and snatched at the door handle.

'I hope you have a nice weekend,' she answered, still fierce, 'although I couldn't care less!' She went through the door and shut it rather violently behind her.

She spent a good deal of the evening trying to cheer up a glum Henry and a disappointed Margaret. 'But he won't be here for Sint Nikolaas,' Henry argued for the tenth time, 'and we've got him a present.'

'He can have it when he gets back,' Eleanor assured him in a cheerful voice which sounded over-loud in her own ears. 'We can give the others their presents and watch the TV, there'll be a special programme and you know you love the colours.'

'But we can't understand what they're saying,' Margaret pointed out in a discouraged voice. 'Do you suppose Fulk forgot?'

'No, of course not, but we have all forgotten that he's engaged to Imogen, and I expect he wants to be with her so that he can give her a present…'

'She could have come here,' grumbled Henry. 'I wonder what he'll give her?'

'Rubies and diamonds and emeralds,' stated Margaret

positively. 'He's very rich, Hermina told me so. If I were just a little older and he were just a little younger, I should cut Imogen out and marry him myself.' She looked at Eleanor. 'I don't know why you don't, darling Eleanor; you're just a nice age for him and though I've never seen a photograph of her, I'm sure you're a hundred times prettier—besides, wouldn't it be lovely for all of us? We could come and stay with you, and mind the babies while you and Fulk go away on marvellous holidays together. I…'

Eleanor knew her voice was sharp. 'Margaret, what nonsense you do talk!' She was helped by Henry's, 'Anyway, you don't like him, do you, Eleanor, you said so in the loft—you said he was a horrid boy.'

'Pooh,' cried Margaret, 'that's a load of hooey, that was years ago; of course you like him, don't you, Eleanor?'

'He's grown into a very kind and—and nice man,' said Eleanor cautiously.

'I wouldn't call him nice, exactly, I mean you don't notice nice people very much, do you? And you do notice Fulk. But he's smashing, all right, his eyes twinkle and he laughs—I mean a real laugh, and when he's cross he goes all quiet instead of shouting.'

Eleanor eyed her sister in some astonishment, agreeing with every word, but all she said was: 'Darling, how observant you are.'

She devised several activities to keep them busy the next morning, and in the afternoon, as it was a fine if cold day, they went for their usual walk before tea, which they had round a splendid fire in the sitting room while they watched the various festivities in honour of the saint. Eleanor switched it off presently, however, because Henry was beginning to look a little tired, and they

all went upstairs to his room where she settled him before the fire in a comfortable chair, fetched the games
table and suggested that he and Margaret might like to
have a game of draughts while she went to the kitchen
to see what was for his supper. She had turned the angle
of the staircase and had paused to admire the prospect
of the hall below her when the front door opened and
her mother and father walked in, followed by Fulk.

Her joyous cry of 'Fulk!' she drowned very quickly
by her breathless exclamation of: 'Mother, Father!' as
she raced down the staircase to fling herself at her smiling parents. 'Oh, what a glorious surprise!' she babbled.
'Won't Henry and Margaret be thrilled—they're up in
his room.' She looked at Fulk then. 'I thought you'd
gone to spend Sint Nikolaas with Imogen.'

He said nothing, although he smiled and his dark eyes
held a gleam which might have been anger, or possibly
amusement as he suggested to Mrs MacFarlane that they
might like to see Henry before they did anything else.

After that the evening went like a bomb. Henry, so
excited that he could hardly speak, consented to lie down
on his bed and rest on the understanding that he should
join the rest of the party for dinner later on, and Margaret
undertook to unpack for her mother, never ceasing to talk
as she did so. Fulk had taken Mr MacFarlane down to
the sitting room for a drink, suggesting that the ladies
might like a cup of tea upstairs, 'For you'll want to gossip,' he declared, 'and there's plenty of time before dinner.'

Eleanor was left to coax Henry to rest, to tidy away
the children's game and then to follow her mother and
sister to the big bedroom in the front of the house, where
she sat on the bed, joining in the conversation and pouring the tea when it came. It wasn't until the evening was

over, with Henry safely tucked up in bed and the rest of them saying their good nights, that she had a moment alone with Fulk. The other three had gone across the hall to look at a particular portrait in the dining-room which they had been talking about, leaving Fulk lounging by the french window in the drawing room, waiting for Flan to come in, and Eleanor, standing, very erect, by the door. She plunged into speech at once, for there was no knowing how long they might be left alone, and although she had thought over what she was going to say, she realized now that she had forgotten every word; better get it over with. She relaxed a little and said soberly: 'Fulk, I must thank you for all the trouble you've taken to bring Mother and Father here, and the expense and the time—I only wish you were as happy as we all feel.'

He had turned his head to watch her. Now he said blandly: 'It merely required a telephone call or two, a couple of free days which I had owing to me, anyway, and as to the expense, I'm sure that by now someone must have told you that I am a wealthy man.'

'Well—yes, Hermina told Margaret and she told me, but you could have had all the money in the world and still not done it.' She gulped, 'Oh, I feel so mean—you see, I thought you'd gone to Cannes again, to your Imogen, and I was beastly enough to mind about it, and that's where you should be really, not here with us. You could have gone out dancing and dining and having fun.' She went on feverishly, seeing it all in her mind's eye. 'There would be sunshine, wouldn't there, and you could have gone riding too and given each other presents, and...'

His short laugh stopped her, his voice was all silk. 'Hardly that. Imogen considers the feast of Sint Nikolaas old-fashioned.' He smiled with a trace of mockery while she tried to find something to say and then went on, still silkily: 'When we came in this evening, you cried my name—oh, you remembered to cover it up quickly, but not quite quickly enough. Why, Eleanor?'

She had hoped that he hadn't heard. She said lamely: 'I was surprised; I thought you were miles away…'

He came and stood in front of her, but she didn't look at him. 'It's nice to think that I'm on your mind, even when I'm not here.' He laughed again, quite cheerfully this time. 'Although perhaps it was those few guldens you owe me which were on your mind—was that it?'

She seized on that, thankful for an excuse, and then, anxious to get away from him, embarked on a disjointed speech which became more and more muddled as she went along, happily unaware of the unholy delight in his eyes. She was brought to a sudden stop by his kiss. 'Your thoughts show very plainly on your pretty face, my dear,' he told her gently, and opened the door and ushered her out.

CHAPTER NINE

SINT NIKOLAAS WOULD BE coming in the evening after tea, which meant that the day was spent, by Henry and Margaret at least, in a state of anticipation. With the exception of Eleanor and her brother, the whole party went to church in the morning, and for the benefit of Mr MacFarlane, Fulk drove them to Groningen to the Martinikerk, so that during lunch the conversation largely concerned this magnificent edifice with its sixteenth-century wall paintings in the choir and its five-storied spire. 'A pity that you were unable to see it for yourself, my dear,' remarked Eleanor's father. 'Should you go to Groningen before you return to Scotland, you must make a point of visiting it.' He turned to Fulk. 'I was much struck by the architecture of the village church we passed on our way home—in the Roman-Gothic style, I fancy.'

Eleanor, eating her delicious ragout of game, wondered if Fulk was bored; he didn't appear to be, indeed, he seemed to know as much about the building of churches as her father did. She listened to him telling her father that that particular style of building was only to be found in the most northerly provinces of the country, and entering into a discussion concerning the differences between the early and late Gothic style of architecture, but he was too well-mannered to allow their talk to monopolize the conversation and switched easily enough to other matters, and soon everyone was talking in a more lighthearted fashion, especially Henry, who, having been a very good boy all the morning, was now inclined to get excited; something which Eleanor saw quickly enough; so did Fulk, for as soon as lunch was finished and before they all went into the drawing room for their coffee, he suggested in the mildest of voices that Henry should have his afternoon rest a little earlier than usual. 'You don't want to miss Sint Nikolaas' arrival,' he pointed out, 'and if you take a nap now, you will be downstairs again in plenty of time for tea.'

Henry agreed cheerfully enough and Eleanor bore her small brother away, tucked him up, admonished him in sisterly tones to be good, and went back to the drawing room, where she spent the rest of the afternoon listening to her mother's quiet voice talking about the various small happenings at home, and answering suitably when she was expected to. But she left most of the talking to Margaret, who had a great deal to say and had them all laughing over her various experiences, for unlike Eleanor, she had been to the village on various occasions, had tea at Hermina's home, and spent a good deal of time with Juffrouw Witsma in the kitchen, watching her cook and learning Dutch at the same time. It was Fulk who remarked: 'I'm afraid that Eleanor hasn't had the same opportunities as Margaret, for she has been tied hand and foot to Henry. I don't know what I should have done without her help, for I have been able to go about my daily work knowing that he was safe with her.'

They all looked at her, and she looked at her shoes, feeling foolish, and her mother said thoughtfully: 'Well, we shall have to make it up to her in some way,' and smiled across at Fulk as she spoke, and he agreed with a smile before enquiring about Mrs Trot. 'Moggy fits very well into our household,' he observed, 'and Flan adores him.' The big dog lifted his head and thumped his tail, drawing attention to himself, and the talk, naturally enough, turned to dogs.

Tea was over and everyone was sitting round talking in a desultory fashion when there was a thunderous knock on the door, and Henry, who had been sitting silently with his ears cocked for the slightest sound, got out of his chair. Fulk got up too, observing that Sint Nikolaas was punctual as usual and they had better see what he had left at the door, and with Henry beside him, went out of the room, to return very shortly with a large, bulging sack. He set it down in the centre of the room, saying: 'Margaret, go to the kitchen and fetch everyone here, will you? And then you and Henry shall hand round the presents.'

There were gifts for everyone there, even for Mr and Mrs MacFarlane, a thoughtful act on Fulk's part which engendered Eleanor's instant gratitude, and when the sack was at last empty, Henry, being the youngest person present, was allowed to open his parcels first.

He opened each gift carefully, and there were quite a number, for besides the presents Eleanor and Margaret had bought, there were a variety of things to please a small boy, and the last package of all, an air gun, complete with pellets and a target board, caused him to shout with delight.

'We'll fix the target up tomorrow,' Fulk promised, and Henry, for all his clever little brain still uncertain about the good saint who handed out presents so lavishly, asked: 'How could Sint Nikolaas possibly know that I wanted a gun?'

Fulk shrugged his broad shoulders. 'It's something most boys want. When you've got the hang of it we'll do some clay pigeon shooting, if you like. Now it's Margaret's turn.'

The pink velvet dress she had so much admired was at the bottom of the pile. She shook it free from its folds of tissue paper and all she could say was: 'Oh, Fulk—it's the dress I showed you when we were shopping in Groningen!' She ran across the room and flung her arms round his neck and kissed him soundly. 'Oh, you really are groovy,' she told him fervently, and raced away to try it on.

By the time it came to Eleanor's turn, everyone was in high spirits; somehow Fulk had managed to create the right atmosphere of excitement and pleasure and the traditional wine they were drinking certainly helped him. She began on the little pile before her, feeling like a child again; the crocodile handbag was in the third box she opened; the very one she had admired with Margaret, and her sister, a charming picture in her new pink dress and perched on the side of Fulk's chair, called out: 'I pointed it out to Fulk, Eleanor, but I never knew—honestly I didn't.'

It was a beautiful thing; Eleanor had never had anything like it before, probably she never would again. She laid it down carefully and looked at Fulk, watching her. 'Thank you,' she said in a voice which quavered a little, 'it's marvellous—you shouldn't have done it, but it's quite—quite...' Words failed her when he asked, laughing: 'Don't I get the same treatment as Margaret gave me?'

There was a little wave of laughter and there was really no way out. She crossed the room and kissed him, aware of the eyes watching her. The kiss was light and brief and she managed some sort of laughing remark before she sat down again and opened the rest of the presents she had been given; it was a relief when she got to the last one and everyone turned their attention to Juffrouw Witsma, whose turn it was.

Being the master of the house, Fulk opened his gifts last of all. His devoted staff had given him handkerchiefs and a rather dreadful tie which he declared was exactly to his taste; Eleanor had no doubt that he would wear it just because they had given it to him, although the blinding paisley pattern was hardly his style. He opened the book last of all, declaring that it was just what he had intended getting for himself, and then went round thanking everyone; when he reached Eleanor his thanks were brief. 'I've kissed all the other women,' he told her in a soft voice, 'but I'm not going to kiss you, Eleanor—and you're welcome to make what you like of that.'

He grinned suddenly at her before going to open the champagne without which he declared Sint Nikolaas Avond was incomplete.

Everything was back to normal in the morning; Eleanor got down to breakfast to find Fulk already behind his paper, and although he wished her good morning, his detached manner gave her the impression that for him at least life was real, life was earnest. There was no one else there and he seemed to feel no need for conversation, but continued to read *De Haagsche Post* while he finished his coffee. Presently he folded it carefully, gathered up his letters, said goodbye to her in the tones of a man who was simply upholding the conventions, mentioned that he would see Henry before he left for the hospital, and went from the room, leaving her feeling strangely hollow. Not that she allowed her feelings to overcome her; when her family joined her a few minutes later, she was the life and soul of the breakfast table.

Mr and Mrs MacFarlane were to stay a week, and it

had already been decided that Henry should remain where he was until a few days before Christmas. He was doing well now, but as Fulk had pointed out, he was living in a strict routine now, with long rest periods, early bedtime and a kind but firm refusal to indulge any ambitious whims he might think up. The longer he kept to this routine, the better chance he had of permanent recovery, and when his parents protested that the boy was giving Fulk a great deal of trouble he shrugged it off with: 'Not in the least. I have already told you that Eleanor takes the brunt of caring for him, and heaven knows the house is large enough for us all.'

A remark, which, when relayed to Eleanor, did nothing to improve her spirits. She and her mother were walking in the garden and Mrs MacFarlane, having delivered this facer, went on: 'Such a good, kind man; he will make a splendid husband. I wonder what this Imogen of his is like? I would have thought that she would have wanted to spend more time with him...'

'Fulk went to see her,' Eleanor explained in a calm little voice, 'just for the weekend—he must love her very much to go all that way just for a weekend...'

'There are other reasons for taking long journeys,' remarked her parent, and before Eleanor could ask her what she meant, she asked: 'What about you, darling? Will you have to go straight back to the hospital, or will you be able to come home for Christmas?'

'I hadn't thought about it.' And it was true, she hadn't. 'I'd better write and find out, hadn't I? Though I'm sure they'll expect me, you know what Christmas is like on the wards, and I wouldn't dare be away.' She fell silent, contemplating Christmas without Fulk, and not only Christmas; the rest of the year, and all the years after that.

It was during dinner that evening that Fulk remarked to the table in general that he thought that Eleanor deserved a day out. 'And now that you are here,' he suggested pleasantly, 'she could quite safely have one, could she not?' He addressed Mr MacFarlane. 'She would have the chance to see the Martinikerk for herself, and there are one or two splendid museums. I have arranged to take a day so that I may go with her.'

He smiled round the table and everyone, with the exception of Eleanor, smiled back, agreeing with him in a pleased chorus, not realizing that the subject of this treat hadn't been given a chance to accept or refuse it.

During the animated discussion which followed as to the best way of cramming as much as possible into a day's outing, Eleanor remained silent; not that anyone noticed; they were all too busy putting forward their own views as to what constituted the highlights of sightseeing. Her father, naturally enough, had a good deal to say about churches, and the Martinikerk in particular, but he was drowned by Margaret's insistent voice raised on behalf of old castles, and her mother, a poor third, voiced the view that perhaps a nice look at the shops would be the thing. Fulk, sitting back in his chair, listened courteously to their arguments, saying little, while he watched Eleanor, but presently he gathered the threads of the conversation skilfully together in such a way that each felt that he or she had contributed a valuable piece of advice and suggested that they should go into the drawing room for coffee. It was a chance that Eleanor took. Mumbling that she would see if Henry was comfortable, she flew upstairs, where she spent quite an unnecessary amount of time shaking up her brother's pillows while she tried to decide what to do. A day out with Fulk would be heaven, there could be no argument about that; on the other hand, he hadn't asked her, had he? Not in so many words. He was making a gesture, rewarding her for her long hours in the sickroom. Well, she didn't want a reward! She gave the surprised Henry's pillow still another shake and went downstairs. The drawing room door was shut and she could hear voices and laughter from behind it; she suddenly didn't want to go in and half turned on the staircase to go to her room when Fulk's study door opened and he put his head out.

'Ah, I thought so—I could practically smell the paint-work blistering under your bad temper.'

'I am not in a bad temper!'

'Come in, then—we'll have a cosy chat.'

She stayed exactly where she was. 'What about?'

'Our day out tomorrow, of course.'

She looked down her nose at him. 'I wasn't aware that I had been invited to go anywhere with anyone,' she informed him coldly.

'Quite right, dear Eleanor, you haven't. You would have refused point blank, wouldn't you, but now that everyone has gone to such trouble to suggest where we should go, and your mother is here to look after Henry, you can't very well refuse, can you?'

'I can't think why you should want to spend a day with me.'

His eyes narrowed. 'Coming from any other girl, I wouldn't believe a word of that,' he told her blandly, 'but from you...' His voice became friendly and warm. 'I haven't had a day out myself for a long time. I need a break.'

She said instantly: 'You went to Cannes to see Imogen.'

He agreed affably, and then: 'You're a little old-fashioned, Eleanor.'

'I'm very old-fashioned, if you want to know. We don't move very fast with the times where I come from.'

'So I realized. It may astonish you to know that the people around these parts don't either—very behind the times, we are. Now, having settled that to our mutual satisfaction, will you spend the day with me tomorrow, Eleanor?'

She knew then that she had never intended doing anything else but that; let the absent Imogen look after herself; she had no one else to blame and she must be a very conceited girl if she didn't imagine that Fulk might need a little female society from time to time. She said frankly: 'I'd like to very much, thank you, Fulk.'

It was pouring with rain when she got up the next morning; cold heavy rain rattling down like a steel curtain from a uniformly grey sky. Eleanor stood looking at it from her bedroom window, resigned to the fact that there would be no day out. It didn't look any better from Henry's room either; she was finishing off a few small chores for him when Fulk walked in. His good morning was cheerful. 'I hope you like rain,' he observed cheerfully, 'for we're going to get plenty of it today—the wind's cold too, so wear a thick coat, you can keep dry under my umbrella.'

She found herself smiling. 'I didn't think we'd be going...'

He looked surprised. 'Why not? You don't strike me as being one of those girls who fuss at getting a bit wet.'

She assured him happily that indeed she wasn't fussy, and went down to breakfast in the best of spirits.

Looking back at the end of the day, she wasn't sure which part of it she had enjoyed most; the great church had been wonderful—all that space and loftiness, so had the Municipal Museum, where she had spent a long time gazing at the regional costumes. They had had coffee afterwards in the Grand Hotel Frigge and then gone on to look at the university, which she found too modern for her taste, although the variety of coloured caps worn by the students intrigued her.

They had left Fulk's car outside his rooms and walked through the rain, arm-in-arm under Fulk's umbrella, for that was the only way in which to see the city properly, he told her. They went through the narrow streets between the two main squares, pausing to admire the variety of old houses lining the canals, peering down centuries-old alleys, looking down into the cold grey water from the small bridges as they crossed them. It was on one of these that Fulk had quite suddenly kissed her, one arm sweeping her close, the other still holding the umbrella and even in this rather awkward situation, he contrived to carry out the exercise with an expertise which took her breath. She had looked up at him, rain dripping down her pretty face, a little flushed now, uneasily aware that she had kissed him back, if not expertly, at least with enthusiasm.

'You're very pretty in the rain,' Fulk had said, and taken her by the arm and walked her on through the almost empty little streets, pointing out anything of interest with an ease of manner which made her wonder if he made a habit of kissing girls on bridges whenever he felt like it. She wondered if she should make some light-hearted remark to that effect, but she had been unable to think of one; silence was probably the best thing, with of course, suitable observations about the house he was telling her about.

They went back to the car after a little while and drove up to the coast to Warffrum, where there was a castle converted into a hotel. They had lunched there, begin-

ning with *Erwten* soup to warm them up and going on
to sole Murat and Charlotte Russe, sitting over their coffee until the afternoon sky began to darken from grey to
black and Fulk suggested that for the last hour or two
she might like to look round the shops in Groningen,
something she was very willing to do, although she had
been very careful not to express admiration for any ar-
ticle which caught her fancy; she wasn't sure, but if he
could buy a crocodile handbag just because she had admired it, he could just as likely purchase any of the trifles
which caught her eye, so she confined her admiration to
the fabulously expensive jewellery, taking care to remark
a cool 'How nice,' to anything she judged to be within
his pocket.

She was quite unaware that her painstaking efforts
were affording her companion a good deal of amusement, but she found it a relief when he suggested that
they might have tea before they went back home, and
she agreed readily enough when he had asked her if it
would be a good idea to buy Henry a book about air
pistols and guns. At the same time he had bought a box
of chocolates for Margaret, pointing out gravely that
children should be treated equally, an opinion which she
shared and which occupied them pleasantly as they drove
back.

They had rounded off the day with a hilarious game
of Monopoly after dinner, and Henry, for a treat, had
been allowed to stay up until nine o'clock. The rest of
them had stayed up much longer than that and the great
Friese wall clock in the hall was chiming midnight when
they went to their beds. Eleanor, lingering to thank Fulk
for her day, had been a little chilled by the cool courtesy
of his reply, so that she had gone up to bed wondering
if his apparent enjoyment of it had been nothing but good

manners. But surely mere good manners didn't necessitate kissing her in the middle of a bridge?

The week went very quickly after that; it was Friday evening again in no time at all, with her parents packed and ready to leave and Fulk, whom she had hardly seen during the last few days, wishing her goodbye with the unwelcome information that he wouldn't be coming straight back this time. 'There's a seminar in Edinburgh on Monday,' he told her, 'and I hope to attend it; I shan't be back until the middle of the week. You know what to do for Henry and if you are in the least worried you can telephone me. Have you any messages?'

She couldn't think of one. She kissed her parents goodbye and wished them all a safe journey, wanting with all her heart to be free to go with them. The house was very quiet when they had gone; the children went to bed and she was left to roam round on her own, a prey to her thoughts, picturing Fulk at her home, driving down to Edinburgh, meeting people she didn't know, living a life in which she had no share. She went to bed at last, feeling lost.

He came back on Wednesday evening and almost as soon as he had entered his front door the telephone rang, and Eleanor, who had heard the car arriving and had come into the hall, paused.

'Yes, answer it, there's a good girl,' he begged her, 'while I get out of this coat.'

She went into the study and lifted the receiver gingerly, hoping that whoever was on the other end wouldn't break into a torrent of Dutch. She said: 'Hullo?' which could do no harm anyway and a girl's voice answered, a sharp voice asking a sharp question.

'Wait a minute,' said Eleanor in English. 'Professor van Hensum is just back, I'll call him.'

The voice spoke English now. 'You are Eleanor? You are still there…' There was a tinkling laugh. 'Fetch Fulk, tell him it is Imogen.'

He was strolling across the hall to take the receiver from her. 'Who is it?' he asked, 'or is it someone speaking double dutch?'

'It's Imogen.' She didn't wait, but went out of the room, closing the door carefully behind her and going back to Henry and Margaret. She had often imagined Imogen's voice, and now she had heard it; it merely served to confirm her opinion of the girl. She embarked on a game of spillikins with the children and when presently Fulk joined them, Imogen wasn't mentioned.

She met him at breakfast the next morning; Henry still had his breakfast in bed and Margaret had taken Flan for a walk and beyond an exchange of good mornings they had nothing to say to each other, only as Fulk went from the room he told her: 'I have no idea when I shall be home, if you want me urgently, telephone the hospital.' His smile was brief, although she heard him whistling cheerfully as he went out of the house.

It was almost tea time when Eleanor, leaving Margaret to entertain Henry, went down to the kitchen to fetch the tea tray; if Fulk wasn't coming home there seemed no point in making a lot of extra work. She was crossing the hall when the front door bell rang and she went to see who it was. Juffrouw Witsma was in her room and Tekla would be busy in the kitchen. A girl stood outside and before Eleanor could utter a word had pushed past her into the hall. A quite beautiful girl, wrapped in a fur coat, her guinea-gold hair tucked up under a little fur cap, her legs encased in the kind of boots Eleanor had always wanted and never been able to afford. She walked into the centre of the hall before she said in English: 'Where is Fulk?'

'You're Imogen,' declared Eleanor, not answering. She got a cold look for her pains.

'Naturally.' She frowned. 'This filthy weather, how I hate it, and this frightful barn of a house...'

'It's a very beautiful house,' said Eleanor sharply, 'and it can't be summer all the year round.'

'Oh, yes, it can.' Imogen walked back to where Eleanor was standing and stared at her, rather as though she were a piece of furniture or something at a fair. 'I came to see you. Mama said that you were pretty, and I suppose you are in a large way, but not in the least chic—I wonder what Fulk sees in you?'

'Nothing,' said Eleanor quickly, 'nothing at all—he's in love with you.'

Imogen smiled, her lovely mouth curling in a sneer. 'Rubbish! You are—how do you say?—dim. Well, I have seen you for myself; I shall go.' She walked to the door and actually had her hand on its handle when Eleanor cried: 'But you can't—Fulk won't be long, at least I don't think so; he usually comes home after tea. Couldn't you telephone his rooms or the hospital and tell him you're here?'

Imogen was pulling her coat collar close. 'Why should I wish to see him?'

'But you're going to marry him—you love him,' declared Eleanor, persevering.

'No, I'm not, and I don't.' Imogen disappeared in a whirl of fur, only her expensive perfume lingering after her as she crashed the heavy door shut.

'Well,' said Eleanor on a long-drawn breath, 'now what?'

It was at that precise moment that she turned her head

and saw Fulk standing in the doorway of his study, his shoulders wedged comfortably against the door jamb, his hands in his pockets.

'There you are!' she exclaimed. 'Just in time—for heaven's sake go after her. It's Imogen—if you run...'

'My dear Eleanor,' said Fulk calmly, 'I never run, and even if I went after her, what would I say?'

'Why, that you love her, of course.'

'But I don't.'

Her brows drew together in a quite fierce frown. 'But you're going to marry her.'

He smiled a little. 'I heard Imogen tell you in no uncertain terms that she wasn't going to marry me.'

She gave him a scornful look. 'Women always say things like that. I expect she's walking down the road crying her eyes out.'

'Not Imogen; she'll have a taxi waiting.'

'Don't quibble—what does it matter, taxi or walking...'

'It doesn't matter at all,' he agreed placidly. 'I can't think why you're making such a business of the whole thing.'

She was bewildered, but she wasn't going to give up. Later on, when she was alone again, she could nurse her broken heart. 'But you're...!' she began again.

'If you are going to tell me once more—erroneously—that I love Imogen, I shall do you a mischief.' His voice was still unworried. 'I haven't been in love with her for quite some time—since, in fact, I climbed the ladder to the loft and saw you sitting there in your old clothes and your hair streaming... You looked—well, never mind that for the moment. And Imogen—she has never loved me, you know, I imagine that she was flattered at the idea of being mistress of this house and having all the money she wanted, but love—no, my dear. All the same, I had to be certain, didn't I? That's why I went to see her; I don't think I was surprised and certainly not in the least upset to find that she was—er—consoling herself with an American millionaire—short and fat and going bald, but still a millionaire.' He added almost apologetically: 'An American millionaire is so much richer than a Dutch one, you know.'

'You're not a millionaire?' Eleanor wanted to know.

'Well, yes—at least, in Holland, I am.' He strolled across the hall towards her. 'I suppose if I were to offer you this house and my millions you would kick them right back at me, Eleanor?'

'Yes.' She had seen the look on his face, and although her heart begged her to stay just where she was, she took a prudent step backwards.

But he had seen that. 'No, don't move, my darling; it would not be of the least use, you know, I should only come after you.' He smiled at her and her unhappy heart became whole once more.

'If I offered you my heart and my love would you throw them back at me too?' he asked.

'No.' Her voice was a whisper. There was no mistaking the look upon his face now. She took another step back and felt the stairs against her heel. She had reached the second tread when she was halted by his: 'Come down off the staircase, dear Eleanor.'

She supposed she would always do what he wanted her to do from now on. She reached the floor once more and he took her hands in his.

'Oh, my dear darling,' he said, 'come into the little sitting room,' and he opened the door and drew her gently inside. The whole charming place smelled delicious; there was an enormous bunch of red roses lying on the table and Eleanor cried: 'Oh, how glorious!' and wrinkled her charming nose in delight.

'Roses for Christmas,' said Fulk, 'just to prove that you do mean something to someone, my dear love.' He pulled a tatty piece of paper from his pocket. 'The last thing on your list, though I promise you they will be the first of many.'

He pulled her close. 'It's been you all the time, my darling. How strange it is that one can love someone and not know it.' He bent to kiss her, not once, but several times and slowly. 'Of course, boys of sixteen don't al-ways know these things.'

She looked at him enquiringly and he kissed her again. 'You were almost five, sweetheart; I pulled your hair and you kicked my shins and fell over, do you remember? And when I picked you up you were warm and grubby and soft and you cried all over me; I lost my heart then, but never knew it.'

His arm tightened around her. 'Will you marry me, Eleanor? And you had better say yes, for I shan't let you go until you do.'

Eleanor heaved a sigh. 'Oh, Fulk, of course I will— and don't ever let me go.' She leaned up to kiss him and sighed again; she had never been so happy. 'I wonder...' she began dreamily, and was interrupted by the opening of the door.

'Juffrouw Witsma has made a cake,' Henry informed them, 'and I'm rather hungry. Do you suppose I might have a slice?'

Fulk still had tight hold of Eleanor. 'Certainly you may—two slices if you wish, and give Margaret some too—and don't hurry too much over eating it.'

'Thank you.' Henry looked at them with interest. 'Are you kissing Eleanor, Fulk?'

'Indeed I am.'

'Are you going to marry her?'

'We were discussing that when you came in.'

'I can take a hint,' said Henry in a tolerant voice. 'I suppose you won't mind if I just mention it to Margaret?'

'By all means do so.' Fulk's voice gave no sign of impatience, but perhaps Henry saw something in his eye, for he turned to go. 'There's a bowl of fruit on the sideboard,' he informed them. 'Might we have an apple too? If we have to wait while you talk, we may get hungry.'

'Eat any of the fruit you fancy,' Fulk told him, and when the door had shut: 'Now, where had I got to? I think perhaps, if you agree, my darling, I'll begin again from the beginning; I rather enjoyed hearing you say that you would marry me.'

Eleanor lifted her head from his shoulder. There was really no need to say anything to that. She smiled and kissed him instead.

ONCE BURNED

by

Margaret Way

CHAPTER ONE

EVEN on the plane Celine couldn't escape media coverage of her grandfather's death. The businessman in the seat next to her was reading a full-page obituary in the morning's paper: Millionaire Property Developer Dies. Centred was a large, smiling photograph of a strikingly handsome elderly man with piercing light eyes and an almost theatrical mane of snow-white hair. Sir Gerald Langton, Late Chairman Harcourt Langton, it said.

Celine turned her head away abruptly, fighting down the compulsion to burst into tears. Three years after she and her grandfather had parted in such anger she was heading home for his funeral. Home to her estranged family. Home to an enforced reunion with Guy. It would be impossible for Guy to avoid her, bound as they were by their shared history and the corporation.

Three years! Could it be *that* long? Her memories had the painful immediacy of yesterday. She had only to shut her eyes to be back in her grandfather's grand, dark-panelled office... She was seated, head bowed, hands clenched in her lap while her grandfather thundered at her for being a ''hopeless little wimp'' and an ''over-indulged ninny incapable of taking up a brilliant challenge''. His temper was legendary, but it had never been directed at her. Until *now*. And why? She had broken off her engagement to Guy Harcourt, for which in some form or other she would be punished for the rest of her life.

Her grandfather had doted on Guy. Guy was the

grandson of his late, lifetime friend and partner, Sir Lew Harcourt. Real estate developers and builders on the grand scale, the two men had been knighted by the Queen in the '70's for their services to the wide community. Guy's father, a senior architect with the corporation, had been killed in an on-site accident when Guy was twelve. The dreadful shock and pain of loss precipitated Sir Lew's fatal stroke barely two years later. It was then Gerald Langton had stepped in, becoming the young Guy's mentor and male role model. Guy's devastated mother and his grandmother, the formidable Lady Muriel Harcourt, had allowed it for a number of reasons, not the least of them securing Guy's future within the corporation. He hadn't started at the bottom and worked his way up. He had real power from day one. Guy wasn't just talented, he was extraordinary. Not only was he a brilliant architect and a visionary, he was a hard-headed realist with a masterful grasp of business principles.

Her response to it all? She had fled him. At nineteen going on twenty, product of an over-restrictive home life and unsure of her own identity, she had lacked the confidence to cope with such a high-powered young man. She only knew she loved him and that paradoxically made things worse. She began to see herself in terms of becoming a future liability. There was an immeasurable gap between them. Eight years her senior, though he never sought to dominate her, Guy possessed a maturity, a natural strength and a toughness that put him far beyond her.

It was her older, sophisticated cousin, Ashley, who had finally put all Celine's anxieties and self-doubts into words. "Let's face it, kitten. You're simply not woman enough for Guy!"

Once said it became central to everything. Guy wanted

her. She wasn't such a fool she didn't know she aroused him, but inevitably as physical passion waned she could come to disappoint him. She couldn't have borne that. The truth of the matter was, she went in awe of him. Then, too, she feared being swamped just as her fragile grandmother had been pushed into a backwater by her larger-than-life husband. Her grandparents' marriage, outwardly serene, was actually a sham. A piece of theatre. They lived separate lives.

She had come to live with them when she was six years old and her parents had been drowned in a terrible boating accident. She could still remember standing in the hallway of Langfield looking down the long gallery at all the wonderful pictures. The colours were like *jewels*. She would have loved them had her mother been there to hold her hand, but tears weighed so heavily on her heart and in her throat she had lost her voice for months and her grandfather had to call in a special doctor to help her find it. Her mother and father were never coming back. Her grandmother told her they had gone to God. Surely God didn't need her parents to make Him happy? She hadn't liked God for a very long time.

Her grandmother, Helena, had always been kind to her, but her manner was so quiet and reserved the young Celine had often found her unapproachable. Her grandfather, so fierce and tall, with his rising loud voice, piercing blue eyes and crown of tawny hair that had once been red-gold just like her own, gave her everything he thought a child could want. She had heaps of expensive clothes, toys, the occasional companionship of a suitable child. She was sent to the best schools. She took ballet lessons, piano lessons, speech and drama. She was taught tennis, riding and golf but no one could teach her to swim. The most docile of children, she turned into a little wildcat when anyone tried. Finally it was decided the unfortunate situation was best left alone.

Until Guy. Guy had cherished her, overcoming her deep-seated fears with his own brand of psychology. She had loved him from the moment he had come into her life, asking her grandfather was she the cherub who had strayed out of one of Sir Gerald's Renaissance-style paintings.

Guy, my love!

Even now that was the way she thought of him. His beautiful ruby and diamond ring still swung between her breasts like an extension of herself. She was conditioned to losing the people she loved. She even *expected* it so early had she been traumatised. Ashley told her, far from being a ''wimp'', she was very brave for breaking off the engagement. ''I have to hand it to you, kiddo, you've got more guts than I gave you credit for.'' Ashley with her sharp wits and powers of observation always made ev-erything perfectly clear. Celine had a sharp mental picture of them sitting in armchairs one lovely summer's afternoon at Langfield watching Guy partner their grandfather against Ashley's current boyfriend and her brother, Michael. When Guy sent the deciding sizzling ace down the centre line their grandfather had run to him, encircling his shoulder. ''Absolutely splendid, my dear boy!''

''Touching, isn't it?'' Ashley had flipped her an ironic look. ''Grandy dotes on Guy and doesn't Guy know how to play up to him! You'd think Guy was the grandson, not Michael. Grandy and Guy are two of a kind. Master manipulators. You're the little sacrificial lamb in the middle.''

She might have made some little murmur of pain or distress but Ashley had continued, oblivious. ''Of course, you're such a pure-minded little thing I dread to think what shocks lie in store for you. Guy's fond of you. No one can deny that. You're a sweet little thing...the way you look, the soft, enticing voice. But the bottom line is Guy is tremendously ambitious. He worked out the way to go on your sixteenth birthday. I spotted it immediately but you, the dewy little virgin, were blissfully unaware of it. The Harcourts aren't going to be manoeuvred out of Harcourt Langton. After all it was Sir Lew who put up most of the money in the first place. What better way to secure the top job than marry the sleeping princess!''

''Then why not you, Ashley?'' Somehow she had found the courage to retaliate. ''You're the glamorous one. Not me. You and Guy are more of an age.''

Ashley had answered that, as well. ''Not me, kitten. I'm much more of a handful than you. Not so easy to control. Besides, you're the one Grandy loves most, if he understands the concept of love at all. They don't call him Tiger Langton for nothing. Except for that, Guy would have made a big play for me. Surely you don't doubt it? Don't hate me, kitten, for pointing this out. I want to protect you. Put you on your guard. You have to stop playing the wide-eyed innocent.''

Her answer was to run. Except, as she had come to realise, she could never run far enough. Guy was always with her. Always. She remembered the violent drama of the night she had told him she wanted out of the engagement. At first he had listened in total silence, his black eyes unfathomable, then her self-contained Guy had suddenly snapped, pulling her into his arms, telling her passionately he loved her and would never let her go. They were closeted in the library and he had shaped her body as he had never done before, kissing her so stormily she had almost fallen in a faint.

Where her strength had come from, she still didn't know. It took a terrible hour but she remained adamant she wanted the engagement over. She was desperate for escape. She could still hear her own frantic cry. "Guy, *please*, I've reached my breaking point!"

After that he switched off. Just like that. Adding weight to her shattering suspicion Ashley had been right after all. Then she had known nothing about real life but she had learned. Her grandfather, expecting her to buckle under, had cut off her allowance, but her grandmother had come to her rescue very quietly, giving her enough money to go interstate to find a place to live and look around for a job. It was her first chance to prove herself and she had. She had gone from playing the piano at the five-star Sydney Beaumont, to personal assistant, to the public relations manager. It was a hectic life involving setting up press conferences, photographic sessions, fashion parades, gala evenings, breakfasts and luncheons with celebrity guest speakers, but she took her job seriously and she handled it very well. She wondered how her boss was going to get on without her for a few days but Max was nothing if not super efficient.

Celine continued to stare fixedly out the porthole, lost in her sad reflections. At this altitude the sky was a gleaming washed-out blue. Beneath the jet airplane lay the thick woolly carpet of clouds. It seemed strange to her Ashley hadn't been the first to ring with news of their grandfather. Ashley was the only one who had remained loyal. Yet she had received the first shattering phone call from Ashley's father, her uncle Clive. He'd sounded as cold and arrogant as ever, talking down to her as of old. She was expected to stay at Langfield. She would be met by someone from the office.

"It's time you started thinking of your duty like everyone else!"

It was grossly unfair but Clive Langton had always been an abrasive man, deeply jealous and resentful of Guy's importance in his father's life; anxious one day Celine would inherit more than her share of the family fortune.

The money didn't really interest her. It wasn't hers. She hadn't earned it. She had learned to stand on her own two feet. Besides Ashley had told her her name was never mentioned from the time she'd left home. Ashley kept her up to date on all the news, in the process unwittingly deepening the rift. Guy hadn't married, but he certainly hadn't remained faithful to Celine's memory. Just as Ashley had expected, he had made a play for her, which she had scorned with the greatest of pleasure. Ashley didn't have a high opinion of men. At twenty-eight, stunningly attractive and an heiress, she hadn't found that special man. Celine had found her special man too early. And as a consequence she had lost him.

CHAPTER TWO

AT KINGSFORD Smith Airport an official met her and escorted her to the VIP lounge.

"Your friend is waiting for you, Miss Langford. A crowd of reporters is out front so we've arranged the private exit."

"That's very kind of you," Celine said gratefully, smoothing her hair. "Man or woman?"

"A gentleman, Miss Langton."

Probably one of her uncle's henchmen or even her cousin, Michael. She felt a little flurry of hurt Ashley wasn't here for her, but the situation was most likely chaotic. Her grandfather, apparently in perfect health and marvellously fit, had suffered a massive heart attack at home. Everyone would be stunned. She, herself, was grateful for the protection. She had no wish to talk to the press, much less fight her way to the car. She was back in the limelight as the "run-away heiress". An old photograph of her had appeared in another of the morning's papers under that caption. She looked amazingly wide-eyed and innocent. Long curling tresses. Little more than a child. She'd been engaged to Guy then.

The official held the door for her and closed it after him as she entered the room. She had endured a long sleepless night so her nerves were tight, but nothing prepared her for the sight that met her eyes. It was like coming face-to-face with an enormous ongoing trauma. She froze momentarily, but the man who had been flipping idly through a magazine threw it down casually and rose to his feet. Tall, immensely elegant, with a fine natural presence.

Guy!

She was pierced to the heart. She even made a soft little sound that signified pain. Whoever said time heals all wounds? Delusion. The ache was as fierce as yesterday.

For a moment Guy said nothing. He simply looked at her gravely. Finally, when she could bear his scrutiny no longer, he spoke. "Ah, the run-away heiress returns to the fold! How are you, Celine? You look shocked to see me."

"I must confess I am." She held out her hand, amazed her voice, though soft and gentle, sounded perfectly calm. "I didn't expect you, Guy. It's very kind of you to come."

"As to that, Lady Langton asked me to," he replied with exquisite brutality. Ignoring her outstretched hand, he bent his dark head and kissed her cheek, the merest gesture, yet it affected her fiercely.

He had changed. Though as achingly handsome as ever, there was a sombre cast to his expression. The sexual radiance so alive yesterday was masked by a brooding austerity. Where was the *sweetness* that had once hovered around his mouth? Gone with the flame of passion that had once burned for her in his dark eyes.

"What a lovely creature you are!" he remarked, the undisturbed calm of his tone telling her her beauty would never sway him again. "Obviously you didn't allow a broken engagement to ruin your life."

"Nor you, Guy." Sadness was in her voice. "I always wanted the best for you."

A gleaming irony shone in his dark eyes. "What a curious way you had of showing it. Never mind, it's all ancient history now. May I offer you my sincere sympathy. I know how much you loved your grandfather.''

Her tender mouth quivered. "I really did."

"I know." His eyes seemed to stare through and beyond her. "*I* was the one who drove you away."

"*No*! Don't say that. I had to find myself."

The air between them was dark and glittering. "You couldn't learn about life with *me*. If it means anything to you, I think you look very poised and adult. That photograph of you in the *Herald* makes you look about fifteen years old."

"I was engaged to you then." She looked straight into his eyes.

"So you were! I'm always surprised I remember. I even recall the exact moment that shot was taken. The evening dress was green. It brushed your eyes with jade. I remember thinking at the time you were so *young*. The '*cherub*' I used to call you. No doubt *that* had something to do with your headlong flight away from me. There's a lot to be said for sticking with the same age group."

Briefly she touched his sleeve. "Please, Guy. Don't be bitter."

Some private thought must have angered him because he frowned. He glanced down at her pale hand against the dark grey cloth of his jacket and for an instant Celine had the sickening feeling he wanted to throw it off. "But I *am* bitter, my dear Celine. In fact I think you soured me on the whole female sex."

"It was never my intention." Despite herself there was a faint tremor in her voice.

"Forgive me, you ran from me as though I were Lucifer himself. I didn't lay a finger on you, either, except for the chastest kisses."

"I loved you, Guy."

"Oh, rot!" He gave a brief, mirthless laugh. "You feared love, Celine. Don't let's talk of it anymore. The whole thing depresses me. You know I suffer from the sin of pride. Still, we can't ignore one another while you're here. The family is shattered enough. Sir Gerald cast a long shadow. I suggest we behave civilly and we'll get through this testing time."

"That's what I want, too, Guy."

He showed absolutely no reaction to her words but turned his head as a porter tapped on the rear door.

"Ready when you are, sir."

"Many thanks. Coming, Celine?" He put out an arm. "We have a drive ahead of us. Some reporter is going to get wind of the fact we've left by the rear exit."

Minutes later they were seated in Guy's Jaguar cruising smoothly through the airport's environs to the open road. It was a glorious, cloudless day. Queensland's blue and gold.

Celine sat quietly, her hands folded in her lap. Only *she* knew her long nails were biting into her flesh. "I can't believe Grandfather has gone," she said finally, to break the silence. "I didn't even know he had a heart condition."

"He hadn't. No one was expecting it. Sir Gerald was in fine form. His death was typical. Attended to without fuss or delay. He spoke a few words to your grandmother. I believe, 'I feel strange,' and that was it."

"Now I can never tell him how sorry I am we parted in anger."

"Why would you *want* to tell him?" Guy asked, his expression quite daunting. "You've had *years* to do it."

"How cruel you are, Guy!" she protested. "You never were."

"If I'm cruel, Celine, you made me."

"I can only say again I meant no hurt. So far as Grandfather was concerned I was told he couldn't bear to speak my name or hear it mentioned."

"Who told you that?" He glanced at her sharply.

"Ashley. She's the only one who remained loyal."

"You think so?" There was derision somewhere in his cool tone.

"I know so."

"You always did champion Ashley. I never understood why. It always seemed to me Ashley was playing a double game."

"You couldn't be more wrong. Ashley has a brittle way about her, I know, but it's only a veneer. You never could see that."

"Or you're a real chump when it comes to Ashley. If she told you your grandfather couldn't bear to have news of you, she was lying. Most likely out of self-interest. Sir Gerald was furious with you. No one can deny that, but he couldn't hide the fact your defection upset and worried him."

"Then why didn't he get in touch with *me*?" Celine asked, unable to believe what she was hearing.

He flashed her a droll look. "You *knew* your grandfather, Celine. The first move had to come from you. That was his way. His natural inclination was toward despotism. But, generally speaking, benevolent. *You* had to make all the overtures. Actually he was proud you were standing on your own two feet."

"You amaze me, Guy." Celine shook her head. "I heard from no one. Not even my grandmother."

"Your grandmother, too, was always anxious for word of you. Of course she *got* it, but only through our contacts."

"I *always* remembered her birthday," Celine said.

"Darling, you never were a liar." His expression was one of distaste.

"I'm not lying now." Celine felt stricken. Ashley had been in charge of delivering the gifts.

He seemed to stifle a sharp response. "Let's leave it, shall we? In many ways this is going to be a very awkward time."

Celine stared out the window. The jacarandas were in bloom all along the hillside overlooking the river. "I won't be bothering anyone for long."

"No doubt you're anxious to get back to your boss?"

Celine's camellia skin flushed. "Excuse me, we don't have that kind of a relationship."

His near-black eyes swept her profile. "Whereas, Ashley, in typical fashion, suggested you did."

"Why do you dislike Ashley?" Celine asked, realising there had always been tension there.

"Don't get in a lather about Ashley. She's more than capable of looking after herself. I'm only repeating what she told me."

"Impossible." Celine's head felt tight. "Ashley knows perfectly well Max looks on me in the friendliest fashion. Much as he would a niece. It would do him a grave injustice to suggest anything else. I can only think Ashley was trying to pay you back in some way."

"Really?" Again the faint undertone of contempt. "And for what?"

"Perhaps for hurting me. I don't know. She always has been very protective."

"I'm sorry, Celine. That would take just too long to work out."

"Would you rather I hadn't come?" she asked quietly.

"On the contrary, I wanted to see how you've turned out."

He hates me, Celine thought. "I've been in control of my own life for some time."

"My dear, it shows!"

She gave a slight shrug. "And who were the *contacts* you spoke about before?"

His eyes met hers briefly. "Your grandfather always kept track of you. Be in no doubt about that. We have our people, Celine. They're necessary."

"Spies?"

"Let's say, minders."

"So there was always someone there watching?"

"Your grandfather very much disliked your stint at the piano bar. I think he was going to do something about it, only you solved the problem yourself. I believe the men gave you no peace?"

"Nonsense! I was well protected."

"Only you couldn't take all the attention?"

"Something like that."

"So rather than have you disappear, Max offered you a job as his assistant?"

"I'm very good."

"I'm quite sure you are. You never did have to prove yourself with me, or maybe you don't recall?"

She flushed, hating the reproach. It was justified. Guy had never criticised her. He had always been supportive. Until *now*. "Uncle Clive rang me," she said in an effort to change the subject. "You know that?"

"Yes," he answered crisply.

"He sounded adamant I should come home."

"Of course. Where else could you be at such a time? I have to tell you, Celine, he still fears you might get more than he considers you're entitled to. He's acting chairman of the corporation in the interim and I expect he'll be appointed executor of the trust."

"I feel sorry for him," Celine said truthfully. "He idolised Grandfather even if they never did get on."

"I agree it wasn't a good situation, but your uncle has more prickles than a hedgehog. I find working with him extremely difficult. With Sir Gerald gone, I fully expect the situation to worsen. *Your* family like to forget *my* grandfather started the business. It was *his* idea: the bulk of *his* money. Sir Gerald was his best friend and invited along on the grand venture. You know the rest. Together they forged a business empire, each as valuable as the other, but in different ways. There's always going to be a Harcourt at Harcourt Langton, Celine."

She glanced at him quickly, hearing the thread of steel in his voice. "I'm glad of it, Guy. Are you saying Uncle Clive would like to see you out?"

"Darling, hasn't that been his main aim from day one?" he asked in a derisive voice. "Clive can't brook a rival. Naturally he has ambitions for Michael, too, but I regret to say Michael can't cut it."

"He never wanted to be part of the business anyway," Celine said. "Uncle Clive is too hard on him. Always was."

"Perhaps another instance of history repeating itself." He glanced again into his rear-vision mirror. "Someone is definitely following us. No doubt an enterprising reporter."

Celine gave a gasp of dismay, checking her own exterior mirror. "I don't want to be photographed, Guy."

"Why not? You look exquisite." Nevertheless he steered the Jaguar into a parking bay, turned off the engine and opened the door. "Stay here," he said briefly, his expression grim. "I'll go and have a word with him."

Celine couldn't resist a backward glance. A white Ford had pulled into the bay behind them. Guy had reached the passenger door and was tapping on the window.

She didn't wait for any more. She turned around, glad of her curtain of red-gold hair. The sun pressed warmly on the windows and she reached into her handbag for her sunglasses, slipping them on. She had been a private person for so long, this was going to be hard.

A few moments later she heard a car start up, then the Ford passed her slowly, the occupants staring in. A sharp-faced, dark-haired woman in her thirties who looked vaguely familiar drove, while her male companion, a heavy-set man with cropped hair, perhaps a photographer, sat in the passenger seat. She saw no more, because Guy rejoined her, sliding behind the wheel.

"They were tipped off, of course," he said, looking intensely irritated.

"To my arrival, you mean?"

"Certainly."

"But who on earth would do that? No one knew outside the family."

"What about your Max?" He pinned her briefly with his brilliant gaze.

"Max would never do such a thing." She spoke with authority. "He's my friend."

"So, forget Max. Who's left? Not Clive. Clive wants you under wraps. Nevertheless someone close to home gave them the tip-off. They told me. Hell and damnation!" Abruptly Guy broke off as the white Falcon cruising in the distance made a sudden U-turn and came speeding back in their direction.

"Duck!" Guy ordered shortly. "These confounded people just can't let anyone alone."

It was too late for ducking. The photographer was all

but hanging out the window, snapping away rapidly with a long-distance lens.

"Blast them!" Guy was furious. "They never keep their word. Now there'll be another entrancing photograph to hit the papers. Ex-Fiancé Rolls Up For The Run-Away Heiress. There would have been more of a story had you actually left me at the altar. I'm only surprised you didn't. It would have appealed to your sense of drama." He leaned forward, switched on the ignition, showed his indicator and eased back into the traffic.

The suburbs peeled away in silence. They were heading for the city, and on to the opposite side of town. A sword lay between them. That couldn't have been more apparent. If she hadn't broken his heart, she had assuredly assaulted his male ego. Guy Harcourt, the brilliant young architect, handsome and dashing, a man who could have had anyone, thrown over by an undistinguished slip of a girl. She could feel the tension in his lean, elegant body, translated as it was into hard mockery.

She sought to turn it aside. "I haven't asked about your mother and Lady Harcourt. I hope they're both well?"

His answering tone was cool and measured. "I have to tell you they're no longer your fans. But yes, they're both well. Thank you for asking."

She swallowed because her throat had gone quite dry. "They love you so much they can't forgive me?"

"Something like that!" The handsome, sardonic mouth turned down. "After all, you gave a marvellous performance of a girl madly in love."

"It was no performance," Celine said quietly. "I loved you, Guy. Never doubt it."

"Oh, for goodness' sake!" He swept that aside.

"Let's get off such a maddening subject. It's a pity you didn't go in for acting. You'd win an Academy Award."

"Does it have to be like this, Guy?" she asked.

"Tragic, but the answer's *yes*."

"You've changed so much."

"Indeed I have," he said coolly. "I'm actually holding you responsible for your actions like any other adult. After all that was between us, with the wedding only months off, you found you had to bolt. Why in heaven's name? You never *did* tell me. All I got was hysteria. And there was absolutely nothing I could do about it. The whole thing came as the most appalling shock." He glanced at her and a kind of lightning flashed from his near-black eyes.

She raised her hand to the gold chain around her throat. Whatever would he say if he knew she still wore his ring? Close to her heart. She seldom took it off. "I'm sorry, Guy," she said. "Maybe I was a little crazy at the time. I've always thought losing my parents so early and in such a way left me tremendously insecure. Everything was going too fast. Shatteringly fast. Grandfather was so thrilled and determined. You outstripped me in every way. I felt I had no real identity."

He made a sound that signified to Celine's mind, contempt and disgust. "At least you don't look the dewy innocent you were."

"That's what Ashley once called me."

"A dewy innocent? Compared to her, darling, you still are." His voice held that derisive note again. "A word of warning about Ashley. I don't suppose you'll listen to me any more than the old days, but Ashley is very jealous of you and no help for it."

"I don't accept that, Guy."

"Then you'll undoubtedly learn the hard way. I'm not speaking idly or because I've never liked Ashley."

She'd have fallen for it once. Dislike didn't preclude sexual attraction.

"You're outnumbered in your own family, Celine," Guy was saying. "I still care about that. Some habits die hard. The problem started when Sir Gerald brought you home as a child. I know he wasn't at all demonstrative, but he loved you in his own way. The rest of the family bitterly resented that affection."

The sun shone through the window striking red, gold and amber from Celine's long, curling mane. "It seems to me *you* were the one they resented. For that matter, the only time I got Grandfather's full attention was when I became engaged to you."

He looked grim. "I'm not going to deny he gave our engagement his blessing, but don't make a scapegoat out of me. Sir Gerald didn't relate to women terribly well. He was the ultimate male chauvinist. I'm not saying anything he didn't admit to himself. He never really relaxed in a woman's presence, for all he attracted them in droves. Men were the natural rulers. Women were only prized for their beauty. Don't you remember the way he used to say no woman is ever married for her *brain*?"

"I know I graduated with honours to no fanfare of trumpets. The only thing I really had going for me with Grandfather was the way I looked. I had his red hair. I had something of him. I didn't need a career. I didn't even have to mature. Grandfather thought a woman should be married young so her husband could mould her. And there, offering for my hand, a young god. *You*. It was a match ordained on Mount Olympus with Tiger Langton playing Zeus."

"But the Dream didn't come off."

"No," she said bleakly. "So what do we do?"

"Certainly not comfort each other." His tone was crisp. "I should warn you, you'll find your grandmother in a state of shock. I don't think she realises Sir Gerald has gone. In a way, he ruled her life."

"Guy, she had *no* life!" A little passion entered Celine's gentle voice.

"I realise that, Celine. I'm as much entangled with your family as you are. Sir Gerald overwhelmed her."

"So you grasp that?"

He glanced at her ironically. "Are you saying I overwhelmed you?"

"You did *then*, Guy."

"Well, we have to thank someone for giving you confidence."

The inference was unmistakable and she looked at him in sudden anger. "Ashley couldn't have told you Max and I were romantically involved. It's a lie!"

"Is it just!" His voice was light but cutting.

"Max is years and years older than I am."

"A father figure?" he suggested suavely.

"You're cruel."

"Perhaps a little. Your Max isn't as over the hill as your tone suggests. He's quite attractive. Not as fit as he should be, but he has a presence. I believe he's been married and divorced a couple of times."

She stared at him, unable to fault the chiselled profile. "Am I to understand you've had Max checked out?"

He nodded quite casually. "In the process of checking on you."

"Let me get this right." She moved in her seat so she could stare at him. "Grandfather did this?"

"My dear Celine, what did you expect? You've intimated you've learned a lot. Why not that? You surely didn't think he was going to let you disappear with no thought for your well-being?''

Bewilderment crossed her brow. "Ashley told me—''

"*Thank you.* I don't want to hear any more about Ashley,'' he bluntly interrupted.

"You don't realise Ashley has been my only friend.''

He looked supremely unmoved, even disdainful. "Even *I*, your much-feared ex-fiancé had to find out if you were quite all right.''

"I don't understand one word you're saying.''

"Darling, I don't think you ever *did*. I would ask you not to upset Lady Langton with talk of birthday presents and the like. She has long since accepted you wanted no part of the family.''

"That is totally untrue!'' Celine defended herself strongly. "As I'm sure Ashley would be only too willing to testify.''

"Ah, but then I don't find Ashley particularly trustworthy.''

"But you're attracted to her for all that?''

He turned his head quickly, with a sharp, thoughtful look. "Is that what she told you?''

"No, of course not.'' Celine covered for her cousin loyally. "I'm just pointing out Ashley is a very glamorous woman. A surface hostility can often conceal attraction.''

"Celine, you're still screwed up,'' he said. He spoke with cool, clinical precision. "I don't think I have ever looked in Ashley's direction.''

"A great many people do.'' Celine stared fixedly out the window. "There's nothing to be gained saying any more. For both our sakes, Guy, it might be best if you leave me alone.''

CHAPTER THREE

THERE were tears in Celine's eyes when they drove through the massive wrought-iron gates of Langfield again. Surely Grandfather would come to the door, autocratic face wreathed in a triumphant smile? With Guy most properly at her side, he would enfold her in one of his rare bear hugs, telling he'd always been certain she would see sense; how happy he was their long estrangement was over. His image filled her mind. Grandfather. *Grandfather*!

"Are you all right?" Guy turned to her, the most unexpected and devastating note of concern in his voice.

"No, I'm not!" she whispered. "I'm full of sorrow and remorse."

"Aren't we all?" he answered bleakly. "Pull yourself together, cherub."

The old endearment obviously slipped out. The next time he spoke, his tone was clipped and controlled. "As far as I know, your grandmother is alone, except for the help."

"Thank you." Celine looked and sounded very subdued.

He brought the Jaguar to a halt at the base of the stone steps but Celine remained in the car, staring up at the house. Now, no less than when she was a child, she found its imposing facade uninviting in the extreme. Langfield was her grandfather's vision of a gentleman's residence. Guy always said it looked like his old school. High Victorian in concept, monumental in size, red brick and tile, a conglomeration of wings, gables, chimneys, verandas, arched doorways, even a square, turreted tower. Sir Lew, whose own plans had been politely declined, had once called it a "lofty monstrosity". Lady Harcourt went a step further and dubbed it a "hideous old pile". Nevertheless it was the sort of place "Tiger" Langton had wanted. Only the magnificent gardens, generously designed by Sir Lew, who hardly ever took offence at anything his friend would do, saved it. The great ornamental trees of the world graced its sweeping grounds. Jacarandas, poincianas, their branches weighed down by dazzling scarlet bracts, frangipani trees in a variety of colours, Indian laburnums, apple blossom cassias, tulip trees, silk trees, giant magnolias, their huge, goblet-shaped creamy flowers rising out of the shiny green leaves. The grounds were splendid with summer fragrance and colour; the famous roses everyone was allowed to see at a pre-Christmas garden party.

Except there was no Tiger Langton anymore. Celine, like her grandmother, was finding it difficult to grasp.

"We'd best go in," Guy said quietly. "I'll have a few words with Lady Langton, then I'll leave you in peace."

Celine pressed her head back and closed her eyes.

"What are you doing?"

"I'm trying to compose myself. Can't you see that?" Her eyes flew open, so liquid with tears they looked like shimmering lakes.

"Here, try my handkerchief."

It was snowy white, beautifully laundered, with his initial in the corner. Just like always.

"Have I done some baby-sitting in my time," he sighed.

"You mean, me?"

He didn't answer.

She dabbed at her eyes, leaving a few little streaks of mascara on the fine lawn. "Damn!" she said softly. "I'm sorry about that. Do I look all right?"

He gave a mirthless laugh, his black eyes moving over her. "The sad truth is you're more beautiful than ever."

"Beauty means nothing. That's all I had going for me with Grandfather." She took a breath, raised her arm to push back her hair, but a long strand caught on a link in her gold chain. "Aaah!"

"Here, I'll fix that." She heard the edgy note in his voice.

"No, it's all right." Nervously she tugged her hair away, using more force than normally she would have done. The chain flew up, exposing the ring pendant.

"Let me see that!" he said harshly.

Her expression held more than a hint of panic. "Leave it!"

"I think not!" He put out his beautiful, long-fingered hand, not caring in the least his fingers brushed the gentle upper swell of her breasts, causing a bone-melting rush of sensation. "My God!" he exclaimed. "Aren't there some mysteries in the world?"

And that was the truth. Colour came and went under her beautiful skin. "I put it on a chain for safety."

"Obviously the ring was worth more than the fiancé!" he said in a hard, ironic voice.

It could have been a showdown of some sort, so strong was the flow of emotion, only Ashley, looking glamorous in a fuchsia silk shirt and matching skirt, chose that moment to appear beside the car. She rapped sharply on Celine's window, a frown on her brow, intensity in her ice-blue gaze.

"Ashley come to check on us," Guy drawled. "She should have been a policewoman."

"She certainly seems anxious to talk to me."

"I dare say she's had a panicky moment wondering if we'd made it up. Personally I find her interference tiresome."

"*Please*, Guy." Celine checked to be sure the ring was inside the neck of the printed black-and-white silk blouse she wore with her Lagerfeld suit. Outside the car, unable to open a door because Guy had pushed a switch, Ashley's eyes were glued to the spot.

"Unlock the doors, please, Guy," Celine said.

"Sure. I was just giving Ashley a bit of aggravation." He put out a nonchalant hand and reversed the switch. Immediately the locks shot up and Ashley pounced.

"Kitten!" she cried, almost pulling Celine from her seat. "What the devil were you doing?"

"What? *What*?" Guy asked with hard mockery from the other side of the car.

"Guy didn't realise he'd pushed the lock button," Celine said. "How are you, Ashley?"

"Fine. Fine. I mean...shattered like everyone else." Ashley was still staring at some point on Celine's chest. "We'd better go up. Grandma has roused herself for the occasion. She's been out of it, I can tell you."

"With good reason surely?" Celine was dismayed by her cousin's rather callous tone.

"When she rights herself, if she ever *does*, she's not going to miss Gramps. Now there was one hell of a husband!" Her gaze shifted direction. "You'll stay for coffee, Guy?" In the sunlight her skin looked golden, her very thick blond hair worn in a straight shoulder-length bob, so meticulously cut not one strand marred the perfect arc.

"No thanks, Ashley." Guy walked on Celine's other side, his every movement full of the fluid grace of the fine athlete he was. "I'll pay my respects to Lady Langton then I must get back to the office. Several matters need urgent attention."

"Aren't we lucky you're there to handle them, darling." Ashley's narrow lips smiled, but Celine caught a flicker of something like hostility in the cool, blue eyes. On the surface there appeared to be no love lost between Ashley and Guy, yet both emanated a strong sexual magnetism. Both were experienced. Ashley had a string of affairs behind her. A lot of men, of a *type*, Celine suddenly realised, found her irresistible. Admired and chased after, perhaps it had always piqued her Guy had never been one of them. Or had things changed? They appeared unusually sensitive to one another.

Coming from the brilliant exterior Celine found it difficult to see inside at first. Then as her eyes adjusted, the paintings began to glow from the walls. They called up a wide range of responses. Pleasure, artistic appreciation, an involuntary desire to shift them around, change the dullness of the embossed wallpaper. But above all, the familiar feeling of loneliness and desolation. It would never leave her. She stood for a moment under the great crystal burst of the chandelier, the sadness of her expression attracting Guy's attention.

"Will the little girl never go away, Celine?"

She shook her head. "No. I'll never enter Langfield without remembering that six-year-old."

"You're lucky you had Grandy to turn to," Ashley pointed out. "You could have been an orphan."

"I'm indebted to him forever," Celine said. "And Grandmother."

"It's a shame, kitten, you forgot to thank her," Ashley said in a voice that ran with uncontrolled malice.

I should have known, Celine thought. *I should have known.*

There was a soft fall of steps on the stairway and as they looked up, a small, frail, elderly lady appeared on the first landing, the colours from the great, lead-light window spilling over her and patterning her dark lavender dress so it looked like she had thrown a brilliant multicoloured shawl over the sombre material.

"Grandma!" Celine didn't hesitate. She flew up the stairs with breathtaking grace, her face reflecting love, concern, sympathy.

"Dearest child!" Helena Langton put up her hands, then her face as Celine gathered the oh-so-fragile body to her, kissing the scented, paper-dry cheek.

"I've missed you, Grandma," Celine said, tears in her eyes.

"I've missed you, too, Celine. You'll never know how much."

"Where shall we go, Grandma?" Celine took her grandmother's arm gently, preparing to guide her down the flight of stairs.

"The drawing room, I think."

Ashley strode forward, looking as though she were about to clap. "I hope you don't mind my coming over, Gran? You were resting when I arrived. I didn't like to disturb you."

"I expected you, Ashley," Helena Langton said quietly, transferring her gaze to Guy. "Thank you, my dear. So very much. You're a young man of heart."

Unexpectedly Ashley gave a little hoot of laughter that sounded shocking in the hush of the house. "Some might quarrel with that, Gran," she said provocatively.

"Not me until the day I die." Helena looked at her

granddaughters, but addressed Celine. "Would you mind going on ahead? I'd like a private word with Guy."

"Of course, Grandma." Celine drew a deep breath and turned back to the silent Guy. "Thank you for bringing me home, Guy."

He gave a slight bow that was immensely elegant. "I'll see you again, Celine."

"Of course it's unlikely he *wanted* to," Ashley remarked as they disappeared into the vast, crimson drawing room.

"You don't have to point it out." Despite the room's opulence and being crammed with valuable paintings and antiques, Celine always thought of it as rococo gone mad. Her grandfather had possessed such sartorial elegance, he had been famous for this dressing, yet his taste in architecture and decorating could only have been described as eccentric.

"Sorry, kitten," Ashley apologised, picking up a jade phoenix, one of a pair, and setting it down carelessly. "What on earth were you and Guy doing in the car?"

"*Doing*?" Out of Celine's gentle mouth came a tone that would have done credit to Queen Victoria as her most disapproving. "I don't follow you, Ashley."

"Hell, Ceci, it looked like he was fondling your breast."

"Don't get excited. He was helping me remove a strand of my hair from my gold chain."

"From where I was standing he got quite a kick out of it."

"I guess I did, too," Celine said sweetly.

"Really?" The superconfident Ashley sounded confused. "You'd be wise not to start any of that up again."

"I'm here for Grandfather's funeral, Ashley. I'm here, hopefully, to be of some comfort to Grandma."

"Good. It's about time!"

Celine moved to a sofa, sat down. "At least I can say I never forgot her birthday."

Ashley, who had been prowling restlessly, swung around. "Listen, I've got to tell you something. You'll find out sooner or later. Gran used to get so upset about you, I judged it best not to pass on any gifts."

"*Did* you?" Even as she accepted it Celine was sickened and shocked by the admission. Ashley in whom she had placed so much trust. Ashley who had exerted so much influence on her all the years they'd grown up. "How the mighty have fallen," she said quietly.

"I didn't want to hurt you, either!" Ashley cried defensively, perturbed by something in Celine's expression. A loss of grace for herself. "Try to see it *my* way. I was caught in the middle of a very difficult situation. Believe me, your running off to Sydney caused an uproar around here."

"Grandma gave me the money. *She* was the one who helped me."

"Don't think she came out publicly on your side. She never did cross Grandy. You were a taboo subject in this house. I was the one on the spot."

"You could have *told* me, Ashley. Instead you let me believe you were passing my presents and messages on."

"You know I've always been very protective of you, kitten. I had to keep your little sun shining. It seemed a harmless enough deception."

"I'm appalled, Ashley," Celine said. "I trusted you as my cousin and my friend."

"Do you have any idea what you're saying?" Ashley demanded. "I went down to Sydney many times to visit you. I listened to your problems."

"I thought you were the intermediary between me and the family."

"Kitten!" Ashley cried, and threw up her hands in frustration. "The family didn't want to know you."

"In fact they put a trace on me. Not that they *had* to when you were reporting to your father."

"Terrific!" Ashley said coldly. "Is this the best you can do? You come home for the funeral and immediately start a fight." She broke off emotionally and walked to the French doors, looking out. The perfume from the rose gardens beyond was amazingly heavy, even faintly cloying in the heat.

"I'm sorry, Ashley," Celine said, feeling sick and faint. "I'm just amazed at these revelations."

"What revelations?" Ashley spun back, anger in her face but choosing a quieter note. "All I'm saying is, I didn't pass on your gifts to Gran. I think they might have killed her. Her health is not good. I believe I was acting on the purest motives. I can see you're upset by it and I'm sorry it happened. We were always best friends, Celine. So far as I'm concerned nothing has changed." She crossed the room and sat down beside Celine, taking her nerveless hand. "Has Guy been talking to you?"

"About what, Ashley?" Celine said, removing her hand slowly.

"About me, of course!" Ashley said disdainfully. "He hates me, you know. Under the suave charm he bitterly resents the fact I told him off."

"When he made a pass at you, you mean?" Celine's tone was unconsciously ironic.

"Not *pass*, dear." Ashley smiled bleakly. "He was hell-bent on an affair. With you gone there was only me."

"That doesn't sound like Guy." Celine shook her

head. "In fact he gave me the impression I had wounded him deeply."

"God, you're incredible, Celine!" Ashley gibed. "Are you *ever* going to grow up? The only thing you wounded was his colossal ego. Let me assure you, you didn't inspire undying love. Surely you've had more experience by now. Men simply can't be trusted. Don't get taken in by Guy again. He's not near good enough for you."

"I can't buy that, Ashley," Celine said, her smoky eyes full of disillusionment. "I'm sure you don't believe it, either. You were the one who told *me* I wasn't good enough for *Guy*. You made sure I understood that fully."

"Oh, Ceci, *please*!" Ashley implored. "You've been thrown off balance."

"I sure have!" Celine agreed, feeling a strong sense of betrayal. "I feel like the wind has been knocked out of me."

Ashley touched her cheek gently, making a soft, saddened sound. "Kitten, what can I do to make things better?"

"You can stop calling me *kitten* for a start," Celine remarked.

Ashley's expression registered disbelief, nevertheless she dropped her hand. "All right. What else am I supposed to call you? I've been calling you kitten since you were six years old."

"I feel it's inappropriate now. I'm twenty-three."

"Well, okay! I hope Ceci's all right?"

"You can call me Celine if you like."

"Precious, I don't want us to fight about anything," Ashley said. "I love you. I can never let *us* be estranged."

Celine looked directly into the ice-blue eyes. "For some reason, Ashley, I now doubt that."

"Then you're not thinking clearly," Ashley said in a strong, persuasive voice. "I blame Guy for that. You've always been under his influence."

"And yours."

Ashley laughed. "I am the elder by nearly five years. Be fair to me, Ceci, I've always looked after you. I used to stay with you for weeks at a time when you lost your voice. I've shared so much with you. All your confidences. I've told you so many things I would never tell another living soul. You know what that swine Alan De Burgh did to me. We've shared torrents of affection. Nothing can change that. Unless you listen to Guy. He's always had it in for me, for some reason."

"He has a funny way of showing it if he wanted an affair."

Ashley gave an exaggerated shrug, moving her straight, wide shoulders. "I didn't say he's not attracted to me in a weird kind of way. You know how these things happen. What makes it even more laughable is, I am attracted to him physically."

"A love-hate case, you mean?"

"Of course not!" Ashley said scornfully. "I know exactly what Guy wants and it's neither you nor me. It's Harcourt Langton. Surely you don't doubt that."

CHAPTER FOUR

CELINE and her grandmother dined quietly that evening. Afterwards, Mrs. Findlay, the very pleasant and competent housekeeper, served them coffee in Helena Langton's private sitting room, a pretty, comfortable retreat she had created for herself away from the overwhelming opulence of the main rooms. There were lots of books and flower paintings, a rather wonderful collection of Meissen figurines locked away in a Regency display case, the colour scheme of the spacious room soft and feminine in a mixture of pastels.

"I'm so grateful to have you home again, Celine." Helena settled herself in her favourite armchair. "It often seems to me you and I are the only gentle people in the family. The others can be so abrasive at times. *Hurting* people if you know what I mean, but then, my nature has always verged on meek."

"I *like* gentle people, Grandma." Celine passed her grandmother coffee in an exquisite cup. Beneath the quiet demeanour she realised her grandmother was deeply perturbed.

"I don't know quite how it happened," Helena continued to muse. "Gerald was always so hard on everyone. Always so demanding. He was never pleased or proud. Except of Guy. I think that's what wrong with Clive. He's always in such a *rage*! Nothing he ever did met with his father's praise. Even when he managed to do well, at school, at university, the business, Gerald's attitude was, so you *should*! I have a theory about my

197

sons. Especially Clive. He couldn't hope to gain ascendency over his father so he sought to dominate the rest of us. It could be neurotic. What do you think?''

Celine was confounded at her grandmother's speaking out. ''I think it isn't power in the sense Grandfather had it.''

Helena nodded, satisfied her views were being taken seriously. ''I share the blame, of course. I was a poor mother. I didn't defend my children against their father as I should have. I believe they've always held it against me, but I was a very dutiful wife. A very dull and dutiful wife. I never had the courage to go against your grandfather in anything. I failed *you* in your time of need.''

Tears sprang into Helena's blue eyes and Celine leaned forward and clasped her grandmother's birdlike hands. They were heavily weighed down by diamond rings, one a ten-carat solitaire, *not* her grandmother, but a bauble that had attracted Tiger Langton's eye. ''That's not *true*, Grandma,'' she said firmly. ''You mustn't upset yourself any more than you already are. These things are in the past.''

''Ah, the past!'' A sad, ironic expression crossed Helena's pale face. ''The past fashions us, dear. We can never get away from it.'' She slowly shook her coiffured head, short, thick and tinted a soft pewter. ''I never thought *this* would happen. I thought Gerald would go on forever. Long after me. He was so vigorous. So bursting with life until the end. Even the way he went was typical. Swift and decisive.''

''No time for *me* to put things right,'' Celine said with deep regret.

''As to that, my dear, your grandfather was proud of you.'' Helena fixed her with large, clear, short-sighted eyes. "He wouldn't *hear* a word of you, but he checked on your every move. That was Gerald."

"Nevertheless I loved him, Grandma."

"I know you did, child." Helena picked up her coffee and took another sip. "I loved him myself though he virtually abandoned me after Nolan was born. Abandoned me to my own resources, that is," she qualified as Celine gave her a dismayed look. "There was no suggestion he would divorce me. Divorce wasn't on the agenda. We led separate lives, though we had *something* to start with I would have thought. I was considered very pretty in my day."

"You're still pretty, Grandma!" Although Helena habitually put herself down, she was, in her own way, a very elegant lady.

Helena smoothed the skirt of her silk dress. "I've looked after myself. I've had to. Gerald would have disowned me entirely had I not looked stylish. Of course I came from a good family, which was what Gerald wanted. But he was such a perfectionist, in the end he came to make me feel truly worthless."

Despite the fact it was the bald truth as her grandmother saw it, Celine was shocked. "That's *dreadful*, Grandma!"

"Dreadful to speak about it *now*." Helena looked past her granddaughter's glowing head, focusing on a painting. "But I can't help it. So many thoughts have been running through my head. Especially when I can't sleep. It's—what do they call it?—a *catharsis*. A kind of purging. Your grandfather's death has brought it all on. I can't pretend our marriage was a happy one. I can't pretend a lot of damage wasn't done. I need you *desperately*, Celine, at this terrible time. I need someone I love in my own camp. Gerald drained my last bit of pride and self-respect. No, don't flinch like that, it's true. I've kept quiet for a very long time, now I feel I'm going to break under pressure. Clive has assumed the mantle of head of the family in no uncertain terms. He is always courteous to me, but he talks to me as though I were lightly retarded.''

"When you're stronger, Grandma, you'll take hold.''

"Do you think so, Ceci?'' Helena looked wistful. "I'm no Muriel Harcourt. Now there's a woman impossible to ignore. Muriel has had to contend with the two greatest blows a woman can suffer in life. The loss of her beloved son, then the loss of dear Lewis. They were a *truly* devoted couple, not a couple of shams like Gerald and me. Lewis was a fine man, so full of kindness and integrity. Such *fun*! Your grandfather for all his abilities was never *fun*. Muriel faced tragedy so bravely. She has that inner strength, that capacity to rise above adversity. I've always been a very vulnerable person. Maybe it's biological? Who knows! I've been treated for depression as you know.''

Celine shook her head. "I *didn't* know, Grandma.'' With her grandmother reaching within herself this could be a night for revelations.

"Oh, yes, for years!'' Helena confirmed. "I must have seemed withdrawn to you?''

"You were always kind to me, Grandma.'' Celine bit down hard on her lip.

"Gerald would never have allowed me to become emotional about you, Ceci. You were Jamie's child. He warned me off.''

"What are you saying, Grandma?'' Celine's expression reflected her dismay and bewilderment.

"I've done, or rather *not* done, many things in my life I'm ashamed of, Celine,'' Helena said in a rambling, exhausted voice. "Yet I used to have good feelings about myself as a girl."

Celine's tender heart melted with love and pity. "It will happen again, Grandma. We'll make it happen."

"I knew what you were going through when you broke your engagement to Guy," Helena spoke more calmly.

"I thought I wasn't woman enough for him, Grandma."

"Nonsense. You were simply too young at the time. I *told* Gerald, but, as ever, my opinion didn't count. I was troubled by Ashley, as well. It seemed to me she wanted Guy herself. But Guy isn't at all like your grandfather, dear child. Not at all. Guy is not a cruel person. He's so *good* with everyone, including your poor grandmother. Guy is a young man who cares. You haven't ruined your chances with him, Ceci. He's never looked at anyone else."

"Are you sure of that, Grandma?" Celine searched her grandmother's tired face.

"I expect Ashley told you differently?" Helena asked with a grim smile.

"Not really." Celine wasn't prepared to reduce Ashley's standing in their grandmother's eyes even to the extent of not referring to all the little gifts that had never been passed on.

"You were always loyal to your cousin," Helena said. "My own view is, she may not be worthy of that loyalty."

Light rain fell during the night, but the morning of the funeral it was brilliantly fine. No tears from heaven for Grandfather, Celine thought. She slipped to her knees, praying for the strength to get through the ordeal that lay ahead. Her own feelings of grief and remorse she would have to hold in check. Her grandmother needed her to be strong. She would have to come up with some strategy to protect them both.

A few hours later she paced outside her grandmother's door still working on all the little tremors that racked her body. She had received two phone calls from her uncle Clive that morning. Admittedly he had worked very hard making all the arrangements but he was running things like a general. Her grandmother had refused point-blank to take calls from him. Less than twenty-four hours back in the bosom of the family, Celine could understand why. Clive Langton had an appalling manner. He had barked at Celine like she was some dim-witted subordinate. Only it was such an inappropriate time, she felt she would have told him where to get off. He had never treated her like a niece, a valued member of the family; more like an imposter who had somehow managed to gain a foothold where she had no right.

When her grandmother finally emerged from her bedroom Celine saw she was dressed in black from head to toe. She even wore a veil draped over her small black hat, something Celine only associated with royalty, but when she caught sight of Celine she put it back.

"I don't know how I'm going to get through this, Celine," Helena said, a statement made all the more piteous because she was trying to square her shoulders. Her small patrician face was lightly made up but her pallor was quite shocking.

"Then why *push* yourself, Grandma?" Celine went to her, kissing her cheek. "Is it absolutely necessary for you to be there? There's the family to represent you." Overnight it seemed her grandmother had lost *more* weight. Her expensive suit looked too big and too heavy on her slight frame.

"No, Ceci. I must do this properly. Gerald would expect it. I must carry out his wishes to the end."

"Then I'll be beside you, Grandma," Celine promised. "We'll get through it together. Uncle Clive said the limousine would be here at 10:30 sharp. He and Aunt Imelda will be riding with us."

"Dear God!" Helena moaned. "Clive defies any attempt to put him off. Arthur could have driven us." Her blue eyes slipped over Celine. "That's a beautiful suit, dear."

"Lagerfeld."

"Your accessories, too." Helena checked Celine's shoes and matching handbag with their famous label.

"You set a high standard, Grandma."

Surprisingly Helena blushed, instantly looking stronger and younger. "Where is your hat, dear? You'll need one."

"Good grief, I haven't got one." Automatically Celine touched her hair. She had decided against leaving it out. She had put it into a thick roll.

"Never mind, Goldie will find one for you. I don't want Clive taking you to task for not wearing one. He's so intolerant of not doing the done thing." Helena turned back to her bedroom, opening the door and addressing her long-time maid, Lily Goldsmith, who was in the act of scooping up discarded clothes and carrying them through to the huge walk-in wardrobe. "Goldie, dear, do you think you could find a suitable hat for Celine to wear?"

"No problem!" Goldie's still-keen eyes swept over Celine's graceful figure. "Give me a minute. I remember a very nice hat your grandmother never wore."

"Too *dashing* for me, I expect," Helena said.

Goldie reappeared almost immediately, holding a wide-brimmed black hat in her hand. It was perfectly plain, but very chic. The sort of hat favoured by the Princess of Wales.

Helena nodded her approval. "Go into the bedroom and put it on, Celine. It's a good thing you've done up your hair. If Clive told you 10:30 sharp, then 10:30 it will be. He's never early and he's never late. He's always right on the *dot*. That's his creed."

When Celine stepped inside the luxurious stretch limousine, property of the Harcourt Langton Corporation, Imelda Langton, a large, handsome blond woman, gave her a sharp, appraising look. "Isn't that hat a bit over the top for a funeral, Celine? I was thinking..."

They were not to hear. "The hat is *mine*, Imelda," Helena told her daughter-in-law in a surprisingly firm tone.

"It seems so unlike you, Mother." There was a malicious gleam on Imelda's sleek face.

"My father is being buried today, Imelda," Clive rebuked his wife sternly. "Why are you worrying about a hat? Mother has excellent taste."

Celine and her grandmother exchanged wry glances but Imelda, flushed of face, stared ahead. It was impossible for Celine to ignore the fact Imelda had always resented her, undoubtedly because of her special position in Gerald Langton's household. Moreover it had always been apparent he had favoured Celine over Ashley, something Imelda found quite incomprehensible. Photographers were waiting even as they arrived. What did it matter it was a time for grief, for family privacy? The media was having a field day with the passing of Tiger Langton. Clive Langton even held up a hand to the crowd. More like a knight on the way to an investiture, Celine thought, putting her arm through her grand-mother's. A somewhat grainy shot of herself and Guy had appeared on page three of the morning's paper under the caption Langton Heiress Returns. Reading on it in-ferred to the arms of her ex-fiancé, the brilliant architect Guy Harcourt, grandson of the late Sir Lew Harcourt, co-founder of Harcourt Langton. Well, she was neither an heiress nor the woman Guy loved. So much for get-ting things right!

The cathedral Gerald Langton had never entered ex-cept for weddings was packed to capacity. Her grand-father would have been well pleased with the turnout. The sun poured through the magnificent stained-glass windows. The organ was thundering out some hymn Ce-line didn't know. Her grandfather's casket was up there before the altar, her grandmother's flowers resting atop it. Celine broke out into a cold sweat.

As they took their places in the front pew she caught sight of Guy's handsome dark head rising above the heads of his womenfolk; his mother, Eloise, a beautiful but retiring woman, and the formidable Lady Harcourt, a woman of considerable distinction. None looked her way. The service began...

At some point Clive Langton spoke, his strong, cul-tured voice resounding up and down the aisles and through the naves. Celine briefly opened her eyes. Clive's powerful hands gripped the lectern. His blue eyes, so like his mother's, had a fanatical gleam. The late Tiger Langton had been a saint no less. Not even Grandfather would have claimed that, Celine thought. She tried desperately to keep a faint grimace off her face, knowing she was in full view of the family and the great many dignitaries who had come to pay their last respects to a formidable public figure. Her grandmother was still gripping her hand. She could feel the trembling. There was worse to come.

At the graveside just as Celine thought they both could make it, her grandmother suddenly crumpled in a dead faint, causing instant panic, dismay, and an outbreak of conversation. There were at least a dozen prominent doctors among the mourners, including Lady Langton's own physician, who immediately took charge. Helena recovered consciousness almost at once but there was no question she could remain a moment more. Despite the fact her two sons, both big men well over six feet, hovered over her, neither thought to pick her up. Lady Harcourt advanced with Guy, giving him instructions to carry Helena to the limousine.

"You'll return with your grandmother, Celine?" Lady Harcourt fixed Celine with still brilliant black eyes.

"Of course, Lady Harcourt."

Alerted to trouble, the chauffeur brought up the car as far as he was able and Guy put the featherweight Helena into the back seat facing the driver.

"She shouldn't have come," Guy said very quietly to Celine. "She's not up to all this." His manner inferred the funeral had been arranged with too much drama. Something Celine couldn't dispute. "Are *you* going to be all right?" He stared down into her face, shadowed as it was by the wide-brimmed hat.

"I hope so, Guy," she breathed. "I'm in enemy territory now."

A great many people came back to the house. Food was set out like a banquet. There was alcohol in case anyone felt the need of it and most people apparently did.

This is crazy! Celine thought. Why do people do it?

Was it a ritual no one thought to break? It was the *last* thing her grandmother needed or wanted, but there she sat enthroned in the drawing room, a small, frozen figure, while streams of people offered her their condolences. It was like some elaborate piece of theatre that had to be played out to the very end. Clive, as heir apparent to his late father, had taken on the role with relish. He appeared to stand even taller, his aggressive chin thrust forward as if to let everyone know they would have to contend with *him* now.

"Dad can't wait for the will to be read," Ashley observed dryly, coming up beside Celine, drink in hand. "Nothing is going to stand between him and the bulk of the fortune. God knows he's worked hard enough, copped enough abuse. There should be enough left over for the rest of us. Even *you*, kitten. I don't suppose even Gramps could die with *you* on his conscience. The little orphan."

Celine turned her head, trying to cover her distaste. "If you don't mind, Ashley, I don't want to talk about money. Not *now*!"

"Oh, don't be so *precious*, Ceci. Everyone wants to talk about money. Even you. What I'd really like is to get my hands on Granny's diamond solitaire. Do you suppose she'd leave it to me?"

"Why don't you ask her, Ashley? I'm sure I don't want it."

"More fool's you! It's *perfect*! It has no flaws and it has that tinge of blue. It looks quite silly on Granny's hand." She held up her own strong, long-fingered hand, the nails long and lacquered to match her lipstick. Like Celine, she was wearing a superbly cut black suit, its starkness relieved by a dramatic black-and-white silk blouse. Both young women had removed their hats and

Ashley's blond hair swung around her face in elegant clean lines. She looked very sophisticated but she sounded very grasping. "Don't look now," she said, "but I think Lady Harcourt is coming our way. I'll skip, if you don't mind. Dear Muriel, worthy though she might be, isn't among my favourite people."

"Nor you hers," Celine couldn't help pointing out.

"I just hope you're aware of *your* fall from grace," Ashley retaliated, looking surprised. "Certainly you caused the proud Harcourt family a good deal of humiliation." With that she flounced off as she had never done before.

Round one, or at least a strike, Celine thought. It was with a degree of trepidation, however, that she faced Lady Harcourt.

"How pale you are, Celine. Come and sit down with me," Muriel commanded. "Have you had tea?"

"I was trying to get a cup," Celine admitted.

"Well, then." Lady Harcourt eyed a passing attendant who hurried over. "Tea, thank you, and perhaps a sandwich. Black or white, Celine?"

"White, thank you."

"Black for me. Slice of lemon if there is one."

The attendant, a young man of girlish good looks, smiled as though he would move heaven and earth to find one.

"So, how are you, Celine?" Lady Harcourt asked quietly. "It must be very hard for you coming back at this time?"

"It *is*." Celine sat quite still, her face composed. "No time now to put things right with Grandfather. Grandma needs me, but I'm not so sure about the rest of the family."

"My dear, they've always been jealous of you. And

Guy?'' Lady Harcourt gave Celine a direct look. The same age as Helena Langton, seventy-four, she looked an astonishing sixty. Her curly dark hair, cleverly cut and tinted, still retained much of its natural colour, her dark eyes were striking, her olive skin in marvellous condition, her tall, upright body as slim and supple as a woman half her age. She was immaculately dressed, as always, but in a somewhat unconventional style. In fact Celine knew she designed most of her clothes and had them made up by an Italian woman who had once worked for the House of Chanel.

''I'm sure he will never forgive me,'' Celine said without a moment's hesitation.

''I've thought the same thing myself,'' Muriel freely admitted. ''Do you have any idea of his pain?''

Celine bowed her Titian head. ''It wasn't any fun for me, either, Lady Harcourt. I had to find myself.''

''And have you?'' Muriel Harcourt asked bluntly.

''What matters is, I'm trying. It's not simple. It's a life's task. I deeply regret the hurt I inflicted but marriage was impossible at that time. Guy had his mother and you: two women who adore him. I had no one.''

''You're dead wrong, Celine,'' Lady Harcourt said with a mixture of affection and impatience. ''You had us. You could have come to us. We were friends.''

''Of course. I want more than anything for that to still be the case, but I was deeply emotional at the time and not thinking clearly. I realise I behaved badly and I've been punished.''

''We've all been punished, dear,'' Lady Harcourt said wryly. ''These things happen, now we must seek to repair the damage. I always did feel for you, Celine. Indeed I spoke out for you from time to time, which Gerald didn't like. He couldn't tolerate any kind of advice. He used to sit there fuming because unlike with other people he couldn't blow his top. The most complete autocrat, Gerald. He won't mind my saying it. Eloise and I were deeply upset when you broke off the engagement. I'm sure you'll understand that. Had you come to us before you took off…''

''You must know what it's like to be under too much pressure, Lady Harcourt,'' Celine argued. ''I was too young, too vulnerable, too *ordinary* for Guy.''

Lady Harcourt showed her disbelief in an ironic bark. ''You were too young certainly, inexperienced in the ways of the world, but *ordinary*? Never! You're an exquisite-looking creature, Celine, as you must know. I know you have little vanity but you do have eyes. You still have your sweet nature and if your grandfather failed to notice your charm and high intelligence, it wasn't lost on any of us, particularly my grandson. Calling yourself ordinary simply won't do!''

''I felt I was *then*,'' Celine said with the ring of truth. ''I never did quite believe it, you know.''

''What, dear?'' Lady Harcourt turned slowly to stare at her.

''That Guy loved me. That he wanted to marry me. I found it a mystery.''

''I can promise you it *wasn't*. Nor did it have anything to do with your being a Langton,'' Lady Harcourt added grimly. ''There were others, of course, to reinforce your sense of insecurity?''

''No.'' Celine denied it, her face troubled.

Lady Harcourt gave her bleak laugh again. ''I don't accept that, Celine. I do have intimate knowledge of the family. It's not going to be easy for you.''

''I won't be staying.'' Celine half expected Lady Harcourt to draw a sigh of relief. ''When Grandma feels stronger, I'll go back to Sydney. I have an interesting job there.''

Lady Harcourt stared at her with those acute black eyes. ''Celine, you'll have to think of something else. You'll have a substantial inheritance.''

''By no means a foregone conclusion, Lady Harcourt.''

''Call me Muriel, dear. I can't think why you're persisting with this Lady Harcourt.''

Surprised, Celine gave her lovely, spontaneous smile. ''Are you sure?''

''Of course I'm sure. It will be a good experience for us both. We were *almost* family, Celine. No matter what, there'll always be something between us. You do realise you won't be able to go back to Sydney. Helena will have need of you. Gerald's death has sapped all her strength.''

''I'm thinking she might collapse again at any moment.''

''She shouldn't be sitting there,'' Lady Harcourt agreed. ''She looks so frail and wretched.''

''She *insisted*, Muriel. There was nothing I could do. Grandma has started making her own choices.''

''I'm not criticising you, dear. Helena has steel in her. She'll find it yet. God rest Gerald's soul, but he was such a domineering man. You all suffered because of it. Helena was terribly affected. She was such a bright, pretty girl. Very appealing. Gerald wanted to seal her up in a display case. No one can survive that. More than anything she'll need your support and love. The rest of the family would have to be described as confrontationist. No, you can't think of going away, Celine.''

''I would have thought you'd want me to go away?'' Celine looked at Lady Harcourt very seriously.

"My dear girl, *why*?"

Celine shrugged, a slight movement of her delicate shoulders. "For Guy's sake. He met me at the airport as you know. A gesture to Grandma. He made it clear he didn't enjoy seeing me again."

"You surely didn't expect him to welcome you with open arms?" Muriel Harcourt said. "Being jilted is a good enough reason for feeling bitter."

Celine lowered her eyes and a flush spread across her creamy skin. "I didn't jilt Guy. I was totally overawed by him."

"You certainly didn't show it," Muriel maintained. "Good heavens, I never saw any two people more deeply in love. You sparkled in one another's company."

"I thought he was being propelled into it."

"Then think again, Celine," Muriel said sternly. "We can't change the past but if we're wise we try for reconciliation. Take it from a woman who *knows*. Guy did love you. I can't speak for his feelings now. He has rather gone into his shell." She paused as the attendant approached them bearing a tray. "Eloise will want to speak to you before we go. We both welcome you back."

"Thank you, Muriel."

Lady Harcourt leaned over and patted her hand. "Generally speaking, dear, yours is not a happy family. You'll need our support."

The reading of the last will and testament of Gerald Connor Langton was scheduled for 6:00 p.m. in the library. Henry Fowler, senior partner of the prestigious law firm of Fowler, Mortensen & Spencer, a firm that had served the family for over forty years, had been appointed trustee and executor and as such would conduct proceedings.

The family began to arrive a good half hour before the reading was due to commence. Celine stood behind the curtain in her grandmother's bedroom relaying information as it came to hand. Helena, fully dressed, was lying on the bed, a hand over her eyes.

Celine looked down at the party disembarking from a brand new, top-of-the-range Mercedes. "It's Uncle Clive and Imelda. I don't know whether to laugh or cry. Aunt Imelda is wearing a bright red dress."

"Triumph!" Helena said. "The children with them?"

"Yes, Ashley and Michael. They've grown very much alike. Yet the sad thing is they're not close."

"There's something about Ashley that reminds me of Gerald," Helena murmured.

"Uncle Nolan is arriving now."

"Do you know they call Dorothy 'Lofty' behind her back? It's her overbearing manner, of course. She's only five feet three."

"Dana and Harris are with them." Celine parted the curtain a little, staring down onto the drive. "Does Dana have a job yet? I didn't like to ask."

"Dana is a professional young socialite," Helena replied. "Apparently it's very demanding of her time. Poor old Harris inherited Gerald's famous red-gold mane, as you did, but unfortunately none of his brain or his striking good looks. Harris has been in and out of trouble since his kindergarten days. When he's finished university, if he passes his exams, he'll go into the business. Goodness knows in what capacity."

"I think he's fighting to find some sort of identity," Celine said. "Of all us grandchildren Ashley is the only one oozing self-confidence."

"And yet she never did anywhere near as well as you with your studies. Neither is she as beautiful. There's a cunning mind behind Ashley's smooth face, Celine. She would fight just as ruthlessly as Gerald for what she wanted. You're older now. I know you're going to be able to cope."

Celine turned away from the tall windows. "You seem to be warning me against Ashley, Grandma."

Helena struggled up from the bed. "I'm letting my instincts roll. They've always been operational. I just never expressed myself, that's all. Smooth my hair for me, would you, please, darling, then we must go downstairs. I have a feeling this will is going to break a lot of hearts."

When they reached the richly appointed library, they found the family scattered about in chairs. Clive got up immediately from behind his late father's splendid desk and went to his mother, inquiring after her well-being. She went to assure him she was quite all right but Clive had already turned away, gesturing to his son, Michael, to get up so Helena could have a central seat. The large room was chock-a-block with armchairs and tables, great globes on stands, high reading tables and a vast collection of books on every conceivable subject, most of them untouched by anyone outside of Celine who, as an extremely lonely and isolated child, had become an inveterate reader.

"We'll have to get that portrait of Gramps down," Ashley said from the depths of a comfortable winged-back chair. "It's giving me the shivers. Didn't he have the most *piercing* regard?"

"It always made *me* miserable," the young, lanky Harris volunteered. "One glare from Gramps was worse than six of the best."

"Had you ever behaved yourself you wouldn't have needed six of the best," Clive Langton rebuked his nephew, who blushed furiously. "What's keeping old Henry?" he demanded in a highly irritated tone. "*I'm* always punctual."

"Obsessively so," Nolan commented promptly, angry Clive had usurped the parental role of correcting Harris.

"It's not six yet, Clive," Helena pointed out mildly. "I do wish you would sit down again. All this raging is going to lead to a heart attack or stroke."

"Well, *thank you*, Mother." Clive collapsed into an armchair, looking surprised and aggrieved. "I really think Henry's getting past it. No one actually goes to him anymore. Now that Father's gone I think it's high time we found ourselves a new firm of lawyers."

"If Henry and his firm were smart enough for your father, they're smart enough for anyone," Helena said, her soft voice actually scratchy. "Surely that's Henry's car now?"

"Who else drives a broken-down Rolls?" Ashley asked derisively.

"I thought it was faultlessly maintained," Celine answered out of loyalty to Henry. Not only was it true, Henry, a courtly gentleman, had always been very kind to her.

"It's as old as the hills, Ceci," Ashley said carelessly.

Moments later Henry was shown in by Mrs. Findlay, ghostly grey beside the sheer drama of the young man who accompanied him.

Guy! Celine's heart leapt. He looked almost unbearably handsome in the black suit he had worn to the funeral, dark, dangerous, aroused. At the expression on Clive's face, his splendid head snapped up. Almost like a mettlesome charger, Celine thought.

Clive, a big, overweight man, crushed Henry's elderly fingers then demanded of Guy what he was doing here. Guy ignored him, went to Helena, bent and kissed her cheek, while she put up a hand to touch his.

"What the hell is going on here?" Clive was breathing deeply, his handsome florid face flushed a deep red. "This is a *family* reading."

"It would seem, Clive, I'm one of the beneficiaries," Guy said in his beautiful, dark timbred voice. "The will will explain. I hadn't intended coming, certainly not without speaking to Lady Langton, but Henry rang me and managed to change my mind. I had an appointment I was committed to late afternoon so there's been little time."

"Please sit down, Guy." Helena indicated a chair beside Celine. "You're always welcome in this house. It's still *mine*, I believe."

Clive looked stupefied. "I think you'd better get on with it, Henry," he snapped.

"All in good time, Clive." Henry went behind the desk, placing his briefcase on the top.

"May I be the first to congratulate you for getting in Gramps's will." Ashley leaned forward, treating Guy to a blue, glittering stare of challenge.

"Nothing is simple and straightforward, Ashley," he told her suavely. "I think you'll find I'm stealing nothing from you."

"Good on you, Guy!" Harris lifted a glass of ginger ale to Guy then set it aside. Harris admired Guy more than anyone he could think of. Guy had helped him so much with his studies. Guy never made him feel the next best thing to a brain dead moron. That was the way his cousin Ashley had always treated him. He gave Guy and Celine a broad, beaming smile. They were impossibly beautiful people, both of them. He was really very pleased to see Ceci back. Ceci had never treated him like a total dolt, either.

"Take that stupid grin off your face, Harris," his mother, Dorothy, admonished him, showing her irritation while his father sat, eyes locked tight, brow furrowed as though trying to fathom the complexities of the human condition.

"Dear Dorothy! Always keeping herself busy putting somebody down," Guy murmured to Celine sotto voce. "I bet you're thrilled to be back in the bosom of the family."

In truth she was immensely glad to have him there beside her. Even a hostile Guy radiated strength for her. Once he had been her true love, her dearest friend, her greatest ally. She must have been *mad*! No woman in her right mind would have fled Guy. No wonder her grandfather had called her a wimp. Seen from his eminence, he might even have doubted her sanity.

Henry had opened his handsome leather briefcase, but to the varying degrees of astonishment of everyone present, instead of withdrawing a great sheaf of papers he placed a black videotape on the desk.

"For God's sake!" Clive burst out, then hastily stifled the rest.

Celine turned in total dismay to seek Guy's brilliant, black eyes.

"Surely you didn't think Tiger Langton would just *disappear*?" he asked in a dry, ironic voice.

"Oh, Guy!" Her sigh was soft and desperate. Like her grandmother, she felt exceedingly frail.

"Hang in there, cherub." The severity of his expression amazingly softened. "It could be worth your while."

"Isn't this just *ghastly*!" Ashley demanded of the room in general. "Surely Gramps isn't going to *talk* to us?"

"It looks alarmingly like it." Imelda began to fan herself though the house was airconditioned. The rest of the family sat like a school of fish, mouths agape, but Helena looked like she was going to slip from her chair to the floor.

Celine sprang up and went to her. "Grandma, are you all right?" she asked anxiously.

"Why didn't I *know* this is exactly what Gerald would do?" Helena moaned. "Even when he's dead he won't lie down."

"Bear with me a moment," Henry appealed to them, looking around him almost absent-mindedly.

"To the right of you, Henry," Guy called. "The large antique cabinet. It houses the TV and video equipment. I'll fix it for you if you like."

"Thank you, dear boy!" Henry looked towards Guy gratefully. "I know I should be up with all these gadgets, but I'm not."

Shockingly, Ashley laughed, a caustic sound, and her father rounded on her, his favourite, but not beyond the cutting edge of his tongue. "If you can't behave in a seemly manner, Ashley, I suggest you go outside."

"Sorry, Dad," Ashley apologised, very meekly for her.

While they all watched in trepidation, Guy set the TV to the appropriate channel, then pushed in the video.

"Now this dreadful, dreadful day is complete," Helena announced in her most dismal tones.

"Amen." Guy glanced keenly at Celine's pale profile, then briskly in the manner of a doctor took her nerveless hand.

Sir Gerald Langton's splendid image came up on the screen. He was seated behind the desk in his grand, dark-panelled office, his expression more sardonic than ever.

"My dear family," he began in his unforgettable voice.

For close on thirty minutes they sat transfixed while Gerald Langton detailed what he wanted done with the family fortune. He spoke to them in turn, but not to complete silence. The deep, authoritarian tones were accompanied by intermittent outbursts of horror, anger, shushes and moans.

There were shocks galore!

Helena, shoved into a backwater all her life, was placed at the virtual mercy of her eldest son, Clive, who would inherit the house and all its contents except the art collection, which would go to Celine as "the only one who knows how to appreciate it," a claim howled down by Clive, Imelda and Ashley in unison. Helena was assured she would be maintained in customary style and her every wish fulfilled. It was obvious Gerald Langton believed Helena would continue to reside at the house after her son and family moved in. It was, after all, an extremely large house.

"How appalling!" Celine edged closer to Guy, quite shocked.

He nodded. "Even to the end Gerald left Helena grief. Clive will take his responsibilities seriously, but at what cost? It's just as well Helena has her own money."

Even Ashley had the grace to take her grandmother's part. "God, isn't that bizarre! Gramps really was the ultimate male chauvinist. Didn't he think Granny could manage her own life?"

"I hope you're not inferring I can't look after Mother, Ashley?" Clive glowered.

"I *know* you will, Pops. But Granny really should have been left the house in her lifetime. I don't want to live in this old museum. I don't imagine Celine will want to live with us, either."

"Of course not!" Harsh colour in her cheeks, Imelda made her position clear. "You won't know the place after I turn my attention to it. It could be splendid if we clear out a lot of the junk."

"You have my permission, Imelda, to go to work," Helena said, demonstrating she couldn't have cared less.

"So Imelda's in charge now and your grandmother is out in the cold," Guy murmured darkly. "Don't you just love it!"

Clive, as the eldest son, the rightful heir, was addressed next.

"This is a farce!" he cried once, as his late father tore his hopes and ambitions apart. "Who gets the yacht and the Lear jet?"

"I wonder, Clive, if you wouldn't mind keeping your comments to the end," Henry pleaded in vain. He remembered now his late client had always said Clive had "more energy than brains". Clive was on his feet now, fists clenched, reminding Henry strongly of a wounded bull about to charge.

Nolan was equally dissatisfied and perplexed, though he retained his seat. When Gerald addressed his two grandsons, Michael and Harris, words to the effect "too much too soon could only ruin young men", Harris broke into near hysterical laughter when told he had inherited his grandfather's collection of gold cufflinks. To add to the aggravations Clive told him not to keep acting the fool.

"Isn't that a case of the pot calling the kettle black?" Guy murmured into Celine's ear. Signals were passing rapidly from one to the other, much as in the old days for all the unhappy state of their relationship. The library was thrumming with shock and ill feeling.

The granddaughters were next. Ashley, Celine and Dana, who was praying she wouldn't have to wait for her windfall like her brother. Ashley was given the string of glamour racehorses in recognition of her love and knowledge of horses and racing, something that delighted her, a luxury unit in Sydney, another on the Queensland Gold Coast and a sum of 10 million dollars free of tax.

"That means I can take off when I feel like it," Ashley said.

Dana, the youngest, unexpectedly came next. Dana inherited the Meissen collection, her grandfather's apartment overlooking the Queensboro Bridge in New York and 10 million dollars free of tax.

"I can't wait to beat it to the Big Apple!" Dana said with a wild grin.

"I'll choose the time you're going there!" her mother thundered, looking on the bequest as a calamity. She needed her children to depend on her for survival.

When Celine's turn came, she tensed then sat straight, prepared for anything. Or nothing. There was nothing her grandfather had enjoyed more than being unpredictable. Gerald Langton began by expressing his regret he had "probably" driven her away, nevertheless, his handsome face deeply serious and frowning, he assured her he still loved her and was immensely proud she had demonstrated she could stand on her own two feet. He was now giving her a portion of his Harcourt Langton shares equal to that of her uncles, twenty percent. She had a seat on the board, various properties including a tea plantation in North Queensland, a hotel in Fiji and the sum of

10 million dollars tax free. She was also to receive the art collection with the exception of the Renoir, which was to go to Lady Muriel Harcourt because she had always loved it.

"This is monstrous!" Clive cried, sagging back in his armchair. "What's the world coming to! Father was a complete mystery to me."

Celine turned to Guy, who was looking very hawkish. "For once I agree with Uncle Clive."

"Why do you say that? You *were* his favourite grandchild."

"The trouble is, he's got several."

"It's hard to feel sorry for them," Guy drawled. "Cheer up, darling Ashley will try to contest the will herself. I wouldn't put it past her. My sympathies are entirely with your grandmother. I have it on very good authority, her *own*, she'd as soon reside on the other side of the moon as with either of her sons. In fact if we don't get her to bed she'll finish up in intensive care."

"I've waited too long already." Celine stood suddenly and was waved down very politely by Henry. "This won't be long now, dear. There are bequests to friends, staff, various charities your grandfather supported, but they are contained in the typewritten copies of the will. Guy is the last one to be mentioned." He released the stop button on the video recorder and Sir Gerald started to speak.

Now it was discovered the fate of the yacht and the Lear jet. Both were left to Guy in recognition of the fact he was the best yachtsman among them and he actually held a licence to fly the jet. Guy also inherited all the shares in a fledgling property company GLRealty, based, in Clive's words "in the Never Never", which his more knowledgeable father had known was coming closer every day. The collection of Rodin sculptures, Sir Gerald's famous set of golf clubs, and all the volumes on architecture in the library.

"As I recall, a lot of them were my grandfather's," Guy told Celine, keeping his voice low. "Sir Gerald borrowed them and forgot to give them back."

"Guy, you're awful!" She had an impulse to laugh, knowing he was similarly affected.

"I know. You used to love it!"

The greatest shock was to come, intensifying the feelings of outrage that so choked the room, and Celine, for one, had difficulty breathing. Guy was to receive fifteen percent of Sir Gerald's shares in Harcourt Langton, which with Guy's own shares inherited from his grandfather gave him the same clout as Clive and Nolan put together. Something their father would have seen only too clearly.

Sir Gerald faded on a challenging note as though he privately believed he would outlast the lot of them.

"My God!" Clive cried in despair. "Robbery! I'm sure I would never wish Father to go to hell, but this will is a perfect *swine*!"

"Which was often said of Sir Gerald." Guy stared into Celine's misty grey eyes. "Don't you just wish you'd married me now? Our combined shares give us control of Harcourt Langton."

She flinched a little at the heavy irony. "I'm not so dumb I can't add up."

"I never thought you were dumb, either, but as it's turned out it seems you were. I suppose this will make me a lot more attractive to Ashley, as well." His brilliant eyes were full of a black humour.

"If only she'd received my share you'd be just right."

''There's that,'' he considered, his handsome mouth sardonic. ''On the other hand I've found it best to do my own thing. Depend on me, darling, to take control *without* you.''

CHAPTER FIVE

"GET me a brandy, darling, to settle my tummy," Helena implored, her mood becoming more melancholy by the minute. "If I were any sort of a drinker, which I may well become, I'd say make that a double."

"Get into bed, Grandma," Celine said, turning back the covers and plumping the pillows. "Come on, now. No more dilly-dallying. Too much has been expected of you."

"What me, the *nobody*?" With a sigh Helena gave in, going to her brass four-poster bed adorned with a blue canopy and allowing Celine to tuck her in. "I have to say this, my family, with the exception of you and possibly Harris, are a shocking lot. Every last one of them was left a fortune but whenever they turn up they're full of complaints. Really, I was disgusted with them tonight. So you and Guy got a lot more than anyone expected? That's rough! I, Gerald's wife for more than fifty years, have been treated like a baby."

Celine put out a hand and smoothed her grandmother's hair from her forehead. "I'm sure Grandfather didn't mean to hurt you," she offered wretchedly. "It's as Ashley says…"

"Please don't mention Ashley," Helena said, the same smooth forehead creasing into a frown. "I hope you realise now, Celine, just how jealous she is of you."

"She has an excuse, Grandma."

"If she's smart enough she won't cross you, but I have the dismal feeling she's going to try. Of course Guy is entitled to a lot more shares. Gerald virtually cheated him out of a large part of his inheritance.''

''*What*?'' Celine stared at her.

''Oh, it was legal enough, but after Lew died and Guy was still a boy, Gerald got up to all sorts of tricks to swing the balance of power. Muriel always *knew* but there was little she could do about it. You could say Gerald in being so generous to Guy has only cleared the slate.''

''So that's why Guy never seemed surprised?''

''Good Lord, Celine,'' Helena said patiently. ''Guy has grown up knowing what a rogue Gerald really was. There are no secrets between Guy and his grandmother. Both are determined a Harcourt will head Harcourt Langton. They don't trust the rest of us. Even Gerald regarded Guy as his natural successor. Clive spends his life trying to dominate people but he's not made of the right stuff. I'll have to move out to survive.''

Celine sat down suddenly in the armchair beside the bed. ''Seriously, Grandma?''

''I may look like a twit, I may even act like one, but believe me I'm not. There is no way I could live under the same roof as Clive and Imelda. I'm surprised they don't want to shove me into some discreet home.''

''So what are we going to do?''

''I don't think we'll have to think long and hard. We'll have to move *out*!''

''Of course. That's understood.'' Celine nodded. ''But where?''

''Get Guy to make inquiries about some property in the Never Never,'' Helena said with a strained smile. ''It will take a miracle to move out *quietly*.''

''They do happen!'' Celine started up and moved towards a circular table covered with innumerable photographs in silver frames and a collection of Lalique birds. A crystal decanter stood atop it with a small gold-rimmed glass and Celine poured a small measure of the finest cognac into it. She walked back to the bed and handed the glass to her grandmother. "This will cause an uproar."

"Gerald should have thought of that," Helena said equably, taking a sip. "Clive might never speak to me again."

"I'm sure in his own way he would do his very best."

"One never knows. Does one?" Helena said. "In any case, I've never been able to swallow Imelda. Thank you, no. I must go my own way at long, long last. All I ask is you don't leave me until I'm properly on my feet. I have the feeling we'll have to weather a few storms."

"I'll go along with that," Celine replied with some feeling. "Why don't I find out what's on the market?"

Helena was silent for a bit, thinking. "What I'd really like is for Guy to design a house for me. A *small* house on one level. All I want is a view and a pretty surrounding garden. You can stay with me for as long as you like. But you're young with your life before you. You'll want a place of your own very likely. You'll marry." Her voice was suddenly very serious. "You won't find anyone better than Guy if you search the whole world."

"That's all over, Grandma."

"*Is* it?" Helena asked laconically. "It seems to me he's as protective of you as ever. I couldn't help noticing he held your hand in the library."

"I was shaking all over," Celine explained.

"Why should he care, if he's as bitter as you say?"

"That's a point, but Guy is a *gentleman* in the same way as his grandfather. Anyway he told me he's going to take over Harcourt Langton without any help from me.''

Helena's expression said this was perfectly acceptable. ''Good for him!'' she remarked. ''I'm not so old I don't find Guy tremendously exciting. Don't forget most of the money that started Harcourt Langton was put up by Lew. It was all tremendously sad, Guy losing his father, then his grandfather. People were always trying to marry Eloise off, but she never recovered, you know. Some women are like that. They care so deeply, no one else will do. Eloise made Guy her life. I expect she'll come into her own as a grandmother. I have to admit some of my grandchildren scare me. I was fascinated to see Michael making a big fuss of you before he left.''

Celine frowned. ''He actually kissed me on the mouth.''

''He's always been attracted to you, Celine, but you never saw anyone else but Guy.''

Celine looked and felt shocked. ''Michael is my first cousin, Grandma.''

''Different mothers.'' Helena shrugged. ''Cousins marry. Especially when they want to keep a fortune in the family.''

''This is weird!'' Celine said, uncertain whether her grandmother was serious or not.

''No, it's life.'' Helena lay back against the pillows and closed her eyes. ''Good night, my darling. A kiss before you go. Do you realise for the first time in fifty years I can no longer call my home my own?''

''I have a feeling, Grandma, it won't be a great loss,'' Celine said quietly. ''What matters most is having a place of your *own*. A house that expresses *you*. Would you like me to speak to Guy or do you want to do that yourself?''

"No, you do it, darling," Helena responded tiredly. "At the moment I feel profoundly *lost*."

The voice on the telephone was almost as arrogant as that of her boss. "This is Ansley Forgan Smythe, Miss Langton," the woman announced herself. "Private secretary to Mr. Clive Langton. Mr. Langton wishes to set up an appointment to see you around threeish this afternoon."

Celine had her own ideas about that. She intended to spend the day with her grandmother. "I'm sorry, this afternoon isn't convenient," she said in her normal dulcet tones. "I could see my uncle the following morning, around elevenish," she added with the slightest hint of dryness.

The voice on the other end sounded enormously put-out. "Mr. Langton has a very tight schedule. I don't know…"

"I could make it ten-thirty if that would be helpful?" What the hell! It was useless trying to evade Uncle Clive.

Miss Forgan Smythe considered that and after a little cough finally agreed.

"What was all that about?" Helena asked after Celine had resumed her seat.

"Uncle Clive wants to see me."

"Of course he wants to see you," Helena said, calmly going about answering the sympathy cards she had kept apart. "He wants to know your plans. Most of them, anyway. I'd say he and Imelda are anxious to move in here. They might describe the place as a horror but it's big and imposing enough, even for them. Lew drew up such wonderful plans for a house, too. All kinds of lovely little surprises, especially for me. Gerald wouldn't have a bar of them. He never did have a good eye for architecture. He wanted a great fortress, someplace nobody could possibly overlook, not an elegant villa that opened out onto a beautiful garden. He had no spirituality, Gerald. Sometimes I feel I was tyrannised into an unhappy lifestyle. Of course I should have had some spunk, but I never learned how. Don't let that happen to you, Celine. Every woman has the right to her dream.''

Miss Forgan Smythe, a handsome, hard-faced woman, turned out to be one of those you're-up-against-a-stone-wall-type of secretaries. In fact it seemed to the gentle-mannered Celine, Miss Forgan Smythe was bent on giving her a hard time. She looked at Celine long and hard as though her one concern was establishing Celine *was* the person she claimed to be. Just as Celine was expecting to be asked for her driver's licence, Guy emerged from the executive floor lift.

"Celine!" He paused as he caught sight of her, then swung in her direction, so handsome and dynamic it was like the power had been switched on.

"How are you, Guy?" Unconsciously she lifted her face and he bent his raven head and brushed her cheek with the same lips that had once reduced her to mindless rapture.

"Fine." He turned to Miss Forgan Smythe, a slight frown on his face, as if asking for an explanation as to why Celine was standing. "What time is Miss Langton's appointment?"

"Ten-thirty, Mr. Harcourt." The secretary suddenly flushed.

Guy shot back an immaculate white cuff and looked at his watch. "Then you might like to buzz through to the office. It's ten-thirty now. I'm sure Mr. Langton wouldn't like to keep his niece waiting."

"Yes, of course, Mr. Harcourt." Miss Forgan Smythe took a deep breath then did as she was told, mouthing "I'm sorry" to Celine.

"May I talk to you when I'm through with Uncle Clive?" Celine asked Guy, while he was still exuding the old care for her.

"Of course. You know where to find me." He gave her a sardonic glance which clearly said "I'm not in the chairman's office. Not *yet*!"

Her uncle Clive was. He sat behind his late father's splendid desk, physically filling the space but lacking Sir Gerald's genuine *presence*. Light poured through the ceiling-high, plate-glass windows that afforded such a magnificent city and river scape but Celine was determined she wasn't going to sit in what she privately thought of as "the hot seat". The room brought back too many unhappy memories. It was the first time she'd been in it since that fateful day. It occurred to her now her grandfather had been an acknowledged business genius, but his private life had not been successful. Each member of the family had suffered in their own way. Had her grandfather been kinder or more understanding of a young woman's anxieties, who knows, things might have turned out quite differently for her. She mightn't have lost her chance at *her* dream.

"So, how are things at the house, Celine?" Clive Langton asked briskly, navigating his way through a pile of files as though she didn't warrant his undivided attention. "How's Mother? I can't seem to get through to her on the phone. Not your doing, I hope?" He glanced up accusingly, blue eyes afire.

"Absolutely not!" Celine spoke so crisply, his head, which had gone down again, snapped up. It had only taken Celine a couple of ticks to realise she had come a long way in a few years. She wasn't about to be brow-beaten by her uncle Clive. "Grandma knows her *own* mind."

Clive actually snorted, then returned to the files again. "Then your knowledge of your grandmother is very small. Mother has never found making decisions easy. I've called you in here this morning, Celine, to confirm a few things. Your aunt Imelda is anxious to move into the house as soon as possible. She's a very impressive woman as I'm sure you agree. She's not overawed by the task of putting the house to rights. It's too startling, too much in Father's manner. There's much to be done and Imelda wants to make a start. If anyone can pull it off, she can. We assume you'll be looking for an apartment?"

"You may be *certain* of it, Uncle Clive," Celine said gently. "I haven't the slightest wish to inconvenience you or get tangled up in the alterations. Grandma and I were discussing it only this morning."

"Good. Good." Clive slapped a file shut with a de-cided thump. "I'm certain I could get you into Falcon Place. We built it, you know. You couldn't do better."

"Thank you, Uncle Clive, but we're thinking of a house." Celine touched a hand to her single strand of very fine pearls. Guy had given them to her for her eigh-teenth birthday. She thought of them as her magic charm.

"We? Who's *we*?" Clive rasped.

Celine lifted her soft grey eyes. "Grandma will want to talk to you herself, but she has authorised me to say she'll be wanting a place of her own."

Clive's heavy, handsome face turned crimson. "This is *your* doing, Celine. I'm not certain what's your mo-tive."

Celine stared at her uncle thoughtfully. "You don't consider Grandma might want her independence?"

Clive almost choked. "My mother has had someone looking after her for *all* of her life. There is no way I would risk sending her out on her own. It would be a crime. Like having her committed. Father instructed me to look after her for the rest of her life. I take my responsibilities seriously, young lady."

"I know you do, Uncle Clive," Celine continued calmly, "but Grandma has reached a point in her life when she wants to make a new beginning."

Clive looked genuinely staggered. "Are you *mad*? Your grandmother is seventy-four. Not the most adventurous time of life, or so it seemed to me."

"A change can be great therapy, Uncle Clive. Grandma is showing courage. She is to be applauded. She's in good health. She's always taken care of herself. She could probably live another ten years or more. Like her own mother."

Clive looked as though he was losing control of what should have been a very minor exchange. "No matter what *Mother* wants, Father's wishes are paramount."

"Not anymore." Ruefully Celine shook her Titian head. "We all know Grandma endured a lifetime of benevolent oppression."

Clive's expression was ludicrous, a mixture of bafflement and anger. "You certainly *have* changed!" he accused her. "Only a few years ago you couldn't say boo to a goose. Ashley explains it as your need to assert yourself."

Celine smothered her hurt and sense of betrayal. "Don't listen to Ashley, Uncle Clive. She doesn't really know me at all. People change. They mature and grow. No matter how much we all loved and obeyed Grandfather it has to be said we all lived in fear of him. The truth fights to get out. Grandma feels the restraints of the past have been lifted from her. It's a kind of rebirth, if you like.''

"What utter twaddle!" Clive gave a bitter laugh. "Old people do get these ideas. I'm telling you now, Celine, there's no way I'll condone Mother's setting up house. Especially not with *you*. Haven't you got enough without starting on your grandmother? Imelda intends doing up the east wing so Mother can have it all to herself. This is *no* time for her to be making decisions. She's in a state of shock.''

"Then why don't you try to calm her?" Celine said in a reasonable tone. "As to what you mean by starting on her, I'm afraid I don't follow.''

"Don't take that tone with me, young lady," Clive said, trying unsuccessfully to stare her down. "You've just about alienated all the family.''

"That's no news, Uncle Clive. You didn't want me from the time I was born. You never offered any love or support to my father, much less my mother. I've never met with anything else but disapproval from you. As I recall, Aunt Imelda took violent objection to the way my hair curled. It's time now to make a stand. Don't make an enemy of me. You might regret it.''

"Oh, my! Who would have thought you'd turn out a hothead!" Clive sneered.

"I think you'd better remember I'm Tiger Langton's granddaughter.''

Silence. Best of all, a modicum of respect. "You'll never get close to Guy again, if you've got any plans there.''

"Guy knows how to separate business from pleasure.''

"You'll never get control. Either or both of you, so

don't press too hard. Don't think I'm not awake to Guy. If he had his way he'd run every last Langton out.''

"That might be the next step," Celine answered wryly, getting to her feet. "I won't take up any more of your time, Uncle Clive. When you do talk to Grandma I'd be very grateful for your understanding. If you love her you'll make it easy for her to move out."

"That I'll never do!" Clive thrust back his swivel chair so violently it crashed into the built-in cupboards. "Mother's future has been arranged. I am the head of the family now, Celine, and I'd thank you not to interfere."

Celine settled the gold chain on her handbag over her shoulder. "It's not interference, Uncle Clive, it's support. Grandma and I have spent enough time doing what we're told, as you're about to find out. I don't think it's too much to ask to be *listened* to. While I'm at it I should mention I'd like a job in the firm. We have a public relations department. I might do well there."

"Job? *Job*?" Clive Langton stared at her as if she'd taken leave of her senses. "My dear girl, you're an *heiress*!"

"Heiresses are people, aren't they? I'm used to working. I've spoken to my boss in Sydney. He understands I won't be able to return to my old job. I'm quite prepared to undertake further study, courses, whatever. I did very well at university though that was between me and the gatepost. Now that I think about it, only the Harcourts remarked on my intelligence."

"This is a very bad decision, Celine," Clive said, reaching for the heavy leather armchair and slumping down into it. "I'm very much against giving women power."

"So are most men your age, Uncle Clive. Hopefully you're a dying breed."

*   *   *

Guy's secretary showed her in; a striking young woman in her late twenties with long, gleaming, dark hair, clear green eyes and a charming manner. She also wore a diamond ring on her engagement finger, something that Celine noted with a sense of relief.

Guy rose immediately at her entry and came around the desk, settling a chair for her. "You look a little flushed."

"That's normal for an exchange with Uncle Clive." She smiled a little wanly.

"He does tend to raise the blood pressure," Guy offered suavely. "Would you like tea or coffee? If you're not due anywhere else I thought we might have an early lunch."

"That would be lovely! Yes to both." Celine slipped gracefully into the chair, crossing her slender legs at the ankles.

"Splendid!" he returned with mild mockery. He picked up the phone and murmured a few words into it, his eyes all the while moving lightly over Celine. She knew there was absolutely nothing about her that he missed. It wasn't exactly a glance of admiration, either. More a cool assessment. She was wearing her black Lagerfeld suit again as a mark of respect to her grandfather, but she had teamed it with a magnolia satin blouse almost the exact colour of her lustrous pearls. Her skin was an even richer cream, a flush of colour over her impeccable cheekbones, but she didn't see that. In any case for such a beautiful young woman Celine was curiously without vanity. Beauty she had found wasn't goodness or wisdom. Sometimes it could cause a good deal of distress.

Guy put the phone down, his expression turning

faintly astringent. "Aren't they the pearls I gave you for your eighteenth birthday?"

She looked down and lightly touched them. "My lucky charm."

"Really?" One black eyebrow shot up.

"If you don't ask you'll never know."

"Then dare I ask if you're still wearing my ring?"

She hesitated only a moment, her flush deepening. "Have you any objection?"

"Maybe one or two. Possibly a dozen. I won't permit myself to dig deeper than that." He stood up abruptly and came around the desk. "I think I'm entitled to take another look at it. Ashley rather ruined the grand moment the last time."

Flustered Celine withdrew the beautiful ring that hung from its fine gold chain. She leaned forward a little and Guy took the weight of it in his palm. "I *do* remember it. Just hazily. The end of a fairy tale. The sleeping princess woke up and ran away and the prince turned into a frog."

"For what it's worth, I've always liked frogs."

He laughed at that. An uncomplicated sound and immensely attractive. Echoes of the old Guy who once would have caught her to him, dipping his head and finding her mouth.

"Yes, don't let's get caught up in all the old pain. Especially not since we're both big shareholders." He let his ring swing back against her breast and Celine tucked it up and slipped it through her blouse. "Grandma has decided to move out of the house. Me, too, of course."

"Great idea!" he said briskly, resuming his seat. "When do you want to go?"

"Uncle Clive is very much against it. In fact he was extremely angry when I told him."

"Domination is central to Clive's dealings. It's at the heart of just about everything he does."

"He could upset Grandma greatly," Celine said.

"It'll be Clive who has the heart attack. Nolan has the ulcers. Three at the last count. It has to be said Sir Gerald was responsible for a lot of that."

Celine nodded. "He never terrorised *you.*"

"No. I'm a sucker for the *soft* touch. So far as Helena is concerned I'm at her disposal at any time. She would know that."

"She does. Sometimes I think Grandma is a little bit in love with you."

"Which makes her rather sharper than her grand-daughter. From now on I expect to be taken very seriously on the marriage market."

"You always were."

"You're kidding me, Celine." His black eyes gleamed.

"So there's no woman in your life now?"

"I've absolutely no intention of telling you. Check with Ashley. I believe she does a brisk trade in gossip."

"I can promise you I don't listen to gossip," Celine said quietly.

"Oh, yes, you do, darling. After all, what happened to our engagement?"

"I was madly, gloriously in love with you, Guy." She lifted her mist-grey eyes.

"Ah, the halcyon days!" He locked his hands behind his elegant dark head and stared at the ceiling. "How sad they will never come again. The old Guy and his dewy Celine have quite disappeared. Maybe we *were* an odd couple."

He broke off as his secretary tapped on the door then entered carrying a tray.

"Thank you, Christine." He gave her a smile that was like being touched by sunlight.

"My pleasure!" She returned the smile with one of her own; one that might have set her fiancé brooding.

The coffee was exactly right and Celine sipped at it gratefully. If anything Guy's sexual radiance had increased. She felt the heat of it so exquisitely it was all she could do not to blow on her coffee.

"I take it Helena hasn't spoken to Clive yet," Guy asked, offering her a shortbread biscuit, which she refused.

"I don't think she can bear the weight of argument."

"So you need some help—right?"

"We can certainly use it. My own brief clash with Uncle Clive has confirmed that. What Grandma really wants is for you to design a house for her."

Guy stared at her thoughtfully. "I'd be delighted, of course. In fact I know just the site. It's a narrow block, part of the old McNally estate but it's high and cool with expansive views. The thing is, it would take a good six months to build and that's going flat out. The plans have to be drawn up and approved and we're looking at top-quality materials and workmanship."

"You can handle it, Guy."

"Of course I can. Where would you want to go in the meantime? The whole thing is already causing comment."

Celine lifted her eyes. "You mean about Grandma's not being left the house? How would anyone know?"

"Dear God, there are people out there who know more about Sir Gerald's will than you do. Besides, don't you think Clive and Imelda would find it a real pleasure to tell their friends they've inherited Langfield? It might have chimneys and towers and turrets popping up everywhere but some people think it's the ultimate stately pile. Imelda's probably been on the phone to the decorators already. If anyone wanted to know what was going to happen to Lady Langton they'd be told she would remain at Langfield where she'd be properly looked after.''

Celine shook her head darkly. "Grandma doesn't need the benefit of their care. She wants to *own* her life. I don't blame her. It's a sad fact but Grandfather didn't listen to one word she said.''

Guy smiled wryly. "No one is going to listen to you, Celine, if you first don't listen to yourself. Being put down has been a woman's lot for countless generations, but it's changing. Look at your own family. You and Helena have come on amazingly.''

"A little miracle?'' she challenged him.

"It's not so easy to tell now what goes on behind those luminous eyes.''

"Yours are uncommonly fathomless, as well.''

"So neither of us trusts the other. It sounds like you're planning on staying?'' He gave her a cool, level glance.

Celine nodded. "I've already spoken to Max. He's disappointed but he knows it's not possible for me to go back to my old job.''

"Such is life for an heiress!'' Guy returned breezily.

"Don't *you* try to put me in a glass case.''

"Terrific!'' His handsome mouth turned down. "When did I *ever* do that? You are one cruel woman, Celine.''

"I'd like to apologise. You never did that. It's important for me, Guy, to find something to do. In fact, I want a job at Harcourt Langton.''

His black eyes sparkled with droll humour. "Darling,

with a twenty percent share and a seat on the board you've *got* it!''

"I'm serious, Guy."

"So am I. Sort of. But I have enough conflicts to juggle without having you at the office. Doesn't it strike you as a kind of insanity?"

"I guess you're entitled to take these little swipes at me," she said.

"We were supposed to be madly in love, remember? Passionate stuff!"

"I didn't have the courage, Guy."

"Really? I thought you were waiting on a better offer."

"Obviously I didn't get it."

"Max was not your lover?" he asked in a hard, sceptical voice.

She lifted her mist-grey eyes. "You've mentioned this before."

"I'm mentioning it again. I enjoy asking questions."

"Believe that, you'll believe anything. Mel Gibson wouldn't have tempted me."

"Was *he* at the hotel? All right—" he held up a conciliatory hand "—let's establish what kind of work you'd like to do."

"Public relations," she said instantly. "I'd *have* to be better than Michael." She referred to her cousin.

"So who's arguing?" Guy shrugged.

"I saw him on television fielding questions about our proposed Manola Bay project."

"Your *uncle's* proposed Manola Bay project," Guy corrected. "They pushed it past the board but I'm not entirely happy about it. I've developed a reputation for my sensitivity to environmental problems. I want to stand by it. Keep the faith."

"I understand that, Guy." Celine was well acquainted with Guy's strong philosophies about architecture and the preeminence of nature. "Michael came out fighting as big business. What's worse is, he kept trying to put the woman environmentalist down. Even to the extent of talking over the top of her."

"Celine, I've seen it all before!" Guy said, an ironic expression on his face. "As it happens, it seems to run in your family. Michael can get nasty, but it's my opinion he thinks it's a way of impressing his father. Ridicule is a weak trick at the best of times. Clive wants Michael to take a higher profile in the firm. He's leaning on me to give Michael more responsibility but believe me he's not ready for it. In any case, Clive doesn't bring out the best in him."

"Maybe he'd be better to get out of Harcourt Langton altogether?"

Guy nodded. "He's at the point where he has to make a decision. The trouble is, and I never cease to marvel at it, Clive has him intimidated into the ground. Which is all the more remarkable he gave you that kiss. I didn't like it much. Did you?"

"Don't be an imbecile. Michael is my cousin."

"I *know*," Guy said bluntly. "Though what that might have to do with Michael's intentions…?"

"Forget Michael." Celine waved her hands.

"I already have. So far as Manola Bay goes, Clive is really pushing the project and that means fast tracking it with the relevant government authorities. He seems to have the townspeople on side. The project would bring jobs, prosperity to the area, but until I have time to look at the environmental impact study I can't make an informed comment. I clash too much with Clive already and this is his baby. Dr. Bertram, the woman you're talking about, is a highly respected marine biologist. She's *not* one of the fanatical fringe. She knows what she's talking about. She must be listened to. There are many environmental issues we have to confront these days. It's a very sensitive area. I saw Michael myself. I can promise you I cringed. Both for him and for Harcourt Langton. Why he was the appointed spokesperson I'll never know. As you say, he's about as sensitive as a school of piranha. At the same time he made me think of a possible alternative site. A big parcel of land the firm bought many years ago. As I recall it was around four hundred acres with a couple of kilometres oceanfront. It's nowhere near as close to the Great Barrier Reef and there are no mangroves to consider. I have to wonder now why Clive and Nolan hit on Manola Bay.''

"I think *money* is the most important thing to them, Guy.''

"Sure. Catch anyone running a business where money's not important. But we're leaders in big property developments. We have to get things right for ourselves and the ones who follow us.''

"And P.R. plays a role.''

"Agreed,'' Guy said briskly. "Let's discuss it over lunch.''

CHAPTER SIX

CELINE arrived home in a turmoil of feelings; excitement, elation, hope, a sense of challenge, as though the world was a different place. Lunch with Guy had been very successful, almost an unsettling replay of their former intense rapport. For sure they had both been a little on edge, more wary than unfriendly, but gradually they had relaxed, trading tales about how each had spent the past few years. At *work*, that is. Any hint of a personal life tended to bring out the acidity in Guy's vibrant tones.

It was all the more distressing then to have Mrs. Findlay rush at her the moment she stepped through the door.

"I'm so glad you're home, Miss Langton," she said, her competent face registering anxiety. "Mrs. Clive Langton is here with Ashley. They're with Lady Langton in the Garden Room."

"Thank you, Mrs. Findlay. I'll go through." Celine put her handbag down on a console table almost grotesquely decorated with ormolu and fat, gilded putti. Uncle Clive hadn't wasted any time! She glanced in the tall, gilded mirror that stood above the console, touching a hand to the radiant masses of her hair. This was going to be a test for herself and her grandmother. Curiously enough she had never been overbothered by her aunt Imelda, but as a shy and retiring schoolgirl she had often flinched at her cousin's sharp tongue.

Celine drew a deep breath as she entered the Garden Room with its high arched windows that led out onto an arcaded terrace. The room was bright with sunlight, wicker furniture and a wealth of tropical plants, golden canes, kentia palms, magnificent philodendrons and boston ferns, flowering orchids in great containers and hanging Tunisian birdcages filled with colourful begonias. All three women were seated at one of the circular, glass-topped tables. Ashley was nursing a drink in a tall, frosted glass, Imelda in a very natty navy-and-white outfit sat to the right of her, while Helena sat a little apart looking very much like a woman under siege. She needed bolstering and Celine regretted now she had spent a little time window shopping.

"You *do* look smart, Celine," Imelda said, somehow, as ever, implying disapproval. "One might even say *glowing*!"

"Having lunch with Guy obviously agreed with her." Ashley held up her glass to Celine in mock salute. "Guy's charm, when he bothers to turn it on, is legendary. *I* should know."

Why was Ashley such a puzzle? Celine thought. Why did she always sound faintly bitter when she was a young woman who had everything?

"Who told you I had lunch with Guy?" Celine asked casually, going to her grandmother, kissing her cheek then pulling up a chair beside her.

"Actually I spoke to him not ten minutes ago." Ashley's ice-blue eyes glinted.

"Really? And he told you we went out to lunch?" Celine could feel her heart racing but she willed herself to be cool.

Ashley let out a little, mocking laugh. "Guy and I are a lot closer than we used to be, Ceci."

Helena turned in her chair to stare at her elder granddaughter.

"What's so amazing about that, Gran?" Ashley asked

in direct challenge. "Celine put herself very firmly out of the picture. I'm sure Guy would ask *me* to marry him if I'd only let him."

"Give it a try," Celine suggested briskly. "I don't like your chances."

"Sour grapes, kitten. It seems like *you're* trying for an encore. This time, I'm afraid, you'll have too much competition. Guy is a rare catch and he knows it. Ask him how many messages he gets on his answering machine." She reached out to stroke Celine's cheek, but Celine leaned away.

"No more about Guy. Not today. He may try hard to conceal his attraction to Ashley but a mother is never fooled. For now we have more pressing things to discuss," Imelda said sternly, turning in her chair to address Celine. "Your uncle tells me, Celine, you've been encouraging Mother to move out."

"He certainly didn't lose any time," Celine said wryly.

"Be that as it may, I've come to see if it's *true*!"

"I've already told you, Imelda, it's my own idea," Helena said in a voice cracking with irritation.

"Mother, you're in need of tender, loving care," Imelda told her in a firm voice. "You're under a great deal of stress."

Helena closed her eyes. "I've no doubt at all about that, Imelda, but I'm not as yet climbing up the walls. Celine is here now to minister to her poor, lame-brained grandmother, and Goldie and Mrs. Findlay wish to look after me, as well."

That came as something of a shock to Imelda, who gasped. "I assumed Mrs. Findlay went with the house?"

"Not at all, Imelda." Helena shrugged tiredly. "She's a human being, not a piece of furniture."

"You're distraught, Granny," Ashley said breezily, draining her glass.

Helena reacted with unaccustomed anger. "I am not. Or I wasn't before you and your mother showed up. You drink far too much, Ashley. It's working against you."

"How can you say that, Mother?" Imelda bristled. "It's only a gin and tonic."

"And it's not yet three o'clock."

"Oh, my!" Ashley threw back her head and laughed, showing her beautiful teeth. "What about all your Valiums, Granny? But that's okay."

Imelda waved a quelling hand at her daughter. "You must look at this properly, Mother," she argued, hunching forward and fixing her mother-in-law with a controlling glance. "It's *far* too late in life to be thinking of starting up again. The house is *huge*! We can all live here quite happily without getting in one another's hair. I fully intend doing up the east wing for you."

"Thank you, no, Imelda. I don't intend to be the skeleton in the cupboard. I'm not living in the east wing. It's so far away I'd have to fire off a rocket to get help."

"Precisely!" Celine burst out laughing at her grandmother's turn of phrase.

"Can't we be *sensible* about this?" Ashley asked flatly.

"It doesn't really have anything to do with you, Ashley," Celine said in a reasonable voice. "One great phase of Grandma's life has ended. She wants to take up the next. She *wants* a place of her *own*."

Imelda gave a clipped laugh and rapped on the glass-topped table. "My dear girl, Mother wouldn't know *how* to survive on her own."

"Please don't speak about me, Imelda, as though I'm not here," Helena implored. "I appreciate your concern on my behalf but you must allow me to go my own way. I don't want to bother anyone and *I* don't want to be bothered.''

"Clive is totally against it,'' Imelda said as though that settled that. "He looks on it as a breach of trust. What would people think if we evicted you from your old home?''

"They'd think my marriage must have been a joke!'' Helena responded, looking both sad and ironic. "Gerald should never have done this to me. The house would have passed to you and Clive in due time. As it *is*, I intend to start a new life. Even the lowliest senior citizen is entitled to an uprising.''

Guy came up with a solution. *Fast*. He presented himself at Langfield that same evening, telling them David Forbes, the Q.C., and his wife, Pauline, were going overseas for an extended holiday. They would be only too pleased to let the house to Helena in their absence. It would be far more secure with a tenant, anyway, as David had pointed out. If Helena was interested they could discuss the matter further.

"Of course I'm interested,'' Helena said, suddenly looking brighter. "It's a lovely place. I've always liked it. I've been there many times, of course, both with Gerald and on my own. Pauline is a tireless worker for charity. Do they know I intend to build?''

Guy nodded. "I thought it best to tell them. They thought it quite exciting. I've secured the site, as well. The old McNally estate. Did Celine tell you?''

Helena looked fondly at her granddaughter. Tonight Celine was wearing a cool summer dress in the palest of pink and her beauty irresistibly drew the eye. "Yes, she did. She told me *everything*. Oh, I'm so going to enjoy this!'' Colour touched her pale cheeks.

''If you're not entirely happy with the site, we can find another,'' Guy said. ''One day soon we'll have to go and look over it. It's a small block compared to what you're used to, roughly a quarter acre, but we can make it very private and containable. You won't want to be bothered with too much maintenance.''

''Perhaps we could take a run out there tomorrow?'' Helena suggested, then immediately looked embarrassed. ''You're far too busy, Guy. I don't know what I'm thinking of.''

''No problem, Lady Langton.''

''*Helena*, dear.''

''Helena.'' He gave her his charm-the-birds-out-of-the-trees smile. ''I have appointments all through the morning, but I'll be free in the afternoon. Shall we say, three o'clock?''

''We'll meet you there,'' Celine suggested helpfully. ''The sooner Grandma approves the site, the sooner you can start on the plans.''

''Helena seems a little happier in herself,'' Guy commented as Celine accompanied him to the door.

''Thanks to you. We had rather a bad afternoon.''

''Oh?'' He paused to look down at her, his black eyes so brilliant and beautifully set they were enslaving.

''Aunt Imelda and Ashley turned up, as you surely know.''

He drew away immediately, his expression tightening. ''What is *that* supposed to mean?''

''Well, you did talk to Ashley,'' she was drawn into commenting, though she kept her tone quiet and matter-of-fact.

He continued to walk. ''You have an *extraordinary*

way of turning things around. Ashley rang *me*. I've no idea where from. She didn't say. I assumed she was at her own home.''

''No, she was here with Aunt Imelda.'' Celine put on a little burst of pace and clutched at his arm. ''I hope I haven't made you angry.''

''Of course you've made me angry.'' He turned on her. ''You're doomed to make me angry. When are you going to learn Ashley is an arch manipulator? Of the lot of you, she's the most like Sir Gerald.''

''I recognise that, Guy.'' Celine stood in the full glare of the exterior lights, her hair a glorious cascade of colour. ''She simply said…''

Guy gave a deep, goaded groan. ''There's no *simply* anything with Ashley. She's very highly motivated. I wondered why the hell she rang me.'' He swung away towards the Jaguar parked in the shadows.

Celine went after him, her near-ankle-length skirt fluttering in the breeze that shook out all the scents of the garden. ''Guy, it's none of my affair if you and Ashley have become friendly. I'm *glad*!''

''Oh, you're just too bloody sweet!'' His voice was taut, pent-up. His anger hit her like a wave of heat.

''What do you want me to say?'' She attempted to disguise her own inner turbulence but it clung to her like an aura.

''My lovely Celine, I refuse to be drawn into your net again. The last time almost destroyed me.''

She couldn't bear to face to face the truth of that so she chose to deny it. ''That's not true, Guy. There have been other women in your life.''

He laughed bitterly. ''I'm sure Ashley has given you a highly coloured account.''

"What's with you and Ashley?" she implored. "You circle one another like a pair of tigers."

"I think you'll find it's claiming territorial rights," he told her harshly. "You carry compulsion about you, Celine. Ashley may be your cousin, but she's *not* your friend. She's possibly even dangerous."

"Oh, Guy!" Celine broke off in distress. "It's hard to accept that. I know Ashley isn't as straight with me as I thought she was. She's let me down. I've found that out, but she seems to be in some kind of pain herself."

"She can't get *everything* she wants," he explained bluntly. "I *must* go, Celine."

"Not on a note of anger. *Please*. We have to meet tomorrow. I'm so sorry if I've offended you."

"I'm sorry, too. I think you can judge your effect on me."

The wave of heat was now so extreme it was *sizzling*. She thought to kiss his cheek by way of apology, but as she swayed towards him he caught her about the waist, locking her to his lean, hard-muscled body.

"What is this, Celine? More of the heartbreaking magic? I've no intention of buying it."

"Guy, I've *known* you for most of my life."

"And you were, quite simply, the most beautiful little girl I've ever laid eyes on. The cherub I thought had escaped from your grandfather's painting. I should have known then you'd find a way to break my heart."

Conscience smote her. "Oh, Guy, I never meant it. I *swear*! It wasn't *you* I rejected. Never!" The words tumbled out in a kind of soft anguish. "Don't look at me like that."

"Like what?" he asked harshly. "With *desire*? Whatever I feel for you, Celine, that just won't die!"

With a burst of electric energy he grasped a handful

of her hair, pinning her head back while he found her mouth. It was as if he still believed he had some claim on it.

It wasn't a gentle possession but dark and turbulent. There was even a flame of desperation in the sparkling violence. She heard herself moan, the merest little sound, but he didn't release her, neither was it over. He crushed her to him with a wilful passion, his mouth locked over hers, their tongues weaving and meeting in a strange mating dance.

Eventually he was driven to find her breast, cupping it with strong, thrilling fingers, the thumb moving sensuously back and forth over the nipple until it budded into a tight rose of sensation.

She was alive at last! The years rolled back. This was ecstasy, even if he was hurting her; an intoxication in the blood. She tried again to speak his name but he wouldn't let her. She could feel the *fierceness* moving through his body, the male power that was only just under control. Everything about him was so *perfect* to her, the contrast between his body and her own yet with the promise of becoming one flesh. She savoured the scent and texture of his skin, the feel of his fine, long-fingered hands as he *electrified* her smooth skin. Sensation was too exquisitely excruciating to speak of caresses.

Just as her admission of love was being forced out of her, he drew back abruptly, making it perfectly clear to her who had the upper hand. The whole dazzling incident had only taken a few moments but she was trembling so badly she might have passed through the eye of a storm.

The night breeze blew, shaking out a cascade of blossom from the jacaranda above them. He still held her with one arm, while she stared up at him dazedly, her hair a wild cloud around her oh-so-aroused face.

"You've kissed me like that only once before."

His chiselled features seemed more tightly etched. "Like then, you drove me to frenzy. Passion has the power to overwhelm the mind. I could make love to you until you ached and burned all over. You're perfectly designed for obsession, but then I remember how it was. The pain and the loss of meaning in my life. The realisation you'd fled me as someone you couldn't trust with your life and your love. Of course you could tell me that's my male ego. Maybe it is. All I know is, I'll never lose control of my life again."

Tears shimmered in Celine's luminous eyes. "So you *hate* me. You really do." She didn't think she could bear it.

"God help me, Celine, I could never hate you." He turned away and opened the door of his car. "Only this time, it's *your* turn to pay."

After that many things happened quickly. Helena approved the site for her new home, emerging as a woman who could make on-the-spot decisions virtually overnight. No one would have thought it possible, but it was. It was as though Helena had rediscovered the identity she had long considered lost. It staggered the rest of the family who reacted as though they had confidently expected her to go into a very serious decline.

"I don't understand it myself," Helena confided to Celine in private. "Maybe it's a last burst of the human spirit. Of course, you're here to add your invaluable support and Guy's always good for real muscle. Clive thinks shouting is what it's all about. He's more concerned with what people will think rather than my well-being."

On the day they shifted out of Langfield, Guy was there to prevent a cheerless departure. Clive and Imelda stood on the front steps loudly bemoaning the fact Helena had chosen to make a "public spectacle of them". Ashley, too, was on hand to help stir the pot, demanding Guy call her just as they were driving off.

"Why don't you get an unlisted number, Guy?" Helena suggested. "Ashley's trying just too hard to be clever."

With her grandmother comfortably installed at the Forbes estate, Celine flew off to Sydney to finalise her own affairs. On the last evening she managed to find time to have a pleasant dinner with Max. Max was in high spirits, confiding there was a new woman in his life, a well-known interior designer in charge of current refurbishment at the hotel.

"Third time lucky!" he quipped.

It would *have* to be if one learned anything, Celine thought, but sincerely wished him well.

A few days after she returned home she was required to attend her first board meeting. It was heady stuff for a twenty-three-year-old. She felt a huge wave of anticipation. Over the past years she had become aware she was of one life's workers. She enjoyed being kept busy, meeting new challenges. She wanted to succeed in life, not as Tiger Langton's granddaughter, but on her own terms. She wanted her life to have some real meaning. It had always seemed very strange to her Ashley had chosen to frolic her life away. Even Aunt Imelda was seriously into charity work.

On the morning she was due in the city she went looking for her grandmother to get her opinion. "So, what do you think, Grandma?" she asked, holding a pose.

Helena put down her newspaper, bending a professional eye on her grand-daughter. "Peachy!"

"Gosh, then I haven't pulled it off. I was going for a touch of power dressing."

Helena made a small scoffing noise. "You're too feminine for that. The suit is lovely. Tailored, yes, but *soft*. The short skirt shows off your dancer's legs. Years ago redheads were supposed to avoid pinks like the plague. Fancy that! All shades of pink suit you beautifully."

"Wish me luck, Granny." Celine bent and kissed the top of her grandmother's head.

"I do, my darling. Don't expect your uncles to clasp you to their manly bosoms. At least you'll have Guy and Muriel. The rest of them will succumb to your beauty but they won't think you'll have anything to contribute. You'll have to change that, Celine."

"I'm going to try, Grandma." Celine picked up her bag, settling the long gold chain over her shoulder.

"And I applaud it. My life would have been very different had I realised my own worth instead of accepting Gerald's one-eyed views. Who knows, in time, you might be capable of running the corporation."

"Guy might have something to say about that," Celine pointed out in a dry voice.

Helena waved an airy hand. "Then run it together."

The atmosphere of the boardroom embraced her the moment she walked in. It actually smelled of big business and decision-making. The room was spacious, mahogany-panelled with a coffered ceiling and Biedermeier-inspired furnishings which included the thirty-foot-long boardroom table and the surrounding chairs. Guy was holding the floor, a group of board members assembled around him. Her uncles were seated heads together at the table, deep in discussion. Near the tall windows Lady Harcourt was laughing at something

Sir Peter Hartford, retired banker and long-time board member, was saying.

All heads swivelled at her entrance. Guy looked towards Clive, naturally expecting him as chairman to be the first to go forward to welcome his niece, but when Clive continued to remain seated, fidgeting with some papers he had before him, Guy lost no time crossing the room.

"Welcome to your first board meeting, Celine." He took the hand she extended. "You look like a peach tree in blossom."

"Should I have worn something more conservative?" she asked seriously.

"Not at all. We men get enough of that. Now, come and meet everyone. Some you already know. Not Nancy, she's new…Ian Prentice, he has a seat on a dozen boards…"

Within moments Celine was surrounded, exchanging greetings or introductions. Lady Harcourt and Nancy Rawlings were particularly pleasant to her and it wasn't long before they took their appointed seats at the big, gleaming table. The meeting began, the first business of the morning to officially welcome Celine to the board and confirm her non-executive directorship.

While the meeting was in progress Celine's face was a study in concentration. She had so much to learn! Public relations, dealing with *people* was a far cry from mind-boggling figures, financial reports, working hours, targets, suppliers, politics. When Guy spoke, which was often, he had everyone's total attention, including, Celine noted, her uncles'. Most of the men in the room were a good twenty years and more his senior, yet it was quite obvious they looked on him as their equal when it came to business; maybe in a few cases, distinctly their superior. Guy had such a mastery of his subject, of "common sense business principles" as Sir Gerald had used to call them, he was now at the top of his profession and still in his early thirties. Obviously the sky was the limit, Celine thought, which meant becoming chairman of Harcourt Langton. It was hard to look away from him. His voice and manner though always completely composed had such *authority* she had no difficulty seeing him as her grandfather's legitimate heir.

The packed agenda was drawing to a close when Guy brought up the subject of the Manola Bay project. He stood up from the table, went to a cabinet and picked up a pile of folders which he proceeded to distribute around the table.

"These are copies of the environmental impact study," he explained as the members began to open them up. "They weren't available up until now."

Clive's face flushed crimson. "Are you saying I've been withholding them?"

"*You* said that, Clive," Guy answered calmly.

"So where did you get it from?" Nolan, too, was red in the face.

"I have my sources, Nolan." The faintest of smiles touched Guy's cleanly-cut lips. "I know you were going to bring it to our attention. I've managed to do it a little earlier."

"Do you have something to tell us, Guy?" Sir Peter asked, his expression indicating he wanted to hear.

Guy resumed his seat. "First of all I'd like you all to read the report. I'll tell you now I'm opposed to the project in its present form. In my opinion, the whole development has to be scaled back. More safeguards have to be worked in. Especially in relation to waterways."

He continued to talk for about ten minutes with the confidence of the expert. Clive scowled and scowled but didn't interrupt. Nolan doodled frenetically. Guy concluded by saying he was confident if the project was pulled back to a more manageable scale and the measures he'd outlined adopted, they would win the support of the strong environmentalist lobby which now opposed the project. He then went on to draw the board's attention to a possible alternative site for the larger scale development.

"Cape Clarence, if anyone remembers. We bought it years ago. As far as I can recall some four hundred acres with a two kilometre oceanfront. Sir Gerald said at the time it was the ideal site for future tourist and residential resort development. I haven't as yet had the time to look it up, but the Manola Bay project jogged my memory."

"Ah, yes!" Sir Peter and one or two others began to recall the acquisition by the firm.

When Celine glanced up at her uncle she was alarmed to see the florid colour had drained right out of his face. "What is it, Uncle Clive?" She stood up automatically. "Aren't you well?"

Clive, in a slumped position, jerked upright. "Of course I'm well," he said icily.

"You certainly don't look it," Lady Muriel intervened, a certain reproof in her tone.

"I'm really not in need of your concern, Muriel."

"You're sure of that?" Lady Muriel asked on a dry note of challenge.

Nolan jumped up as if he meant to restrain his brother. "Perhaps we can bring the meeting to a close? This is our first meeting without Father. Naturally Clive and I are feeling it."

"Shouldn't we include Celine?"

"Of course, Celine," Nolan said hurriedly, not meeting Lady Muriel's fine, dark eyes.

Guy took charge. "That's okay with me." He looked around at the other board members who unanimously nodded their heads. So the meeting was concluded with the Manola Bay project still up in the air.

"What was that all about?" Celine overheard Lady Muriel ask of her grandson. Everyone had begun to disperse in a flurry of goodbyes.

"Something gave Clive *and* Nolan a nasty shock!" Guy's brilliant, black eyes were narrowed, as though trying to fathom what it was. "It seemed to coincide with the mention of the Cape Clarence site."

"You'd better look into it," Lady Muriel advised. "You don't suppose they could have possibly sold it off?"

"Not unless they were mad, and they're not! That land today would be worth a fortune."

"Perhaps Clive was just furious with you for undermining his pet project. Be *careful*, darling. You have an enemy there."

"Really? I never noticed." Guy gave a brief, ironic smile. "So where are you off to?"

"A luncheon in honour of Maggie Hoffman." Lady Muriel mentioned a well-known woman politician. "She's really a wonder! She has the respect of both sides of the house."

At this point Celine wandered over to say her own goodbyes.

"Lots to learn, Celine?" Lady Muriel smiled at her.

"So much! Did Guy tell you I wanted a job?"

Lady Muriel nodded. "Good for you, Celine. You have all you need to succeed. So when are you coming to have dinner with us? I'd ask Helena, of course, but she tells me she's not going out for a while. I have to say she sounded a whole lot better."

"She is, in a number of ways. Would Wednesday be too soon?"

"Wednesday would be fine. Shall we ask Guy to come?"

Was Lady Muriel trying to reconcile them? "He might say no."

Guy's answer was a fraction slow. Like a man put on the spot and too gracious to decline. "Not if Gran serves a good old-fashioned lamb roast," he managed smoothly.

"I'll be happy to see Maybelle does. Shall we say 7:00 p.m? Guy, you'll pick Celine up?"

"Whatever you say, Gran." He gave her a challenging stare not unlike her own. "If you've got some time tomorrow, Celine, I'd like to show you around the various departments. There have been lots of changes. I understand you can't start work immediately, but you can get to meet the staff."

"Not Miss Forgan Smythe." Celine smiled wryly. "I've already had the pleasure."

"Why don't we all pray for her to find a husband," Lady Muriel said.

CHAPTER SEVEN

WHEN Celine presented herself at the executive suite of offices, "the hub of the empire" as her grandfather had used to call them, all very grand and beautifully furnished, she found Guy in a decidedly crisp and businesslike mood. He rose with a smile that showed his beautiful, white teeth but the smile didn't reach the intense dark of his eyes. She felt it in her head and in her heart. Life was very much a shuffle, she thought. One step forward, two steps back. Nevertheless he took her on the grand tour, stopping in each department to introduce her to key personnel and occasionally the lowliest on the chain. Harcourt Langton employed architects, engineers, draughtsmen, surveyors, lawyers, accountants, administrators and their own public relations people.

Michael Langton, who had not shone academically but had been exceptionally good on the sports field, had been dumped in that department. As they reached his big, corner office, he jumped up from behind the desk and came around, grasping Celine's arms and kissing her yet again a bare inch from her mouth. Celine just stopped herself from wiping it off, something that was lost on Michael. He gestured them into chairs, sitting back on his desk, arms folded, his thickly lashed blue eyes sparkling with uncousinly admiration. Over the past few years he had filled out and Celine realised he would look *exactly* like his father in time. He was blond, handsome, sensual in the way Ashley was sensual.

"This is going to be *fun*, Ceci, having you on the premises."

"Fun? I don't think so, Michael," Guy said.

"I'm hoping to fill my time with work, Michael," Celine added with a pleasant smile.

"Really?" He looked amazed. "Some days I go potty looking for something to do."

"I'm sure we can fix that," Guy commented, looking deadly serious.

"Just joking, Guy." Michael grinned. His eyes travelled down Celine's slender body in a citrus yellow silk dress to her legs and elegantly shod feet.

Whatever Celine had expected, she hadn't expected this. In fact, she felt an element of shock. She remembered the time she had played the piano at the Beaumont when some of the men had looked at her as if she were a peach to be plucked. She didn't expect it of her cousin, but it was happening right in front of her eyes. Ashley had told her all the girls in Michael's department were madly in love with him, but there was something about him she found distinctly off-putting. Guy must have thought so, too, because his tall, lean body moved restively.

"Would you like me to show you around?" Michael suggested, sounding expansive. He was, after all, the chairman's son.

"We did stop to speak to a few people on the way in," Guy returned, slightly repressively.

"Good, good!" Michael boomed, reminiscent of his father. "So where are we going to put Ceci? There's room enough in here. I don't mind sharing. Quite the reverse!"

"You're too nice, Michael," Guy said in his smoothest voice. "We can fix Celine up with an office of her own."

"Not too far away. I get lonely," Michael said. "Let's do lunch one day, Ceci. I haven't had a chance to talk to you properly since you got back."

"Fine, Michael. I'll give you a call when I'm available."

"Still tickle the ivories?" he asked.

"That's certainly a cute way of putting it," Guy said.

"I don't practise as much as I should," Celine intervened without missing a beat.

"That must have been one hell of a job playing at that piano bar?" Michael grinned. "Gramps was *livid*! There are too many crazies running around out there. You're one beautiful girl!"

Celine felt a sharp stab of irritation. "I managed to survive. The Beaumont is a five-star hotel, Michael. I was well looked after. The job was short-lived in any case. I spent nearly all my time in P.R."

Something faintly malicious crept into Michael's bright, smiling expression. "It must have been tough on you leaving your boss. Wasn't there just a hint of romance?"

"No, Michael." Celine denied it gently, refusing to take the bait. She could have added Max was shortly to remarry but didn't think it was any of Michael's business.

"That's not the way I heard it!" Michael crowed, sounding much like Ashley. "I heard he came on pretty strong. A real womaniser!"

"Obviously a wild story," Guy said in a curt voice, and stood up, glancing at Celine in an indication she should do the same.

"Or that's all you're going to tell us, eh, Ceci?" Michael persisted. "You've lost a lot of that head-in-the-clouds, little-angel look. Why, you're downright sexy!"

"Surely that's an inappropriate remark?" Guy asked abruptly.

"Well, she *is*, Guy. Extremely sexy."

Something changed in Guy's face. Enough to give Michael pause. "You've made your point."

"Ceci knows I mean no offence."

"I really should be getting back to Grandma," Celine said, more to end a bad moment than anything else. "Apart from which, Guy, I'm taking up your valuable time."

"So how's dear old Gran?" Michael asked at once, not bothering to wait for an answer. "Say hello to her for me. Better yet I'll come over soon for a nice long chat."

"I'd wait a while, Michael," Celine advised. "Grandma is taking things very quietly at the present time."

"You're pulling my leg!" Michael rolled his eyes heavenwards. "Gran's escapades have set the whole town on its ears. Mum and Dad think she's gone bonkers!"

"Perhaps they like to look on the negative side of things," Guy said shortly. "No, I have an urgent appointment in about half an hour. We'd better go back upstairs, Celine."

"Take care of yourself, Ceci!" Michael called. "It's going to be a real pleasure having you around the place."

"To my way of thinking Michael ought to be turfed out of Harcourt Langton," Guy said, turning to face Celine at the lift. "All he's ever had going for him is muscles!"

Celine groaned. "Why on earth is he making a play for me?"

"It's called common lust," he told her bluntly.

"Thank you. Now I know."

They stepped into the lift, which was mercifully empty.

"I presume you want to stay with P.R.?" Guy asked, looking stern.

"You think Michael might be a problem?"

"I think you could handle it but you'd have to have an endless reserve of patience. It might be an idea if you spend time in each department in turn."

"Whatever you think, Guy. Ashley told me all the girls in Michael's department are in love with him."

Guy gave a laugh just the least bit menacing. "They've got better taste."

In his office he handed her a medium-sized padded bag, the kind issued by all post offices.

"What's this?" She looked down at it, noting it was addressed to Guy at the Harcourt Langton building, not the private box. "I'm supposed to open it?"

"It's of you, after all!"

"All right," she said faintly, disturbed by his tone. "What a one you are for mysteries!"

"What a one you are for deceptions."

"I don't buy that. Not at all." She drew out a couple of glossy photographs, staring down at them blankly. "What the heck is going on?"

"Something I might ask you."

She looked up into his brilliant black eyes. "Who took these and why would they send them to you?"

"Certainly not for the stamps," he said at his most sarcastic. "I suppose *some* people might think I still care."

"This is *wrong!*"

"You mean, there are *more*?"

"Please, Guy, I know nothing about this." Celine stared down at the photograph on top. It was an excellent one and she didn't stop to think she looked lovely. It showed her bent over Max, both hands clasped on his shoulders, hair cascading while she kissed his cheek. Max had his head thrown back, obviously enjoying it immensely. The second photograph showed them staring at one another soulfully, hands interlocked. To anyone who didn't know the situation it might have appeared they were lovers. Max was years older, overweight, but even the photographs revealed he was a man who was extremely attractive to women.

"This was taken the last night I was in Sydney," she tried to explain.

"I guessed that. It must have been a very pleasant dinner indeed."

"It was delightful!" Celine stared at him.

"My own feeling is he's too old for you and he's starting to go to fat."

Celine shook her head. "He looks heavier in the photographs. Guy, there's something I must tell you."

"*Don't. Please!*" He came around the side of his desk, wearing his most cynical expression. "I'm on my way. I told you I had an urgent appointment."

"This will only take a moment." She gripped his jacketed arm. "Max is remarrying."

"Of *course* he is!" Little brackets of scorn etched themselves into the sides of his beautiful mouth. "And you're the lucky woman?"

"Not at all!" She blinked. "Holly Lewis is."

"And who the hell is she?" he asked pleasantly.

Celine was amazed. "You *don't* know Holly Lewis?"

"That's right!" He sounded testy. "Is she a well-known person?"

"Why, she's possibly the finest interior decorator in the country."

Guy stared at her a moment longer, then he passed a hand across his eyes. "*That* Holly Lewis?"

"I was surprised when you said you didn't know her. It's a wonder you haven't met her at some time."

"I think I have." Guy unceremoniously dumped his disclaimer. "You're telling me Max Kenton is marrying Holly Lewis?"

"Isn't it splendid!" Celine's grey eyes lit up. "The moment Max told me I swooped on him with a kiss."

"I can't help thinking he didn't deserve the degree of ardour, but all right, I accept that."

Celine laughed for the first time, a sweet, engaging sound. "So you *should*! Naturally I'd enjoy your apology."

"You're going to get it!"

His movements were so swift and supple, so masterful in their intent, Celine had the sensation of losing her balance. She clutched at him while his hand encircled her chin. "Your mouth is the colour of watermelon," he murmured hypnotically, his thumb moving up to slide over it.

"You used to love it." Her heart shook with a desperate passion.

"So I did!" Time seemed to stop. He bent his head and took possession of her mouth in a kiss so brief, yet so deep and urgent, her body *flowed* towards his.

Oh, God, Celine thought. *I love you...love you...love you.*

"Remember where you are, Celine," he admonished her, his warm breath mingling with hers.

"You started this," she whispered. It was true his kiss had left her feeling so vulnerable she didn't quite know where she was.

"And I'm not following it up with a marriage proposal." He kissed her very quickly again, determined to make light of it.

"I don't expect you to." The expression in her misty grey eyes was as soft as a peace offering.

"I've been burned once. Twice is too much!"

"That sounds fair to me." She followed him a little breathlessly to the door. "Do you intend to remain a bachelor?"

He made another of those lightning turns. "Not unless I can't catch myself a rich dolly bird."

"But you're rich yourself."

"Well, not to *excess*! In any case, I'm talking nonsense. Come along, Celine. Business calls."

It was only as she was driving home Celine began to ponder in earnest who might have sent the photographs. Clearly they were intended to muddy her image in some way, so they were personal. She hadn't told a soul she was having dinner with Max at the hotel. Correction, she had told her grandmother when she had rung home during the day, but her grandmother was the last person in the world to have any involvement in such a sad little ploy. The photographs were the glossy variety taken by a professional. Was it possible, now she was a minor celebrity, she would be prey to this kind of thing? No one could deny it happened. But why send the photographs to Guy? That was as good a lead as anything to the sender's motive and identity.

Irresistibly she thought of Ashley. Ashley had a rather peculiar sense of humour. Neither was she to be trusted. She had learned that the hard way. But how could Ashley have known, let alone have found the time to set it up? She was being naive. All it would take was money and a phone call. She gave a little shiver of distaste. It wasn't nice to know she was the object of someone's malice.

Celine spent a quiet but rewarding fortnight keeping her grandmother company. Then on Helena's insistence she started work, not as an executive or anything like it, more an apprentice in training. Clive had told her from the beginning he was against the move, but Nolan greeted her the first morning albeit with no obvious sign of pleasure. Guy on the other hand told her he was delighted she intended to take her training seriously, then immediately threw her in the deep end, clearly expecting her to survive.

She was to spend a few months in each department in turn. If she'd hoped or expected to start with the glamour department, architecture, she was doomed to disappointment. The very first morning she went into accounting, where she was greeted in friendly fashion with no hint of deference. That suited Celine fine. She wanted to be treated just like any other employee. After the first week it was apparent her wish had been granted in spades.

She was swamped in the humdrum, but no one ever heard her complain. In fact she won some admiration for her cheerfulness and level of commitment. She sensed one of the girls was vaguely hostile to her, but she couldn't think why and she didn't dwell on it. She waded through mountains of invoices, checking and entering into the computer, which sometimes gave her a headache. She reconciled accounts, fielded telephone enquiries and took photocopies. In short, she did everything that was asked of her.

The only real problem was Michael. He took to lying

in wait for her, or more embarrassingly, coming down
to the accounts department pestering her for a lunch date.
Finally to get it over, Celine gave in. On the particular
Friday she was combing her hair and touching up her
lipstick in the rest room when the hostile girl, Marcy,
followed her in.

"So where are you off to?" she asked with more than
a hint of challenge. She had oddly coloured eyes, one
brown, one greenish brown.

"A lunch appointment," said Celine pleasantly, leaning towards the mirror, lipstick pencil in hand.

"With Michael?"

"As it happens. Why?" Celine was aware her voice
had cooled.

The strange eyes flashed. "No need to get off your
high horse. Michael and I had a thing going at one time.
Surely he told you? Of course I knew it wasn't going
anywhere. The rich stick to their own when it comes to
marriage."

Celine turned, giving the other young woman her full
attention. "Was it as serious as that?" Marcy was very
attractive in her fashion. Olive-skinned, brunette, her
eyes set at a provocative slant. Now she looked as though
she was fighting hard to hold in her jealousy and resentment.

"No, it *wasn't*. Michael was always out of reach, but
he knew where to take his pleasure."

So that explained the odd hostility, Celine thought.
She put her lipstick back in her bag and shut it. "I'm
sorry you've been hurt, Marcy, but this isn't any of my
business."

"I thought it might be since Guy Harcourt slipped
your net. You've turned our attention to Michael. He *is*
one sexy hunk!"

"He's also my cousin. *Family*."

"That's not the sort of vibes I'm getting."

"I have to tell you, Marcy, I don't care." The sooner I get out of here the better, Celine thought.

"Do you mind if I ask you a question?" Marcy persisted, following her to the door.

I must be crazy, Celine thought, but she relented. "Get on with it."

"My God, you must know how I feel!" Marcy cried emotionally. "There's *your* ex-fiancé romancing your cousin, Ashley."

There was a moment Celine thought all the blood had pumped away from her heart, leaving her icy cold and bereft. "I wasn't aware he was." She was astounded her voice remained calm.

"He *is*, dear." Marcy snorted. "Unlike *you*, apparently, I know a lot about it. Michael would tell me everything in bed. Besides, I caught them together in the executive lift of all places."

"Surely you shouldn't have been there," Celine retorted, sounding for the first time like the Langton heiress. "In any case, both of them are free agents. Why *exactly* are you telling me all this? You obviously aren't in any way kindly disposed to me."

"Maybe I'm more on your side than you think. Both of us, *losers*," Marcy explained. "If you're not romantically interested in Michael and I have to say you sound convincing, I have to warn you he's one persistent guy. He keeps at it and at it until he gets what he wants. The *chase* is everything with Michael. Once he's got you he very quickly tires."

"I'll be sure to remember." Celine was fighting hard to keep her composure. She put her hand on the doorknob.

"Don't let me stop you," Marcy called. "You wouldn't want to keep cousin Michael waiting."

The maître d' showed them to their table, one of the best in the riverside restaurant. Though Celine kept her eyes trained ahead, she couldn't help but be conscious of the interested gazes all around her. In fact the hum of chatter had abruptly subsided the moment they walked in. Langton was a prominent name in the city and as such the family was used to attracting curious and often envious eyes. Michael had her rather possessively by the elbow, shepherding her through the tables while continuing to wave expansively here and there. It was now well into November so Celine had dressed for the heat in finest white linen. The purely simple dress was oval-necked and sleeveless but she had added a wide belt worked with azure, emerald and turquoise adornments. Her handbag matched and she had strappy high-heeled sandals on her feet. Michael, with the build of a fullback, wore an expensive summer-weight suit in an attractive caramel shade and she realised they must have made an eye-catching couple. There was no family resemblance between them. She had inherited her grandfather's brilliant red-gold hair but her features and her light-limbed frame were inherited from her mother. Michael was all Langton, big, blond and handsome with the Langton ice-blue eyes. No one would have taken them for first cousins.

As soon as they were seated Michael ordered a bottle of chardonnay even though Celine shook her head. She had no intention of drinking in the middle of the day. In any case she had to go back to work. Mind and body in disarray, she gazed out the window at the river; deep and wide, a paddleboat was wending its way upstream, its decks filled with tourists and patrons who delighted in a long, leisurely seafood lunch. On the opposite bank, one of the oldest parts of the city, the great spreading poincianas were breaking out into sumptuous orange-red blossom, the radiant colour enhanced by the bright green of the delicately leafed fronds and the intense blue of the sky. *Everything*, the water, the trees, the paddleboat and the old white-washed buildings shimmered in the soft luminosity of the heat haze. It was a lovely, relaxing scene, but no way Celine could enjoy it. Could it *possibly* be true? Guy and Ashley? Michael would know, but she knew she could never bring herself to ask him.

"You're a little pale, Ceci," Michael said, blue eyes skimming over her face and breast. "Not that I don't adore your skin. It's like a baby's. Poreless, flawless. Makes you want to touch it." He picked up the menu. "Now, what are you going to have? We've got all afternoon."

"No we *haven't*, Michael," Celine roused herself to say emphatically, "I have to get back to work."

"You're joking, sweetie!" Michael scoffed.

"I'm not laughing. I'm working, Michael. Not playing at it. I just have the hour."

"Don't be absurd!" Michael looked at her narrowly, reminding Celine vividly of his sister Ashley. He leaned across the table, speaking confidentially. "What are you playing at, Ceci? Here you are looking like a dream and you're talking about going back to work. *Accounts*, for God's sake! If I didn't know you were so intelligent I'd say you needed your head read."

"Then there's nothing more to be said. I'll go now." Celine began to gather up her handbag and sunglasses.

"Ceci, sweetie! Have a care!" Michael very quickly put his hand over hers. "Just about everyone in the restaurant is staring at us. If you're serious, all right. I just didn't think you would be. Don't let's spoil what time we have.''

Celine just had to speak; to put the developing situation right.

"Michael, forgive me if it's out of order, but you're speaking as though we're on a *date*!"

"Aren't we?" Michael looked at her strangely. "I've always been attracted to you, Ceci. At the same time I've always been afraid of Guy."

Celine considered that in amazement. "Afraid of Guy? Guy isn't the sort of person to inspire fear. Admiration, respect, hero worship, if you like, but not fear. Grandfather was the one to do that."

"Let me put it another way," Michael said, staring at her. "I've always been in some awe of Guy. He may not be forbidding or anything like that—he has too much charm—but he's very formidable when he has to be. Guy's going to end up chairman of Harcourt Langton, don't you worry. It's going to kill Dad but it's going to happen. Sooner rather than later. Just between the two of us, Guy's our man. He's in another league from Dad. Why do you think Gramps gave him so much power? Even with Dad interim chairman, Guy is the real boss. Look how he got his way over the Manola Bay project."

"He did, but we all voted on it. What has this got to do with *us*, Michael?"

Michael started to trace patterns on the salmon-pink tablecloth. "You always belonged to Guy. I swear he fell in love with you when you were six years old. You captivated him then. The thing is, I fell in love with you, as well, only I didn't know it at the time. You were the very opposite of Ashley. You were always so sweet and sympathetic and gentle. Just to be with you was to stop hurting. Ashley's my sister and I guess I love her. I know

I'm supposed to, but she's very intolerant. She would never permit me to be her friend. I was always dumb, or a nuisance. You were her little pet. She loved you.''

"She doesn't now?" Celine asked with a saddened expression.

"You've grown up, Ceci. You don't run to Ashley anymore for comfort. You're a lot of things she isn't and it stings her to the quick. Besides, you're in competition."

"How? Ashley wants no part of Harcourt Langton."

"I mean *Guy*!" Michael groaned. "God, Ceci, she's mad for him. Surely you know?"

"Things might have been different if I had. I thought they were incompatible. No love lost between them."

"That's just Ashley's way," Michael assured her. "She's always wanted Guy and why not? Who the hell else is like him? The tragedy was he wanted you. Ashley had to accept it. These days it's a different matter. Guy didn't take being jilted too kindly. Frankly I don't think he'll ever forgive you. They're all being very polite, the Harcourts are like that, but I can tell you they were devastated for Guy. Why *did* you do it, Ceci? I would have thought the two of you meshed perfectly, like two pieces in a puzzle."

"I thought I wasn't woman enough for him, Michael."

"I don't believe it."

"It's true."

"Well you've lost him, sweetie," Michael said gently. "Ashley told me, not that I can accept every word she says, she's inclined to be a little careless with the truth, the two of them have been playing at a silly love-hate. That's apparently over. I suppose it's quite possible even while he loved you he was attracted to her. She's supposed to be very sexy.''

''She is as *you* are, Michael, but I have to tell you I look on you as *family*.''

''Well, I hope to change that, Ceci,'' Michael said with a faint swagger. ''There's no impediment to any relationship between us. We're close, sure, but we had different mothers.''

''Michael, what you're suggesting is quite out of the question,'' Celine said as kindly as she could. She felt sick with dismay, all appetite gone.

''I'm nothing if not persistent, Ceci,'' Michael warned her, lifting a hand and signalling a waiter. ''We'd better order if you've got so little time. Next time I'll make it dinner. I suggest the catch of the day. Red Emperor, with whatever you fancy, vegetables, salad. Are you absolutely sure you want to run away?''

''Very sure, Michael.'' It was something she was good at. Running away.

CHAPTER EIGHT

CONDITIONED to heartbreak from her earliest years, Celine had developed a number of defence mechanisms which she quickly put into place. Over the following weeks she came into contact with Guy many times but managed to throw up a protective shield which he instantly detected and accepted with stunning indifference. She has hurt him once. She will never do it again. Her behaviour has always been erratic. Who should know better than he?

She ached. She was sad and angry, but it was all kept beneath a surprisingly convincing show of serenity.

Guy and Ashley! When she wasn't working like an automaton her heart and mind recoiled in horror. Theirs had *always* been a strange relationship. The love-hate Ashley spoke off. Now her worst fears had been made known to her. Ashley would do anything to get Guy. Somehow her perfect knight had succumbed. Sexual attraction could strike anyone, anywhere, anytime. Nature's driving force.

Guy. Her Guy!

To counteract her depression she undertook an intensive crash course of study on the Harcourt Langton group of companies. There were many non-property interests including a travel company, a computer company, a TV station, country newspapers and a supermarket chain. The family still held a considerable stake in a major maritime business. She thought she might do well to consider further study, perhaps in commerce law. She had no intention of sitting back and letting the men take over the empire though she fully expected to hit her head on the glass ceiling.

The weeks slid by and Christmas was upon them. She had finished her stint in accounting, not without effecting some change. Some of her ideas were being considered for incorporation into the accounting package.

The next phase of her training was the legal department where she expected to sit in as an observer. All this was to happen in the New Year. Meanwhile she rode the seesaw of emotions. At least nobody knew about it. She battled the jagged edge of distress through many a long, sleepless night. To love was to lose. Life had taught her that.

A few days before Christmas, Clive sent for her. His secretary had become strangely respectful. In no time at all Celine was shown into the chairman's office, more like a room in an exclusive gentleman's club, now Aunt Imelda had had her way with it.

Her uncle waved her down, his nose buried in the pages of a thick file. Why was he so rude? she thought. Was he trying to put her in her place? If so, he had failed. "Now then." He looked up abruptly, his expression stern. "I wanted to talk to you about what's happening at Christmas. Mother won't give me a firm answer, indeed she won't give me an answer at all." His ice-blue eyes smouldered. "I want you both at Langfield for our traditional Christmas dinner. It would be unthinkable if you didn't come. The whole family will be gathered."

Celine had one word for that. Hallelujah! "I'll speak to Grandma, Uncle Clive," she answered diplomatically, knowing her grandmother's mind.

"Good girl." Clive Langton looked mollified. "House going ahead, is it?"

Celine nodded. "Building will start in the New Year.

Grandma is over the moon. Guy has designed her something special.''

"Oh, he's clever!" It came out like a jealous snarl. "Too clever by half! I'll never forgive him for crueling the Manola Bay project."

"In its original form, Uncle Clive. The board voted on it."

"Ah, yes, the board!" There was a hard edge of bitterness in Clive Langton's voice. "He put in a lot of work there."

"We're talking about the most successful and prominent business people in the city. It was a wise decision. It's been applauded in the press. Harcourt Langton must be seen to respect world heritage values."

"You mean, we allowed ourselves to be scared off!" Feelings of anger and resentment continued to hold sway. "With his sympathy for the greenies, Guy will probably ruin us."

Celine shook her head but remained silent.

"One day that young man will come a cropper," Clive warned. "He's after my seat. Don't think I don't know it. *My* father made Harcourt Langton what it is, not *his*. That grandmother of his encourages him in every way she can."

"Above all, so did Grandfather," Celine pointed out quietly. "Are you enjoying life at Langfield, Uncle Clive?"

It took an extreme effort but Clive Langton calmed down. "Imelda has fixed it up unbelievably well. She's got style. We thought you might spare us a painting as an act of goodwill. You've got so many."

"Certainly, Uncle Clive. I intend to offer each member of the family a painting. As you say, there are far too many and so *valuable*. I don't want to live in a fortress."

"In safe storage aren't they?" Clive boomed, knowing perfectly well they were at a Harcourt Langton facility. "Imelda and I thought one of the Sydney Nolans. The big central Australia landscape. It would look well in my study. Imelda's had it done over."

I can imagine, Celine thought. Imelda, too, had the reputation for going over the top. "Would you have a second choice, Uncle Clive?" Celine asked politely. "I'd like to give the Nolans to the State Art Gallery."

Clive, who had been looking majestic, took an eternity to speak. "You *what*?" he cried finally, his head cocked forward in horror and alarm.

"I think it's the way to go," Celine explained in a serious voice. "Great paintings are to be enjoyed by as many people as possible, don't you think?"

"Absolute lunacy!" Clive offered. "Father would turn in his grave. He acquired the collection for the family, not for every Tom, Dick and Harry!"

"Tom, Dick and Harry *will* represent a fair proportion of the crowd, but it's not going to stop me, Uncle Clive. You had to know sometime. We have so much we can afford to share. I won't give them *all* away. I'll keep a few and the rest of the family can take a painting each. The most significant, however, will go to the gallery. We could call it the Langton Bequest."

If Celine thought that would soften her uncle his expression became even more ferocious. "Celine," he said determinedly, "I really believe if you go through with this you ought to be committed."

"You won't hear the art gallery agreeing with that. I'm sorry if you're upset, Uncle Clive, but the collection is mine. It's just too important to hang in a *house*. Ever since I can remember, Grandfather had security people crawling all over the place. I used to think one would leap out and shoot me."

"If Father had known what you intended to do he would have said 'go ahead'!"

Celine stood up. "I'll speak to Grandma about Christmas dinner, Uncle Clive. Don't be disappointed if she decides not to come."

"I didn't excuse you, young lady!" Clive Langton lashed out.

Celine whirled. "I have a *name*, Uncle Clive. I wish you'd use it." Her gentle, elegant voice darkened with resentment.

"It's your youth and stupidity that numbs me. You sit so demurely, butter won't melt in your mouth, then you tell me you're going to give away the collection. Lunacy is the word, young lady. Lunacy! It suddenly occurs to me your father was a fool, as well."

"You mean a fool as in honest, brave, independent! Isn't your greed a bit vulgar?"

"Oh, my!" Clive leaned back in his chair. "So the little kitten knows how to spit and snarl."

"I'd have to learn, wouldn't I, with *my* family?"

"Then you're completely outclassed, my dear. We're *real* tigers."

"Without teeth beside Grandfather."

Clive Langton glared at her. "You may go now, Celine. I can't recall any other member of my family being so rude to me. It was a sorry day Father left you so much power. Clearly it's gone to your head."

"I'm sorry, Uncle Clive," Celine said quietly, "but if you're going to talk down to me this is what's going to happen."

On the other side of the door she literally ran into Guy. The shock was electric. He reached out and steadied her.

"Is the sky falling?" she asked wryly.

The expression on his handsome face was dark and formidable. "If it did, *your* family wouldn't be in the clear.'' He grasped her wrist. ''You might as well come with me.'' He advanced on the chairman's door.

''Mr. Harcourt, Mr. Harcourt!'' Miss Forgan Smythe jumped up from behind her desk, looking as though she was coming apart around the edges. ''Please let me ring through to Mr. Langton.''

But Guy was blazing mad. He ignored her, if he even saw her. ''Come on, Celine. You're a smart girl. You and I are going to talk to your uncle in private.'' Guy threw open the door and shut it firmly behind him.

Celine's last glimpse of her uncle's secretary was of an agonised woman wringing her hands. Fancy working for Uncle Clive, she thought faintly. No one could do that and remain in a mellow mood.

''See here, see here!'' Clive Langton often spoke this way. He staggered to his feet, spluttering his outrage. ''What the devil are you up to, Guy? What is Celine doing back when she was so anxious to leave?''

''Celine is a major shareholder in Harcourt Langton,'' Guy clipped. He spoke so forcibly Clive sat down heavily as though he had momentarily lost the power of his legs. ''Thank you, Guy. I'm well aware of that.''

''So you can't make a move without her. Or me.''

Clive laughed grimly. ''What is this? A consolidation of power. Could you *stand* another humiliation? Isn't Celine the little bolter?''

Celine was startled. ''What's all this about, Guy?''

''What do you think it's about, Clive?'' Anger flashed in Guy's brilliant, dark eyes.

''My dear boy, I've no idea!''

''Don't *dear boy* me!'' Guy generated so much rage and contempt, Clive's ice-blue eyes flickered.

''A term of affection, Guy,'' he said, clearing his throat. ''Something has obviously upset you.''

''Sit down, Celine.'' Guy looked at her. ''This may

take a while. Would you like to get Nolan here?'' He turned to Clive, who shrugged.

"Can't say I would. The fact is, Nolan's out to a meeting with Ian Brinkworth. They want to merge with us."

"Then forgive me for asking. Was Nolan the best person to send?"

Clive interpreted that as an insult. He flushed. "It's adding up, isn't it, Guy? *You* want to run Harcourt Langton."

"Not only want to run it, I am!" Guy announced without a moment's hesitation. "Harcourt Langton *needs* me, Clive, and you're going to step aside."

"Is there any possibility you might tell me, Guy, what's going on?" Celine asked.

He looked down at her. A ray of sunshine was touching her skin. It had the perfection of porcelain. "Remember a couple of board meetings ago when Clive had a sick turn?"

"Yes, I do!" Celine's grey eyes fled to her uncle, who seemed to be shrinking back in his chair. "We were talking about the Manola Bay project and how you could modify it to meet all environmental protection requirements. You spoke about an alternate site for the big development. Cape Clarence."

"God!" Clive writhed in his chair and covered his eyes.

"Exactly!" Guy agreed harshly. "Cape Clarence and the four hundred acres Sir Gerald bought more than twenty-five years ago. It took me a little while to unravel the complex set of manoeuvres you put in place, Clive, but at last I hit on the sole owners and partners in Nucleus Ltd. Clive and Nolan Langton."

A high flush had come to Clive's cheeks. "You'd do anything to discredit me."

"I've done nothing, Clive." Guy spoke in a terse

voice. "You did it all to yourselves, but *why*? It's unethical, illegal, it's against the interests of the board and ultimately the shareholders. How did you think you were going to get away with it?"

"We did, didn't we?" Clive had raised a sweat, which dotted his brow and under his eyes. "With *all* our property holdings why did you have to hit on Cape Clarence? It was one of our *forgotten* assets.'

"You don't have the necessary vision, Clive," Guy told him bluntly. "But even then you knew *one* day it was going to be extremely valuable. Haven't you got enough?"

"We have *now*!" Clive did his best to rally. "You wouldn't know what it was like, Father doling out money in drips and drabs. He liked to keep us tied to him. We thought he'd go on forever. That parcel of land was a little protection."

"You're going to give it back, Clive." Guy looked at the older man directly. "Harcourt Langton is not going to buy it back, you're going to hand it over."

"The hell we are!" Clive laughed shortly. "You're talking millions of dollars."

"Would you and Nolan prefer to be thrown out?"

"See here, Guy." Clive sounded genuinely shocked. "We're major shareholders. Our father with your grandfather started this great firm."

"Can you imagine what he would have said, Uncle Clive?" Celine's breath caught in her throat. "You and Uncle Nolan tried to rob *Grandfather*?"

"That's an exaggeration, Celine."

"I don't think so." She shook her head. "I know you've suffered, Uncle Clive. I suffered myself at Grandfather's hands, but what you've done is *stupid* as well as illegal. I agree with Guy. You have to right this wrong and do it immediately before anyone else finds out. Can you imagine the disgrace! Clive and Nolan Langton thrown off the board of Harcourt Langton. In effect, major shareholders robbing themselves.''

"You don't have any option, Clive,'' Guy summed it up. "Chalk it down as a hard lesson. We should really put this before the board but even Sir Gerald wouldn't have wished it.''

"It should have taken you a long, long time,'' Clive told Guy bitterly.

"What, following the paper chase or becoming chairman?''

"Both. I have to discuss this with Nolan.''

"I think I want to discuss it with Uncle Nolan myself,'' Celine said. "Don't think you can write me off as a Barbie doll. I have plans for Harcourt Langton myself.''

"And why not?'' Guy returned briskly. "I've always told you you had a good brain.''

"You did when nobody else seemed to care. Certainly not my family. It's even possible later in life I might qualify for the position of chairman.''

"So, let the good times roll!'' Some of the hard tension had left Guy's face.

"How do I know you two are going to keep your mouths shut?'' Clive was back to demanding.

"You don't know, Clive,'' said Guy, shrugging. "You're not hurting for money. You should retire. At any rate, this is the beginning and end of your little corrupt ventures.''

Clive Langton fought hard to cover his desperate humiliation. "Return of the land, my resignation as chairman, that will clear it?''

"We'll give you a call, Uncle Clive.''

"Thank you!'' Clive was shocked into saying.

Miss Forgan Smythe wasn't at her desk. It was possible she had gone off sick. "You were pretty impressive in there," Celine told Guy as they walked down the silent corridor.

"What was impressive was he fell into the trap."

Celine wondered if she had heard right. "You mean, you didn't *know*?"

"I'd have forced their resignations if I had. I was acting on my strong suspicions and a certain amount of evidence. Not enough, I'm afraid. They covered their tracks extremely well. I took a calculated risk, that's all."

"It could have misfired, you know."

"It didn't." He shrugged again.

"So you have every chance of being voted chairman when the six months are up?"

"Probably, if *you* don't work too hard." His black eyes glinted. "I've always known there was a brain behind the angelic face. How's Michael?"

"All right," Celine answered casually.

"The word is you two have become very close."

"We are close. We're cousins."

"The word is he might become something else?"

"I promise you, Guy, the word's wrong. I feel sorry for Michael."

"*Tell* me about it."

"Don't be sarcastic. Michael's not doing the things he ought to be doing."

"Darling, I've known *that* ever since he started."

Celine's delicate, winged brows knitted. "There's terror in having to succeed for Michael. All the help in the world couldn't get him through university. But he did shine on the sports field. He plays a marvellous game of golf and tennis."

"As do I." Guy sounded bored. "Are you suggesting we could make a fortune?"

Celine ignored the irony. "You have a very secure sense of yourself, Guy. You were born with it. There's never been a lot of pressure on the home front. Your mother and grandmother adore you. Michael has always known he's a disappointment. I have to admit it. We're a dysfunctional family. Michael has such a poor relationship with Uncle Clive just as Uncle Clive had such a bad relationship with Grandfather."

"A little more of this, Celine, and I'll go to sleep."

"It could even explain why Michael gets into so many meaningless relationships."

"Not a one of us who couldn't be saved by the love of a good woman!" Guy glanced down at her radiant head. "My own view is Michael is deliriously in love with you."

"Don't say that! I couldn't handle it."

"Yes, you do have problems in that department. You're quite right, Celine. Michael is hungry for love and affection. Intimacy with the right woman."

"There's no intimacy between us. Nothing like that!" She shivered delicately.

"Despite which he has a very nasty habit of kissing you on the mouth."

"He's a toucher."

"Then tell him to keep his hands and his mouth to himself."

"I already have." Celine stopped walking and looked up at him. *Her* Guy. Her one perfect love. She had broken the relationship and there was no way to mend it.

"Don't look at me like that," he said, his chiselled face going taut.

She sighed. Softly, sadly. If you loved someone why couldn't you tell them?

"You have the most beautiful eyes. It's like getting lost in a mist," he murmured.

Lost in *love*. The silence grew as did the extraordinary flow of sensuality.

"I have a mild objection to being made a fool of," he rasped.

She flushed. "No one could make a fool out of you, Guy."

"Not the *second* time."

She dipped her head, the lustrous waves and curls glinting every shade of gold and copper and red. "My God, Guy, I know I should have done things differently. I've had to live with my mistake."

"So don't let's make one more."

"That won't happen." She had driven him into the arms of Ashley. "Anyway, I was trying to speak to you about Michael."

"Why do I hate myself for not finding him interesting?" Guy began to walk on.

"We have a TV station, don't we?"

"It's in South Australia. Why, are you hoping to get on it?"

Celine caught him up, her head just coming to his shoulder. "For all you know they may be genuinely pleased to see me. It's Michael I'm thinking of. He has an encyclopedic knowledge of sports. It's his one great area of expertise. His biggest enthusiasm."

"I *know*. He's often given me a bad migraine."

"You could help him, Guy. Michael has no real place here. No sense of self-esteem. There are too many brilliant people."

"Well, definitely me," Guy agreed facetiously.

"Why don't we give him a chance as a sportscaster? Is that what they call them? He looks fabulous on TV. He has an attractive speaking voice. That should win over the women viewers."

"Actually half the female population as soon as they realise his wealth."

"Wealth hasn't made any of us happy."

"It should *help*. You're serious?"

"It's only just occurred to me. I'm concerned about Michael, Guy."

"Oh, he'll survive," Guy retorted philosophically. "If only you'd felt this bad about *me*."

"But you're over me." So why did this current always crackle between them?

"Is there any good reason why I shouldn't be?" he asked airily. "I can take all your little blows without flinching."

"*Blows*? What do you mean?"

"Come on! You've got a real knack for it. Just when I thought we might be able to pick up a few pieces you go cold on the idea. I can't spend all my time trying to fathom your emotional shifts."

"Especially not when you're looking in Ashley's direction."

As always the mention of Ashley affected him powerfully. "This business with Ashley," he said tersely. "It drives me *wild*!"

"It happens though, doesn't it?" she offered sadly.

"*What* happens?" He appeared to grind his perfect white teeth. "Oh, who the hell cares!" He spun on his heel. "I'm busy, Celine. I *used* to love you. I still want you to have a long and happy life, but for God's sake, leave *me* alone."

"We used to be able to communicate, Guy," she called after him. "We've been through so much together. You were *everything* to me. Almost a brother."

He walked back to her, holding a hand to his temple. "Is this one of life's profound statements? You thought of me as a *brother*?"

"I thought of you as every important person in my life. Mother, father, the brother I never had. The most *precious* person in the world!"

"Don't cry," he said, reaching out for her at the same time.

"*Guy*!" She rested her head against his breast, dizzy with her love for him.

"My God, isn't life a struggle," he said. "I'm so used to looking out for you I can't stop."

"Be my friend," she whispered. "I can't lose you."

"You've lost *something*," said Guy. "Maybe the ability to make a commitment." His hand stroked her hair. "The fear of a little girl persists through time. Your family offered you very little. We've always recognised that. Is that the reason for all the defensive shields?" Grasping a handful of her hair, he lifted her head.

He knew all about her defensive shields, but he didn't seem to know the reason. Suddenly she wanted terribly to tell him. His eyes rested so meltingly on her face. Velvet black, deep, exquisitely passionate. They raced her pulse even as they moved her to tears. Guy was her hero, her soul. She would never change.

"*Tell* me!" His urgency dazzled her. "You can plead so eloquently for everyone else."

Her lips parted. She longed to give him the answers he was so impatient for, only the doors of the executive lift opened and Ashley stepped out, long legs flashing.

She stopped in full flight as she caught sight of them, just managing to mask her expression. Her blond hair, almost white from a tropical sun, swung around her lightly tanned face, her blue eyes glittered like icefloes with an Arctic sun on them. They all knew one another so well it was apparent she had caught the mood of extreme emotional tension.

The moment, so crucial to Celine's interests, was utterly spoiled.

In the quiet, Ashley's light, arrogant voice resounded. "This is carrying things a bit far. Shouldn't you two be working?"

"*You* want to try it," Guy remarked as though he disliked her.

"No, thank you, darling!" She gave him a brilliant, triangular smile. "My one aim in life is to enjoy myself. You have to admit I know all the right things to do."

Ashley's eyes were drilling into Guy with such intensity Celine found their expression quite scary. "So how was Fiji?" she asked in an effort to normalise the atmosphere.

"Glorious, Ceci!" At last Ashley turned to her, seeing behind Celine's assumed calm. "You should've come with me instead of playing at this ridiculous 9 to 5. I had a lovely time. An absolute idyll. Still it's wonderful to see both your faces." There was a peculiar blaze at the centre of the icefloes. "Dad busy? I don't see that old witch, Forgan Smythe. We had an appointment for lunch."

"He hasn't anyone with him at the moment," Celine volunteered.

"You're a sweet little thing, aren't you?" Ashley said in a strange voice.

"When did you recognise it?" Guy asked.

"*Spiritual*, that's it!" Ashley continued as if she hadn't heard him. "A *bright* soul. You mightn't be a Langton at all."

"Are you in some sort of crisis, Ashley?" Guy continued, still in that subtle, attacking tone.

Ashley turned to him and laughed. "You're *amazing*, Guy! You know so many things." She might as well have added, *about me.*

"Yes, Ashley, I do," he replied sombrely. "If you'll both excuse me, I must be on my way."

"You're dropping in Christmas morning, aren't you, Guy?" Ashley sought to detain him, her hand on his sleeve. "Anyway, I'll be seeing you before then."

Not if I can help it, the severity of Guy's expression seemed to say. Was he fighting to overcome this unholy attraction? Celine thought. Ashley's overt sexuality would test any man.

"Do you want to walk with me, Celine?" he asked.

"I'd like to speak to Ceci for a moment, Guy, if you don't mind."

For a moment Celine thought he was going to challenge her, but he lifted a hand in a salute and walked on to the lift.

"An odd triangle, aren't we?" Ashley murmured when they were alone.

"*Triangle*?" I can't bear to believe it, Celine thought.

"Both of us in love with Guy." Ashley spoke so softly Celine could hardly hear her. "Guy plagued by the violence of his feeling for me. He really wants to love you, Ceci, only I keep getting in the way."

Celine felt a burst of anger and jealousy as old as time itself. "I don't think think he *likes* you, Ashley. That could be the problem."

"What's liking compared to desire?" Ashley gave her a steamy look. "I wouldn't have had this happen for the world!"

"If it's not too much to ask, *what's* happening?"

"Do I have to spell it out? God, Ceci!" she muttered.

"I don't care if you *shout* it. All this secrecy. The hints, the intrigue, the lies. Why must we endlessly shuffle around in the dark? If you love Guy and he loves you, what can I do about it?"

Ashley's eyes froze. "You can leave us alone, instead

of trying to get him back. But *no*! You're everywhere like some lingering perfume.''

Celine was startled. ''I think you overrate my power.''

''You *underrate* it.'' Ashley cut her off. ''You always did. I suppose that's a manifestation of your spirituality. You're so damned noble. Running off because you thought you weren't good enough for Guy! Who the hell else would have done that? When he called you a fool, Gramps had a point.''

''I think you and Gramps would have to accept some of the blame,'' Celine said with a hint of disgust. ''That was years ago anyway. I wasn't twenty. Not even a modern twenty. I was overprotected, over-isolated. Maybe that was why I kept trusting you. You put yourself into the role of big sister. You helped me fight out of the shadows, then you turned on me. It was Guy. When you told me so often how you disliked and mistrusted him, you wanted him with every fibre of your being.''

''Not only that, I intend to get him!'' Ashley's voice rose dramatically. ''I don't have any of your precious scruples, as you'll discover. I don't want to hurt you, Ceci. You must believe that. I love you. You're a far better person than I'll ever be. But we have this terrible conflict.''

''*You* have this terrible conflict, Ashley,'' Celine pointed out quietly. ''I'd be happy to see if I could find you a good counsellor. It's not the first time you've fallen in love with the wrong man.''

Affronted, Ashley grasped hard at her silver earring. It fell to the floor with a clatter and she was obliged to pick it up. ''You're talking affairs, Celine. Sex. I'm talking about a magnificent *obsession*! I can't remember the time when I didn't want Guy. He was the first excitement I ever had. He was fired into me. My demon lover. I used to fantasise about him endlessly. I still do.''

"Then that strikes me as extremely odd. Why would you fantasise about him when you've supposedly had the real thing?"

Ashley touched her blond hair, momentarily looking confused. "He's fighting it, Ceci. Surely you can see that? It's a classic example of a love-hate. Why are you so *blind*? Guy has to be in total control. That's one reason why he became engaged to you. You were such a sweet, compliant creature."

Celine clicked her tongue. "You really make me sound attractive. Why don't you add 'goofy' for good measure?"

"You were never stupid, Ceci. In many ways you were extremely bright. Just not about Guy."

"And you're the femme fatale?"

"That's how my mamma raised me!" Ashley answered flippantly. "She never wanted me to be a *brain*."

"Maybe that was her way of acknowledging you were never going to be a straight-A student."

Ashley laughed, reaching out to touch Celine's cheek. "Touché, Ceci. Don't let's fight. Fighting with you is the hardest part of all. We were so close. You mean more to me than my own family. You're closer than Michael."

"Poor Michael!" A few words could capture the essence of a life.

"And you want to watch your step there," Ashley advised, sounding, of all things, pious. "Michael fancies he's in love with you. Isn't that sick?"

"I see it as he's had precious little affection. If he could break away from the family, he might heal."

"Well, we are a terrible lot," Ashley admitted with a mirthless smile.

"You didn't know Max got engaged to Holly Lewis?" Celine slipped in so casually, Ashley answered on automatic.

"No, I didn't!"

"So that little business with the photographers didn't work."

Instantly Ashley's expression grew so uncharacteristically defensive it told Celine all she needed to know. "What photographs? What are we talking about?"

"The photographs of Max and me you sent to Guy."

Ashley arched her eyebrows high. "My dear Ceci, you're talking in riddles. I know nothing whatever about any photographs. I keep telling you you can expect that sort of thing now you're in the public eye, but you won't listen. Now, I have to pop in and collect Dad. You and Gran are coming to us Christmas Day?"

"I wouldn't count on it, Ashley."

Ashley threw her a stern, reproving look. "But we *are* counting on it. We've never missed having Christmas dinner before. We are family, you know."

"Sometimes I try to forget that," Celine said quietly, and turned away.

CHAPTER NINE

CELINE recalled with great vividness Christmas Day. Helena said from the moment she left she never intended to set foot on Langfield again and it appeared she meant it. These days Helena was acting more like a woman who had recovered from a long illness than a grieving widow. Even her mental and physical health was much improved. There was a brightness in her eyes, a sheen on her skin, a sense of purpose in her step. It was as though she had regained the good spirits and optimism of her youth.

"I'll be damned if I'm going over to Clive and Imelda," she told Celine when she broached the subject. "Not this year and maybe not ever. I want peace and tranquillity in my life. Not my overbearing, overpowering family. I resent what has been done to me and quite rightly. I've been turfed out of my own home. Not that I ever liked it much. I always expected Gerald's security people to come in and shoot me by mistake. I know you did, too."

"Could we ask them to call Christmas morning, Grandma?" Celine suggested. "They genuinely want to see us."

"That's the truly peculiar part. All right, darling, call them and ask them to pop in Christmas morning. That should do it. Make it fairly early. I've promised we'd stop over at Muriel's for a few minutes to say hello. I do so admire Muriel. I know you never knew this, the Harcourts would never put it about, but Gerald had quite a yen for Muriel in the old days. She was such a dynamic young woman. The very antithesis of me. Of course she loved Lew. A one-man woman was Muriel and he gave her such a happy life!'' Helena sighed.

''But this is extraordinary!'' Celine said, really meaning it.

''Oh, yes.'' Helena patted the collar of the lovely blue-and-white printed dress Celine had chosen for her. ''It was a big secret even from me, but I knew. I wasn't prepared to discuss it, that's all. Not that there was anything *to* discuss. The want was all on Gerald's side, the need to best Lew, who was his very best *friend*. Your grandfather, rest his soul, was a very strange man. The strangest man I've ever known and that includes Clive. Of course it would never have worked with Muriel. They would have *roared* at each other, possibly taken to each other with whips. Such strong-minded people! I was the little puppet Gerald could put back in its box. I'm sorry to say my mother taught me to defer to my husband in all things. A crime really. Don't *ever* do it. Now I'm my own woman and I love it. Does that sound too awful, darling?''

''It sounds honest, Grandma. And sad.''

''I spent too much time brooding. It was my own fault. I should have made a life for myself.''

''It's not too late, Grandma!'' Celine took her grandmother's hand, feeling the tight, loving response.

Christmas morning, ten o'clock on the dot, the family descended on them en masse, laden down with so many presents Celine thought they were really in need of a forklift. Ritual kisses and greetings were shared. This was only done once a year. They all sat in the large, airy living room while Helena, the recipient of the bulk of the gifts, examined each present in turn.

"This is splendid, Imelda," she said of a weighty sterling-silver tureen designed like a cabbage. "Polishing it will give me something to do."

"I'm glad you like it, Mother," Imelda said, glancing sideways to try to ascertain the exact expression on her mother-in-law's face.

"It's not too late to come to us, Mother." Clive did something he hadn't done in years. He spoke kindly.

"You can't be serious staying here, Mother," added Imelda, very festive in green slacks and a red blouse with an enormous bow. "Why, it isn't even your own home!"

"I was never more serious in my life, Imelda," Helena told her daughter-in-law pleasantly. "I thought I had my own home when I married, but it appears I was wrong."

"I hate you to say that, Mother." Clive sounded desperately hurt. "You haven't been thrown out onto the streets. Father meant you to be properly looked after by us. It was entirely your own decision to set up house elsewhere."

"People need their independence, Clive. As much when they're elderly as at any other time. Oh, thank you so much, Warren," she exclaimed as her youngest grandchild came forward to present his gift. "You painted this yourself?" Helena looked up with a smile.

"What it's supposed to represent God only knows!" Ashley mocked. *It* was a small acrylic on canvas, sensitively framed.

"I call it 'Solitude', Gran!" Warren put his arms around his grandmother's frail shoulders.

"That's certainly the mood!" Celine had moved forward to study the small painting. "You have talent, Warren,'' she said warmly. "You should take your painting more seriously.''

"Do you think so, Ceci?'' Warren blushed.

"Celine is not qualified to give advice,'' his mother said repressively from the sofa where she was huddled up with her husband Nolan, thick as thieves. "Warren has quite enough on his hands trying to pass his exams.''

"A lot of people can't paint!'' Celine looked down at the canvas again. Why was Aunt Dorothy such a domineering woman? If her intention was to make Warren resent her, she was doing a great job.

When Michael gave Celine her gift, a heavy gold necklace that looked like it might have been worn by Nefertiti, he hugged her to him tightly. "With my love! That was a brainwave of yours thinking I could get a job as a sportscaster. I've already put out a few feelers and the feedback has been promising.''

"I'm pleased for you, Michael.'' Gently Celine disengaged herself before some damage was done to her spine.

"Don't for the love of God say anything to Mum and Dad,'' he begged.

"I wouldn't dream of it!'' Celine replied with considerable fellow feeling. "I've already been shot down for suggesting Warren might take his painting more seriously.''

"Painting?'' Michael laughed derisively, almost an echo of Ashley's. "No one could cop an *artist* in the family.''

"When Grandfather was such a notable collector?''

"It was the money, wasn't it? Money was the big part.''

"You're wrong!'' Celine shook her head. "Grandfather loved his paintings.''

"If you say so, Ceci. I couldn't care less about any of them. I'd sooner have action shots of my favourite football players. You're the only one of us who's genuinely artistic. The Harcourts are the real art patrons. Family tradition and all that. Guy, the brilliant architect. You expect that sort of thing. As to that, Guy can draw exceedingly good faces. He did some marvellous sketches of you. Whatever happened to them?"

"They probably got pulped."

"Or he made one big fire!" Michael grinned. "God, jilting Guy has to be the most reckless thing you've ever done. Here, let me put the necklace on for you. It cost me a pretty penny I don't mind telling you."

"A box of handkerchiefs would have done fine." Celine held up the silken masses of her hair so he could secure the catch.

"And make me look mean? You deserve the best, Ceci," he said hotly.

"Don't start talking like that, Michael," she warned him.

"It's the little glass of sherry. The last time I had sherry I was four years old and sick under the table. Did I tell you you look wonderful?"

Celine walked towards a tall, gilt-framed mirror. "A couple of times." She was wearing a very pretty sheer silk dress in a swirl of colours from pink through to violet but the necklace, far too opulent for day wear, made her look as though she was all dressed up for a party at Buckingham Palace.

"That's terrific!" Michael held her by the shoulders.

"It does indeed make a very strong statement. Thank you very much, Michael. I shall treasure this gift from my cousin. Do you mind if I take it off now? It's too decorative for day wear."

"No, *please*, leave it on!" Michael made a grab for her right arm. "If anyone can wear jewellery, you can. You have perfect skin and no amount of dazzle could top your glorious hair." His voice trailed away as Ashley in a bright red shift dress with a scalloped neckline sauntered up to them.

"I insist on knowing how much you paid for that, Michael," she said, staring at the necklace. "It looks like a stage piece. Quite bizarre!"

"Ceci loves it!" Michael responded angrily. "Why do you have to spoil things, Ashley?"

"Listen to the boy!" Ashley crowed. "It's my rotten nature. I really mean, the piece is quite spectacular."

"Promise me you won't take it off, Ceci," Michael begged as though her decision was very important to him.

"Of course, Michael." Not for anything, at that moment with Ashley looking on, could she have disappointed him.

"Thanks, Ceci," he sighed.

"That boy's heading for trouble," Ashley muttered as Michael responded to a signal from his father. "Why don't you tell him he's being absurd?"

"I'm trying to be a little kinder than that, Ashley," Celine said. "This little…whatever it is…will pass with no encouragement."

Ashley's narrow, finely shaped mouth turned down. "He's always been a bit wacko about you. We're kind of an obsessive family. The hell is, everyone tends to love you and hate me."

"You're unhappy, Ashley. You lash out. That might be part of it."

"Do you ever say *anything* nasty?" Ashley smiled.

"I once hissed at a young punk who tried to steal my bag."

"I wish you were coming over, Ceci." Ashley sounded genuinely regretful.

"I can't leave Grandma."

"Why the hell not? Gran is dreary at the best of times."

"No, she *isn't*! She can be very funny."

"You'd have fooled me." Ashley shrugged. "So why not come over tonight? Stay the night. We have so much to catch up on and you'll love what Mamma has done to the house."

"I'll come soon, Ashley," Celine promised. "Not tonight."

"I bet you're going to the Harcourt's New Year's Eve party, Gran or not?"

"I've been invited." Celine met her cousin's ice-blue eyes.

"We've *all* been invited," Ashley mocked. "It's obligatory, don't you know. We're Harcourt Langton, after all, though that could change if our Guy has his way. Can't you see it at the front of the building in big, tall brass letters. The Harcourt Corporation?"

"He might like it, but I think we'll manage to keep the Langton alive."

Ashley's mood switches were amazing. "Sweet Ceci, you astonish me!" she said on a wave of laughter. "Have you any plans to see Guy today?"

"I expect I will for a short time," Celine answered casually. "Grandma traditionally sees Muriel and Eloise Christmas morning for a quick hello."

"Do you mind if I tag along after you?" Ashley asked. "I promise I'll leave after I give Guy his present."

"But you never give presents to the Harcourts, Ashley?"

Ashley thought a minute before she answered. "If one *starts* giving presents, where does it all end? I've never thought Muriel and Eloise liked me. I could be wrong. As for Guy! This year it's different. I really want to give him something he'll treasure."

"Are we talking an object of great rarity?" Celine asked more tartly than she intended.

"Wait and see." Ashley smiled.

It simply wasn't possible to make any further objection.

Eloise, a beautiful, retiring woman whose life had been blighted by the early tragic death of her husband, greeted them with open pleasure and no hint of surprise Ashley had tagged along.

Kisses were exchanged Euro-style; seasonal greetings.

"Muriel is waiting for us in the drawing room," Eloise told them with her gentle smile. As usual she was beautifully dressed, her taste as quietly elegant as Muriel's was dramatic. "Guy hasn't arrived yet. He's taken Greg Maitland to the airport. Greg's having Christmas dinner in Sydney with his parents."

In the gracious Harcourt drawing room with its soaring ceiling and grand dimensions Muriel sat enthroned like a queen before the splendid fireplace. The mantelpiece behind her was adorned with a fabulous decorative Christmas swag featuring dark evergreen foliage, gold and scarlet baubles, Christmas angels, bows and tassels and tiny, sumptuously wrapped presents tied with scarlet ribbons. It was a work of art and Celine exclaimed aloud.

"Guy's idea this year." Muriel beamed. "Doesn't it give such a festive look to the room?"

"Guy's *idea*, Eloise put in a lot of time getting it all

together.'' Muriel rose to greet them, giving Eloise a warm, loving look. ''Our house is always beautiful with Eloise in it. She arranged all the flowers, as well.'' She gestured around the room at the strikingly beautiful arrangements, all continuing the festive air.

Helena almost moaned. If only she'd had a daughter-in-law like Eloise! Muriel genuinely loved her like a daughter. The two women had lived together in perfect harmony since the Harcourts' double tragedy. It was true Muriel had wanted her daughter-in-law to remarry and pick up the shattered pieces of her life, but something vital in Eloise had died with her husband.

Helena looked at her lifelong friend Muriel with a little smile. Even in her mid-seventies Muriel's looks were dramatic. Today she wore a wondrous Middle Eastern type garment, obviously of her own design, with a necklace of gold links at her throat. Her presence had a *force* that was palpable. Muriel had passed it on to her grandson along with her glossy, crow-black hair and the brilliant midnight dark of the eyes.

''I bet you weren't expecting to see me, Lady Harcourt.'' Ashley gave her curious little crack of laughter.

''You're very welcome, Ashley, at any time,'' Muriel said graciously. As fibs went it was a great success, for the sophisticated Ashley blushed with pleasure.

Muriel saw them all comfortably seated, then almost on cue, Maybelline, the Harcourt housekeeper, wheeled in a trolley laden with the silver tea service, exquisite Spode china and a selection of mouth-watering little pastries and small cakes.

''A choice of teas.'' Muriel smiled, preparing to do the honours. ''Your favourite, Lapsang Souchong, Helena, dear, and a particularly fine quality Darjeeling.''

Ashley looked like she wanted to laugh. Tea wasn't her favourite beverage.

Afterwards presents were exchanged. A Hermès scarf somehow materialised for Ashley, who eyed it so intently it might well have been a bomb. Celine was rather embarrassed by Ashley's manner. Ashley wouldn't have come at all, only for *Guy*!

Celine's gift to Eloise was a small bronze head of a boy. It had reminded her of Guy the moment she laid eyes on it amid an array of small artworks in an antique shop. Eloise saw the resemblance, too, because she held it to her heart.

"This is truly beautiful, Celine," she said, her large, grey-green eyes misted over. "It might almost be Guy at the same age."

"That's what drew me to it." Celine didn't realise how revealing was her expression until Ashley gave another one of her ironic laughs.

"It's been difficult for you to get over Guy, hasn't it, Ceci?"

"Guy and Celine will always care about each other, Ashley," Eloise said quietly.

Celine's gifts included a Bally handbag and a beautiful gold lace vest which she thought she could team with her wide-legged evening trousers.

Guy arrived ten minutes later, like his mother and grandmother, betraying no hint of surprise at Ashley's unexpected appearance.

"Happy Christmas, darling!" she said boldly, handing him a richly gift-wrapped box.

"This is such a surprise, Ashley!" He took the box into his fine hands. "The first Christmas present I've ever had from you."

"And not the last! I've gone to considerable trouble choosing it." She gave him a brilliant smile.

There was a kind of wariness in Guy's expression. While they all watched he unwrapped the box, put the paper and trimmings down on a small table then lifted out a silver-gilt goblet Celine thought for one minute might have gone missing from a cathedral.

"This is really something, Ashley!" Guy looked down at her. "I'm only *asking*, mind you, is it a liturgical vessel?"

"Of course it's not!" Ashley said a touch anxiously. "What made you think of *that*?"

He shrugged. "It sprang to mind at first sight. I think those grapes and wheat ears mean something."

"I knew you'd love it." Ashley placed a beautifully manicured hand on his arm. "It's supposed to date from the eighteenth century."

"When my wits settle, I'll thank you," he said crisply. "I can't produce a similarly unique gift for you but you must allow me to find you something you can admire."

"I'd rather see *you* happy." She flashed him another of her brilliant smiles. "Now I really must go. Mamma will expect me home to lend a hand. I saw you looking at Celine's necklace, Guy, when you came in. It's fabulous, isn't it? Maybe a touch heavy. Ceci and Michael have certainly come a long way. I've never seen Michael so over the moon!"

"I'll walk you to the door, Ashley," Guy said.

"Lovely!" She looked up at him with lazy sensuality. "Have a wonderful day, everybody. It might be a touch gloomy for Gran and Ceci, but not even Michael could persuade them to come to us."

"What's all this talk of Michael?" Muriel asked in some astonishment as Guy escorted Ashley to her car.

Helena answered, putting it in polite terms. "Ashley can be very naughty when she wants to be. Michael has been a little in love with Celine since they were children. A puppy love sort of thing. My own theory is Celine was always so sweet to him when his sister was a little monster. Now Ashley's putting it about they're having a romance. It's all for effect."

If that's what it was, it was getting results, Celine thought. Guy's dark eyes had been locked on Michael's gift as soon as he'd entered the drawing room. He even looked as though he knew who had given it to her. *Why* had she promised Michael she would wear it all day? It was too heavy, too *gleaming*. It just could spoil things.

"I do wish you could stay and have Christmas dinner with us," Muriel was saying. "Ashley's right, in a way. It will be quiet for you."

Helena shook her head regretfully. "Thank you so much, Muriel, but I think I've given the family enough of a shock. They would be mortally offended if I declined their invitation and stayed here."

"Of course, my dear. Well, come along and see the dining room, anyway. Eloise has worked magic."

While the others moved into the dining room to admire the festive decorations and the table, Celine edged towards the French doors that led out onto the loggia and the blazing summer gardens beyond. She was a little ashamed of her action, but she was desperate to see how Guy and Ashley acted towards each other when they thought themselves alone. There was such a sense of confusion, even disbelief, mixed up with her feelings of loss and betrayal. Ashley could weave such a web of deceit. The most terrifying thing was she was often believed. How well she remembered the distraught weeks before she had broken off her engagement. Behind Ashley's counselling had been a sinister self-interest. Behind the smiling face, the dark shadows.

The rich, beguiling scent of the roses wafted to her nostrils. There were at least a hundred varieties in glorious display; hybrid tea roses, floribundas, old-fashioned roses, climbers trained over arches, the great double hedges of the pure white Iceberg leading down to the octagonal summer pavilion where Guy first told her he loved her.

He had meant it. *Then.* His eyes had held such intensity and passion she had lost herself in their dark spell.

Now Ashley and Guy were standing close together beside Ashley's brand new B.M.W. Even to someone not familiar with them, there was acute tension in their body language. It was like looking at lovers in the midst of a furious quarrel. Ashley was staring up into Guy's face, her blond hair lifting in the breeze and fanning across one cheek. She jerked it away and Celine caught her expression. It was *raw* with feeling. She wouldn't have believed it had she not seen it with her own eyes. Ashley who had given voice to a thousand denials was madly, terribly, in love with Guy. For a moment the compassionate Celine felt a great burst of pity. Ashley was in agony. Wanting to be loved, she must be finding Guy was having difficulty with the relationship.

Almost in a state of hypnosis, Celine watched as Guy turned away, his handsome face dark and stormy. Ashley stumbled after him, catching at his arm. Celine thought Ashley was crying. Ashley, her cousin. Ashley who had filled the role of big sister. The fact she was a traitor didn't strip away the old affection from Celine's tender heart. Ashley was far more vulnerable than Celine would ever have believed.

Was it possible Guy sought to humiliate her? He

wasn't normally callous, but, drawn to her against his will, did he deeply resent her compulsive hold on him? Was the rage all against himself? There was *something* peculiar about the intensity of his feeling. In her passion Ashley had flung up an arm, catching at Guy's head. He threw it off, yet with the strength of desperation Ashley succeeded in pulling his head down to her, rising on tiptoe to seize the exquisite warmth of his mouth.

Not even Guy was proof against such temptation, Celine thought. She turned away abruptly, trembling with shock. Ashley went after what she wanted just as their grandfather had. Both of them predatory people with remarkable needs.

Celine's joy in the beautiful day turned to ashes. For each of us comes the moment, she thought. The moment when we know we've lost our one chance at true happiness.

From close by she heard her grandmother asking to see the roses. Moments later she caught sight of the three ladies strolling contentedly down the famous Iceberg Walk. The flowering was prolific. Masses and masses of pure white roses, a spectacle beautiful enough to stop the heart with delight. It didn't seem unusual they had wandered off. Obviously it was intended she have a private moment with Guy.

From somewhere on the terrace she heard him call her name, then he appeared at the French doors. He still had a brooding expression on his marvellous face.

"Everything okay?" she forced herself to ask.

His sudden smile was like the sun breaking through clouds. "The girls are working in together. They've gone off to see the roses so we can be alone."

"That seems to be the idea. Enjoy seeing Ashley off?"

"My God! What a character she is. A real case!"

"You look tense."

"I assure you I wasn't before Ashley showed up with that chalice. Do you suppose she stole it?"

Celine shrugged. "It might be worth knowing where she got it from."

"And your necklace!" Guy said suavely. "Tell me about it. It looks like it might have been lifted from an Egyptian tomb."

"Michael and Ashley seem to have similar taste." Celine glanced down at the wide, glittering band.

"Indeed they have." Guy moved towards her. "They bring to mind Sir Gerald at his most flamboyant. Helena told me the other day she's going to have her diamond solitaire cut off."

"Well, I know who'll be there to catch it. Ashley adores it."

He smiled wryly. "I can't think why. Helena always disliked it but Sir Gerald insisted she wear it. Don't you think now we've all admired your necklace you could take it off?"

"Michael asked me, begged me really, to keep it on," she said a little shakily.

"I'm not sure I'm ready to listen to that. Since when have you obeyed Michael's every fond wish?"

That deep humming current of sexual energy was pulsing between them. "It seemed important to him." Celine advanced, conscious she was provoking him but unable to stop it.

"Let's try to get it off, shall we? It looks too heavy for your slender neck."

His determination was apparent so she lifted the masses of her hair and presented him with her pearly neck.

"Do I leave your gold chain or not?"

"Leave it," she said, easing out a ragged breath.

"It's unclear why you still wear it." He released the catch of the heavy gold necklace, unburdening her of its almost oppressive weight.

"In memory of the old magic," she heard herself saying. She let her hair fall once more around her shoulders, lifting her head and seeing them both reflected in a tall, giltwood mirror that stood atop a handsome console. They looked rather magical in the antique, silvery glass. Perfect foils. At the height of summer Guy's olive skin had a rich, golden sheen, hair, brows, brilliant eyes, a gleaming black. She looked almost ethereal in contrast, a gossamer creature with a long, graceful neck and slender arms. She had lived protected from the sun so her skin remained porcelain, her long, red-gold mane a blazing radiance.

That used to be us, she thought. Guy and Celine. Soon to be married. She made a little involuntary heartbroken sound, then, realising it, ducked her head.

"Regrets, Celine?" he asked, with his uncanny ability to read her mind.

"A few."

"All the days, the nights, the weeks, months and years you've been away from me," he said in a low, intense voice.

Tears formed in her cloud-soft grey eyes. One trailed down her cheek.

"You used to fit into my arms as though you *belonged*."

"I suppose I do still," she whispered.

"Except there's no happy ever after!" He moved behind her, encircling her willowy body with characteristic mastery. "I should have held you fast," he muttered. "I should have taken you, made you pregnant if I had to, instead of all this torment!''

Her senses were flooded with bittersweet nostalgia. Her head fell back irresistibly. Came to rest against his shoulder. Her tender mouth opened like a flower.

''What is it you're offering?'' he asked harshly. His hand moved, caressed her delicate breast.

The sensual arousal was so powerful she gasped. ''I can't bear the thought I've hurt you.''

''You'd do it again,'' he said tautly, yet covered her mouth with a kiss that betrayed a deep, silent hunger.

How could they solve this? It seemed impossible.

The New Year came in promising big things for Harcourt Langton. Approval had been granted by the Fiji government for an international tourist and residential development on one of their beautiful islands. Celine had already studied the project in detail; the executive summary, the financial report, and Guy's brilliant design plans. It was a major development on a spectacularly beautiful site.

Clive Langton had already announced to a stunned board he wouldn't be standing for the position of chairman at the end of his six-month stint which was drawing to a close. He had put it about he wanted to ease the workload, leaving some to speculate he might fear a heart attack. It was well known he suffered from high blood pressure. This left the way clear for Guy. The Cape Clarence parcel of land, once more a company asset, would be developed at some future time.

On a more modest level, Helena's new house was rapidly taking shape. While Celine was at work, Helena and her ever-faithful Goldie had taken to driving over every day to check on work in progress. Both women enjoyed themselves immensely with their innocent, newfound pleasures.

"I can't wait until the roof goes on," Helena told Celine cheerfully. "We'll have a little party."

Celine had deliberately missed the New Year party at Harcourt House. She felt miserable about it, she hated telling lies, but she'd invented a migraine. She had suffered migraines on and off throughout her life, so as an excuse it was plausible enough, except her decision did its own damage.

Guy became more mettlesome than ever. His natural wit found a devastating sharpness that sometimes took Celine right to the edge. In the following months his photograph appeared many times in the newspapers, in the business section and in the social pages. On two occasions he was photographed with the same brunette, a partner in a public relations firm; another two had him with an incredibly glamorous-looking Ashley at his side. Celine well remembered the particular functions. She had been invited to both and attended for a very short time, dodging Guy, her family, and the photographers all the while.

True to her promise Helena gave a little party for the workmen when the house was finished. She stayed to sip a glass of champagne and afterwards Celine drove her home. Guy had been invited as a matter of course but at the last moment he had been called away to confer with their senior engineer on an onsite problem. Traffic had held Celine up so she didn't get to see as much as she wanted to, so Helena gave her a set of keys to look over the house at her leisure the following afternoon.

Her first thought was Guy had created a grand feeling in a compact space. Helena had wanted a "small" house, or what she considered small, which was a lot of house

to most people. Guy had come up with a masterpiece of
modern design, yet classical in its symmetry and without
the corridors Helena had hated at Langfield. The master
bedroom, library, living and dining rooms were aligned
along the length of the lot to take advantage of the view
of the river and the parkland on the opposite bank filled
with towering blue gums and acacias that in winter
turned the natural reserve into a soft golden glory.

Celine wandered around the silent rooms, feeling
Guy's presence beside her. How well she knew and
loved his great gift. Late afternoon sunlight slanted in
through the floor-to-ceiling glass doors that led from the
main rooms onto the spacious rear terrace. She unlocked
one door and walked out, moving dreamily across the
thick, springy grass. Six-foot-high fences in white-
rendered brick and wrought iron divided the house from
its neighbours on both sides. This was a long established
area. Her grandmother's house was actually built on
what was once the tennis court and part of the garden of
the house to the left. The wrought iron on both sides was
ablaze with thick bracts of the showy pink bougainvillea.
At the bottom of the garden banks of blue and white
hydrangea continued to bloom, sheltered to one side by
a massive jacaranda that at Christmas had borne pink
flowers instead of the familiar lavender-blue. Her grandmother had already engaged a well-known designer re-
nowned for her ''romantic'' gardens to draw up a plan.
There was to be a ''white'' garden, a scented garden,
and a sitting arrangement down by the river, as silver as
a smoked mirror with the rays of the sun on it. It was a
beautiful, peaceful spot, the house a delight after the for-
tresslike grandeur and opulence of Langfield.

She had just reached the open doorway leading in to
what was to be the master bedroom when she was ar-

rested by the sound of footsteps coming through the house. She stood poised like a fawn, nerve endings tense, until a man came into view and she looked straight into Guy's brilliant eyes.

"Hello," she said brightly, except her heart was hammering and her blood was shooting sparks.

He didn't answer for a moment, just staring at her, half in and half out of the sunlight. "Where have you been hiding all this time?" He started towards her, his blazing vitality never more apparent.

She caught her lower lip between her teeth. She felt trapped, yet savouring a fierce happiness, the physical exhilaration of being alone with him. "I've been busy, Guy," she evaded, when she was filled with torrents of words and emotions and no way to express them. "I thought you wanted me to take my job seriously?"

His beautiful mouth twitched. "Not to the extent you show the rest of us up. I thought I'd take the opportunity to look over the house. I'm sorry I missed Helena's little party."

"She understands. Did you manage to solve the problem?"

A frown appeared between his brows, a look of determination. "We're working on it. There are a lot of hazards in construction."

"Yes." Celine looked away. No one would know better than Guy, who had lost his father. "The house is marvellous," she told him, trying to will the tumult inside of her to die down. "I love it. So does Grandma."

"It must seem like a playhouse after Langfield." He gave a lazy smile.

"That's exactly what Grandma wants. Even entering the front door one feels joyful."

"No higher praise!" Guy glanced out at the rear terrace which he had designed as an outdoor living room with tall pillars supporting the sky-lit roof. "What it really needs out here is a reflecting pool running the length of the living, dining rooms. Helena would enjoy it. I've overscaled the windows and doorways, as you can see. It adds to the feeling of spaciousness. Helena wouldn't have found it as easy as she thinks coming down to normal scale."

"She's wonderfully happy about everything, Guy. She can't wait to move in."

"So, how long are you two going to stay together?" he asked, turning a searing gaze on her. "Until some man with an exceptionally high degree of commitment sweeps you off your feet."

"*You* did." Once said there was no way to call the words back.

"And look where it got me." Immediately Guy's expression was back to taunting awareness. "Do you still wear my ring? May I see it?"

"I'm *not* wearing it, you might as well know!" She stepped back very quickly so the full blaze of the setting sun engulfed her. It radiated light from her body and turned her hair into a fiery cloud.

"God, Celine," he murmured feelingly, "seeing you now is like witnessing the sudden visit of an angel. Is it any wonder you send shivers down my spine?"

He sounded as though he really meant it but then she knew her physical beauty had always moved him. She, his bright angel. Ashley, his torment.

"It's my colouring," she managed to say.

He shrugged as though the brief moment had passed. "Well, Titian hair *is* a mark of extraordinary beauty." He reached out idly and brushed away a cobweb that had already formed on the exterior wall. "I ran into Michael before I left. He's all excited about the weekend."

"Why, what's on?" Now he wasn't about to touch her, the hammering of her heart slowed.

"Aren't you two going out on his boat? Cruising the islands?"

"Of course I'm not!" She made the mental note to tell Michael to stop making things up.

"You really should tell Michael," Guy said, sounding cynical.

"Or maybe Michael should tell me."

"Surely you're not saying he was *lying*?"

Celine hesitated. "What Michael *wants* to happen, he convinces himself is true."

"That's definitely *Ashley*," Guy said with some fervour. "Let's face it, some of your family are quite odd."

Her grey eyes darkened. "We *all* do strange things, Guy. Even *you*!"

"Mention one," he challenged her bluntly. "*What* strange thing, Celine?"

She thought only of *one*. "You have a very curious relationship with Ashley."

Even the sound of her name made his lean body tense. "Would that have anything to do with *you*?" he asked coldly.

"I have to leave now, Guy." She felt ragged with emotion, close to tears. "I'm taking Grandma and Goldie to the ballet tonight. It's the first time Grandma has been out."

"I won't keep you." She heard the terseness in his voice.

"Goodbye, then." She took a deep breath and went to move past him, her creamy skin pale.

He grasped her arm, staring down into her face. "Do

you *still* wear my ring?'' His question rang with challenge.

She felt her emotional control slip from her. ''What do you think I am, a masochist?''

He raised his black brows. ''I suppose you could be. I hadn't figured it from that angle. Weren't *you* the one to inflict pain?''

''For which you will never forgive me until hell freezes over.''

''So there it is!'' he agreed. ''I have to admit it went deep as you might discover if you ever allow yourself to love.''

''I *loved* you!'' She lifted her shimmering eyes.

''Extraordinary!'' It came out as total disbelief. He lifted his hand to her throat. She was wearing a sunflower-yellow silk shirtdress with several strings of necklaces around her neck. He wound his fingers through the multicoloured swirls until he isolated the gold chain that held his ring.

''Don't do this to me, Guy!'' Beset by emotion, Celine tried to break away, only he compelled her back against the wall.

''Why do *you* do *this*?'' he countered in an intense voice. He let the exquisite ring come to rest in the palm of his hand. ''You must wear it every day of your life. I see the gold chain all the time. *My* ring nestling between your breasts. It doesn't make sense.''

''It makes sense to me. You gave it to me. It belongs to me. Do you want it back?''

He grasped a handful of her hair, making her look up at him. ''If I said I wanted *you* back, what would you say?''

Her mouth trembled. ''I'd say it couldn't work.'' There was sadness in her voice, deep and constant.

"Tell me *why*?" he demanded in fierce frustration. "Stop struggling, Celine. I don't want to hurt you. I want to understand. What *is* it you can't tell me?"

She tried to turn her head away. "It's complex. You know that."

"I know you're still the lost child who can't find her way. Too much love means too much pain. You *did* love me, didn't you? I couldn't have mistaken it. It shone out of your eyes. How can so much love be lost? How could it have ended like that? *Tell* me. I can't bear not to know." His voice resonated with the emotions that burned in him.

She looked up at him directly. "I loved you, Guy, far more than you will ever know."

"And just to prove it, you fled me, without words, without an explanation. Just some strange gibberish, half hysteria, I was supposed to accept?"

Frantically she shook her head. "So many factors went into my decision, Guy. The way I was brought up. I was too young, too vulnerable, too full of private doubts."

"Then why the hell haven't you overcome them?" Goaded beyond endurance, he gave in to the overwhelming impulse to shake her.

She seemed to slump against him and he stopped. "Oh, Guy, *don't*! You accuse me of fleeing you, but what was your truth? What is it now?"

His answer was stark and immediate. He lifted her head, his fingers hard along her jawbone, crushing her mouth beneath his just as he crushed her resistance.

"I'll never be free of you, *never*!" he muttered, his mouth covering every inch of her face and throat. "Sick of you. Sick with you. Sick of the long, lonely nights. The whole wretched business." His hands smoothed her body urgently, her breasts, inciting her flesh. He had touched her like that once before. Her recollection was vivid, timeless in its power. It had stayed with her every day, the angry ecstasy, her sensation of utter defence-lessness.

"You were too innocent to take *then*." Guy gave voice to a restraint that had tested him. "But you're a woman now."

Celine felt the great wave of desire coming for her, deep yet towering. She let him slip the buttons of her dress, cup her breast in a bra so thin it might have been a second skin.

"*Guy!*" She was seduced into a long, trembling sigh.

He stared down into her upflung face, her full, sensitive mouth faintly swollen from the violence of his kisses. "I don't know what's worse," he raged, "being with you, or being without you!" Yet the touch of his hand, the manipulation of her tightly furled nipple, was delicately, *exquisitely*, strong and arousing. She felt the pull of it at her body's core.

He continued to excite her until she had a sensation of falling and locked her hands behind his neck. Their bodies were crushed together as though he sought to make them one. The flame of love in her heart rose high. She had been betrayed and inarticulate those years ago, she had to speak now.

Celine threw back her head, thinking the expression in her eyes mirrored the love in her soul. "*Please*, Guy!" She was pleading to overcome her doubts and anxieties, only he took it as a familiar manifestation of withdrawal.

"Don't *stop* me," he gritted, his handsome face full of a terrible frustration. "I just might strangle you. You deserve it."

"No—*no!*" She covered his mouth with the pearly

tips of her fingers. "I want to tell you how I feel. How I felt *then*."

"A miracle!" He laughed bitterly, extraordinarily on fire.

"Please listen, Guy. I couldn't properly express my love, my terrible self-doubts."

"You're telling *me*?" The midnight eyes were brilliant with remembered pain and humiliation. "There ought to be a law against women being able to do so much damage."

"I'm so sorry," she murmured, broken-heartedly. "How long do I have to pay for it?"

Abruptly his hands caught her face, cupping it, a certain pressure in his grip. "Never leave me," he said.

She was stunned by his words, the burning look in his eyes. "Guy?"

"You heard me," he said tautly. "I can't really say I love you, although I've loved you for most of your life. I know the bitter taste of rejection. It's still in my mouth. But things are a little different now. I've divined your secret. I'm prepared to live with it."

"*Secret*?" Her eyes glistened as though he had stabbed her to the heart.

"Celine, don't let's pretend anymore," he groaned. "You're terrified of being loved. You're terrified of returning it. It's a reaction to your childhood tragedy. You've carried the terror since you were six years old. You came closest to loving me but I wanted you totally. Body and soul. You couldn't handle any of it. You ran away."

"It wasn't as simple as that," Celine said in a low voice. "I admit to bouts of panic, a fear of being dominated in our relationship…"

"Is there any other man you've been drawn to?" Ruthlessly he cut her off.

"No." She shook her head. She hadn't even toyed with the idea.

"So you're still a virgin?"

"And if I *am*? Surely that's not a scandal?"

"It could mean you can't conceive of loving."

"I love you," she said very quietly.

His lean body went very still. "You just could go to hell for lying."

"I'm *not*!"

"Prove it. Marry me. It's up to you. But, lady, never run away from me again."

She shivered, knowing she was approaching a subject fraught with danger, but one that had to be addressed. "And what about Ashley?"

Convulsively he threw her off. "I *detest* Ashley," he said, white teeth gritted. "I never liked her when we were children. Now I positively loathe her."

That could well be true. "Is it possible that you also *desire* her?" Celine asked, just a little afraid of him, as though she had brought out the *wildness* beneath the so-civilised veneer.

For answer he paced halfway across the room, putting her in mind of a highly strung racehorse full of power and recklessness. "Steady," he was saying to himself. "Steady." He swung on her, his polished skin sheened with the heat of their love-making. "I desire Ashley like the proverbial hole in the head," he said in his most cutting voice. "You're *amazing*, Celine, you really are. A few minutes ago I was mad to have *you*. Mad. Enraged, obsessed. Nobody else can do it to me. And you're talking *Ashley*?"

Wretchedly she persisted. "We must face this, Guy. She loves you."

He came right up to her, his height and splendid physical fitness never more accentuated. "Celine, listen *hard*. Ashley believes, like your grandfather did, they've only got to want a thing badly enough and it's theirs. Determination is the thing. I saw it time and time again. Determination and some kind of malignant desire to take something of value from someone close to them. It may seem unlikely to you now, but *your* grandfather got up to every strategy possible to try to break up my grandparents' engagement. It may shock you, but it's true. Delve any deeper and we'll open up a Pandora's box. I know your loyalties go deep, at least to *Ashley*, certainly not *me*, but how can any man deal with a woman like that? She spends her time fantasising, romanticising, inventing all kinds of crazy scenarios. She really ought to write books. Hell!" He looked away, his expression plagued. "Listen to me trying to explain something to someone who can't or won't listen. Ashley is your blood, but she's not your friend. I've warned you before."

"And I really did listen, Guy," she protested.

"Rubbish!" he said deliberately. "You're far more prepared to believe Ashley than you'd ever believe me. I suppose that's the way of it with liars. They score far too many victories. It happens every day."

"I'm sure of it!" Celine agreed. "But, Guy, I saw you both Christmas morning, when you walked Ashley to her car."

"Ah, the new B.M.W. That should make her more dangerous. Ashley is the last woman to put in a high-powered car."

"You can't have been arguing fiercely about *that*?"

"No, her new car didn't make me blazing mad," he returned shortly.

"She kissed you."

"Shock, horror! How could you have known? Were you *spying* on us, Celine?"

She flushed at his look of open contempt, the colour staining her porcelain skin. "My only excuse is, since I've been home, a number of people have told me you and Ashley are having a relationship."

"Who are these people, Celine? If you tell me Ashley, it's likely I'll need a straitjacket."

"Ashley was only one of them."

His striking face registered disdain. "Why did I have the feeling she was? So that condemns me, does it? Honestly, Ashley's a real snake. If she were a man she'd get one where it hurts and that would be the end of it, but a man's got lots of problems with women. Especially ones who live to stir up trouble. I suppose in your simple-mindedness you didn't consider it might be to their advantage to make me the prime suspect?"

Celine shook her aching head. "Guy, the whole issue has kept me awake at nights."

"That's okay. I don't sleep that well, either."

"It wasn't *impossible*?"

"Sure. I kept telling Ashley to get lost, but she was certain that meant I loved her. Actually she's not the only one in your family who's crazy."

"Isn't that the truth!" Celine agreed miserably. "So you *deny* any relationship with her?"

His eyes flashed a deeply felt resentment. "You stand there accusing me like a solemn *child*. Who needs it? You're a woman now. When are you going to put faith in your own judgment? I'm not going to spend my time trying to clear my name. Of what, for God's sake? Your

cousin Ashley has always been eaten up with jealousy.
I remember, if you don't, how she always tried to di-
minish your pleasure in anything. Some little snide comment followed by her familiar laugh. I refuse point-blank
to tolerate your mistrust when one of *your* relatives needs
intensive psychiatric help. You've only seen me gentle
with you up until now. Maybe that's hindered your development. But get *this*. I want you now and I'm going
to have you. Think of it as shock therapy. Now run away
and tell Ashley. That should bring on some loopy reaction.''

CHAPTER TEN

IT WAS mid-afternoon Saturday when Ashley decided to visit them, hard on the heels of Michael, who found it difficult to accept Celine didn't want to go out with him on the boat.

"No romancing you, Ceci," he promised her. "I'll keep my hands to myself, right?"

"Why did you tell Guy I was going out with you this weekend?" she challenged him directly.

Michael shrugged. "So I could get back at him a little. Guy's got everything. Looks, brains, charisma. Just tell me he hasn't got *you*?"

Celine shook her head. "I can't do that, Michael."

"But you rejected him?" Michael frowned, concentrating intently on her. She was wearing a long, jersey, slip dress the colour of Parma violets that turned her grey eyes iridescent.

"*Never*, Michael. I allowed myself to be *frightened* off."

"Does this involve my sister in some way?" Michael looked a little shaken.

"You know Ashley better than I do."

"Well, she's always been your rival," Michael said dully. "I can't change your mind to come with me?"

Celine strolled with him to the veranda, gently touching his arm. "I'm always your friend, Michael, but you must get on with your life. One day soon you'll find the right woman, then you'll be amazed you thought of me."

"I don't think so, Ceci." Michael put his arm around

her willowy body and gave her an expansive hug. "There's never going to be anyone like you. By the way, I've taken a step nearer to my television career. I've been asked to do a mock-up."

"When's this?" Celine looked up, warm lights in her eyes.

"End of next week. Friday. You're the only one who knows."

"Congratulations!" She gazed at him with open pleasure. "I think this could be the start of a whole new life."

"And if it is, I have you to thank." Michael couldn't bear not to kiss her cheek, savouring the scent of her skin. "I'm not looking forward to telling Dad."

"It's your life, Michael. Time to get involved in something you care about. Time to go after that worthwhile woman. They're out there. Just remember they have certain expectations."

"I can make a commitment, you know," Michael said. "I just want someone to *need* me. Not the money and so forth."

"Then nurture the right woman. You'll find someone special."

"What a tragedy you're my cousin," he said dryly, walking down the steps to his car.

"Yes, Michael," Celine called softly. "We're very, very close."

She waved him off, hoping her words and her attitude had finally sunk in. With the promise of a new job where he could actually perform well, Michael might see life altogether differently. Not that he wouldn't have a battle royal with his father. Celine could see where she would get the blame. It was unlikely she would ever have a good relationship with most of her family but that's the way it was.

Thirty minutes later Ashley arrived, a spectacle witnessed by Goldie. Celine and her grandmother were in the comfortable family room going through swatches of fabrics to pick out what they most liked for sofas, curtains and bedspreads for the new house. It was a pleasant and absorbing task and when Goldie tapped on the door, both women gave a little start.

"Yes, Goldie?" Helena looked up.

"Ashley's arrived in her plush new car. I clocked her at one hundred miles per hour through the front gate. It's a mercy it was open."

"She does drive too fast," Helena said worriedly. "Tell her to come through, would you, Goldie?"

Sprightly Goldie nodded laconically. "I think she's found something important to talk about, maybe."

Ashley made quick work of visiting her grandmother.

"Have a good time last night, Gran?" she asked, giving Helena a quick peck on the cheek. "Ballet's not my scene."

"Too many parties are not a good idea," Helena retorted. "Michael told us it broke up around 3:00 a.m.?"

"So?" Ashley shrugged. "Life's too short not to make the most of it. Are you coming over for an hour, Celine?" she demanded. "You promised."

"You mean, Langfield?" Celine felt an involuntary clutch of dismay.

"Where else? Everyone is agreed Mamma has made a marvellous job of the place," she added blithely, ignoring her grandmother's feelings on the matter.

"As long as you can live with it, Ashley," Helena responded tartly.

"No offence, Gran." Ashley gave her mocking smile.

Like Celine, she was dressed for the heat in a sleeveless blue dress as light as a zephyr. "Sure you won't come with us?"

"I didn't really know I'd received an invitation?"

"Do family need that?"

"Not a one of us should forget our manners."

"What happened about Michael?" Ashley glanced away from her grandmother to ask. "I thought he was supposed to be taking you out on the boat?"

"That doesn't ring too true, Ashley." Helena sat back in her chair, frowning. "If that were the case, why are *you* here?"

"Oh, I thought it was possible Celine mightn't go. She's still carrying the torch for Guy, aren't you, Ceci?"

"I could have sworn you were, too!" Helena looked at her grand-daughter coolly.

"Correct, Gran!" Ashley gave her crack of laughter. "Only this time I have a chance."

"Why don't we go, Ashley?" Celine asked, not wanting to further upset their grandmother's pleasant afternoon. These days Helena wasn't keeping her opinions under lock and key.

"I won't keep her long, Gran," Ashley promised, picking up a swatch of Colefax & Fowler silk taffeta in various colourways and putting it down without comment. "An hour or two. It's Carla Freeman's engagement party tonight. I have to look in. Guy might turn up. Strange you didn't get an invitation, Ceci. Carla used to be very fond of you."

"Maybe you put it about Celine doesn't go where Guy's invited?" Helena said with a crispness that appeared to stagger Ashley.

"*What* did you say, Gran?"

"I happened to run into Carla over a week ago," Celine explained. "She was under that impression."

"We wanted you to know." Helena shook her head severely. "You have a lot of your grandfather in you."

"I take that as a compliment, Gran. I did tell Carla having the two of you together at the same party might upset you. I did it for you, Ceci. I thought you mightn't be able to handle it. Guy *had* to go, of course. He's one of Terry's closest friends."

"In any case it doesn't matter," Celine said smoothly. "I wouldn't miss it for the world."

Once inside Langfield it was hard to tell if Imelda had made an actual improvement. From an overcrowded museum Langfield now looked like an opulent Russian railway station.

"So what do you think?" Ashley asked.

"Splendid! Very…very…" Celine sought but failed to come up with another word. The walls minus the collection seemed to cry out for graffiti.

"Splendid will do. Come up and see my bedroom," Ashley invited. "Suite of rooms, really. I have what was going to be Gran's."

"I expect Grandma thought it was all going to be hers," Celine said, following Ashley up the stairs.

"Anyway it's worked out well. She looks so much better, years younger. I didn't know she had such a sharp tongue."

"Possibly because she had to spend so much time keeping quiet."

"That's never going to happen to me, darling. I hate it the way men try to control you."

Ashley's bedroom was decorated in her own blond and blue colours, with lace bed hangings filtering the morning sunlight. The adjoining room with its leaded-glass windows was used as a luxurious sitting room with a continuation of the blond-and-blue colour scheme.

"Naturally I selected the fabrics," Ashley said casually. "Mamma has been known to go over the top. If I'd left it to her the sitting room would have looked like a compartment on the Orient Express. I'm glad it's finished. I'm looking for new treasures, but nothing could match *this*." She walked to an elegant rosewood desk by the window, picking up a silver gilt-winged female figure that stood near the lamp.

"It's beautiful!" Celine said. And so it was except it had an ambiguous feel to it more erotic than chaste. Perhaps it had something to do with the line of the draperies and the exposed breasts.

"Guy's belated Christmas present to me," Ashley said, her voice pulsing with some secret emotion. "He called it 'Dark Angel'. I suppose it's the way he sees me."

For the first time in her life Celine felt fully prepared to confront her cousin. "Ashley, one day you're going to get hung up on your own lies. Guy didn't give you that. I know that in my bones."

Ashley sighed helplessly. "Ah, Ceci, I was afraid if I told you, you wouldn't believe me. There's part of you that will never accept Guy's no longer yours. Maybe in a weird way he was *never* yours."

"Is this what you got me here for? To show me the statue and tell me Guy gave it to you?"

"No." Ashley smiled at her. "I got you here to talk. We have so much in common."

"But nothing more important than Guy. He *doesn't* love you, Ashley."

"I guess we do have to battle over him." Ashley sat

down in an armchair, her ice-blue eyes fixed on Celine's face. "He told me he never stopped thinking about me. What would you call that?"

"Wishful thinking," Celine suggested sharply. "He denies any involvement."

"You mean, you've discussed me?" Ashley's voice crackled with anger. She leaped up from the armchair and went to the window.

"Things have to be settled between us."

"My God!" It came out like a howl. "I've done everything I possibly could to protect you and you betray me?"

"Don't start turning the tables, Ashley," Celine warned. "I know you're very good at it. The betrayal was all on your side."

A long shudder took Ashley's square shoulders. "That's a lie!"

"You love to confuse people," Celine said. "You make up stories. Now that I think about it, you always did."

"How did I ever confuse *you*?" Ashley's ice-blue eyes glittered.

"You deliberately played on all my insecurities to break up my engagement. You wanted me out of the way and you knew that I'd run. You didn't care how much damage you did. Even when you had me safely on the way you tried to destroy my relationship with Grandma."

"Why would I do an ugly thing like that?" Ashley launched herself away from the window to stand over Celine.

"You've got problems, Ashley. Problems with me."

"With a wimp? Oh, my God, I'm sorry. I didn't mean

that. I love you, Ceci. All I've ever done is try and help you.''

''You drove me away.'' Celine said it quietly, simply, a plain statement of fact.

Ashley stood over her, wringing her hands. ''Ceci, you were desperate to *get* away. Please take responsibility for your own actions. If I once said you weren't woman enough for Guy I was only articulating your own feelings. Remember when you were little and you lost your voice? I used to say things for you. Remember?''

''I remember our shared history. But somehow, Ashley, you came to resent me. It started *before* Guy, but Guy brought it all to a head. I think you would have tried to take *anyone* I loved off me. It didn't have to be Guy.''

''You're talking pure melodrama, Ceci.'' Ashley brushed a hand across her eyes. ''It's indefensible. Everything that's happened to you you did to yourself. You lost Guy because you couldn't match him. You shrunk from it. Now you're trying to take *my* chance from me.''

''When you spent so much of your time warning me against him?''

''I knew he'd never make you happy, Ceci. Can't you see that? Guy needs a dynamic kind of woman. A woman who knows her way around the world. You're much too sweet-natured. Admittedly not so vulnerable these days but you don't have my self-assurance. You'd finish up like Gran, living in a man's shadow.''

''Wake up, Ashley. That won't work anymore. For all you've done I still don't want to see you hurt. Guy doesn't love you. He's asked me to marry him.''

For a moment Ashley stood riveted as though trying to grapple with something incomprehensible, then she exploded into sudden rage.

"You're lying!" she cried, her expression hard and bitter, full of a furious scorn. "Guy's finished with you, hear? Finished. He told me so himself. He could never forgive you for what you did to him."

"Then it's a measure of his love he still wants me," Celine answered, white-faced but resolute.

"This is a trick, Ceci." Ashley's blue eyes narrowed to mere slits.

Celine shook her head. "You're the manipulative one, Ashley. You try through your lies to make *your* wishes come true. You lied to me, to Grandma, to Michael, to friends. And for what? Some impossible dream? Guy's a one-woman man and that woman is *me*. Time now to give it all up."

"And who are you to talk to me?" Ashley sneered. "You stole everything I ever wanted. I was supposed to feel sorry for you just because your parents had been drowned. So the Titian-haired doll moved into Langfield. With Gramps. He actually preferred you to me. *I* was the first grandchild. The first grand-daughter. But no, you had to have this strange magic about you. Gramps paired you with Guy. It should have been *me*. Guy would have done whatever Gramps wanted. You ruined everything for me. God damn you, Ceci!" Ashley put her head into her hands and began to sob with a dreadful intensity.

"Ashley, don't!" Celine went to her and grasped her cousin by the arms. "You'll make yourself ill. I'm so very, very sorry about all this. Grandfather had a lot to answer for."

"Let's hope the old devil is burning in hell!" With a movement swift and violent Ashley threw Celine off. She went to the rosewood table, picked up the silver-gilt statue and hurled it with considerable force through the open window.

"Good God, Ashley!" Celine cried in alarm. "Someone could be down there." She made a rush for the window, looking down.

The statue lay almost directly beneath her. It had cleared the line of sasanqua camellias and lay on the thick grass, the tip of one wing buried in the turf, the sun burnishing the silver gilt to a dazzling gold.

Celine groaned aloud with relief. "It's landed on the grass."

"Forget about it," Ashley snapped, going to the dressing table mirror and wiping mascara from beneath one eye.

"It's a mercy no one was around."

"Who would care!" Ashley answered viciously.

"I wouldn't want to be the person to hit your mother on the head."

"I guess the world would roll along without her."

Celine turned back to look at her cousin. "Ashley, don't sound so bitter. You break my heart."

"There you go, so sweet and generous. You make me sick."

At some distance they heard Imelda's voice. Ashley didn't move, as though she had absolutely no intention of opening the door, so Celine crossed the room, admitting an extraordinarily upset-looking Imelda.

"I couldn't believe my eyes!" Imelda looked almost blindly from one to the other. "We were coming up the drive and something came sailing out your window, Ashley. It looked heavy, too."

"It wasn't mine, Mamma." Ashley's answer had the inveterate liar's ring of truth.

"Yours, Celine?" Imelda looked at her niece with confusion. "You really can't do things like that. Somebody could have been hurt."

"It was only fun and games, Mamma."

"It looked totally irresponsible to me." Imelda made a sudden distraught movement, throwing up shaky hands. "That's not what I came to talk to you about. We just heard on the car phone there's been an accident at the Matson site. Someone's been injured or…killed. Pray God it's not the latter. Your father let me off and drove straight back. Are you all right, Celine?" Imelda asked worriedly. "You've gone as white as a sheet."

The room that had tilted, swung back into focus. Celine was experiencing the worst dread she had ever known. No one ever recovered from terrible trauma. The resignation to a crushing fate was always there. "Guy!" she murmured in a near whisper. There was a sensation of bitter cold on her skin.

Something maternal moved Imelda's heart. She went to Celine and put her arm around her. "There was no mention of Guy, dear. Don't let's jump ahead." Still, damp broke out on Imelda's white brow. Almost twenty years but she remembered the dreadful day Guy's father had been killed as though it were yesterday.

"I must go. I must see what's happening." Celine's expression was torn with a terrible anxiety. "Guy's the senior architect. He could be on call."

"I'll drive you," Ashley offered.

How strange her voice sounded!

"I'll come, too," said Imelda. "Better to know than remain here with our worries."

"You won't be needed, Mamma." Ashley turned on her mother almost fiercely.

The distressed Imelda was furiously jolted. "How *dare* you, Ashley?" she thundered. "Sometimes I think I failed badly with you. Don't tell *me* whether I'm needed or not. You forget yourself. Let's go!"

*　　*　　*

It took them half an hour of speeding to reach the Matson site; an office block high-rise. Celine was too desperately worried to care much about Ashley's driving, but Imelda called out several times a cruising police car would surely pull them over. No one, but no one, was this lucky.

In the event, they were. The city slumbered in the late Saturday afternoon heat.

"Something tells me it's bad trouble!" Ashley muttered. Jaw tight, she ran a red light then turned downtown.

Even three intersections away they could see the flashing lights. Police cars, a fire engine, an ambulance, people standing in little groups in the street. The area had been blocked off. A young policeman held up a warning hand, clearly expecting to be obeyed, but Ashley made her own decision. She swept up to the back bumper of a parked police car and braked just short of hitting it.

"You're a dreadful driver, Ashley," her mother said, breathing fast.

"I got you here, didn't I?"

"You can't stay here, miss!" The policeman walked towards them as though Ashley might start up again at any moment. Even ram the police car.

"Can't I?" Ashley muttered, looking hard and tense.

"Please don't cause trouble, Ashley," Imelda begged. She opened the door of the car and stepped out in her normal regal style.

"Oh, it's *you*, Mrs. Langton," the policeman said in obvious relief. Imelda Langton was almost daily in the papers. He recognised her.

"What is it? What's happening?" Imelda shaded her eyes, looking up.

There was no need to ask. A man stood at the extreme

edge of the scaffolding some thirteen floors up. The sway on his body and his dangerous position heralded imminent disaster. Another man had eased out to a few feet away obviously in the hope of talking the man back to safety.

Celine swallowed convulsively. "It's Guy!" She hadn't missed his blue Jaguar parked in the street.

The policeman glanced at her quickly, responding to her agonised tone. "Mr. Harcourt offered to try to talk the man down. He's already broken a mate's nose. He's been threatening to jump for some time. Somehow Mr. Harcourt has managed to keep him there. Family breakup. We're trying to contact the wife, but with no success so far."

"What about a psychiatrist?" Ashley asked harshly.

"One's coming, miss," the policeman said pleasantly, thinking this one was a real charmer. "I don't think he could do a better job than Mr. Harcourt. The fellow knows him well. Worked for Harcourt Langton for years. Yugoslavian, I believe."

Clive Langton disengaged himself from his group to come back to them. "Bad business," he said, giving Celine the kindest look she had ever received from him. "Poor devil has simply cracked up. We've had a few worries with him but no one wanted to sack him. Guy's managed to get him fairly calm. Or calm compared to what he was."

"He could take Guy with him when he falls," Ashley pointed out harshly.

Clive looked shaken. "It was Guy's decision. God knows I didn't want to put him at risk. We've had our differences, but he's almost *family*." He broke off as the man began to call out in an excited voice.

The small crush of onlookers fell back as though expecting a body to come hurtling at them.

"What's he saying?" Imelda moaned, her face paper white.

"The fool!" Ashley's body shook with violent temper. "If he wants to jump, *let* him!"

"Don't you dare say that!" Clive looked appalled. "He's a good man. He's lost his children and he's been worried sick about them. Where's your heart, Ashley?"

"Don't you *know*?" Ashley was nearly dancing in her rage. "It's up there with Guy."

Anger gave way to pity as Clive realised what his daughter was saying. "I should have stopped this years ago," he said bleakly. "There's no other woman in the world for Guy, but Celine. It's always been Celine, my poor child."

"Quiet. Please be quiet!" Celine implored. She was ready to surrender Guy forever if it would only keep him alive. He was far too close to the edge. Far too close to a dangerously unstable man.

One tragedy too many, Celine thought. This will be one tragedy more than I can possibly bear.

She bowed her head and began to pray. If God failed her…if God failed her…

During the next ten minutes a psychiatrist arrived but decided not to intervene at that point, because Guy Harcourt was doing as good a job as anyone could hope for. The distraught man had quietened. He had even waved to the crowd in the street and amazingly they had all waved back. Except Celine, who was shaking with nerves.

The policeman suddenly exclaimed. "He's got him. Bewdy! He's actually got him."

Clive Langton grunted his intense relief. "Looks like

it. This isn't my idea of a peaceful Saturday afternoon, being half frightened to death. We'll have to help this poor fella!''

The man came quietly, apparently drained of all resolve. As he was led out onto the street by the police, a patrol car pulled up, discharging the estranged wife. She jumped out, then suddenly hurled herself at her husband whether in anger or relief Celine couldn't say.

She only had eyes for Guy. The police chief was thumping him on the back, probably commending him for his courage. Guy lifted a hand, then walked on, fending off questions from the press.

''We might as well go home now, Ashley,'' Imelda said quietly to her daughter.

Ashley's lips twisted into a bruised smile. ''I suppose even I have to accept the inevitable.''

''Yes, darling.'' Imelda nodded soberly.

Celine kept on walking until she was locked in Guy's waiting arms. It was a marvellous, intimate moment that said very clearly what was in their hearts.

''If I *lost* you,'' Celine murmured, her face buried against his chest.

''Not even death could separate us,'' he said. ''I love you, Celine. I love you with all my heart.''

''Let's go home,'' she said, lifting her face and staring into his eyes.

''Home?'' He smiled a little quizzically.

''To *your* place,'' she said. ''Your little penthouse in the sky.''

''You know the first thing I'm going to do to you, don't you?'' His beautiful dark eyes fairly blazed, revealing the depth of his exultation.

''I'll settle for making love all night!'' Celine's pale cheeks were flushed to sudden radiance.

"It's a deal!"

It wasn't said flippantly, but with an intensity to take her breath away.

A photograph appeared in the following morning's paper. It was brilliant, touching. It caused much comment. The camera had caught lovingly two young people utterly focused on each other. The caption read,

A Harcourt Langton Merger?

A SUITABLE
HUSBAND

by

Jessica Steele

CHAPTER ONE

IT WAS not unusual for Jermaine to work late. She was
part of the sales support staff at a busy plant and ma-
chinery manufacturers and was used to working under
pressure. Her work was varied, but mainly she dealt with
reports from Masters and Company's top-notch sales executives when they either rang in or visited head office
in London.

This week she had nothing in particular to rush home
for. It didn't matter that it was going on for eight o'clock
when she let herself into her small flat.

She had been going out with Ash Tavinor for three
months now, only for the last two weeks Ash had been
working away from home in Scotland, too far away for
him to return to London, or for them to spend any time
together. He could have flown down, of course, but he
preferred to work at the weekends, the sooner to get his
business done.

Jermaine smiled as she thought of him. She had
missed seeing his happy sunny face. She would be glad
to see him again. He was tall, good-looking and—her
smile dipped a little—had broached the subject a month
ago of some kind of 'commitment' from her. In fact Ash
had called her old-fashioned in the extreme, because she
was not prepared for them to become lovers in the true
sense of the word.

She had wondered herself, since knowing him, if it
was time to yield her stand. The stand she had taken six
years ago when her beautiful sister, Edwina, had clapped

her eyes on Pip Robinson, Jermaine's first boyfriend, and decided that she'd like him for herself.

Jermaine recalled again the hurt she'd experienced then. She supposed she couldn't have been all that fond of Pip because it hadn't been his defection that had hurt so much. She had been more bruised by the fact that her sister—whom, it had very soon became apparent, had had no particular interest in Pip other than as another conquest—didn't care that he was Jermaine's boyfriend.

Suddenly Jermaine didn't feel at all like smiling. Pip hadn't been the only boyfriend Edwina had clapped eyes on and taken from her.

Jermaine made some coffee, musing that it wasn't any wonder that, over the years, her decision not to make the sort of commitment Ash wanted her to make had become deeper and deeper entrenched.

But her smile came out again; all that had been before Ash. Ash was different. When she had been going out with him for about a month, she had grown to like him so much that she had begun to ponder occasionally about introducing him to her sister and taking the risk of everything falling apart.

She had pondered needlessly. Ash had met Edwina and—nothing. Not that Jermaine had ever come to any decision about introducing him to Edwina. Neither of the Hargreaves daughters lived with their parents any longer. But Jermaine and Ash had been driving through the Oxfordshire countryside one early September afternoon when she had happened to mention that her parents lived close by.

'Don't you think it's time I met them?' he had teased, as ever smiling. She had smiled back—most men ran a mile at the thought of meeting a girl's parents.

She had tensed up, however, when, turning into her

parents' drive, she'd seen that she and Ash were not the only visitors that Sunday afternoon. Edwina's sports car had been parked outside.

'My sister's here,' she'd informed Ash, and had hidden her reluctance to go into the large old house she had been born in.

She need not have been concerned. Ash had been pleasant and courteous to her parents, and had smiled and been polite to Edwina, and that was all. Jermaine hadn't missed the way her sister had gone into action—the smile, the breathless laugh, the big blue eyes attentive, absorbed in every syllable Ash uttered.

Ash had been unmoved as Edwina had flattered his choice of car and enquired—after an interval—what sort of profession he was in. 'I'm in computer software,' he had answered, and, probably because he was proud of his elder brother, 'I work for my brother's company, International Systems—I don't know if you've heard of them?'

Edwina hadn't, but Jermaine hadn't doubted as her sister's glance had taken in Ash's discreetly expensive shoes and clothes, that she would soon be finding out all about the forward looking company—and its wealthy chairman—not to mention Ash, the chairman's far from impoverished brother. Edwina liked money. Regretfully, Jermaine realised, that had been one of the chief reasons for Edwina calling on their parents that afternoon: because her bank account could do with topping up. Their father thought the world of Edwina and, although Edwin Hargreaves's income had greatly reduced when the stock market had received something of a massive hiccup, Jermaine guessed that her father's cheque was already residing in her sister's purse.

Jermaine made herself some cheese on toast to go with

her coffee, reflecting how more than two months had passed since that Sunday. It was now the beginning of December and, although she had since paid quite a few more visits to her family home—especially when her mother had gone down with flu—she had not again met Edwina there.

Jermaine's thoughts drifted to her parents for a moment or two. She was aware that she was not her father's favourite, but her mother had always sought to be scrupulously fair to both her children. Though, thinking back, Jermaine realised her pain over the Pip Robinson business had caused her mother pain too. Even then, though, when annoyed at her twenty-year-old daughter's heartlessness, she had not remonstrated with her beautiful blonde offspring but had striven instead to bolster up the shattered confidence of her younger platinum-haired daughter.

'She doesn't want him!' Jermaine recalled complaining, vulnerable, shaken by Pip's behaviour and hardly able to believe her sister could have acted in the way she had. 'Just because she's beautiful…'

'You're beautiful too,' he mother had cut in gently, much to Jermaine's astoundment.

'Me?' she'd gasped, conscious only that she was thin and seemed to be all arms and legs.

Grace Hargreaves had given her sixteen-year-old a hug. 'You,' she'd smiled, and, at Jermaine's look of surprise, 'You're losing that gangly look, filling out in all the right places. Give yourself another year and you'll see.' And when Jermaine hadn't looked convinced she'd added, 'Your complexion is flawless, match that with your lovely violet eyes and you're going to be outstanding.'

Jermaine had never known her mother tell her a lie,

but wasn't very sure about 'outstanding'. 'You don't think the colour of my hair's a little bit weird?'

'Not in the slightest. Learn to love it,' her mother had urged. 'You really are a sight for sore eyes, sweetheart.'

Over the next couple of years, when her burgeoning curves had fulfilled their promise, Jermaine had come to accept and quite like her white-blonde hair. By that time, however, Edwina had used her wiles on any male friend her sister brought home, and it had soon become clear to Jermaine that, while there might be only four years' difference between their ages, there was a vast difference between their natures. She would never, and could not ever, behave in the way Edwina did.

Edwina had not been at all happy when her father's finances suffered a reversal—though not unhappy so much for him as for herself. Jermaine had been sixteen then, and had left school at once and got herself a job, but Edwina had no intention of working for a living. Her father had indulged her—she regarded it as her right.

Edwina was greedy but, when in sight of men, could be most generous if, by being so, it would get her what she wanted.

After another couple of boyfriends had succumbed to Edwina's charms, Jermaine had known that she was never going to commit herself to any man unless she was certain that he wanted her and nobody else. There was no way she was going to give herself or go to bed with any man until she was two hundred per cent posi- tive that it was her, and her alone, that he wanted. She was just not interested in any fickle affair where her sis- ter could waltz in, bat her big blue eyes, smile that par- ticular smile kept for such occasions—and take over. Good grief! Jermaine came to with a start, realised she had finished her light meal without being conscious of having eaten—and wondered what on earth had sent her off into reflective mode of things past.

Ash and the commitment he wanted from her, very probably, she realised. But Ash was different. True, her own tastes had changed. She had moved on from the lightweight males she had been drawn to up until a couple of years ago.

She supposed it was all part and parcel of growing up. Two years ago the company she worked for had invited her to transfer from their Oxford branch to their head office in London. It had been a very flattering offer. To go had not been a difficult decision to make. Edwina, while returning home when it suited her, had already moved out several times. She had then, however, been back again, and was lazy, untidy and given to treating Jermaine's wardrobe as her own. Edwina was, in fact, generally a pain to live with, and at that time had shown no sign of moving out again.

'Will you mind very much if I go?' Jermaine had asked her mother—her one regret about leaving.

'It's not as if you're going to Timbuktu,' her mother had smiled—and with her blessing Jermaine had left Oxfordshire for London, and had taken residence in the small flat that Masters and Company had found for her.

Two years on, Jermaine was an established member of the sales support team. She worked with, and liaised with, the best field people in the business. Hard-working family men in the main. Sophisticated executives who had come to rely on her input, trusting her to follow up anything they initiated. She was good at her job, and loved it, and enjoyed the maturity of the men she worked with.

Three months ago she had been at a party with Stuart Evans—a man she shared an office with—when she had met Ash Tavinor. They had immediately got on well, and Jermaine hadn't been totally surprised when a few days later Ash had phoned her at her office and enquired would he be stepping on anybody's toes if he asked her out?

She'd liked him, and dined with him the very next evening. In no time she'd learned that he had just sold his apartment, more quickly than he had anticipated, and had not as yet found anything that had everything he wanted. He was still looking. In the meantime his brother had said he could move into his place and was welcome to stay as long as he liked.

'That's very good of him and his wife,' Jermaine had remarked, only to learn that Ash's brother, Lukas, was not married.

'Lukas is away more often than he's at home so we're unlikely to see each other all that often,' Ash had smiled.

A month later Ash had met her parents and—her sister. He had been totally impervious to Edwina's charms, and from then on Jermaine had allowed herself to grow fond of Ash.

But now Ash had grown weary of her backing off every time the amorous side of his nature reared its head. He wanted that commitment from her. And she—wasn't she being just a tiny bit stubborn? Hadn't Ash proved himself? He was sincere. It was her and her alone that he wanted. Wasn't she, as he'd said, being just a little bit old-fashioned? Wasn't it time she…? The phone rang. Ash!

It must be him. He had been away two whole weeks now and she had thought every day that he might think to give her a call, but he hadn't. True, he had told her he was going to be extremely busy…

She hurried to answer it. 'Hello?' she enquired brightly. It *was* Ash.

'Jermaine—um…' he began, though not cheerfully, not in his usual sunny tone. She was eager to talk to him, to ask how he'd been, how was work—she thought they knew each other well enough by now for her to ask when was she going to see him again. But—something wasn't right! Instead of sounding eager to talk to her, Ash was sounding reluctant to talk to her at all and had said nothing after that 'Jermaine—um…'

'What's wrong?' she enquired, ready to help, wanting to help if he had a problem—or so she thought *then!*

'I've—er—I've been putting off making this call,' he confessed, and sounded so much as if he would by far prefer to be talking to anybody else but her that, as shaken as she was suddenly feeling, Jermaine felt her mammoth pride spring urgently into life.

She and Ash had spent some very good times together, but if his silence this past fortnight—no matter how busy he had been—meant he had gone off the idea of her and commitment, then she wasn't about to let him think she'd be broken-hearted if he'd rung to say that this was 'bye-bye' time.

'Let me make it easy for you,' she answered lightly. 'While I've truly enjoyed the good times we've shared, your absence this—er—past couple of weeks has shown me that, well, to be blunt, I'm not ready to make the commitment you spoke of. In actual fact,' she hurried on, pride to the fore, 'I've come to the conclusion that it would be better if we didn't see each other again.'

'Um…' Ash still seemed stuck for words. 'Actually, Jermaine, I wasn't calling to—er—um…' She waited. She still liked Ash, was still fond of him, but if he wasn't phoning to say 'It's been nice knowing you', then she hadn't the first idea what his fourteen days of silence, or his stated, 'I've been putting off making this call' was all about. 'The thing is...' he seemed to gather himself together to begin to explain '...Lukas came home unexpectedly on Saturday.'

Two days ago. 'You're phoning from home? Your brother's place?' Jermaine questioned. Ash was still looking for the right property to purchase. 'You're back from Scotland?'

There was a tense silence from the other end. Then, to her surprise, Ash confessed, 'I didn't go to Scotland.'

He'd been away two weeks but hadn't been where he had told her he was going? 'Your plans changed?' She concentrated on keeping her tone light. She still had no clue as to why Ash, if he hadn't called to say goodbye, had put off making this call. But she was more astonished than surprised when at last he answered.

'I never intended to go to Scotland,' he confessed.

'You never...? You lied to me?' The lightness had gone from her tone.

'I—couldn't help it,' Ash admitted. Jermaine's feeling of astonishment went up tenfold and, at his next three words, it mingled with a sudden familiar sickness in the pit of her stomach. 'Edwina and I...'

'Edwina?' Her voice had risen in her shock. 'Edwina, my sister?'

'We couldn't help it. We fell in love, and...'

'You've been seeing Edwina?' Jermaine couldn't take it in. 'All the time you've been ringing me, dating me, you've been...'

'It didn't start out like that,' Ash jumped in quickly.

Jermaine was reeling, but holding on—just. 'I'm sure it didn't!' Oh, weren't we on familiar territory! 'It started out with me introducing her to you at my parents' home over two months ago—have you been dating Edwina since then?' Jermaine questioned sharply.

'No!' he protested. 'And it didn't start out as a "date".' Tell me about it! 'Edwina was near my home, Highfield, Lukas's place, when she had a puncture. You must have given her my phone number because, poor darling...' *Poor darling!* I'm just loving this! '...she rang me with no idea what to do.'

Jermaine knew for a fact, since she had seen nor heard nothing from her sister this past couple of months, that by no chance had she passed on the telephone number of Highfield. 'You had, of course?'

'Yes,' Ash answered.

'You never mentioned Edwina's "puncture" to me.'

'She asked me not to.' I'll bet she did! 'She thought you might be upset that she'd bothered me. I said you wouldn't be but Edwina said she'd feel better if it was our little secret.'

How sweet! 'So you asked her out and...?'

'I didn't. We—er—that is, Edwina found a glove in her car—it was your fathers, but she didn't know that then. Not until after she'd called in at my office one day when she was passing. And, since it was close to lunch time, suggested that the least she could do after the inconvenience she'd put me to was to take me to lunch.' Hook on to my line and let me pull you in! Edwina obviously hadn't lost her touch. 'Then you couldn't see me—that weekend you went home to look after your mother when she had flu—and...'

'Thank you for *at last* having the decency to tell me!' Jermaine chopped him off. She didn't want to hear any more; she could guess the rest. 'Goodbye, Ash,' she added with quiet dignity.

'That wasn't why I phoned!' Ash cried in panic before she could put the phone down.

She hesitated. She needed time, space to lick her wounds. Edwina had done it again! 'It wasn't?'

'Edwina's had an accident!'

Fear struck her. She did not particularly like her sister—but that didn't stop her from loving her. 'What sort of an accident? Is she badly hurt? Where is she? Which hospit—?'

'She isn't in hospital. It isn't as serious as that. She's here—at Highfield.'

Highfield! 'Your brother's place? Edwina's at your brother's home?'

'We've—er—had a little holiday here,' Ash owned reluctantly. 'She intended to go back to her place yesterday, but...'

Edwina had been holidaying with Ash! A two-week holiday! Jermaine was shaken anew. She supposed she shouldn't really be shaken by anything Edwina did, so perhaps it was the fact it was Ash—her own boyfriend—correction, *ex*-boyfriend—who was her sister's holiday boyfriend that was the real shaker. All this while Jermaine had thought him too up to his ears in work in Scotland to get near a phone—and he had been holiday all the while with her sister at his brother's home in Hertfordshire!

But—Edwina was hurt in some way. 'What's wrong with her—what sort of an accident?'

'As I said, Lukas came home unexpectedly on Saturday. He's been away for about a month and was pretty shattered. So, to give him a chance to unwind a bit, I took Edwina down to the local riding stables and we hired a couple of horses. Only Edwina's mount was a bit more spirited than we were told, and galloped off with her. When I caught up with them, Edwina was lying on the ground, stunned. She'd taken a dreadful tumble and hurt her back.'

'What does the doctor say?' Jermaine asked urgently.

'Poor darling, she's so brave—she's refused point-blank to see a doctor.'

'She's refused…? Can she walk?'

'Oh, yes. But with great difficulty. Between us, Mrs Dobson and I—she's Lukas's housekeeper—' he explained, 'got Edwina upstairs and into bed. She's there now. She tried to insist on getting up, but when she fainted I made her stay exactly where she was.'

Fainted! Suspicions which she did not want began to stir in Jermaine's mind. How well she remembered how conveniently Edwina would limp with some knee injury or other should she be called upon to do some errand she wasn't keen on. Jermaine clearly recalled when she had been thirteen, Edwina seventeen, and Edwina, who had had her own small car, had been in a fury because her mother wouldn't allow her to borrow her much larger and zippier car. There had been a fearful screaming match, Jermaine remembered. It had ended with Edwina flouncing out of the drawing room. Her mother had gone after her a minute later—and had found Edwina in a dead 'faint'. Only Jermaine, who had rushed out at her mother's call, had seen the way Edwina had surreptitiously peeped beneath her lashes to see how her 'faint' was going down. Not many weeks afterwards Edwina's car had been changed for her first sports car.

'So you see, Mrs Dobson has looked after Edwina, but now she's busy with her other duties,' Ash was going on. 'And although I know I've got a colossal neck to ask it of you, I just had to ring to ask if you'll come down to Highfield and look after your sister?'

'Colossal neck' was putting it mildly. 'I'd better have a word with her,' Jermaine answered coolly, feeling mean for her suspicions, but years of living with her sister had left few blindfolds.

'She doesn't know I'm ringing!' Ash exclaimed. 'She'd have a fit if she did. I didn't want to ring at all, which is why I'm ringing so late after her accident. But Lukas has just asked what family Edwina has and seems to think that you, as her only sister, would be sure to want to come down to Highfield to look after her, so...'

'Now wait a minute!' Go down to Highfield? Go to look after her back-stabbing, excellent horse-woman sister who, more than probably—if past knowledge of her was anything to go by—had not hurt her back as badly as she was making out? 'I've a job to go to. I can't drop everything and come dashing down to Hertfordshire just because...'

'Just because?' He sounded horrified. 'Edwina's your sister...' he began to remonstrate.

'And she's *your* girlfriend!' Guilt at the small percentage of doubt that remained, because maybe Edwina had seriously injured her back, made Jermaine's voice sharp. 'You look after her!' she told Ash, and discontinued the call.

She couldn't rest, of course. Jermaine paced her small flat, furious with Ash, angry with Edwina—but plagued by conscience. Drat, and double drat. Then she remembered the mobile phone from which Edwina was never parted. In seconds Jermaine had dialled the number.

'Hello?' enquired a sweet, totally feminine voice.

'Thanks for pinching Ash. How's your back?' Jermaine opened with sisterly candour.

'He *rang* you?' Edwina was clearly outraged, her sweet tone swiftly departing, sounding not the slightest abashed that Jermaine knew about her and Ash. 'He had no right...'

Edwina could talk of *right!* 'Why wouldn't he ring—with you "suffering" the way you are.'

'Stuff that—you should see his brother!'

Click. In that one sentence Jermaine, who knew her sister so well, had it all worked out. The wealthy elder brother, bachelor brother, had returned home unexpectedly and Edwina—never one to miss a chance and already established at Highfield—had no intention of removing herself from his orbit. Due to leave Highfield the next day, Edwina must have had her greedy little brain working furiously in her endeavour to find some way of lingering on at Highfield. Jermaine saw it all. Lukas Tavinor would be a much better catch than his brother. Poor Ash; like the proverbial hot coal, he would be dropped.

'You're a better rider than Ash?'

'He'd barely settled in his saddle when I took off,' Edwina boasted.

'He wants me to come down and "look after" you.'

'Don't you *dare!*' Edwina shrieked.

'Don't worry, I wasn't going to,' Jermaine retorted, and hung up.

Well, she had no need to feel guilty any more, Jermaine fumed. All too plainly there was nothing wrong with Edwina's back. Her 'accident' had merely been a means to an end. By the sound of it, the globe-trotting Lukas Tavinor was back in England for a short while—Edwina wanted to be 'on the spot' while he was still around, and before he went away again. And what Edwina wanted, she invariably got.

Jermaine was familiar with her sister's tactics, yet even so it still shook her that there had not been a scrap of remorse from Edwina, or apology, for 'holidaying' with her younger sister's boyfriend. Edwina had cared not a bit, nor felt any need to pretend when they'd been on the phone just now. She had not hurt her back, but took Jermaine's loyalty for granted, assuming without question that she would not tell anyone what a humbug Edwina really was.

And the devil of it was, Jermaine fumed, Edwina was right. Edwina had done nothing to earn her loyalty, but she had it. She knew Jermaine wouldn't be telling Ash what a fraud she was. But he had enough to learn. Jermaine went to bed wondering if he knew yet that he and Edwina were history.

By morning Jermaine was coming to terms with her ex-boyfriend's duplicity and was starting to feel a little incredulous that she had ever given more than a passing thought to the sort of commitment Ash had wanted. Good grief, he was as fickle as the rest of them! She had been so sure about him too. So sure that he wasn't remotely interested in Edwina.

Well, it was doubly certain now that the next man who dated Jermaine Hargreaves had better not try the 'commitment' angle. She positively was not interested. Come to that, she wasn't interested in dating again either. She had a good job; she'd concentrate on that.

Thinking of which, Jermaine left her flat and drove to her place of work, aware as ever that something seemed to cut off in her when her boyfriends strayed in her sister's direction—Jermaine was no longer attracted to them and Edwina was welcome to the spoils. One or two had come back, pleading for a second chance, but Jermaine just hadn't wanted to know.

It was the same with Ash—she had lost interest in him. She had enjoyed his company but should he ever again ask her to go out with him then she would tell him, quite truthfully, thanks, but no thanks.

And, having moved on, Ash Tavinor would become someone she once knew, and would be no more than that—Jermaine got on with her work.

'Coming for a swift half?' Stuart Evans invited when they were clearing their desks for the day.

She had nothing else pressing, and Stuart was more a friend than anything else. No way could his invitation be construed as a date. 'Since you ask,' she accepted, and the 'swift half' turned out to be a bar meal. Jermaine arrived home around nine to hear her phone ringing.

'It's Ash,' he said as soon as she answered.

Ash who? or *Hi?* Since she knew full well that there was nothing whatsoever the matter with Edwina, Jermaine simply couldn't bring herself to enquire how she was. 'How's Ash?' she enquired instead.

'Look, Jermaine, couldn't you come and look after Edwina? Not that there's a lot to do,' he added quickly. 'The poor darling's talking of going back to her place— she doesn't want to be a nuisance. But I can't let her do that and…'

'In case you didn't hear me last night—I have a job to go to.' Jermaine cut him off, with no intention at all of going down to Highfield to hold her sister's hand.

'I never knew you were so hard!' Ash complained.

Hard! 'Let me put it this way. Edwina's your holiday companion—take an extended vacation.' There was a brief silence, but if Ash was drumming up some kind of an argument, Jermaine didn't want to know. 'Goodbye, Ash,' she bade him, and had barely put the phone down before it rang again.

'Have you no concern at all about your sister?' enquired a harsh voice she had never heard before—though her mind was working overtime as to whom her caller might be.

Jermaine only just managed to bite back a snappy retort. She swallowed hard. 'Good evening,' she managed pleasantly.

'Your place is here, looking after your sister, not staying out half the night.'

It was only a little after nine o'clock! Which monastery had he sprung from? Jermaine strove hard for control. 'Have we been introduced?' she tossed in shortly.

'Lukas Tavinor!' he barked—as she'd surmised, Ash's brother. 'Ash has an important meeting he can't miss tomorrow. You'd better come now and...'

At which point Jermaine lost the small control she had over her annoyance with the whole lot of them. '*I've* got an important meeting tomorrow!' snapped she who hadn't, not caring at all for his tone, much less his orders. 'Edwina's your guest—*you* look after her.'

A tense silence was her immediate answer. Followed by a clipped, 'Ash was wrong to suggest I should try ringing you. You *are* as hard as he said you were.'

Jermaine's breath caught. She didn't even know this man, yet here he was ready to brand her—when all she'd done was to go out with his brother. This, and his brother's duplicity, was what she received for her trouble!

'That's right,' she agreed.

'You won't...?'

'I won't.'

'My...' He seemed to find her insensitivity beyond words.

'Oh—go and play with your train set!' she erupted, and abruptly terminated his call.

Suddenly she was the bad lot in all of this! Jermaine

felt like throwing something. She didn't even know the man. He didn't know her. Yet, even so, he was ready to believe her to be heartless!

Well, on reflection she supposed it did look bad. But it wouldn't look half so bad if Lukas Tavinor knew the truth—that all time she'd believed his brother was her boyfriend he had been dallying with her sister. Not that Jermaine was likely to tell him. And it certainly didn't sound as if Ash had. But she could sit back with a feeling of relief; at least her parting remark had ended any odd chance that Lukas Tavinor Esquire might telephone her again.

Strangely, when the day before Jermaine had thought frequently of how when she had been cosily imagining Ash slaving away in Scotland he had been cosily having a fine old holiday with her sister, it seemed the following day to be his brother that occupied quite a few spare moments.

She'd got the impression that Lukas Tavinor had rather a nice voice, though there had been little to hear of it in the harsh way he had spoken to her. Who did he think he was anyway? He didn't know her. In fact, he knew nothing about her. Other, of course, than what Ash and Edwina had told him.

While Jermaine wouldn't put it past her sister to put a little poison down if it would elect some sympathy from Lukas Tavinor, Jermaine couldn't think that the three months she had gone out with Ash counted for nothing. She had always thought him to have honesty and integrity. Which, if that was true, must mean he was pretty besotted by Edwina to have been carrying on a liaison with her while still going out with her sister.

All of which meant that Ash was going to be the one to be hurt when all of this was over. For, as sure as night followed day, Edwina was going to dump him when it suited her.

It was at that moment that Jermaine, finally over her shock at Ash's behaviour, all at once realised that she would never have made that commitment to him which he had at one time wanted. She had been fond of him, but her emotions, she now knew, had not been any deeper than that.

Jermaine went home from her office having come to terms with Ash's duplicity and realising that she still felt a little fond of him. Fond enough anyway to know that she didn't want him to feel very badly hurt when Edwina gave him the big heave-ho.

Jermaine made herself something to eat, wondering again about his brother. Lukas sounded a particularly nasty piece of work. She smiled. Wouldn't it be wonderful if Edwina pulled it off? From the little she knew of Lukas—and, thank you very much, she didn't want any more communication with him—they seemed exactly right for each other.

She was still having rosy dreams of one Edwina Hargreaves and one Lukas Tavinor giving each other hell when there was a ring at her doorbell. Thinking it might be one of her neighbours, Jermaine went to the door. But, on opening it, she saw not a neighbour but a tall, dark-haired, firm-jawed, mid-thirties man standing there.

The fact that he was immaculately suited told her he hadn't come to read the electricity meter. Add to that the grim look about him, and Jermaine's own anticipatory welcoming smile went into hiding.

He said nothing, this man, until those steady grey eyes had fully taken in her platinum-blonde hair—loose about her shoulders—her large violet eyes, and her slender yet curvaceous body.

'And you are?' She hadn't intended to say a word.

'Tavinor!' he clipped.

Her insides gave a funny little squiggle. Grief—and she'd not long since decided she didn't want anything further to do with him! 'Which one?' she snapped right back, knowing full well he had to be Lukas—surely there couldn't be three of them!

'You're already acquainted with my brother, Ash, I believe.'

Like we'd had something going from strength to strength before I introduced my sister—oh, does she have a nice surprise waiting for you, Lukas Tavinor! How fast can you run? 'We have met,' Jermaine concurred.

'Are we going to have this discussion on your doorstep?' he demanded.

It wouldn't have taken much for her to have said no and shut the door; end of discussion. But manners were manners, and, regrettably, she had a few. 'Come in,' she invited, and led the way to her small but, thanks to her mother's insistence, very pleasantly carpeted and furnished sitting room.

Jermaine knew why he'd come. She opened her mouth to tell him 'Not a chance' but he got in first. 'I thought perhaps I should call to personally appeal to you to come to Highfield to do your duty to your sister,' he said without preamble.

You don't appeal to me personally or any other way, Jermaine fumed, not taking kindly to that 'duty' dig. 'I trust you haven't come very far out of your way, for nothing,' she hinted.

'Aren't you interested in your sister's well-being?' he demanded, her hint not lost on him.

For a moment she was stumped for a reply, but, since

loyalty forbade her from telling him what a fraud her sister was being, Jermaine settled for, 'I'm sure Edwina must be feeling better by now.'

'Is that all you can say?' he enquired harshly.

Jermaine had suddenly had enough of the whole of it. Ash, Edwina, and now *him*. 'Look,' she said snappily, 'if you're that concerned somebody should look after her, hire a nurse!' He'd got pots of money—he could afford it.

'I've offered to get a nurse in. Your sister wouldn't hear of robbing some other patient of a nurses' expert services.'

I'll bet she wouldn't hear of it. It wouldn't take a nurse very long to realise that there was very little the matter with Edwina's back. 'Then Edwina will have to put up with it without a nurse!' Jermaine stood her ground to tell Lukas Tavinor.

He didn't like it; he didn't like her tone. Jermaine could tell that from the slightest narrowing of his eyes. She had an idea that few opposed this man and got away with it. Oh, my word, that jaw looked tough.

'And that's your last word?' he questioned grimly.

'"Goodbye" seems a better one,' she said sweetly, and didn't miss the glint that came to his suddenly steely grey eyes the moment before she moved round him and went and opened the door wide.

Without a word he strode straight past her, and Jermaine closed the door after him and went back to her sitting room—and found that her hands were shaking.

For heaven's sake, what was the matter with her? She'd repeated to Tavinor what she'd told him on the phone last night, that she was not going to go anywhere near Highfield, his home, to look after her sister. And that was the end of it—so why did she think that, somehow, she hadn't heard the last of it?

CHAPTER TWO

MEMORY of a pair of grey eyes glinting steel made Jermaine leave her bed the next morning well before her alarm went off. Ridiculous, she fumed, as she showered and went over yet again Lukas Tavinor's visit last night. She was giving the man far too much space in her head. For goodness' sake, she hardly knew him—and no way on this earth could he make her go down to Highfield to 'look after' her sister.

Jermaine tossed him out of her head. Overbearing pig—who did he think he was? She went to work, however, with the feeling starting to creep in that she wasn't too happy that anyone should think her the unfeeling kind of monster that Tavinor, and his younger brother, obviously believed her to be. But, since she couldn't very well tell either of them what an utter sham her sister was, Jermaine knew that she was stuck with the 'unfeeling monster' label.

'Come out with me tonight and make all my dreams come true?' Tony Casbolt, ace flirt, waltzed into her office with his usual Thursday offer.

'I'm shampooing the dog,' she answered without looking up.

Tony knew as well as everyone else that she didn't have a dog; he never gave up. 'One of these days you'll say yes, and I'll be shampooing my cat,' he threatened.

She laughed. She liked him. But she wasn't laughing a half an hour later when she took a call from her mother. Her mother rarely phoned her at her office.

'Are you all right?' Jermaine asked quickly; her mother sounded rather strained.

'I think so—but your father's getting himself into a state.'

'What's the matter with him?' Jermaine questioned, ready to drop everything and dash to her parents' home.

'We've just had a visit from Ash Tavinor's brother.'

'Lukas!' Jermaine exclaimed in absolute astonishment.

'Oh, you know him?' her mother asked, but didn't wait for a reply as she went on, 'I know you went out with Ash several times; you brought him here once. But he's apparently been going out with Edwina since you stopped seeing him. Anyhow, she's been staying at the Tavinor home, and has injured her back slightly. Since Lukas was passing this way, he called in to personally tell us not to be alarmed, but that she might feel better if one of us went to see her.'

He'd been to see her parents! Jermaine couldn't believe it. The utterly unspeakable swine. Since Tavinor was *passing,* my aunt Mabel! The devious toad had made a special journey or she was a Dutchman.

'I've spoken to her on the phone, and she's fine.' Jermaine immediately put her mother's mind at rest.

'You have? But you've not seen her?'

'No,' Jermaine admitted carefully.

'I shall have to go and look after her. Your father won't rest until one of us does, and you know how hopeless he is in a sickroom.

'Mum, there's no…' 'Need' she would have said, but her mother interrupted.

'I'll have to. You know your father.'

Indeed she did. And at that point Jermaine knew, galling though it was to accept, that Tavinor, L. had won.

'I'll go,' she said, as she knew she must. Her father would go on and on until one of them had seen and reported on Edwina. He would be beside himself if anything happened to her—it would be pointless telling him that his eldest daughter hadn't hurt herself at all.

'Will you love? I'll go if...'

Jermaine wouldn't hear of it. The bout of flu her mother had suffered had been particularly exhausting and she was only now getting back to her former strength. No way was Jermaine going to have her fetching and carrying for Edwina—as she knew full well Edwina would let her.

'I'll go and see her tonight after work. How's that?'

'And you'll ring as soon as you can?'

Jermaine promised she would, and ended the call with steam very nearly coming out of her ears. How could he? How *could* he? Okay, so her parents weren't in their dotage, but Tavinor hadn't known that when he'd gone to see them.

Barely knowing what she was doing, she was so incensed, Jermaine grabbed the phone and dialled the number she had occasionally dialled when she'd needed to delay meeting Ash when work had taken precedence.

'International Systems,' answered a voice she remembered.

'It's not Ash I want this time—' Jermaine put a smile in her voice '—but Lukas Tavinor. Is he in?' Too late Jermaine realised what, in her fury, she had overlooked. If her parents had only just had a visit from Lukas Tavinor, then he couldn't yet be back at his office.

'I'm afraid he's not answering, and his PA is off sick. Is it personal, or can anyone else...?'

'May I leave a message for him to ring me? Jermaine

Hargreaves.' She gave her name, and also where she might be reached.

She was still angry when she went out for some air at lunchtime. Seeing the brightly lit shops all festive with Christmas decorations did nothing to calm her sense of outrage. In fact the more she thought of what Tavinor had done, the more furious she became. Suddenly a date with Tony Casbolt that night seemed a better idea than what she was committed to do.

She was still kicking against what she had to do when Stuart left the office, saying he'd be away about fifteen minutes. Only seconds later her loathing of what she had to do peaked, and she quickly dialled her sister's mobile phone.

Unbelievably, Edwina wasn't answering. Jermaine let go an exasperated sigh. So much for her notion to get Edwina to phone their parents to tell them she was fine. Not that there was any guarantee that Edwina *would* phone, even if she said she would.

Hating that Lukas Tavinor should dominate not only her thoughts but her actions as well—no *way* did she want to make that journey tonight—Jermaine rang his home. Ash answered. She put the phone down without speaking. What was the point?

It was just after four when the phone on her desk rang. Jermaine was glad that she again had the office to herself—her caller was Lukas Tavinor.

She did not thank him for returning her call, but in less than a second went from standing still into furious orbit. 'How *dare* you descend on my parents?' she blazed. 'How *dare*...'

'You have my address?' Obviously a very busy man, he chopped her off mid-rant, and Jermaine hated him with a vengeance. This arrogant pig of a man, this overbearing, odious rat, was totally confident she would be going to his home that night. She was too choked with rage to speak. 'Or perhaps you'd prefer me to call for you on my way home,' he suggested smoothly.

Jermaine took a deep and semi-controlling breath. 'I'll make my own way!' she snapped. 'Where do you live?'

She hated him afresh, because there was a smile in his voice as he gave her directions. And she wasn't sure, had he been near, that she wouldn't have hit him, when, silkily, he added, 'Don't forget your nightie and a toothbrush.'

Jermaine slammed the phone down. What a skunk! She wasn't staying that long. A quick look at Edwina so she could truthfully tell her parents that Edwina had 'fully recovered', then she would be back in her car and on her way. She would be sleeping in her own bed that night.

Events, however, transpired against her. She was ten minutes away from leaving her desk to go home to grab a quick bite to eat—no way was she going to dine at *that* man's table—when Chris Kepple, one of her favourite executives, phoned in asking her if she could get a quote and some brochures out that night.

'I'm sorry to drop it on you this late, but I've been with my client all day and I wouldn't like him to feel our efficiency is any less brilliant than he's sure it is. You can scold me the next time you see me,' he promised.

Jermaine laughed. 'I'll hold you to that,' she answered, and took down the details of his day's business and got on with it. She eventually finished her day's work at seven-thirty, and was halfway to her flat before she unwound sufficiently from that last couple of hectic hours to consider she might have done better to have driven straight to Hertfordshire. It was a foul night—wind, rain, storm and tempest—and she could have been part way there by now.

Rain lashed the windows as she stood in her kitchen eating a hasty sandwich and drinking a quick cup of coffee. She still had not the smallest intention of staying overnight at Highfield but, just in case she hadn't found the place by midnight and had to put up at some hotel, she tossed a few things in an overnight bag and went out to her car.

The rain had lessened as Jermaine headed her car in the direction of Hertfordshire. She drove along reflecting that, for the sake of her parents' peace of mind, she was going to have to fulfil this wild goose chase—and realising that no matter how late she got there she would have to telephone them; they were waiting for her call.

Rain began again before she was anywhere near to Highfield. Deluging down thick and fast, too fast for it to drain quickly away from the country roads on which she was travelling. The result being that she had to check her speed and cautiously make her way.

She mutinied against her sister, she mutinied against Ash Tavinor, but most of all she mutinied against Lukas Tavinor, who that day had had the unmitigated effrontery to go and see her parents.

By the time Jermaine eventually came to Highfield she was not very taken with any of its inhabitants. This was ridiculous, totally ridiculous. There was nothing in the world the matter with Edwina. Nothing at all. It was only because of wretched sisterly loyalty, Jermaine fumed, that she had been unable to tell anybody about it. That Edwina did not feel the same loyalty to her, or she would never have made a play for Ash, didn't seem to alter anything. Jermaine sighed. Stupid though she knew it was, she couldn't help remaining loyal to Edwina.

Highfield, as its name suggested, was built on highish ground, and as Jermaine steered her way she was glad to find there were no more stretches of water to negotiate around; all water was running downhill.

Her feeling of mutiny against the house's occupants dipped slightly when she noticed that someone had left the porch lights on, as if to guide her. She studied the stone façade of the elegant old building; she found it truly quite lovely.

But this would never do. Giving herself a mental shake, Jermaine left her car and sprinted for cover from the torrential downpour. Under the cover of the stone-pillared porch, she rang the doorbell. She was not kept waiting very long.

Lukas Tavinor himself pulled back the stout front door and for several seconds just stood looking at her. But Jermaine had had enough of this. He might be tall, he might be dark, he might be good-looking, but rain was pelting in at her and she did not want to be here anyway.

'You want a discussion on *your* doorstep?' she questioned disagreeably, and disliked him some more when she actually thought she saw his lips twitch. If he was laughing at her she'd...

'Where's your case?' he asked.

Jermaine, confused that he might be laughing at her, angry at him and this whole wretched business, and having fallen instantly in love with his house, found she was telling him, 'It's in my car.'

In the next second she had got herself into more of one piece, but by then he was ushering over his threshold while telling her, 'I'll get it later. Come in out of this rain.'

The inside lived up to the outside, all lush warm wood panelling hung with various oil paintings. But as she stood there while Tavinor closed the door Jermaine reminded herself that she wasn't here on any pleasure trip, and her case, in this instance her overnight bag, was staying exactly where it was—in her car.

'Where's Edwina?' Jermaine questioned promptly. Get this over with and she was out of here.

'In the drawing room.'

She'd managed to drag herself out of bed, then? Though, of course, since Lukas Tavinor and his bank balance were what Edwina cared about, she'd hardly be likely to ensnare him while hiding herself away in bed.

'You've told Edwina I was coming?' Jermaine asked as he escorted her along the hall.

She was looking at him as he glanced to her and shook his head. 'I thought we'd give her a nice surprise,' he answered blandly, so blandly that for a fleeting moment Jermaine had an uncanny kind of feeling that this clever man staring down at her so mildly had seen through Edwina. Had seen through her and was on to all her wiles.

Oh, heavens! Though before she could blush from the embarrassment of thinking that Edwina was making a fool of herself, Jermaine countered any such idea. Men fell for Edwina like ninepins. Lukas Tavinor might be clever in business, but he was a man, wasn't he? Besides which there was nothing in his expression now to so much as hint that he knew Edwina was playing to the gallery.

Then he was opening the drawing room door. How cosy! There was Edwina, feet up on the sofa. There was Ash… Though, come to think of it, Jermaine had seen him looking happier.

'Jermaine!'

It was not her sister who exclaimed her name but Ash, as he beamed a smile at her and hurried over. 'You came!' he cried, and appeared so pleased to see her he bent as if to kiss her.

Jermaine gave him a frosty look for his trouble, but as she pulled back of out his reach she caught his elder brother speculatively observing them. She met Lukas's gaze full-on, and let him have a helping of frost too.

She wanted out of there! None of these people were doing her blood pressure the slightest good. One way and another she seemed to have been in a permanent state of anger ever since Ash's phone call three days ago. Since his brother had joined in the act, two days ago, she had gone from mere vexation to a constant state of uproar!

Jermaine decided to ignore both men and approached the sofa where her sister was so prettily draped. Edwina was too good an actress to show her displeasure while the others were in the room, but Jermaine knew her well enough not to miss the hostility in her 'What are you doing here?'

'How are you feeling?' Jermaine asked, hating the role she was forced to play—but it was that or show her sister up as the fraud she was.

'Oh, I'm much, much better.' Edwina smiled fragilely.

'Edwina's been so brave.' Ash joined them to look down at his new love.

There didn't seem much of an answer to that, Jermaine fumed. But she'd already had enough of perjuring her soul by asking Edwina how she was. Jermaine turned and saw that Lukas Tavinor was still silently observing the tableau. Though, since his expression was inscrutable, what he was thinking was anybody's guess.

'May I use your phone?' she asked, tilting her chin a proud fraction. It was humiliating having to come here and start play-acting—but it was all his fault. If he hadn't deliberately gone to see her parents...

'There's a phone in the hall,' he replied evenly, and went with her from the drawing room and out into the hall. Though his tone had toughened, she noticed, when, as she looked about the wide and splendid hall for a phone, he abruptly challenged, 'Won't the boyfriend wait?'

Get him! 'For ever, if need be,' she answered snootily—like she was going to tell him she'd been dumped by her boyfriend, his brother, in favour of her sister.

'You've only just got here—did you promise to ring him as soon as you'd landed?'

Jermaine stared at him, her lovely violet eyes going wide. What *was* this? 'Thanks to you, and your colossal cheek in alarming my parents, I need to ring them to tell them that Edwina isn't as badly hurt as you must have made out to them,' she hissed.

He smiled. She hated him. 'Perhaps you'd like to make your call in the privacy of my study?' he offered, and was leading the way before she could hit him.

She hadn't seen him smile before, though. And, while she was still angry with him, she had to admit there was something fairly shattering about him when he smiled. His smile seemed infectious, somehow. Not that she was going to smile back—perish the thought.

Nor was she smiling a minute later when—so much for privacy—he closed his study door—but with him on the inside. 'Thank you,' Jermaine said nicely. He didn't budge. She looked pointedly at the door—he seemed to find his turned-off computer of interest. Jermaine turned her back on him, picked up the phone and dialled. Her father answered straight away. 'Edwina's fine,' she told him, knowing that that was what he wanted to hear in preference to anything else.

'You've seen her?'

'I'm with her now.'

'Can't she come to the phone herself?'

'Well, I'm not actually in the same room,' Jermaine explained. 'I'm at Highfield, Ash's place.' She was aware of the elder Tavinor breathing down her neck and, though when she never, ever got flustered, she started feeling all edgy inside. 'Well, it's his brother Lukas's place, actually,' she corrected.

'That would be the man who came to see us this morning?'

'He shouldn't have,' she rallied. If he was staying to hear her private conversation, he could hear this as well. 'He had no right at all to call and to worry you so. He...'

'He had every right, Jermaine,' her father retorted sharply. 'I've since spoken to Ash, and he tells me *you* knew on *Monday* that your sister was injured. You should have told me straight away!'

'But...'

'It was you who had no *right* not to tell us. Your mother said you'd spoken to Edwina, but I thought it was only today you'd spoken to her. Ash Tavinor told me you've known she was injured since Monday.'

Jermaine was not very happy at being taken to task by her father, and, had not Lukas Tavinor been listening to her every word, she wasn't sure she wouldn't have told her father that his dear Edwina was only pretending to have hurt her back for her own ends. He'd be furious with his younger daughter, of course, but, while he had never been able to see any wrong in Edwina, surely he couldn't be so completely blinkered to some of his eldest daughter's less loveable traits?

But Lukas Tavinor *was* listening and all Jermaine could think of to say to her father was, 'I'm sorry.'

'So you should be. Ash wants you to stay with Edwina—just mind that you do.'

Jermaine sighed. She was used to coming second where her father and Edwina were concerned. 'I'll get Edwina to ring you tomorrow,' she promised.

'Not if it's going to cause her pain to come to the phone. You can ring me to tell me what sort of a night she's had.'

'Give my love to Mum,' Jermaine said quietly and put the phone down ready to strangle her sister—and not feeling too well disposed to the man who strolled into her line of vision either. 'I hate you,' she snapped, tossing him a belligerent look.

'That makes a change,' he replied urbanely. 'Women are usually falling at my feet.' Jermaine added seething dislike to her look. He grinned. 'Did your father give you hell?'

'Thanks to you.'

'You should have come when you were called,' Lukas replied, totally unabashed.

'I came, I saw,' she answered shortly, 'and I'm going home.'

'Oh, your father wouldn't like that,' Lukas mocked.

'You'd tell him?' she questioned, staring at him in disbelief.

'You bet I would.'

What a swine the man was. 'Why?' she asked angrily.

'Why?' He shrugged. 'Because Mrs Dobson, my treasure of a housekeeper, is getting on in years, that's why. Because she gets upset at the thought of retiring and wants to keep on working, I wouldn't dream of letting her go. That doesn't mean I want her running upstairs ten times a day to attend to your sister when that job is so obviously yours—that's why!'

Jermaine came close then to telling him that there was nothing wrong with her sister. But he wouldn't believe her anyhow, would again think her hard and unfeeling and prepared to blacken her injured sister's name rather than stay and do her sisterly duty. Jermaine felt then that she had taken enough. But, having come near to denouncing her sister and letting them all go to the devil, she discovered that family loyalty was still stronger than her own fed-up feelings. Because she couldn't do it. Instead, her tone firm and unequivocal, she told him bluntly, 'I'll stay tonight. But I'm going to work—at my office—in the morning.'

Grey eyes stared hard into her wide violet eyes. Then he smiled, a gentle smile, and her insides acted most peculiarly. 'Allow me to show you to your room,' he suggested quietly.

That gentle smile, his quiet manner, seemed to have the strangest effect on her. Because, instead of mutinying some more that her plans appeared to be getting away from her, Jermaine found she was standing meekly by while he went out into the foulness of that stormy night and collected her overnight bag from her car.

Unprotesting, she went up the wide wooden staircase with him, turning right and going along the landing with him to a room at the far end. He opened the door to a beautifully furnished room with not a speck of dust to be seen, the double bed already made up. Jermaine did pro test then.

'I shouldn't have come.'

'I asked you to come. Pressed you to come,' Lukas reminded her.

'All I've done is given your Mrs Dobson more work.'

'My Mrs Dobson has help during the week,' he answered, a teasing kind of note in his voice, his grey eyes fixed on Jermaine's regretful look. 'Sharon probably "did and dusted". Now, you get settled here and I'll get you something to eat.'

That surprised her. '*You* will?'

'Knowing you were on your way to look after your sister, I have given Mrs Dobson the night off. What kept you, incidentally?'

'I worked late,' Jermaine replied—before it abruptly came to her that she was being far too friendly with someone who had more or less coerced her to come to his home that night—a man she had not so very long ago declared she hated. 'And I've already eaten,' she added snappily, 'so you can leave your chef's hat on its peg!'

His eyes narrowed at her tone, and he took a step towards the door. 'And there was me trying to be pleasant,' he commented, and she guessed he had more from instinct than desire accidentally fallen into the role of host—ensuring that his guest wanted for nothing.

'You don't have to bother on my account,' she retorted. And just in case he thought she might be joining them downstairs once she had 'settled', 'I'm going to bed!' she announced firmly. 'I need to be up early in the morning.'

'Presumably you intend to help your sister comfortably into bed before you put your lights out. That, after all, is why you're here.'

Jermaine glared at him. Ooh, how she hated him. She was here because she had no option. She did not thank him that he had just reminded her that, but for her being there to do her family duty, he wouldn't have given her house room.

She sent him a seething look of dislike, which speared him not at all, and he favoured her with a steely grey-eyed look and went from her room.

Men! She hated the lot of them. Well, perhaps that was a bit sweeping. She liked the men she worked with, and her father most of the time. But the Tavinor brothers—pfff!

Because she knew she was going to go and have a few words with her sister at whatever time the 'invalid' decided she must return to her room, Jermaine unpacked her bag, showered and donned her nightdress and the lightweight robe she had thought to throw in. A very short while later she heard sounds that indicated that Edwina was being 'assisted' up the stairs.

Some minutes later Jermaine was wishing she had thought to ask Tavinor which room was her sister's. She didn't fancy going along the landing trying all doors until she came to the right one—though she wouldn't mind waking up Tavinor if he was already fast asleep.

Then someone came and knocked at her door. She discounted that it might be Edwina—she'd be 'struggling' to walk at all. Jermaine went and opened her door, and as Lukas Tavinor stared down at her, his eyes going over her face, completely free of make-up, so she felt stumped to say a word.

He seemed pretty much the same, she thought, then immediately cancelled any such notion. Because, although that gentle look was there about him again, he wasn't at all stuck for words. However, what he had to say was the last thing she would have expected him to say.

For softly it was that he murmured, 'You know, Jermaine, you're incredibly beautiful.'

Her heart gave a jerky beat and she wasn't sure her mouth didn't fall open. She firmed her lips anyway, when she saw his glance go to her mouth, and from somewhere she gained some strength to tell him acidly, 'I'm still not falling at your feet!'

He was amused; she could see it in his eyes, in the pleasant curve of his mouth. He didn't laugh, but stared at her for a moment longer before, 'Damn!' he mocked. 'In that case—your sister's in the room three doors down. The first one at the top of the landing.'

Which, Jermaine realised as he turned and went back the way he had come, was what he had come to let her know. Clearly he didn't fancy his sleep being disturbed if she tried his room when she decided to go looking for her sister.

Jermaine found Edwina's room without any trouble. Her light tap on the door before she went in ensured that Edwina was sitting down looking suitably helpless when Jermaine had the door open. By the time she'd closed the door after her, however, Edwina was angrily on her feet, her glance on Jermaine's night attire having made it plain she was staying the night.

'It didn't take you long to get established,' she snorted.

'I didn't expect you to be thrilled.'

'Why did you have to come at all?' Edwina demanded hostilely.

'You think I wanted to? Lukas went to see Mum and Dad this morning. He…'

'Did he now?' Edwina was soon smiling. 'He must be worried about me to do that. Perhaps he's falling in love with me.'

Jermaine was side-tracked. 'What makes you say that? Has he…?'

'There are signs,' Edwina purred. 'Little looks here and there. Small indications.'

Jermaine didn't want this conversation after all. 'What about Ash? I thought he was your "man of the moment".'

'You can have him back any time you want him.' Edwina shrugged. 'I'm no longer fishing for tiddlers.'

Thanks for nothing! 'How does Ash feel about this?'

'Good Lord, I haven't told him—and don't you, either,' she warned. 'Naturally, being in so much pain, I at once made sure I had my own room. Ash moved my stuff out of his, like the gent he is, and Lukas will probably never know that Ash and I were *that* close.'

She really was a heartless madam, Jermaine fumed. She might have been in love with Ash, for all Edwina knew, but did that stop her from letting her know that she and Ash had been bedroom lovers? Did it blazes! Jermaine knew then that she would be wasting her time remonstrating with her.

'Mum and Dad are very worried about you,' she said instead. 'I told Dad you'd ring him tomorrow.'

'The batteries are flat on my mobile. I didn't think to bring my charger.'

'I'm sure somebody will carry you to a phone if you ask nicely,' Jermaine suggested, knowing from experience that Edwina would ring if she felt like it, but if she didn't she wouldn't bother.

Edwina obviously didn't take kindly to Jermaine's manner. 'And I'm sure you've stayed long enough to have helped me into bed half a dozen times,' she hinted nastily.

Jermaine looked at her lovely blonde-haired, blue-eyed sister, and suddenly no longer felt it would be justice if Edwina managed to ensnare Lukas Tavinor. Somehow, just then, Jermaine felt that he deserved better.

CHAPTER THREE

IT WAS still dark when Jermaine awoke the next day. She lay there for a while, recollecting where she was. For someone who had never intended to stay the night, she realised, she had slept very well.

She knew she should get up and start her day—but not just yet. Strangely, where spending a night at Highfield had never been in her plans, now she somehow felt most at home here.

Which was absurd, she decided, pushing back the covers and reaching for the lamp switch. Light flooded the superb room. Work, she decided firmly. She had a long way to go, and she wanted to get Edwina's breakfast and take it up to her. Correction. She didn't want to do anything of the sort. But if she didn't get Edwina's breakfast Mrs Dobson would be expected to do it.

Dawn had not broken when she showered and dressed. Since she could not hear noises of other occupants astir, Jermaine lingered in her room, stripping her bed and putting her belongings into her overnight bag. When one last check of her room showed there was nothing else she could do to save Mrs Dobson more work, Jermaine silently left her room.

A light burning in the hall indicated that either someone was up or that the light had been left on overnight. Someone *was* up, Jermaine realised when she went to the main door and found it was already unbolted.

She saw neither hide nor hair of anyone, though, when

she took her overnight bag out to her car and triggered off the outside security lights.

She didn't get to stow her bag, however, because, looking about this idyllic spot, she found her attention drawn to the elegant lamps which stood on stone posts way down the long, long drive. They had been switched on, but it was not the grounds of Highfield that particularly interested her just then—but what lay beyond. It—couldn't be? Light reflecting on—water?

Staring incredulously, Jermaine set off down the drive. She did not want to believe what her eyes were telling her, but the nearer she got to the end of the drive so she had to believe it. The road beyond was flooded!

With dawn starting to break, but determined not to trust the evidence of her eyes, she skirted the rain-sodden gardens—only to find yet more water. Unbelievably, they were *cut off!* No way was she going to be able to drive through that lot—she'd be waterlogged long before she came to any main road.

Still staggered, and unwilling to admit defeat—she had a job to go to, for goodness' sake—Jermaine trudged on. She was going to go to work. She was, she *was!* Though, as she surveyed the scene, she owned that she didn't very much fancy being stranded in the middle of a moat, should her car go so far, decide it wasn't amphibious and pack up on her.

Jermaine was some way from the house, and had skirted round the rear of the building and its outbuildings, when she came unexpectedly to a little footbridge. She went over to it and stared down at the torrent of water that was splashing about in the small stream below. Then she spotted a nearby bench and went over to it. Strangely, then, as she sat down to collect her thoughts, a feeling akin to peace started to wash over her. Should that torrent ever steady down to a ripple this would be a most tranquil spot. Even now the scene—grassy banks, the bridge, even the water—had great charm.

She guessed it hadn't rained for a couple of hours now; the bench she was seated upon was wind dried. Yet, oddly, the lighter it got and the longer she stayed there—while she was still extremely anxious to leave Highfield this morning—Jermaine discovered she began to feel less anxious than she had.

It was this place, this spot, she realised, having, without being aware of it, started to take in her surroundings. It was winter now, of course, but even when damp and flooded, and with half of the trees having shed their leaves, there was something exquisite, serene, about the spot, about the willow tree bending over the stream, the dear little wooden bridge, the silence, the peace and quiet, the…

'You're up and about early,' remarked a voice, well modulated and, strangely, not disturbing the scene.

Jermaine looked up. 'It's lovely here,' she answered Lukas Tavinor, quite without thinking.

'You find this corner a bit special?' he enquired, coming to share her bench.

'Isn't it, though?' she replied. 'So serene. You could just sit here and forget all your troubles…' She broke off, astounded—wasn't that exactly what she had just been doing? She didn't even like Lukas Tavinor, yet here she was having a friendly conversation with him! She swiftly remedied that. 'How are you going to get to work today?' she demanded.

Her change of tone was not lost on him. 'I'm not,' he replied evenly.

'You're taking the day off?'

'I doubt I'll sit at home and do nothing.'

Lucky him! He'd got a study. 'How long before this floodwater clears?' she asked grumpily, with ideas of perhaps being able to drive out around mid-morning.

'Difficult to say. If it doesn't rain again before Monday...'

'Monday!' she gasped, and had her attention drawn to her feet when, ignoring her exclamation, it appeared Tavinor had been studying them.

'While I have to say I doubt I've ever seen a prettier pair of ankles, those shoes are never going to be the same again,' he remarked.

Jermaine stared at her neat two-and-a-half-inch-heeled shoes. They were black, but since they were now caked in mud they could have been any colour.

'I've got better things to do than sit here all day,' she abruptly decided, and was on her feet and marching away from him.

He did not fall into step with her, and she told herself she was thankful for that. No doubt he'd been out and about checking for any damage to his property from the storm. Pretty ankles indeed! Was that the sort of nonsense he used on her sister? Was that the kind of thing that made Edwina think he was falling for her? Jermaine thought not. Edwina knew men and...

Edwina! Oh, grief. Monday! She could be stranded here until Monday! Play-acting—going along with this ridiculous farce because Edwina was after Lukas Tavinor! Going along with it for the next *three* days!

It was farcical. She wouldn't... Loyalty, family loyalty tripped her up. Even while Jermaine fumed against it and made herself remember how, from childhood onwards, Edwina had always taken anything that was hers, be it a toy, a game, a boyfriend, she still felt this nonsensical family loyalty to her, and knew that no matter how much she kicked against it she wouldn't give Edwina away.

Feeling thoroughly out of sorts, and this morning revising her last night's opinion and deciding that Lukas Tavinor did deserve a fate going by the name of Edwina, Jermaine slipped off her shoes and re-entered the house.

By instinct she found the kitchen, and Mrs Dobson. 'I'm Jermaine Hargreaves,' she introduced herself to the plump, sixty-something housekeeper. 'Am I going to be very much in your way if I clean my shoes at your sink?'

'I'll do them for you...'

Jermaine wouldn't hear of it, and for the next half an hour stayed in the kitchen chatting with Mrs Dobson, when that lady wasn't popping in and out to the breakfast room. And, since Jermaine had told Tavinor that she had better things to do, yet wasn't able to get to her place of work, she assured the housekeeper that she was there to help.

Jermaine had a bit of breakfast with the housekeeper, and, having got on famously with her, insisted on preparing Edwina's breakfast. Another half an hour later and Jermaine was carrying a tray up the stairs.

She was nearing the top when a door opened on the opposite side of the landing from where she and Edwina had their rooms, and Jermaine saw Lukas appear from what she presumed was his room.

They met at the top of the stairs. 'Looking after your sister, I see,' he remarked with a glance to the tray she was carrying. Jermaine wasn't sure, had not her hands been full, that she wouldn't have thumbed her nose at him—she was certain she'd heard a mocking sort of note in his voice. As it was, all she could do was walk past him without a word.

Edwina was still in bed, but wasn't pleased to see her. 'I didn't expect you to still be here!' she exclaimed nastily.

That makes two of us. 'It's either me or a nurse, apparently,' Jermaine answered, unable to resist seeing the whites of her sister's eyes.

'Heaven forbid!' Edwina roused herself.

Jermaine took the tray over to her. 'How long do you intend to keep up this pretence?' she asked forthrightly.

'What's it to you?' Edwina asked disagreeably, her sneering tone flicking Jermaine on the raw and causing her to say more than she would have.

'Since you ask—and aside from the fact that you've got both your parents, your father in particular, in a state worrying about you, not to mention that you're disrupting the whole household here, expecting to be waited on—were it not for your injury, I would be at work today, earning my living. And talking of earning a living,' Jermaine flared, 'it wouldn't hurt you to get off your back and find yourself a job.'

'Work! Me!' Edwina exclaimed as if she'd been shot. 'I wasn't brought up to work!' That was true, Jermaine had to agree. Their father had indulged Edwina past spoiling. 'Dad wouldn't want me to soil my hands…'

'But you must know he can no longer afford to be as generous to you now as he was in the past.'

'He doesn't have to be, not for much longer,' Edwina purred, and Jermaine knew then, if she hadn't known already, that Edwina would latch on to any man who had money. In this case, Lukas Tavinor. Wasn't that the sole reason Edwina was still at Highfield? 'I'll say goodbye now,' Edwina went on as Jermaine, again for some unknown reason not thrilled that Lukas might be ensnared, went to the door. 'Just phone Lukas at his office and tell him that I became so distressed at taking you away from your boring old job that I insisted you leave at once.'

When life dealt you the occasional sticky end there were sometimes other rewards, Jermaine found, and she smiled at her sister. 'I'd love to do that, Edwina, believe me I would. But if you take a look out of your window you'll see there's water, water everywhere...'

'Water?'

'The rain came; the roads are flooded. With luck—' Jermaine smiled '—I may be able to leave on Monday.'

'*Monday!*' Edwina shrieked. Jermaine left her. She was still smiling. It was nice to score one once in a while.

She bumped into Ash as she was going along the hall to the kitchen. 'Jermaine.' He waylaid her. She stopped and looked at him. 'You're still speaking to me?' he asked, and looked so vulnerable that she realised she was still fond of him—yet, oddly, in a different sort of way. Suddenly he seemed more a friend than a boyfriend.

'Of course,' she assured him.

'I—cheated on you,' he said. 'And—I'm sorry I hurt you—I just couldn't seem to help myself.'

Jermaine had wondered how she would feel on seeing him again, but all that was there was the same sort of affection that she had for Stuart in her office. As always happened, Ash's predilection for Edwina had killed instantly any warmer romantic feelings Jermaine might have had for him. Edwina had again cast her net and, as far as Jermaine was concerned, Edwina was welcome to him. But Edwina would very shortly be giving him her sad regrets—and Jermaine just felt sorry for him.

'We were never going to be serious, Ash,' she told him quietly.

'We weren't?' He looked surprised.

'We weren't,' she confirmed.

Ash looked a tinge put out, but that was male pride, she rather supposed. So she smiled at him, and he smiled back, and they went to go their separate ways.

'It's flooded up to the bridge,' she heard Ash say, and turned to see that Lukas was standing in his study doorway, that his brother had made the comment in passing. How long Lukas had been standing there watching her and Ash in conversation was anybody's guess.

As Ash went on his way so Jermaine strolled back to the man standing at the study door. 'I need to make another phone call,' she told him bluntly.

Without a word he stepped aside so she should enter his study. She did not expect him to vacate it this time, so wasn't disappointed when he followed her in. She took up the phone and dialled her office number.

'Mr Bateman, please, Becky,' she asked the girl on the switchboard, and glanced at Lukas while she was holding.

'You seem very pally with my brother?' he remarked.

'Perhaps he inherited *all* the Tavinor charm,' she replied sweetly, and turned her back on him when she heard the voice of her immediate boss coming down the wires. 'Matthew. It's Jermaine. I'm sorry, I won't be able to get in today. I...'

'You're not ill?'

'No, I'm fine,' she assured him. 'The thing is, I stayed the night with a relative in Hertfordshire and I can't travel in this morning.'

'Floods?' he enquired. 'That was some storm last night.'

'I'm sorry,' she apologised again, knowing how busy they always were at the office on a Friday.

'That's all right, sweet love,' Matthew answered good-humouredly. 'I'll let you work late on Monday.'

Jermaine laughed and rang off, and still had a smile on her face as she turned about. She caught Lukas's glance on her, on her laughing mouth—he seemed to enjoy seeing her happy. On reflection, she supposed that for the most part he had only ever seen the grumpy side of her.

'Thanks,' she tossed at him, and got out of there to go and see what assistance she could be to Mrs Dobson. Poor woman! Prior to Ash moving in temporarily the housekeeper had only had to cater and take care of the household for just Lukas—and from what Ash said Lukas wasn't there half his time. And now not only did she have Ash to cater for, but two other guests as well.

But, with the house running smoothly, there was only so much that the housekeeper would allow her to do, and Jermaine went to the drawing room. The house was silent, no one about. She went and looked out of the window—it was raining again, pouring down. There seemed scant hope of leaving today. But she was definitely going to work on Monday, Jermaine determined, even if she had to swim it.

She mooched about; there was no sign of Ash, and Edwina would still be languishing in bed. Jermaine thought of all the work waiting to be done at her office. Work she enjoyed doing. She owned that she needed something to do.

She went back to the kitchen; Mrs Dobson wasn't there. There were many doors along the hall. Jermaine knew the drawing room, and she knew the study. She didn't want to pry. Oh, hang it, she was a sort of guest here—albeit reluctantly, albeit unwanted. She went and knocked at the study door, and went in.

Lukas was seated at his large desk, a sheaf of papers before him. He put down his pen and leaned back in his chair, waiting for her to state her business. Even before he'd said anything, she didn't care for his attitude. 'Where do you keep your bookshelves?' she asked belligerently, adding—as her normal good manners gave her a prod—'Please.'

Lukas stared at her for a few moments. Then mockingly taunted, 'I do believe the lady's bored.'

'I'm used to being busy,' Jermaine informed him stonily. 'Mrs Dobson's run out of jobs to give me—and it's tipping it down outside so I can't go for a walk.'

Again he stared at her, studying her. 'Any good at typing reports?'

'Brilliant,' she answered, hating that she had felt the need to explain anything to him.

'You wouldn't care to type something for me, I suppose?'

It was enough that she was incarcerated here, without having to work for the wretched man. 'You suppose correctly. I wouldn't,' she replied. 'I'd rather read a book.'

He shrugged, a 'suit yourself' kind of shrug, but got up to escort her to the library. Without another word he left her there, and that was when Jermaine started feeling the meanest thing on two legs.

She had no reason to feel mean, she tried to console her conscience. She didn't want to be here. If *he* hadn't had the audacity to call on her parents, she would never have come here.

With her conscience prodding away at her, however, Jermaine found the strength of her anger against Lukas Tavinor weakening. She discovered too that she seemed unable to concentrate on searching for a book to occupy her. She didn't want to be here—she wanted to be at work.

Conscience bit again as she realised that Tavinor probably didn't want to be here either. He worked hard, and must want to be at his London office. But, in the event of not being able to get there, he couldn't even have his house to himself.

Jermaine strove desperately to keep her mutiny going. She wasn't going to type his mouldy old report; she wasn't, she wasn't. His PA could do it on Monday, when… Ah, but his PA was away from work sick.

Jermaine abandoned all pretence of looking for something to read. Wouldn't she be doing his PA as much a favour as him? His PA would have other work to catch up on when she returned to work, of that Jermaine felt sure. Really, when she thought about it, to type that report was hardly a favour to anyone. Both she and Edwina were under his roof, enjoying his hospitality. True, in her own case it was hospitality she would prefer not to have to endure, but she had no wish to be beholden to anyone, and certainly not him. To type that wretched report would perhaps go some way to repaying him a little.

The matter was settled. Before she could change her mind, and not giving herself chance to think further lest she sailed on straight past the study, Jermaine went briskly from the library. She was so against doing what her conscience dictated, though, that she didn't this time even pause to knock, but went marching into the study.

She stopped dead. Tavinor looked up—he was on the telephone to some female named Beverley. Had she followed her instinct, Jermaine would have promptly turned about and got out of there. She was sure she wasn't remotely concerned at hearing him making arrangements to meet Beverley at some art gallery in a week's time— Edwina would be thrilled. But Jermaine knew then that if she turned about and left Tavinor's study she would never enter it again. Besides, *he'd* stayed around while she'd made two telephone calls. What was sauce for the goose...

He put the phone down—too busy to stay chatting to Beverley all day, obviously, Jermaine mused sourly, hardly knowing why she felt so anti-Beverley. She didn't even know the woman!

Lukas Tavinor sat silently watching and waiting, and the moment passed when Jermaine would have told him not to curtail his love-phone calls on her account. 'So where's the computer?' she snapped instead.

Again she experienced previously unknown pugilistic tendencies when his lips twitched. 'I've an idea, deep down, you're rather a nice person,' he mocked.

It was touch and go then that Jermaine didn't turn about and march straight out of there. 'I wouldn't bank on it!' she retorted, and—when he got to his feet and moved the computer to a workstation for her—she stayed.

She had told him she was brilliant at typing reports; too late now to wish she'd been a bit more modest. For the first ten minutes she concentrated hard on being as brilliant as she had said she was. Then she became absorbed in the report she was working on, and as her fingers flew over the keyboard she could not help but admire the subject matter and the conciseness of its author.

'I think you should take a break now.' Lukas Tavinor's voice cut into her absorption with the work in hand.

Jermaine looked up. 'What?'

'Mrs Dobson will have some sort of a meal ready for us.'

Jermaine got herself together. 'You're good,' she said

begrudgingly, and started to print what she had so far typed.

'Not brilliant?'

Was he teasing? Looking up at him, she stared into serious grey eyes. For the moment that steely glint was missing, but she thought she saw a gleam of something else—humour, perhaps. Her heart gave a crazy little flutter—which she at once denied and went to check the first of the printing.

But Lukas was there before her. Their hands touched as they both reached for the same piece of paper. She pulled back quickly, realising this whole nightmare was having more effect on her than she'd thought—she had felt tingly all over for a moment or two then.

She watched as he read what she had so faultlessly typed. 'You were speaking the truth,' he observed admiringly, taking his eyes from the paper in his hands.

Strangely, she wanted to laugh. 'I never lie on a Friday,' she commented—and made hastily for the door.

She went to the kitchen wondering what on earth was the matter with her? She knew for a fact that some of the executives at Masters asked especially that she should do their work. Her pride and accuracy in her work was appreciated. Indeed, her employers said as much. But never, when receiving compliments from one of them, had she ever felt so flustered as just now, when Lukas Tavinor had intimated she had been speaking only the truth when she'd said she was brilliant at typing reports.

'Anything I can help you with?' she asked Mrs Dobson on going into the kitchen.

'That's most kind of you, but no,' the housekeeper declined. 'You were such a big help this morning, preparing the salad for lunch and doing the vegetables for tonight. Ash has taken your sister's tray up, so I can put my feet up for an hour or so. I've laid for lunch in the dining room.'

From preference Jermaine would have chosen to eat with the housekeeper. By the sound of it Edwina had no intention of leaving her room until this evening, which meant she would have to eat her lunch with Lukas and Ash—and she had nothing very much she wanted to say to either of them.

As it happened Jermaine wasn't called upon to say very much at all. Ash was solicitous and, while seeing to it that she had all to eat that she required, seemed to put himself out to entertain her. Jermaine wondered, had she not discovered he had 'feet of clay', if she would have been flattered by his attentions. Involuntarily she glanced at Lukas—and thought not. Somehow Lukas, who was saying very little but, she didn't doubt, missed nothing, seemed more of a man of the two—Ash, by comparison, seemed quite shallow.

Jermaine blinked and wondered at the way her thoughts were going. She'd never used to think of Ash as shallow. She had in fact been quite taken with him! But, now, she all at once she felt quite grateful that Ash had defected. It endorsed for her the fact that they had been going nowhere and that their non-relationship would have eventually, sooner rather than later, petered out.

She looked at Lukas and found his eyes on her. She flicked her glance away as the craziest notion struck that, beside Lukas, any man would appear shallow. *Good grief!* Get your head together girl, do!

'More fruit?' Ash enquired.

Jermaine shook her head and, with a quick look at

their empty plates, said, 'If you've both finished?' she took charge bossily, 'I'll clear this table and you...'

'I'll help,' Ash volunteered—Jermaine noticed 'Big Brother' stayed silent.

Lukas had gone by the time she returned from the kitchen with a tray. She was glad he had gone. She was feeling a touch unnerved and wasn't quite sure why. Though it was true she was hating this farcical situation she had been forced into.

She was busily stacking the tray with used dishes when, looking up, her glance lighted on Ash—she had never seen him looking so down.

'What's the matter, Ash?' she enquired quietly.

'Oh, sorry,' he apologised at once. 'I was trying not to let it show.'

'You're upset about something?'

He shook his head—but then, as if unable to keep it bottled up any longer, 'Edwina,' he said. 'I know she's in pain but—well, I arranged to have today off so I could be with her, so she wouldn't have to suffer alone, but she doesn't seem to want to know.'

Jermaine was at something of a loss to know what to say. She supposed she could have reminded him that with the roads being flooded he'd have had to take the day off anyway. But that wasn't the point. He was hurting and, knowing that Edwina was likely to ditch him any day now, Jermaine didn't see how she could give him false hope with regard to her sister.

'I'm—sorry,' was the best, the inadequate best, she could come up with, and she disliked it intensely that Edwina had put her in this position, where she couldn't give Ash the hope that everything would come out right for him.

'No, *I'm* sorry!' Ash exclaimed quickly. 'Whatever

was I thinking of, complaining to you after the shabby way I treated you?'

'Oh, Ash,' Jermaine said helplessly. But as he moved towards her, and she received the distinct impression that because he was so upset he was coming over to her for a hug of comfort, she quickly changed the subject. 'Come on,' she brightly donned her bossy hat again, 'Let's get these dishes back to the kitchen.'

Ash helped with a few chores in the kitchen—which was rare, she guessed, because Mrs Dobson seemed quite bemused by it happening. Not so Jermaine, for it became clear to her, when he asked her to go for a walk with him in the grounds of Highfield, that Ash was very much at a loose end.

'I've already been up to my ankles in your brother's grounds once today, thanks all the same,' she declined.

'I'm sure Mrs Dobson has a pair of wellingtons somewhere she can lend...'

'I'm mid-way through typing a report for Lukas,' Jermaine interrupted, and escaped from the kitchen, Ash already gone from her thoughts. How peculiar! For all Lukas's name had come out sounding quite natural, she had felt all kind of chaotic inside on speaking his name.

By the time she arrived at his study she was consigning any such nonsensical notion to the bin. Since she had started a precedent, she opened the door and went in without knocking.

Lukas Tavinor looked up as she entered. 'I'm back,' she said, unnecessarily, she knew, but she somehow felt the need to make some small comment—though why just seeing this man should make here feel all kind of out of step with herself, she was baffled to know.

She took her seat thinking he might have likewise made some pleasant reply. A 'So I see' wouldn't have hurt. But forget that, and forget pleasantry. He did have something to say, however, albeit more grated than said as he questioned toughly, 'What's with you and Ash?'

Taken slightly aback, Jermaine stared at Lukas wide-eyed. Talk about accusing! Where did he get off...? 'Nothing's with Ash and me!' she retorted hotly. 'Except in your imagination,' she added for good measure—and ignored him from then on, slamming into finishing the report, wishing she was the kind of person who could leave work only half done.

Pig! Watchful swine! Those keen grey eyes didn't miss much, did they? Not that there was anything very much to miss—except, she qualified, that perhaps she and Ash might seem to know each other that bit better than merely having been introduced once by Edwina. Trust eagle-eyed Lukas to notice. Though it wasn't so much what he said which she found so annoying as the way he said it. Arrogant devil!

An hour later and Jermaine found she had worked her anger with Lukas out of her system. A half-hour after that and, her respect for his work extremely high, she began printing off what she had that afternoon typed, and was once more on as much of an even keel as she was likely to be, given the circumstances.

The phone rang as she was collecting the papers together. She almost reached automatically for it. She checked, and left Lukas to answer it—only he didn't, and she realised he was too involved with what he was doing. Either that or he wasn't expecting a call and had left Ash or Mrs Dobson to take the call elsewhere in the house. But the ringing reminded her that she needed a telephone.

She inspected her work for mistakes, found none, but when she decided to leave her work by the computer for

Lukas to pick up, a glance in his direction showed he had broken off from what he was doing and had his eyes on her.

'I think that's it,' she murmured calmly, taking her work over to him instead.

Lukas took the papers from her, scanned quickly through, and he too, by the sound of it, had recovered his temper, for it was pleasantly that he remarked, 'With people like you working for Masters, it's no wonder the firm's the success it is.'

Oh, my word—did he know how to turn on the charm when he felt like it! 'You don't have to go overboard—it was only a report,' she answered dryly, but needed a favour. 'Talking of telephones,' said she, quite well aware that they hadn't been, 'do you have one of the portable variety?'

He didn't bat an eyelid. 'You're thinking of taking a stroll down to the bench by the bridge and calling up a few friends?'

She almost smiled, but didn't. 'Edwina wants to ring our parents,' she replied, and made the mistake of look-ing into a pair of steady grey eyes which seemed to her to be clearly accusing, *I thought you didn't tell lies on a Friday.*

Lukas soon found her a phone and Jermaine took it upstairs, unable to again refrain from wondering—had he seen through Edwina? Oh, it would be just too sham-ing if he knew that there was nothing the matter with her—other than that she was after *him*. But what had that look in his eyes been all about when she'd asked about a phone? Did he know that Edwina had not the smallest intention of phoning her parents?

Jermaine went to her sister's room and found Edwina bathed and dressed and taking her ease on a sofa. She looked up from the magazine she was flicking through. 'Is Lukas still working?' Ash, Jermaine gathered, must have told Edwina that he was.

'He's still in his study,' Jermaine answered.

'How tiresome. I'm getting really fed up with this room.'

In Jermaine's view, it was a lovely room. 'There's nothing to stop your leaving it,' she reminded her.

'Not much! The minute I set foot downstairs Ash will be there, wanting to know what he's done wrong.'

'You've obviously started the "Don't ring me, I'll ring you" treatment, then,' Jermaine realised, and when Edwina didn't deign to answer Jermaine decided to do some ringing of her own. She dialled her parents' number.

'What are you doing?' Edwina screeched, plainly having a very good idea.

Jermaine ignored her, and, when her father at once answered the phone, said, 'Hello, Dad, it's Jermaine. Edwina's waiting to speak to you.'

'How is she?'

'She's fine.' And, walking over to the sofa, she continued, 'I'll put her on,' and held out the phone to her sister.

For a moment Edwina just sat there looking sulky and said not a word. But, when Jermaine was starting to think she might have to find some other way of getting her sister to speak to their father, Edwina snatched the phone from her with an angry, impatient movement. 'Hello, Daddy,' Edwina cooed, adopting her little-girl voice. 'Yes, I've been in very great pain...' Jermaine could have slapped her, worrying him like that. Though she felt marginally better when it seemed her father wanted to send a consultant to examine his elder daughter's back. 'What? A specialist? Here?' Edwina said, barely hiding her alarm. But, as quick as ever, she at once assured him, 'Oh, that won't be necessary. As Jermaine has said,' she went on, throwing her sister a venomous look, 'I'm fine now. Just a bit achy, that's...'

Jermaine didn't wait to hear any more. Edwina would hate her for about a week. That was the norm when, pushed beyond bearing, Jermaine sometimes retaliated. She went along to the room she had used last night. By the look of it, she was going to have to spend another night here.

She remade her bed, and, prior to going downstairs to collect her bag from the car, she popped into Edwina's room to collect the phone. Edwina wasn't speaking. Good. Jermaine didn't feel much like speaking to her either.

When she returned to her room she surveyed her scant wardrobe. Two shirts, the deep blue suit she had on, and some spare underwear. Edwina would have a whole wardrobe full of surplus clothes, but Jermaine wouldn't ask her. Instead she rinsed out yesterday's shirt and underwear, and knew she was going to have to settle for today's shirt to wear at dinner.

She took a shower and washed her hair, but was ready to go downstairs long before she heard sounds of Edwina being assisted down to the drawing room. It sickened Jermaine that Edwina could play-act in this way. Jermaine felt sick with herself too that, out of sisterly loyalty, she was having to go along with it.

When she was certain that the 'stretcher party' were safely downstairs and behind closed doors, she left her room and made for the kitchen to give what help she could.

Edwina was fit enough to come to the table for dinner,

and had Jermaine, who knew her sister well, had any doubts about which Tavinor brother she was after, then those doubts disappeared into thin air as she watched her in action.

Here we go, Jermaine inwardly squirmed, wondering why neither Lukas nor Ash could see through Edwina's putting on the allure. But perhaps they could. Perhaps they were both too well mannered to notice it.

But, whether they had or whether they hadn't, Jermaine grew quieter and quieter with every breathless word Edwina spoke as, occasionally tossing a light remark to Ash—mustn't be entirely obvious, Jermaine observed—Edwina concentrated, in the main, solely on their host.

Their host, who was too sophisticated perhaps to give her the put-down she deserved; too good-mannered, for the very reason that he was host, to tell her to go and bat her baby-blue eyes elsewhere. It could have been, of course, that he was answering all of Edwina's breathless questions with a certain degree of charm because he, like his brother before him, had fallen for her.

That thought gave Jermaine something of a jolt, and she darted a glance at him—to find he was looking her way. She averted her eyes. She didn't want to be here; she wanted to go back to her flat. She felt sick inside— and the only reason she could come up with to explain that was the notion that Lukas might be treating Ash in the same way that Edwina treated her; the notion that Lukas would have no regard for Ash if he felt like stealing Ash's girlfriend.

Yet she couldn't quite believe that of Lukas. She'd seen the way he and Ash were in each other's company. The greatest of friends. No, Lukas wouldn't... But, then again, what did she know? She was glad everybody had finished dessert. She wouldn't hang about for coffee. She'd go and see Mrs Dobson and then go straight to bed.

'I had a call from an estate agent this afternoon,' Ash announced generally, but Jermaine saw his eyes were on Edwina. 'He says he has the very property for me.' And, definitely addressing no one but Edwina, 'I'm going to view it tomorrow—do you think you'll be well enough to come with me?'

Jermaine willed her sister to say yes even while, if her assessment was correct, she knew full well that she wouldn't. 'Oh, Ash, I'm sorry,' Edwina answered, and managed to look it. 'I wouldn't be able to sit for that long.' To Jermaine's knowledge he hadn't said how long or how far away the property was! 'I know I'm sitting now,' Edwina added quickly, before anyone should remind her of that fact, 'but all that bumping along in a car... And in any case,' she went on, glancing down at the table, Ash no longer worthy of her 'special' look, apparently, '...according to what you were saying earlier today, the roads will be flooded for a few days yet, and we wouldn't be able to get out.'

In spite of the way Ash had behaved to her, Jermaine felt quite sorry for him. But as he went on to explain to Edwina, 'Lukas says I can borrow his Range Rover,' so Jermaine was too instantly furious to think of anyone but Lukas Tavinor. He had a Range Rover?

She stared at him, thunderstruck for the moment before her feeling of outrage peaked. 'You've got a Range Rover?' she exploded, flames of fury storming in her violet gaze. 'A *high off the ground* Range Rover? One that can go through floods?'

Lukas held her gaze, her fury not lost on him for all that his voice was mild as he calmly replied, 'It's advisable to have one in this area.' He smiled, the swine, he actually *smiled!* 'If we're not rained in, we're snowed in,' he explained pleasantly.

Jermaine drew breath, ready to go for his jugular—but Edwina, an angel by contrast, was batting her eyes at him and trilling, 'But a price so well worth paying to live in this most heavenly of heavenly places.'

Jermaine knew her control was thin. If she didn't leave the room right now she'd be throwing something at Lukas. She didn't bother saying goodnight—stuff manners—but jerked out of her chair and went quickly from the dining room. To think she had been stuck there all day when Tavinor could have given her a lift to the railway station! Instead of which she'd had to stay cooling her heels while the work on her desk piled up. And, to add insult to injury, instead of being at her job doing *her* work—she had been hard at it in his study, doing *his!*

Oh, it was intolerable! He had a Range Rover, parked, ready, waiting, doing nothing! She wouldn't mind betting he had never intended to go to his office but, even before the storms of Thursday, had planned to work from home today. Had he *wanted* to go to his office that day, the Range Rover would have got him there—anyone else, forget it!

CHAPTER FOUR

As soon as it was light enough to see out the next morning, Jermaine was at her window. She sighed—there was still too much water about for her to risk driving her car, indeed, it would be the height of folly to try to drive through the floodwater. She felt defeated even as she tried to tell herself that Saturday was not a work day and that there was no urgency for her to leave.

There was no urgency to leave to get back to her job, she amended, but there was an urgency to leave. While it was true she had been invited to Highfield, because of Edwina's play-acting Jermaine was very aware that she was there under false pretences.

But—that wasn't her fault, she rallied. She'd tried hard to avoid coming to Highfield. In fact she'd done her very best *not* to. But, no, his lordship wasn't having that, was he? Well, it was his fault, not hers, going to see her parents the way he had, she fumed.

He'd just jolly well have to put up with it! Let him deal with having his home invaded. Not that she'd even intended to stay one night, much less two. Jermaine stared helplessly out from the window. If this little lot didn't clear up today, she could be there a *third* night.

But *he* had a Range Rover! Jermaine played for a while with wonderful wild thoughts of taking a temporary loan of the vehicle—in the circumstances she didn't care to term it stealing. Two things were against that, however. For one thing she had no idea in which of the probably locked outbuildings the four-wheel drive was garaged, and for another she just hadn't a clue how one started such a vehicle without a key.

She admitted she was not feeling at her most cheerful as she headed down the stairs. But, since the housekeeper was the only one Jermaine considered blameless in all of this, she pinned a smile on her face when she went into the kitchen. 'Good morning, Mrs Dobson,' she greeted her brightly. Though she was very tempted to let Edwina go without breakfast, she set about making her some.

Jermaine returned to the kitchen after she had delivered the breakfast tray, and spent the next twenty minutes assisting where she could, before the housekeeper assured her she could cope very well now.

Jermaine would have been happy to have had her breakfast in the kitchen, only just then Ash came looking for her. 'Now, why did I think you'd be here?' He smiled. 'Come and join me for breakfast,' he insisted.

By the sound of it Lukas wasn't at breakfast. Good. Jermaine left the kitchen with Ash, but when she preceded him into the breakfast room she saw that three places had been laid at the table—one of them already occupied.

Lukas Tavinor wasn't her favourite person just then. She would have ignored him, though found it difficult when, his grey eyes steady on hers, he enquired pleasantly, 'Over your little tantrum?'.

Ooh, was he asking for a thump! She glared at him for his trouble, but otherwise ignored him anyway. Ash, who seemed to be in a world of his own all of a sudden, pulled out a chair at the table for her. Too late now to wish she had stayed in the kitchen.

Quite inexplicably, Jermaine found she suddenly felt tongue-tied. Her? It was almost as if she was shy. Shy?

Oh, for heaven's sake! Shy of what? The elder Tavinor, who was sitting there, totally unconcerned, eating his breakfast? Ash, who was quiet all at once—as if he had a lot on his mind?

Jermaine helped herself to some toast from the toast rack, but looked up when Ash called her name. 'Jermaine,' he said again, his look somehow pensive. 'You wouldn't care to come and have a look at this house I'm going to see this morning—would you?'

Jermaine didn't think she *would* care to. On the other hand, what else was on offer but to stay at Highfield, kicking her heels while she waited for the road conditions to improve? She was still undecided, however, when for no reason she glanced at Lukas. Oh, my word! Grey eyes, highly disapproving, bored into hers. She remembered Lukas yesterday, his grated 'What's with you and Ash?', and a defiant light entered her eyes.

She turned from Lukas and smiled at Ash. 'I'd love to,' she answered. Perhaps he'd drop her off at some nearby railway station afterwards. 'What time are we going?' Lukas Tavinor, obviously having sufficiently breakfasted, left the breakfast room without saying another word. No doubt, Jermaine mused sourly, he thought her place was there, taking care of her sister. Tough!

Jermaine did look in on Edwina before she went, however, and found Edwina had roused herself to eat some of her breakfast. The room was a mess, so while her sister lounged in bed Jermaine set to tidying it and putting Edwina's discarded clothes away.

'I'm going with Ash at eleven to view the property the agent phoned about,' Jermaine informed her—and didn't miss the way Edwina's eyes lit up at the prospect of having Lukas to herself for a while.

'Don't hurry back,' Edwina instructed, and, having a lot to do if she was to be stunning by eleven, she got out of bed and headed to inspect her wardrobe. 'Come to think of it, don't come back at all,' she further instructed.

'I suppose it's not your fault that you're so unbearable!' Jermaine commented tartly.

'Dad should have taken his belt to me,' Edwina agreed, and because Jermaine loved her despite all she just had to laugh. 'Keep Ash out as long as you can, will you?' Edwina requested seriously.

Jermaine sobered. Poor Ash. 'You're impossible,' she told her sister candidly, and left Edwina to make herself ready for her five past eleven onslaught on the master of Highfield.

The house which Jermaine went with Ash to see was some twenty miles distant. At the start of their journey, there seemed to be water everywhere. But, for all it was a gloomy, overcast kind of day, the roads further on were dry as they left the flooded area behind.

Mr Fuller, the estate agent, was waiting for them when they arrived at the attractive four-bedroomed residence. After he had shown them from room to room he left them so they should look over the property on their own.

It was a very nice property, but in Jermaine's opinion it didn't have the charm of Highfield. There was, she reluctantly had to admit, something rather special about Highfield. Too good for its wretched owner, anyway. Now why did she have to think about *him?*

'What do you think?' she asked Ash quickly, for some reason not wanting to dwell on thoughts of Lukas Tavinor.

They were inspecting the upstairs rooms when she asked her question. But Ash stopped dead and turned, and Jermaine nearly cannoned into him. 'I think Mr Fuller thinks you and I are contemplating setting up home together,' Ash answered quietly. Taking a hold of her arms, he tried to draw her close. 'Oh, Jermaine,' he exclaimed miserably, 'how I wish he was right.'

Good heavens! Jermaine stared at Ash in amazement. 'Aren't you forgetting a little something?' she reminded him, resisting the pressure he was using to take her in his arms. 'A little something by the name of Edwina?'

'These last couple of days—ever since you arrived—I've started to see that Edwina isn't the one I want,' Ash stated. The old Ash was suddenly there as he smiled his old smile—and Jermaine was appalled. She'd used to love his little-boy smile. What had happened to her? Now, instead of smiling back, she felt only irritation with him.

His head started to come down. She moved her head out of range, and his kiss landed on her cheek. 'Don't you dare!' She pushed him impatiently away. Ash stared at her, his expression changed from smiling to astonished as she angrily fumed, 'What the dickens do you think I am?'

'I've offended you? Oh, Jermaine, forgive me, I never intended to do that. I never...'

'Give me the keys—I'll wait in the Range Rover!' she demanded shortly.

'Jermaine, I...' She held out her hand for the keys. But Ash had seen all he wanted to of the property, it seemed. 'I'll come with you,' he said.

They were silent on the way back, save for Ash once trying to explain that it had come to him last night that he had made one colossal mistake, and that he had allowed lust to rule his head. He also tried to explain that it was only when he'd seen Jermaine beside her sister that he'd…

'I am *not* interested,' Jermaine cut him off. 'And if you have any regard for me at all, you'll just shut up.'

After that, all was quiet on the return journey to Highfield. Jermaine owned she was not over her annoyance with Ash—and it had nothing to do with his defection but everything to do with the fact that any man should believe he could pick her up, and drop her down, and then think she would be grateful when he tried to pick her up again. He had even attempted to kiss her!

The journey back didn't seem to take as long as the outward journey, and they were at Highfield before Jermaine recalled she had been thinking of asking Ash to drop her off at the nearest railway station.

'Jermaine, I…' Ash began, turning to her as he halted the Range Rover at the top of the drive.

'Forget it, Ash,' she cut him off. She didn't think she was cross with him any longer—just plain weary of the whole messy business. With that, feeling down, she left Ash to garage the vehicle and walked over the drive and indoors.

What she didn't need in the mood she was in was to have Lukas Tavinor come out of his study just as she was passing the door. If he'd been watching for her from the windows, he couldn't have timed it better.

But one glance at his unfriendly expression was all Jermaine needed to know that their meeting was accidental—her sister's efforts in her absence didn't appear to have put him in the sunniest of moods, Jermaine observed. She began to feel more cheerful.

She had intended to walk by him without a word, but then discovered she had been wrong in her belief that, likewise, Tavinor had nothing he wanted to say to her either. Because, before she had taken more than two steps, his right hand suddenly snaked out and caught hold of her right arm—and the next she knew she found he had pulled her into his study and slammed the door shut.

Jermaine was gasping at how fast it had happened, but as he let go her arm it wasn't very long before she gained her second wind and was ready to pitch into him in no uncertain terms.

Before she could, though, *he* was going for *her* main artery. 'The reason you're here is for your sister's benefit, not my brother's!' he clipped aggressively.

Jermaine's jaw fell open from the shock of this onslaught. 'You obviously didn't care to play nursemaid in my absence!' she slammed straight back.

'Ash is your sister's boyfriend!' Lukas reminded her grimly.

So he'd noticed? 'She's welcome to him!' Jermaine retorted—what in blazes was all this about?

'You're not moving in with him?'

She stared at him thunderstruck. 'Because I've been to see a property with him?' she questioned, astounded.

'There's more going on with the two of you than that!' Lukas gritted aggressively. 'I saw the way he greeted you when you arrived. Yesterday he was all over you, and you haven't hurried back today, so don't tell me there's nothing between you...'

'Oh, for heaven's sake!' Jermaine exploded. 'What is it with this family?'

Lukas stared at her—and Jermaine knew she had said more than was wise. He was clever, was Lukas Tavinor—he'd work it out. 'You've had a spat with Ash?' he questioned, right on target.

'He—annoyed me,' she admitted.

'How?'

Jermaine glared at Lukas Tavinor. He cared not but waited, determined, it seemed, to have an answer. She went to sidestep him and open the door—he was there first.

'So, what's with you and Ash?' he demanded.

She sent him a seething look of dislike, but could tell he wasn't going to let up until she told him. 'If you *must* know,' she snapped, 'Ash was my boyfriend to start with.'

It was humiliating to have to confess that. But, when she had been expecting something sarcastic in the line of 'either you've got it or you haven't' in relation to Ash dumping her in favour of her sister, Lukas said nothing remotely like it, but rendering Jermaine very near speechless, his look toughened, and it was harshly that he gritted, 'You're saying Ash had you between the sheets first?'

'I'm...' She was flabbergasted. 'Well, that *would* be the way your mind works!'

'He didn't?'

'Look here...' she began angrily, feeling sorely like bashing his head in. 'It...'

'How long were you and Ash going out?' he cut in, staying with his theme to challenge.

'Three months!' she answered furiously—then, remembering the last two weeks of her and Ash, 'Maybe a little less, but...'

'And in all that time you and he never...?' he began sceptically. But Jermaine had had enough.

'Look here, you!' she flared, 'Not all women *do*.' That made him raise his eyebrows.

'You—don't?' he questioned disbelievingly.

'I don't!' she flared. 'Honestly!' she huffed. 'I don't

know why I'm still standing here having this conversation with...'

'Well—I'll be... You—haven't—ever?' he double-checked.

'I didn't know it was compulsory!' she answered furiously.

He continued to stare at her for a few seconds. And then, unbelievably, she saw his expression soften. 'You're scared?' he probed gently.

She didn't want him gentle—it undermined her anger. 'I haven't met the right man yet!' she tossed at Lukas airily—and saw him smile.

'Oh, get thee behind me, Satan,' he said softly, his meaning obvious—he saw her answer as a challenge!

'Fat chance!' Jermaine scorned, and, giving him a disgusted look, went to push him out of the way of the door. But only to find, when he caught a hold of her and her heart started to beat erratically, that he wasn't ready to let her go yet. But as she looked into his eyes, her heart started thundering. There was mischief there, and teasing, and, staggeringly, his head was coming closer. She panicked.

'You're as bad as your brother!' she railed—that sent the teasing look on its way.

'Did Ash kiss you while you were out?' Lukas demanded stonily.

'Tried!' Jermaine snapped. '"Tried" being the operative word—it landed on my cheek.'

For no reason she could think of, his good humour appeared to be restored. 'Oh, naughty Jermaine,' he teased. 'Did you give him a set-down.'

Her lips twitched at the old-fashioned expression. She didn't want to laugh. No way did she want to laugh. But there was just something about this wretched man that had her doing things she didn't want to.

His glance went to her mouth. 'You're lovely,' he said. 'And even lovelier when you laugh,' he added, and, leaning down, he gently kissed her.

Something was trying to tell her that she shouldn't be standing there allowing him to kiss her. But as his lips touched hers and a tingling kind of sensation washed through her, right down to her toes, so her senses seemed to go absolutely haywire. She was still standing there when Lukas pulled back and looked into her eyes. She looked back, feeling mesmerised—what a wonderful, tender, absolutely sensational mouth he had.

How long she would have stayed there, just standing there staring at him, had he not been the first to move and break the spell she was under, Jermaine had no idea. But he did move, to kiss her again, and, even while a pounding started in her ears, Jermaine somehow managed to get herself more of one piece.

'I—er...' she mumbled, drawing back out of reach and voicing the first excuse she could think of—though why she should need an excuse she had no idea. 'I'm—er—going for a shower,' she mumbled.

His hand went down to the door handle, but she didn't miss the sudden wicked light in his eyes when, just before he opened the door he enquired nicely, 'Want company?'

'Our requirements are different,' she answered as coolly as she could. 'I'm for a hot shower—I suggest you take a cold one!' His laugh followed her from the room.

Her lips twitched too, so she was glad she had her back to him as she crossed the hall and sailed up the stairs—but she was still staggered. What was it about the man? He seemed to be doing most peculiar things to her.

Up in her room she convinced herself that she didn't find him in the least bit funny. She was not amused. What she was, was stuck here—stranded—and he had a vehicle that would get her out. Against that, of course, there was pride. She wouldn't ask him, she'd be hanged if she would. And, anyway, why was she getting so stewed up? She would need her own vehicle to get her to work on Monday. Just supposing she did leave here in the four-wheel drive, she would only have to make a special trip back to collect her car.

Chafing against force of circumstance, Jermaine joined Edwina and the Tavinor brothers for lunch—and grew more and more embarrassed at Edwina's less than subtle attempts to ensnare Lukas. True, both he and Ash were polite to Edwina as she twittered breathlessly away. But, from Jermaine's point of view, if it was a fact that Ash had switched his allegiance back to her, then he most probably no longer wanted Edwina in his brother's home.

Which made it all rather splendid, didn't it? Lukas wanted neither of them here at Highfield, and the same went for Ash. Intolerable? It was beyond that. With her pride battered, Jermaine glanced at Lukas, her gaze falling on his splendid mouth. So, okay, he hadn't made a meal of it, but he had kissed her and... Her heart missed a crazy beat at the memory of his tender, gentle kiss.

She flicked her glance upwards—and to her consternation saw that Lukas was watching her. She went scarlet when, every bit as if he could read her mind and knew her every thought, Lukas Tavinor smiled.

Jermaine was back to hating him again and was silently calling him a swine. She was glad that he wasn't at dinner that night, and had fresh reason to hate him that he—he with his transport—could go out, leave the house whenever he chose. No doubt he was out somewhere, wining and dining with *Beverley!*

Jermaine did not sleep well that night and was showered and dressed early. As soon as it was light enough to see outside she was off down the stairs. As soon as she was able, she was leaving.

Her first port of call, however, was the kitchen, where she found the housekeeper having her first cup of tea of the day. 'Will you join me?' Mrs Dobson invited, heading for the teapot.

'Not just now, Mrs Dobson.' Jermaine smiled. 'But if you've a pair of wellingtons I may borrow to take a look around?'

Ten minutes later, dressed in a pair of wellingtons and an over-large, heavy topcoat, which the housekeeper was certain Jermaine would 'catch her death' without, Jermaine was going quickly down the drive to take a look at the road beyond.

There was still plenty of water about, she observed, but not so much. Good—she was going to risk it. Strangely, Jermaine felt a most decided pang at the thought of leaving Highfield. Then wondered, why shouldn't she? It was a lovely house, not to say a beautiful house, and since it was most unlikely she would ever set foot here again, to feel that little twinge of regret was only natural, surely?

She wouldn't feel the slightest pang at saying goodbye to its owner, though. Nor would she feel any anguish at the thought of never seeing him again. But, manners being manners, she would thank him for his hospitality— and get out of there.

Though first... Somehow Jermaine felt pulled to go

and look again at that idyllic spot by the little footbridge. Unable to deny that pull, she made her way to the rear of the house and then to the small wooden bridge, where the waters beneath were much less of a tiny torrent now than they had been.

Because she couldn't resist it, Jermaine went over to the bench and sat down, and for some moments enjoyed the peace, tranquillity—quiet solitude.

She was, however, just feeling grateful that Mrs Dobson had insisted she borrow her topcoat, when her quiet solitude was broken by the sound of someone approaching.

'I thought it was you—even if I did recognise the coat,' Lukas Tavinor commented as she turned.

'Mrs Dobson loaned it to me—and the wellingtons,' Jermaine answered.

'Why wouldn't she?' Lukas smiled. 'You're her favourite.'

Favourite! Jermaine stared at him. 'Me? Why?'

'According to Mrs D, you've been more than pulling your weight. You've seen to it that your sister has breakfast in bed.' Guiltily Jermaine remembered how yesterday she had been in two minds about letting Edwina 'starve.' 'She says you've also made sure that neither of you need trouble her. You're always cheerful and friendly, and eager to do any small task, no matter how menial. You're...'

'Stop! I can't live up to this,' Jermaine cut in, and, wanting to change the subject, she honestly told him, 'I could quite miss this wonderful spot.'

She wasn't sure what she expected him to say, but it certainly wasn't his sharp, 'You're thinking of going somewhere?'

His tone annoyed her. It had no place in this enchanting spot. 'In half an hour!' she answered bluntly.

'You can't!' he rapped.

'Watch me!' she tossed back. 'And thank you for your hospitality.'

He threw her a murderous look, clearly not wanting her thanks, and her pleasant mood evaporated. He had spoiled everything. Without another word, Jermaine got up and left him.

Lukas Tavinor was nowhere around when, a little over half an hour later, Jermaine put her overnight bag in the back of her car. Ash was, and came out to her car with her.

'You'll drive carefully, Jermaine,' he instructed.

'Don't I always?'

'There'll probably be a lot of debris around after the flooding.'

'I know. I'll be careful.'

'Jermaine.' She looked at him. 'May I kiss you goodbye?' Ash asked.

She suddenly felt sorry for him. And yet, oddly, when they had kissed in the past and she had quite enjoyed his kisses, she didn't want his mouth against her own now. She was sure it had nothing to do with the fact that his brother had yesterday kissed her—and she had tingled all over. Good grief! This enforced incarceration at Highfield must have turned her brain. But, in any event, she offered her cheek to Ash.

'Goodbye, darling. Take care,' he said, and saluted the cheek she offered.

As soon as she arrived at her flat she telephoned her parents. She did her best to assure them that there was little the matter with Edwina—naturally her father thought Jermaine was being very hard-hearted. Her mother, however, was for once slightly ascerbic, remarking, 'Edwina always did have the flu longer and much worse than anyone else in the area,' causing Jermaine to realise that their mother saw more than she'd been aware. How much longer Edwina was going to continue playing the martyr down at Highfield was anybody's guess. Highfield…

Jermaine was glad to be extra-busy the next day. The hours she had spent at Highfield seemed to have disturbed her more than she'd appreciated. At any unsuspected moment she would find herself thinking about more or less everything that had taken place since giving in to coercion last Thursday and driving down to Lukas's home. She thought about Edwina, who didn't want Ash. And about Ash, who apparently no longer wanted Edwina. Though, mysteriously, Jermaine found she was thinking more about Lukas than any of them. Lukas, who was a law unto himself and, by the look of it, didn't want anybody.

Two days later, Jermaine was so busy at her office she didn't have time for lunch. But, having at last caught up, she left work on time and reached her flat to hear her phone ringing. Lu… Abruptly she strangled the thought before it could go further. Just because Lukas Tavinor knew her phone number—just because he was in her head a lot just lately—it didn't mean he was going to call her.

Heavens above—as if she wanted him to! She picked up the receiver. 'Hello,' she said, and heard Stuart Evans, her friend and work colleague, asking her how she felt about keeping him company at the nearby Chinese restaurant.

'We needn't stay late,' he added.

'Which means that there's football on one of the TV

channels at nine o'clock,' she interpreted, and owned she didn't feel much like cooking a meal for herself. 'I'll meet you there in half an hour?' Stuart lived a few streets away in an apartment the company had likewise found for him.

'I'm passing your door—I'll pick you up in ten.'

He was obviously starving. Jermaine freshened up a little and ran a comb through her shoulder-length platinum-blonde hair. She was ready when Stuart drew up outside.

He was uncomplicated and easy to get along with, was Stuart. She had dated him a couple of times, but when she'd told him plainly that she wasn't interested in anything but friendship, he, unlike one or two others she had said the same thing to, had accepted it. That was when they had become friends.

'I asked you—my treat,' he said when she drew her purse from her bag. 'You can pay next time.'

Since she knew that she might well call him next week and invite him to keep her company at the local Indian restaurant, she put her purse away and Stuart drove her home. Equality of the sexes aside, Stuart got out of his car at her flat and saw her to her door, as he always did.

He watched while she opened the door, then gave her cheek a friendly kiss. ''Night, Jermaine,' he bade her.

'Enjoy your football,' she bade him, and they both laughed.

Jermaine watched in the light of the streetlamp as he pulled away, and had turned back to her door when, making her very nearly jump out of her skin, a curt voice demanded, rather than asked, 'Who was that?'

She spun about. Lukas Tavinor! Where the…? What…? She got herself together, the question of where he had sprung from fading as, regaining her composure, she offered sarcastically, 'You should have come out of the woodwork sooner—I'd have introduced you.'

Her sarcasm was wasted. 'Is he the reason you didn't want Ash to kiss you?' Lukas questioned toughly.

She'd had enough of him—and they were on *her* territory. 'If you've got a report you want typing—forget it!' she bristled.

He smiled and she could feel herself weakening. 'I could do with a cup of coffee,' he hinted.

And there was such charming persuasiveness in his voice that Jermaine found she had answered, 'So could I,' and had invited him to, 'Come up,' before she'd had time to think about it.

How long had he been there? she wondered as he followed her inside the building. And why, when she had climbed these stairs hundreds of times, was her heart pounding so? She had *run* up them sometimes, if she'd felt like it, and had never experienced such inner commotion.

'Come in,' she called over her shoulder as she opened the door of her small flat, suddenly realising that her meal must have restored her flagging energy. After a hectic day, she had been feeling a degree or two weary, but now, all at once, she felt brimful of vim and vigour. She put her bag down and went into the tiny kitchen. There was barely room for two and he was tall and broad-shouldered. 'I'll bring the coffee through,' she commented pointedly, when he followed her.

'I make you nervous?'

She gave him her best cool look. 'Not remotely,' she replied, and remembered to smile pleasantly as she added, 'This place isn't big enough for both of us.'

Jermaine was glad when he strolled to her sitting room; she realized, as she reached for a couple of cups and saucers, that her hands were shaking. Oh, get your-self together, do, she instructed herself impatiently. Why, she didn't even like the man half the time! In fact she quite hated him sometimes, so why on earth was she getting into this state?

Had he just finished work? Had he eaten? She popped her head round the sitting room door. Lukas was stand-ing casually eyeing a rather expensive piece of porcelain she had always loved and which her mother had insisted she brought to the flat with her. 'Er—do you need a sandwich?' Jermaine enquired jerkily. For goodness' sake—if he were hungry he'd go and eat!

For a moment he looked at her speculatively. Then he smiled. 'I grabbed something earlier,' he replied, but added, 'You're rather a nice person, aren't you?'

Jermaine dived back into her kitchen. Nice! *Nice!* Who wanted to be *nice?* Nice, safe, predictable. She poured two cups of coffee, heartily wishing she had never issued an invitation for him to 'come up'.

Lukas relieved her of the tray when she carried the coffee in. Perhaps he liked to drink it scalding hot and wouldn't be but a few minutes, she hoped. 'Your friend obviously has an early start tomorrow,' he remarked, to confuse her totally.

'Sorry?'

'Your escort just now.'

'Stuart…' Light dawned—though she had no intention of explaining Stuart. 'You're working late?' she en-quired. Or was he killing time before going on to meet someone? 'Why are you here?' she asked bluntly on that thought, belatedly wondering why the dickens she hadn't asked that question before. It was his fault; she blamed him, he confused her.

He smiled congenially, and she didn't like the feeling

that he knew every thought that went through her head. 'In answer to your first question, I've stayed at my desk clearing any loose ends prior to flying to Sweden early tomorrow morning.' Jermaine refused to smile back and he took a drink of his coffee, and then went on, 'In answer to your second question, and since I won't be back until Friday afternoon, I thought I'd stop by on my way home to see how you felt about coming with me to an art exhibition on Friday evening.'

Jermaine was little short of amazed. He had called, in person, to ask her for a date? 'I wouldn't dream of coming with you,' she replied coolly.

'Don't prevaricate—tell me straight,' Lukas tormented.

She had been determined not to smile. Her lips twitched. He was impossible. 'I thought you were taking Beverley?' Jermaine reminded him sharply.

He looked amused. 'Did you?' he answered, which was no answer at all other than it told her that he felt it was nothing to do with him if she had misinterpreted the arrangements she had heard him making over the telephone. Even though Jermaine was sure he had been arranging to take Beverley to some art gallery or other this Friday.

'Huh!' Jermaine puffed. 'I fully appreciate it's unheard of for anybody to turn you down, but in case you didn't fully comprehend my answer the first time, no thanks.'

Sarcasm hadn't dented him, and neither did her repeated refusal. 'Oh, come on, Jermaine, you know you love art.'

She stared at him. She barely knew him, yet he seemed to know so much about her. 'Who told you I do?' she asked, and he looked long into her violet eyes, and Jermaine owned—she was weakening.

'I have an instinct about these things. Say you'll come, and I'll go to Sweden a happy man.'

His look, his smile, his charm, were potent forces. But, even so, she was ready to refuse a third time. And, what was more, she knew he was expecting her to. Then, oddly, at that precise moment, she thought of 'nice, safe, predictable', and something came over her. When she knew that Lukas was fully expecting her to again refuse, some inner rebel against 'nice, safe, predictable' rose up and refused to be pushed down. 'Well...' she began. 'Well, I suppose I can't really let you go to Sweden an unhappy man.'

Lukas was on his feet—if he was surprised, hiding it well. 'That was a definite "yes," if ever I heard one,' he stated, adding swiftly, 'I'm going before you change your mind.' Jermaine went with him to the door and, as if he couldn't resist, he gazed into her violet eyes for a moment and then dropped the lightest of butterfly kisses on her mouth.

He had gone before she could protest. But whether she would have done so or not Jermaine was hard put to it to tell. She seemed to be breaking all her own rules since knowing him.

She, who had a most decided aversion to being treated as second best, had—when clearly Beverley, the *numero uno,* must have broken a leg or something, and couldn't see Lukas on Friday—had accepted to be just that. She had accepted to go in her place.

She had made a date with him—and Edwina would hate her because of it.

She, Jermaine all at once realised, had—to crown it all—made a date with a man who, when she had as good as told him that she was a virgin, had as good as told *her* that he saw her as a challenge!

She should be wary of him; she knew she should. And yet all she felt was tremendously excited at the thought of seeing him again in two days' time. Oh, what on earth was happening to her?

CHAPTER FIVE

EVEN though she was extremely busy the next day, Jermaine found that thoughts of Lukas Tavinor still kept coming into her head. As common sense reasserted itself she knew she should never have accepted his invitation for tomorrow evening. What on earth had she been thinking of? So okay, she'd objected to being thought nice, safe and predictable, but where in blazes had her brain been?

And yet, five minutes later, she was wondering why in creation shouldn't she go to an art gallery with him? As he'd surmised, she did like art—well, most of it anyway.

Against that, though, she, who was never, ever going to be second best, had been Tavinor's second choice. Had to be. Beverley was his first choice—and must be severely incapacitated, since Jermaine was sure the gods decreed nothing less would prevent Tavinor going out with the first woman of his choice.

The phone on her desk rang. She answered it, discovered it was one of the newer executives, Nick Norris, phoning through about business. But, business done, he stayed on the line to ask her out the following evening.

'I'm—I've got something arranged for tomorrow,' she answered, and was aware—even if she could have got a message through to Lukas to cancel—that she was committed to going to the art gallery with him.

'Of course you have!' Nick accepted. 'It was a long

shot, anyhow. But you're not engaged or anything like that, are you?'

Oh, crumbs. She liked Nick; his work was good and she seldom had problems with it. But she didn't know that she wanted to see him outside of a work environment. 'No, nothing like that,' she agreed slowly.

'You're going to tell me you're fully booked all next week?'

There had been a smile in his voice, and Jermaine wished she knew what the matter was with her, but she just didn't feel she wanted to go out with anyone just then. And it had nothing to do with the way Ash had behaved—two-timing her with her sister. But... Suddenly visions of his brother Lukas were in her head.

Heavens above, surely Lukas Tavinor wasn't the reason she didn't feel like dating anyone else! Oh, for goodness' sake, pull yourself together, do. 'Actually, Nick, with Christmas so close, I'm a bit pushed to find any spare time just now.'

'You must have the same large family I have,' he accepted. 'When there's only two weekends to go before Christmas, I've got three sisters all determined I should spend a weekend with them and their families when I deliver their Christmas presents. I don't suppose you'd care to...? No, I'm sure you wouldn't. I'll see you at the firm's Christmas dinner,' he promised. 'Are you bringing anybody, or...?'

'I'm going with Stuart,' she invented on the spot— and as soon as she'd said goodbye to Nick saw that Stuart had looked up from his desk.

'Where are we going?' he asked, having caught some of her conversation. 'And am I being used as an excuse?'

'Are you taking anyone to the staff dinner next Wednesday?' Jermaine asked.

'You, if you promise not to drink so I can?'

'You're on.' She laughed; she had been going to drive herself anyway. It would be no hardship to pick Stuart up and be his chauffeur for the evening.

Stuart went out of her head and she found she was wondering what Lukas Tavinor was doing next Wednesday. Which, to her way of thinking, was just *too* much. Anybody would think she wanted to ask *him* to partner her! Jermaine gave herself a severe talking-to.

Although, by Friday evening, she could not deny that she was feeling a little excited at the thought that at any moment now Lukas would call. She had been unsure what to wear, but in the end had opted for a deeply blue suit that enhanced the colour of her violet eyes.

For no reason, she felt dithery inside—and owned it was ridiculous. As it was ridiculous, she admitted—not for the first time in the see-saw of her thoughts—that she had accepted Tavinor's invitation in the first place. Again she gave herself a talking-to, and in the end decided that, provided she wasn't called upon to tell lies about her 'invalid' sister, she was going to enjoy the art gallery affair. In any event, it wasn't going to last more than an hour, was it? Just how long did it take to look at a few pictures?

Her apartment bell sounded. She swallowed, and was cross with herself that she did so. Picking up her dainty bag, she left her flat and went down the stairs. No point in inviting Tavinor up.

Ridiculously, she had to swallow again before she opened the door. She pinned a pleasant look on her face and felt her heartbeat quicken as she pulled back the door. 'Hello,' some actress addressed the tall, broad shouldered man standing casually there.

'Not a girl to keep a man waiting, I see,' Lukas remarked pleasantly, his grey eyes warm as he looked back at her.

'I thought it was raining,' she lied—as though she'd hurried to the door in case he might be getting soaked. 'How was Sweden?'

'Fine,' he answered as he escorted her to his car. 'Been busy?'

'Enjoyably so,' she replied, and sank down on to the leather upholstery of his smart car. While Lukas went round to the driver's side, she felt the need to take a few deep and steadying breaths.

After her initial nervousness, however—and she could never remember being so uptight on a first date before; first and last she made a mental note—with Lukas keeping up a light conversation as they drove along, Jermaine began to relax. So much so that by the time they reached the art gallery, which was more or less one huge ground-floor room with a selection of movable partitions here and there, she was, as she had previously decided, all ready to enjoy the viewing.

'Lukas!' A short, slim, slightly intense-looking man broke away from the group he was with and came hurrying over as soon as he spotted them.

'How's it going?' Lukas asked, shaking hands with him.

'Fingers crossed—I've been in such a state!' the man confessed.

Lukas grinned, which Jermaine didn't think was very sympathetic of him. 'This is the man whose work you've come to admire,' Lukas said, turning to her.

'You're the artist?' she smiled, before Lukas could complete the introductions.

'Beverley Marshall,' he answered, and Jermaine's smile became a grin too—though she wouldn't look at

Lukas. He knew darn well she had thought Beverley was a female, while of course Beverley could be a man's name too.

'Jermaine Hargreaves,' she supplied, and shook hands with him.

A hired waiter hovered near and Beverley called him over. Jermaine opted for a Buck's fizz and nursed her drink as the three of them fell into conversation.

It was not long, however, before people who appeared to know Lukas came up to them, and, the art exhibition a side issue, by the look of it, they seemed prepared to chat in a group all evening.

'You'll excuse us,' Lukas murmured suavely after a few minutes. 'There's one picture in particular I'm interested to see.'

Jermaine never discovered which picture that was. What she did discover was that there was one picture in particular that caught *her* eye. She was moving around the room with Lukas, stopping before each picture, sometimes making a comment, sometimes not, when they came to a pastel abstract entitled *Boy With A Barrow*. She could detect neither the boy nor the barrow at first, yet something about the picture appealed to her.

Lukas went to move on. 'You're impressed?' he enquired when she didn't move.

She stared at the painting. 'I can see a wheel,' she told him eagerly as she spotted it.

'Where?'

'You don't believe me?'

'Sure I do. I just need to have your in-depth vision,' he explained.

'There.' Jermaine pointed to a fine swirl of red on the otherwise pale blue and pink canvas.

Lukas's eyes followed her finger. 'Didn't I say you had an artist's eye?' he smiled.

Jermaine laughed at his light humour and moved with him on to the next picture. Several people came over to them once they had been round the room. But when the conversation appeared to be more about business than anything else, and one of the wives took a couple of paces away from the group to study a nearby picture, it seemed a good idea to Jermaine that she should do the same.

Lukas was involved answering a point about which some man named Akerman had asked him when, believing she'd be back without Lukas ever having missed her, Jermaine casually meandered away. The picture she went to have a second look at, however, was not nearby.

Yes, that was most definitely a wheel, she decided, and stared fascinated at the blue and pink and the merging of a swirling wisp of red. She was sure the barrow was just coming into focus when she was suddenly aware that she was not looking at *Boy With A Barrow* alone.

'Something tells me you like this one more than any of the others,' Lukas observed.

'Give me long enough and I'll find the barrow and the boy,' she smiled. But, not wishing Lukas to think her rude, 'I didn't think I'd be missed for a few minutes.'

'You were away ten,' he informed her.

'You noticed me slipping away?' she asked, astonished, having thought him deeply involved in a business discussion.

'I may not have your eye for unscrambling abstract art, but I knew at once when the most beautiful woman in the room left my side,' he answered—and her heart crazily seemed to miss a beat.

She opened her mouth, sorely needing some witty retort, but found she was too stunned. 'There's no answer to that,' was the poor best she could come up with.

Shortly afterwards they were in conversation with Beverley Marshall again, and, having complimented him on his exhibition, Lukas said they were leaving. Whereupon, once she was seated in the car next to him, Jermaine discovered that her idea that she would spend about an hour with him and that once they'd left the art gallery that would be it was erroneous.

'I thought we'd eat at my club,' Lukas announced as he swung the car out into the traffic.

'I didn't know you were feeding me as well!' she exclaimed.

'You're suggesting I don't know how to treat a lady?' he teased.

Jermaine, having formed the very opposite view—that Lukas Tavinor knew all there was to know about women, and how to treat them—said nothing. She had to own that she had no objection to having dinner with him— she had been planning to have something on toast later anyhow.

His club—what she saw of it, apart from the dining room—was all leather furniture and antiques. 'What time did you arrive back from Sweden?' she enquired once they were seated, an innocent enough question, since she couldn't sit there all through dinner and say not a word.

'Late this afternoon,' Lukas answered as the waiter brought their first course; they were both starting with fish.

'You must have called for me straight from your office,' Jermaine realised—he must have gone from his plane to put in time at his desk. 'Have you had chance to relax at all?' she wondered. She worked hard, but the pace of his life seemed to leave hers standing.

'I'm relaxing now,' Lukas replied, his grey eyes holding hers.

She felt nervous and excited at the same time suddenly, and again wanted to say something witty. But all she could come up with was a dull, 'Good.'

'You've had a busy but enjoyable day too, you said?'

She shrugged. She had no intention of boring him out of his skull by telling him about work, so confined her answer to, 'Today's just flown by.'

'Have you worked for Masters and Company very long?'

'I worked for them in Oxford when I left school—at sixteen', she inserted. 'I stayed there four years then transferred to their head office here two years ago.'

'That makes you twenty-two.'

'Your maths teacher would have been proud of you,' she laughed, and felt all sort of squiggly inside when she saw he seemed to like the sound of her laugh—there was an upward curve on his breathtaking mouth anyhow. Breathtaking? 'How old are you?' she asked abruptly.

'Thirty-six,' he answered without hesitation. 'You're younger than your sister?'

She didn't want to talk about Edwina. To do so might mean she would be called upon to varnish the truth a little—and Jermaine felt then that she didn't want to lie to Lukas. 'That's right,' she said brightly.

'Edwina doesn't have a job—when she's well?' he enquired.

'Edwina—we—that is…' Lukas silently waited, and Jermaine started to wish she had told him she wasn't hungry and that she didn't require feeding. But too late now to wish, as well, that she had told him to take her back to her flat. 'At—er—one time… That is, my father didn't want either Edwina or me to do anything—er—

work-wise, in particular. Um, we used to be quite...
Well, we had money and...' She broke off. This was
ridiculous! 'No,' she said bluntly, 'Edwina doesn't have
a job.' Oh, heck, that didn't sound very good for Edwina.
'She's looking for the right opportunity,' she added, and
looked straight into a pair of steady grey eyes... And
you're it, she almost told him.

And could have hit him when he contributed, 'And
meanwhile she has time on her hand in which to snaffle
your men-friends?'

'Snaffle?' Jermaine repeated indignantly, not thanking
him for referring to something which stung more because
of Edwina's utterly disloyal trait than the fact that Ash
had defected.

'Ash was your boyfriend first,' Lukas documented,
when Jermaine refused to answer his question. 'Which
explains why you were, naturally, reluctant to go down
to Highfield to look after your sister.'

For the pure joy of letting him know just how wrong
he'd got it, Jermaine was very much tempted to tell him
that the reason she hadn't wanted to go to Highfield was
because she had known full well that Edwina didn't need
'looking after'. That in fact there was absolutely nothing
wrong with Edwina—other than that she'd got the master
of the house in her sights. But, while Edwina had no
qualms about being disloyal, Jermaine knew that she
couldn't be the same. So she said nothing, but just glared
stubbornly at him.

That was until, quite quietly, but, oh, so seriously,
Lukas asked, 'Are you in love with my brother?'

Jermaine stared at him, and was quite dumbstruck to
find an answer to his most unexpected question. 'Is that
what this evening is all about?' she questioned tautly

when she had her breath back. 'You looking after your brother's interests?'

It was Lukas's turn to stare at her, but he wasn't giving up on his question, she found, when he replied, 'I think Ash is quite big enough to look after himself. Are you?'

'Big enough to look after myself?' She had no intention of playing the game his way.

Lukas kept his gaze steady on her. 'Are you in love with him?' he insisted.

'He's a very nice person,' she prevaricated.

'Which means you're not in love with him,' Lukas decided; in Jermaine's view he was much too clever with his summing up. Though he was way off course, she realised, when he further reckoned, 'I've been stupid. Ash didn't prefer your sister over you—you were the one to do the honours.'

Was Lukas upset that she might have thrown his loved brother over? Jermaine didn't see how he could be. Not since he must have realised it hadn't taken Ash any time at all to turn his affections elsewhere.

'Strange as it may seem,' Jermaine replied loftily, 'you got it right the first time.'

'Ash told you on your last date…?'

She'd had enough. 'I don't want to talk about it,' she butted in bluntly.

'You're hurt! I'm…'

Jermaine shaking her head caused him to break off. 'Edwina's welcome,' she said and, determined to end this conversation, she glanced at his newly arrived main course and remarked, 'Your Beef Wellington looks better than my fricassee of chicken,' and had the shock of her life when, without more ado, Lukas swopped plates with her.

She went to protest, but instead burst out laughing,

and, to her surprise, the mood immediately lightened. Lukas laughed too. And—she fell in love with him.

'*Bon appetit,*' he grinned, and her heart thundered.

'Likewise,' she said, and concentrated fiercely on her Beef Wellington, that or go to pieces. She couldn't love him, she barely liked him sometimes, but—love him she knew that she did. 'When are you going away again?' she asked, after some seconds of desperately searching for a safe topic.

'I've only just got back!' he protested

'I know.' She risked glancing up, her heart raced again. 'But Ash said—' or she'd thought he'd said—her brain seemed to be having an off few minutes '—that you were always jetting off somewhere.'

Lukas smiled, his grey eyes did too, and her heart flipped. 'So—I fly off again on Monday,' he said, and asked, 'What will you be doing while I'm away?'

'Nothing very much, I don't suppose,' she answered, and glanced from him to realise how feeble that sounded. She injected a little stiffening into her enfeebled backbone. 'Though, of course that depends how long you'll be away?'

'The soonest I can possibly make it back is Christmas Eve,' Lukas replied, and, because she wanted to hear regret in his voice, she actually thought she heard it when he said that he'd be out of the country all that while— with no earthly chance of getting back to take her to another art gallery.

Get real! 'Ooh, I'll be doing more than nothing very much in all that time,' she laughed.

'Such as?'

She looked at him again, looked into his interested eyes, and went momentarily brain-dead again for some seconds. Grief, it sounded pathetic, but the only outing she'd got planned was the firm's dinner.

'Well, among other things,' she who hadn't wanted to lie to him lied cheerfully, 'there's the company's Christmas dinner next Wednesday...'

'You're taking a partner?'

Thank you, Stuart, wonderful Stuart. 'You almost met him,' she replied prettily.

'Stuart?'

Good heavens, he'd remembered Stuart's name? Though, on thinking about it, it wasn't that difficult a name to remember, and she had a sort of idea that Lukas forgot very little of anything.

'The same,' she replied.

'Are you serious with him?' he wanted to know, and, when Jermaine just sat and looked at him, 'Of course you're not,' he decided.

'Oh?' she questioned, not sure she cared for his calculations, even if they were accurate.

'While I can see that you owe Ash no allegiance whatsoever, I just don't see you as someone who'd be serious with one man and be out dining with another.'

He was right there, but she didn't thank him for it. Or, rather, she said, 'Thanks!' But didn't mean it.

'Now what have I said?' he teased.

'Add your last comment to a previous one of "nice", and it all adds up to "dull",' she answered sniffily— and, even if she did love him, could have thumped him when he laughed.

'You dull? Never!' he decreed. 'You're beautiful and charming, and far too spirited to ever be anything so mediocre as dull.'

Her heart fluttered—beautiful and charming? Oh, my word! 'What are you having for pudding?' she asked.

'I'm not swopping this time,' he threatened, and she laughed. Her world righted itself and the next half an hour just flew by as they talked and smiled, talked and laughed, and generally struck companionable sparks off each other.

They lingered over coffee and, because of her newly discovered love for him and the need she had just to be with him, Jermaine could have lingered the night away with him. But because of that love, and a pride that said he should never know about it—though the way she was laughing or smiling at his smallest quip he might soon guess—she knew she had to put a stop to the evening.

'I've had a splendid time tonight,' she hinted.

She didn't have to say more. All too soon Lukas was guiding her from the building, starting up his car—and pulling up near her door.

She thanked him. 'The art gallery was super.'

'Especially the *Boy With A Barrow*,' Lukas ribbed her as he escorted her to the outer door of where she lived.

'It was rather a special picture. Well, I thought so anyway,' she added defensively.

'And you're quite right,' he agreed, taking her keys from her and inserting one in the door-lock.

She wanted to invite him up. She didn't want the evening to end. Lord knew when, if ever, she would see him again. Surely it wouldn't hurt to invite him up for coffee? Pride, girl, pride. Do you really want him to see, as surely he will if you don't get your act together, exactly how you feel about him?

'We've just had coffee, so you won't want another,' she said as she turned to face him.

He laughed. 'You're wonderful,' he said.

'Now what did I do?'

'At the risk of sounding immodest, most women can't wait to get me inside to give me a cup of coffee.'

Oh, she did love him. She laughed too. 'Have a safe trip,' she bade him.

He took a step back and gazed at her, then, to her astonishment and joy, he asked, 'I don't suppose you'd consider coming up to Highfield tomorrow?'

He wanted her to go down to his home? Her heart thundered. She could see him again tomorrow. 'Er...' She murmured only slightly, not wanting to miss this quite unexpected but fantastic opportunity.

'I wouldn't ask, but unfortunately Edwina isn't sufficiently well to make her own bed yet—a back injury can be the very devil—and with you there to help, it would give Mrs Dobson a bit of a break,' Lukas explained.

Jermaine's heartbeat evened out. Idiot, idiot! You thought he was inviting you, personally. Oh, Jermaine, you fool!

'What do you say?' he pressed.

'What *can* a girl say?' Jermaine returned lightly.

She saw him smile, and she forgot totally about Edwina when Lukas further invited, 'And you'll stay the weekend?'

'Oh, I don't know about that,' she hedged, even while everything inside her screamed to accept. But, having hedged, she felt honour-bound to follow through with, 'I need to be back here on Sunday evening.'

'So you'll stay until after lunch on Sunday? Good,' he said, before she could get the words out to confirm. 'And you'll drive down in the morning?'

I'll come with you right now, her wayward heart cried. 'I'll come as soon as I can,' she answered soberly, and, grabbing at a moment of sanity, opened the door. 'Goodnight,' she smiled.

But as she went to move away so Lukas took a step closer, and as her heart began to race, so he took her into his arms. She was barely breathing when his head came down, and while the racing of her heart picked up yet more urgent speed Lukas gathered her closer, and gently, lingeringly, and without hurry, he kissed her.

'Goodnight, Jermaine,' he murmured softly, and let her go.

Blindly she turned from him and floated on auto-pilot up to her small apartment. She had been kissed before, and with more passion. But never had she been kissed so wonderfully, so beautifully, so—oh, his sensational mouth—so sensationally, and—by the man she loved.

CHAPTER SIX

JERMAINE lay awake for hours just thinking of Lukas. She supposed she must have slept at some stage, but she awoke early and he filled her head again, and she was once more enthralled as she remembered his magical kiss

She was no more certain this morning quite why Lukas had invited her to go with him to the art gallery in the first place—not forgetting he had taken her to dinner afterwards. Yet she smiled as she thought—it hadn't been because he had been let down by any female named Beverley. Her smile became a grin. Lukas had known jolly well that she'd thought Beverley had been a female of the species.

Jermaine fell to pondering again why Lukas had asked her out. It couldn't have been purely to persuade her to go up to Highfield today to give Mrs Dobson some help. He could have done that when he'd called on Wednesday.

So why had he asked her out? Could it be—her heart started to beat energetically—that for all they had got off to a 'spikey' start, Lukas had come to like her a little?

Oh, she did hope so. Liking wasn't love, of course, but... Suddenly her heartbeat slowed down to a dull pattern. Grief, woman, have you forgotten? Edwina is in his home! Why would any man waste time with you when Edwina's around?

Stop that, do, Jermaine ordered, only then realising more fully how much Ash's defection in favour of her sister's charms had shaken her confidence. Jermaine decided there and then that Lukas had asked her out for no other reason than he *did* like her. Must do. Edwina was in his *home,* for goodness' sake! He hadn't been rushing back to her, had he? And, don't forget, he hadn't made a dash to get home as soon as he could after his Swedish trip, had he?

For a moment or two Jermaine dwelt on the blissful pleasure of realising that, when Lukas had known Edwina before he had known her, it was the younger Hargreaves sister he had chosen to spend time with. Did that signify, or did it not, that Lukas preferred her to Edwina?

Jermaine's bliss was short-lived when she recalled that for all she knew Lukas might think that Ash was in love with Edwina. While it was said that all was fair in love and war, Jermaine could not help but know that Lukas looked out for his younger brother. That being so, wouldn't Lukas perhaps deny his own inclinations and deliberately keep away from Edwina's charms—even if he did desire a closer liaison with her?

With her thoughts in more of a tangle than ever, Jermaine got out of bed, musing that the only thing she knew for sure was that while she had been strong enough to deny Lukas a cup of coffee last night, she had not been strong enough to deny herself the chance of seeing him, of perhaps spending some time with him today.

It was a little after eleven o'clock when, endeavouring not to be too eager while at the same time telling herself that the sooner she got to Highfield the sooner she would be able to give Mrs Dobson some assistance, Jermaine drove her car through the gates of Highfield.

An emotional tide of warm colour rushed to her face when, obviously on his way out for a walk or something of that nature, she saw Lukas step out onto the drive. Memory of his wonderful kiss swamped her.

He glanced down the drive and saw her and paused, waiting for her to pull up next to him. Jermaine was outwardly under control by the time he was opening the driver's door.

'I'm glad you're here,' he greeted her, and ridiculously, because she was sure he didn't mean anything by it, her heart leapt. He retrieved her overnight bag from the rear of the car. 'You're in the same room as last time,' he informed her pleasantly, and walked with her back inside the house.

Jermaine found her voice. 'Don't let me stop you from what you were doing.'

'Come down as soon as you've dropped off your bag. I'll get some coffee sorted,' he answered.

Was he going to have a cup of coffee with her? She felt all fluttery again at just the thought: the two of them, Lukas and her. 'I'll make it,' she determined. 'I'm not here to be waited on, and Mrs Dobson has enough to…'

'Mrs Dobson has Tina here to help her this weekend,' Lukas interrupted, stopping her dead, mid-flow.

'Tina?'

'Sharon's sister,' Lukas explained.

'Sharon—who helps Mrs Dobson during the week?' Jermaine remembered.

'Apart from the other Friday when Sharon's little boy was unwell,' he agreed.

Jermaine went to go on, but as she quickly realised that Tina's help must have been arranged in his absence, so Jermaine also very quickly realised that if Tina was there to assist Mrs Dobson today and tomorrow there was no reason at all for her being there. She stopped stock-still at the bottom of the staircase.

'You should have phoned me,' she protested. Oh, no, she was going to have to go back to London—and she didn't want to part from him, not yet.

'While it's always a delight to hear your voice, Jermaine, why did you want me to phone?' Lukas enquired, and Jermaine stared at him wide eyed.

'Why, to tell me not to come. With Mrs Dobson having all the help she requires, there's no need for me to be here,' she replied, promptly adding, 'I'll go.'

Lukas looked astounded. 'No, you won't!' he stated categorically, no ifs or buts about it.

'I won't? Why won't I?' Embarrassment that she was here at all under the circumstances made her voice short.

'Because...' he began to answer just as shortly, but then paused. Paused, and smiled, and said winningly, 'Because you type reports so absolutely accurately.'

Jermaine blinked, but a moment later was inwardly smiling. 'You rogue,' she admonished him nicely. 'You've a meeting before you fly off on Monday and you want your report on your Swedish trip typed and ready before then.'

He looked steadily at her, and then, making her tingle all over, he stroked a sensitive finger down her cheek— every bit as if he couldn't resist touching her. 'Say you will,' he coaxed.

She was seduced by him, seduced by his charm—and that was without the added bonus of being able to spend some time alone with him in his study. What could she do? 'Well, if you put it like that,' she replied sedately, joy just to be with him bursting in her heart.

'I'll rustle up that coffee,' he said decisively, and Jermaine again floated up a staircase.

Fearing her mood of high euphoria might be dampened if she saw Edwina, Jermaine sailed straight by her sister's door at the top of the stairs and went straight on to the room she had used that last time she had been at Highfield. She would look in on Edwina later.

It took Jermaine but a few minutes to unpack her overnight bag. But she took another couple of minutes in which she checked her appearance. Normally she wouldn't have bothered, but if Lukas was going to join her for coffee, and she rather thought he was, she needed the confidence-boost of knowing that she looked all right.

The mirror confirmed that her pale complexion was flawless, that her platinum-blonde hair needed no attention—she ran a comb through it just the same—and that the small amount of make-up she had used looked all right.

That was as long as she could bear to be away from Lukas. Wanting to see him again, she hurried from her room—but only to bump into Edwina, limping from hers. Jermaine's feeling of excitement plummeted.

'Where on earth did you spring from?' Edwina, the first to recover, demanded.

Jermaine never had been fooled by the limp. 'How much longer are you going to keep this up?' she counter-demanded.

'Lukas is proving a tougher nut to crack than I'd anticipated,' Edwina answered, gladdening Jermaine's heart. But only to make her spirits dive when she added, 'But I see signs that he's cracking...' She broke off, and then, a calculating smile touching her mouth, she added 'I don't know why you're here, but since you are you can make yourself useful and take Ash off my hands—and leave Lukas to me.'

'No can do,' Jermaine replied as Edwina, not risking to be caught out if anyone should be lurking unseen, held her 'injured' back with one hand and limped down the stairs with her sister.

'Why not?' Edwina demanded.

'Because I'm here to work this weekend. Lukas has some typing he wants doing.'

'You're staying overnight?'

Jermaine ignored the aggressive question. 'Have you phoned Dad this week?' she asked.

'Don't be a pain!' Edwina retorted, but as she spotted Lukas crossing the hall she was suddenly all smiles. 'Did you know Jermaine was here?' she called down to him.

He halted as they slowly descended. What he was thinking Jermaine had no idea, for his expression was bland. 'I invited Jermaine to join us,' he replied smoothly.

'Well, you mustn't work her too hard, you naughty man,' Edwina scolded archly, and as they stepped onto a level with him Jermaine felt her face flame with warm colour. Edwina made it sound every bit as if she had been complaining to her elder sister about being pressed into work.

Jermaine caught his eyes on her and, embarrassed, she looked quickly away. But she fell even more hopelessly in love with Lukas when, suavely, he told Edwina, 'I won't. Though I've a feeling Jermaine would be the last to complain.' And while Jermaine was glowing from that, he asked Edwina solicitously, 'Can you manage as far as the drawing room? Mrs Dobson will bring in some coffee presently.'

Edwina, taking a hold of his arm and leaning against him, swiftly put paid to any remaining glow Jermaine had been feeling. Spiteful darts of jealousy bombarded her and she couldn't bear to watch.

'I'll get the coffee,' she announced as evenly as she

could. 'I wanted to go and say hello to Mrs Dobson, anyhow.'

With that she turned and made for the kitchen, acknowledging that her newly discovered love for Lukas had not come alone. It brought with it a whole gamut of other, unsuspected emotions. She who had never hated anyone in her life had hated Lukas on occasion when she had first met him. Oh, how could she ever have hated him? Was it all part and parcel of falling in love? She felt confused suddenly that she didn't know anything. Though she corrected that. The one thing she did know for sure was that there was nothing whatsoever the matter with Edwina.

'I'm here again, Mrs Dobson.' Jermaine found a smile as she entered the kitchen.

While the housekeeper seemed genuinely pleased to see her again and introduced Tina, who had been busy with a coffee pot, Jermaine spotted that a tray had been laid with two cups and saucers.

'May I have an extra cup?' she asked, and passed a pleasant few minutes in conversation with the housekeeper and her helper. Then, insisting she would take the tray, Jermaine carried it to the drawing room.

The extra cup and saucer was not going to be necessary, she discovered. Lukas was there, but got to his feet as she went into the room. 'If you'll excuse me,' he addressed both his female guests, 'I need to go and look at some fencing.'

'He's never still,' Edwina complained the moment he had gone.

'Poor you,' Jermaine replied, and found another unsuspected trait when, having enjoyed Lukas's company last night, she quite enjoyed saying, 'Just now must have

been the first time you've seen him since he went to
Sweden on Thursday.'

It was not a very nice trait, she knew. But she got paid
back for it in full when Edwina, favouring her with a
short look, stated, 'I had a very late night last night. In
fact, I was still up when Lukas came home.' Jolted,
Jermaine instantly visualised her beautiful sister draped
prettily on one of the sofas, waiting to go into action the
moment Lukas walked in through the door. 'He rang me
from Sweden to ask how I was getting along.' Edwina
put her delicate size five boot in.

Somehow Jermaine managed to stay civilly in the
same room with her while they shared a pot of coffee
and spoke of nothing in particular. She should have
known, Jermaine inwardly sighed; Edwina always won.

With pictures flashing through her head of Lukas rushing home after he had left her, so that he could dally
with her sister, Jermaine finished her coffee and returned
the tray to the kitchen. What she would have liked to do
then was to escape via the rear door and take a walk
down to the picturesque brook. It was such a tranquil
spot—and she needed a tranquil spot. She was, in truth,
feeling anything but tranquil.

But Lukas was in the grounds somewhere, checking
out fences. And, when not long ago she had left her room
in a hurry to join him, to spend some time with him, she
was now not ready to see him again so soon—should his
fence inspection area be anywhere near that brook.

Jermaine, aware that her sister wouldn't be bothered
whether she went back to her in the drawing room or
not, went upstairs to her room. She would have to go
down again for lunch, politeness alone decreed that, but
she would by far much prefer to return to London.

But that was a lie. Falling in love with Lukas had

made a liar of her—a liar to herself. Because, had she felt that strongly about returning to London, nothing would have stopped her. As it was, despite being in a state of turmoil—not knowing if Lukas, needing a report typing, had deliberately set out to entertain, to charm last night, even to the extent of that oh so wonderful kiss, in order to ask her to come to Highfield today—Jermaine knew she wanted to stay.

She was being weak, not to say pathetic, but she loved him so that even if he was being a rat of the first water she wanted to stay in his home, where she stood the best chance of spending some time with him.

With the passing of the next fifteen minutes Jermaine started to get on top of her emotions, and was then able to think more logically. Come on, buck your ideas up, she instructed. Do you really believe that a man of Lukas's standing, a man of his undoubted wealth, would—*before* he went to Sweden, mark you—arrange to take you out so that on his return he could persuade you, deviously, to come and do some work for him?

Jermaine realised she didn't believe any such nonsense. If he needed someone to work over the weekend, he'd hire somebody. The same way in which he must have instructed Mrs Dobson to hire any help she needed while there were extra people in the house. Clearly Mrs Dobson must have accepted that she couldn't cope without weekend assistance, and had contacted Sharon's sister in Lukas's absence.

Jermaine was still in her room when, glancing from her window, she saw Ash's car turn in at the gates. It puzzled her why if, as he'd hinted, he was not so enamoured of Edwina, he was still harbouring her as his guest. A whole week had passed since he'd stated that he had made a mistake—so why was Edwina still here—though ultimately as Lukas's guest?

At that point Jermaine realised that jealousy in relation to Lukas and Edwina was starting to get to her again, and she was impatient with herself. For goodness' sake, she could hardly expect either Lukas or Ash to send Edwina on her way—not when she was playing the suffering delicate damsel.

Jermaine left her room and, on entering the drawing room, felt jealousy nip again, because Lukas was back from his fence checking and was seated in conversation with Edwina. He broke off what he was saying and was on his feet as soon as he saw her. 'Jermaine,' he greeted her pleasantly. 'Can I get you something to drink before lunch?'

'No, thanks,' she replied, her thoughts on the work for which she would need to keep her full attention focused that afternoon.

She was half turned when someone else came into the drawing room. 'Jermaine!' Ash exclaimed, and again looked as though he might kiss her in greeting. Perhaps remembering the last time he'd tried it, he controlled himself, but still looked delighted to see her as he added, 'This is a wonderful surprise! You're not dashing back to London, I hope?'

'I'm here until tomorrow,' she answered. But, feeling a little awkward, and as if needing an excuse for being there, she explained, 'Lukas has a report on his Swedish trip he wants typing.'

Ash looked from her to his brother. 'Has he now?' he questioned.

'Since we're all here, we may as well go into lunch,' Lukas suggested, and it was *prima donna* time as Edwina winced and nibbled prettily at her bottom lip as she struggled painfully to stand. Naturally, gentlemen both, the two males went to assist her.

The two men seemed a little preoccupied over lunch, but Edwina was obviously insensitive to the vibes Jermaine was certain she was picking up. Edwina kept up a steady flow of conversation to which, when addressed, everyone present politely replied.

It was near to the end of the meal when Ash commented that he thought he would go and take a second look at a property he had almost made up his mind to purchase. Before being asked, Edwina declined. 'You won't mind if I don't come with you?'

Ash smiled. 'You must rest as much as you can,' he answered. Then he turned to Jermaine, seated next to him. 'And you're about to tell me you're going to be busy,' he commented regretfully.

But before she could agree that she would be busy, in his brother's study, Lukas was stating quietly, 'I'll come with you, Ash.' And all eyes went to Lukas. But it was Jermaine to whom he looked as he stated charmingly, 'With the speed you type, Jermaine, we'll have ample time to complete that report tomorrow morning.'

She had straight away decided that if there was nothing there for her to do, then she was here under false pretences—double false pretences if you took into account the charade Edwina was playing to the full—and that she would go back to London right now. But Lukas stating they would work in the morning gave her pride the fillip it needed—he still expected her to stay overnight, then? 'Of course,' she answered evenly.

'You could come with us this afternoon,' Ash suggested.

But somehow she sensed—and could only suppose her senses were more acute to Lukas now than they had been—that he wanted to talk privately to Ash. Something to do with business, obviously, so she smiled, unoffended, and entered her sister's charade. 'I think it would be better if I stayed and kept Edwina company,' she replied.

The two Tavinor brothers departed soon after lunch, and with Edwina comfortable back in the drawing room, with a seemingly limitless supply of magazines, Jermaine went and found the portable telephone she had used on her previous visit. She rang her parents and chatted to them for some while. After confirming that she wouldn't dream of spending Christmas anywhere but with them, in their home, she handed the phone to her sister. Edwina stuck out her tongue to her, but took the phone and assured her father that she was making excellent progress and that she would be leaving Highfield shortly. No, she quickly answered their father, there was absolutely no need for her to go home to be looked after.

Jermaine heard her promise that—as was usual and expected—she also would be home for Christmas. But only one sentence stuck in Jermaine's mind as Edwina ended the call and idly handed the phone back to her. 'You're leaving here?' she questioned.

'Even I can't keep up the pretence of a bad back for ever,' Edwina answered. 'Although were it not for Lukas going away on Monday I'd have given it a shot.'

'You're leaving because Lukas is going abroad?'

'You know as well as I do that he's the only reason for my "incapacity". I'm not sticking around here all next week with only Ash and that odious Mrs Dobson for company!'

Mrs Dobson, odious! Jermaine gave up. 'Got everything you need?' she asked a touch sarcastically as, taking the portable phone with her, she headed for the door.

'No,' Edwina replied, a calculating look there in her eyes, 'but I will have.'

Jermaine blanched and felt quite ill. She'd seen that look in Edwina's eyes before. When Edwina set her mind on something, she always got it—and Edwina was set on getting Lukas.

Jermaine stayed in her room until close to dinner time, when she felt it would be rude to stay there any longer. She had no idea where the property was that Lukas and Ash had gone to see, but they had been absent an absolute age. Jermaine knew, because she had had her ears tuned for every passing vehicle, they had returned a little over half an hour ago.

Dinner was a pleasant enough affair, but Jermaine found she was having a hard time trying not to be forever glancing across to Lukas. Determined not to focus all her attention on him—she'd just shrivel up and die if he observed that she hung on his every word—she turned to Ash.

'Have you decided about the property you saw this afternoon?' she asked.

Ash looked at her and smiled. 'I have. I'm going to make an offer for it.'

'You'll be pleased your long search is at an end.'

'You must come and see it,' Ash invited enthusiastically, but paused, glanced quickly to Lukas, and then looked at Edwina, seated across from him. 'You, too, Edwina. If you feel up to it, of course,' he qualified.

'I'd like to,' she accepted, but, as Jermaine knew full well, Edwina was quite able to find an excuse not to go when the time came. Now, having spent enough time on Ash apparently, Edwina turned the battery of her blue eyes onto Lukas. 'What did you think of the property,

Lukas?' she asked in her breathless way. She even
touched his arm.

Jermaine concentrated her attention on a roast pars-
nip—she was finding the vicious assault of jealousy difficult to cope with.

They retired to the drawing room for coffee. 'Would
you care for a liqueur?' Jermaine looked up and found
Lukas had come to stand near. 'Cointreau? T...?'

'Cointreau would be lovely,' she accepted, her voice
suddenly husky. She looked quickly away from him—
about the only way she could get herself back together
again.

This was dreadful! She'd gone to pieces over him like
some lovestruck schoolgirl! Though, recalling the burning pain of jealousy not too long back, this was no
schoolgirl crush. Lukas returned with her liqueur, but
when he did no more than sit down next to her Jermaine
was again left struggling to get herself together.

'Um—what time would you like to start in the morning?' she asked.

'Any time to suit you,' Lukas replied.

'Nine?'

He smiled. 'I think we can be a little more relaxed
than that.' His smile became a grin. 'How do you feel
about nine-fifteen?'

She loved him—she burst out laughing. 'Nine-fifteen
it is,' she said.

And stopped laughing when Edwina, not caring very
much to be sharing her sofa with Ash, suddenly pouted.
'Are you going to share the joke?'

Jermaine realised then that she was laughing too freely
with Lukas and might be in danger of giving away her
feelings for him. She wanted to stay with him, to be near
him, close like this on the sofa. Against that, though, she

knew her pride would never recover if he, or anyone in the room, saw the love which she was so desperate to hide. She felt panicky suddenly, and needed to be on her own. She shouldn't have accepted that will-weakening liqueur. Not that she'd done more than have a sip or two, but she needed to be alert, on her toes—needed to be out of there.

Because she'd asked for the Cointreau, she finished it while Edwina, giving Lukas her undivided attention, pulled out all the stops in the allure department. When jealousy again sent fast and furious spiteful darts, Jermaine knew it was more than high time she made herself scarce. It was even more painful to her that Lukas didn't appear at all unhappy that Edwina was dedicated to his every utterance. Surely he must be aware that Edwina was making a play for him? Perhaps he was— and was enjoying every moment.

Jermaine yawned delicately. It wouldn't hurt him to know that such goings-on bored her totally. 'I'm sorry,' she apologised prettily. 'Would anyone mind if I went to bed?'

'Must you?' It was Ash—how she wanted it to be Lukas.

'I've had a busy week.' She smiled at Ash.

'And it isn't over yet,' Lukas said, getting to his feet with her.

'Nine-fifteen, you said,' she reminded him, wished everyone goodnight, and went without obvious haste from the room.

She lay sleepless for a long time that night, then had sleep of the fractured variety and wanted quite urgently to get up and leave. Yet, at the same time, she began to feel quite desperate—because when she did leave she might never see Lukas again.

Jermaine was glad to see dawn break, and, still in the same troubled frame of mind, showered and got dressed. She felt restless and fidgety, and, unable to take it any longer, she shrugged into her coat and decided to take a walk.

Letting herself quietly out of the house, she skirted round to the rear. Supposing that she had known in advance where her feet would lead her, she was very soon walking down to the bridge with its little stream gurgling cheerfully beneath.

She stayed on the bridge for some minutes, then moved to the bench that seemed to call a welcome. It *was* a tranquil place, as she had previously discovered, and gradually Jermaine became more at peace with herself. She was then able to recognise that, probably because she had never been in love before, she had been thrown in a total heap by it and just hadn't known how to handle it.

She still didn't know how to handle it, particularly, but this morning she seemed more reconciled to the fact that, while she loved Lukas, he was never going to return that love—and so she had better get used to that foul companion, jealousy, whenever any female flirted with him.

Jermaine was just wryly musing that since she was unlikely to see him again after today there was nothing to get used to, when she was suddenly shaken to realise that she had company of a very special kind.

'Couldn't you sleep?'

She looked up, a smile in her heart, in her eyes, as she stared at Lukas. 'Early to bed, early to rise,' she trotted out.

'Shall I join you?' he asked.

'Of course,' she replied, and, on a sudden thought, 'I

didn't disturb you when I left the house, did I?' she asked hurriedly.

He shook his head. 'I was in my study when I heard dainty footsteps going over the gravel on the drive,' he answered. 'Now, how did I know I'd find you down here?'

'I'm bewitched by this spot,' she smiled, but, her head jerking up, 'You—followed me?' she asked, her already hurried heartbeat picking up more speed at the notion before common sense landed. 'You wanted me for something?' she dully realised. 'You wanted to have a word about…?'

'I need to have a reason?' Lukas teased—and her heart fluttered again.

'Er—no,' she replied, telling herself she mustn't take any of this personally. 'They're your grounds, after all.'

Lukas didn't answer. He didn't move away either, but seemed perfectly content at that hour in the morning to sit quietly with her, watching the clear waters of the dancing brook as it leapt over pebbles.

Then suddenly, astonishingly, she heard him say, 'So who's this man you've got to rush back to London to see tonight?'

'Sorry?' she queried blankly, staring at him mystified.

'You said you couldn't stay until Monday morning,' Lukas reminded her—she didn't remember saying any such thing. 'When I asked you to stay the weekend, you said you needed to be back in London for Sunday evening.' Now she remembered—she hadn't wanted to appear too eager. 'Is it the diabolical Stuart that takes you away from us?' Lukas wanted to know.

She laughed. She didn't want to laugh. She had an idea that just being with him made her so happy that laughter just kind of bubbled up inside her. Still, all the same, she didn't feel like telling Lukas that she had absolutely no need whatsoever to dash back to London that afternoon. At the very least he would think it odd that she had said she had to in the first place. She saw his glance move from her violet eyes to her laughing mouth, and she reined in her inner happiness to tell him primly, 'Stuart isn't diabolical. He's…'

'You're not in love with him, I know that much,' Lukas cut in.

How did he know? She panicked for a moment, until she recalled Lukas saying on Friday that he didn't see her as someone who'd be serious with one man and be out dining with another. 'I don't need to be in love with him,' she replied, and, in the manner of some newsworthy film star, she ended, 'We're just good friends.' She started to feel a mite anxious that with this mention of love Lukas might probe deeper—though why he would was ridiculous—and stood up. 'I've an appointment at nine-fifteen,' she mentioned lightly. 'I shall have to go.'

Lukas gave her an amused look, but left the bench too. Together they walked back to the house, each occupied with their own thoughts. They parted at the stairs with little else being said, apart from Lukas commenting, 'If I miss you at breakfast, I'll see you in the study.'

Jermaine went up to her room with her insides all wobbly—partly from her unexpected meeting with Lukas, and partly from her anticipation of shortly seeing him again.

She delayed going down to breakfast for as long as she could, and discovered from Ash that Lukas had breakfasted some while ago. 'So you're stuck with just me,' he smiled, and was so exceedingly pleasant and likeable that Jermaine realised that, had circumstances been different, they could have been very good friends.

'Must dash,' she said when she had finished the bacon and scrambled eggs Tina had brought her.

'Don't let that brother of mine work you too hard.' Ash smiled.

Jermaine returned briefly to her room to wash her hands, clean her teeth and to check that she was looking all right. Her platinum-blonde hair was shining and needed little attention. Likewise her make-up required little attention. It was her insides that she could do nothing about.

She wanted to see him. She so wanted to see him. So what are you doing, dithering up here? It had never been her habit to wait until the clock struck nine to start work. If she arrived at the office early she began work straight away.

At five past nine, passing Tina in the hall carrying a tray, obviously on her way to Edwina's room, Jermaine made it to the study door. She took a steadying breath and went in, her heart performing a jig when she at once saw that Lukas was there first.

'Oh, good,' she smiled. 'You're here.'

'Here and waiting,' Lukas answered quietly, his serious grey eyes taking in her shoulder-length hair, her superb complexion and her slender but shapely figure. 'Come in and sit down,' he said when she hadn't moved, and smiled.

Jermaine hung the jacket of her suit over the chair she had used before—and in no time they were deep into his work concerning Sweden.

It could, she supposed, have been some deadly boring business report. But, possibly because of her own business background, and because of the overwhelming love she felt for him, Jermaine thought his report little short of terrific.

'Shall we take a break?' Lukas asked at one stage. But suddenly she felt strangely shy.

She shook her head. 'Shall we get on?' She made the mistake of looking at him, and at the warm look in his eyes for her her pulses raced.

'A woman after my own heart,' he said softly, and while Jermaine wanted to tell him, yes, yes, she wanted his heart, he continued from where they had left off.

It was nearing half past twelve when everything was neatly typed and many copies printed and checked over. Jermaine felt Lukas come and stand behind her.

'You've worked like a Trojan,' he commented, and she looked up, awash with pleasure.

'I enjoyed doing it,' she answered truthfully, turning and basking in the warm look in his eyes. They stared at each other, and she felt transfixed to look away. Her heart started drumming and there was a pounding in her ears too. But abruptly she stood up. 'I'd b-better go and tidy up before lunch,' she mumbled huskily, desperately trying to get herself together; with Lukas looking steadily at her like that—a certain indefinable warmth in his eyes—something, she knew not what, was happening to her, and she urgently needed to find some sort of control.

She went to shoot past him, failed to clear him, violently bumped into him, and they ended up facing each other. His hands came to her arms as he steadied her. 'Now what are you panicking over?' Lukas asked, not letting her go.

'N-nothing,' she said. 'I'm not…'

'You're afraid I'm going to kiss you?'

Please, oh, please do. 'Of course not!' she answered, her voice coming out nowhere near as firm as she would have liked to have heard it.

A frown crossed his intelligent forehead. 'You're not scared of me, Jermaine?' he asked quietly—and suddenly she was remembering how he had gently probed 'You're scared' when he had learned she was a virgin.

Because she loved him, and had all at once realised that he had a fine sensitivity, she was not thinking but just acting on instinct alone. Jermaine showed him in the only way she could that she was not scared, or afraid he would kiss her. She stretched up, and she kissed him...

Then found she didn't want to break away. Her hands went to his waist—just the feel of his excellent mouth against her own and she seemed to need to steady herself.

She quickly pulled back; that, or kiss him again. 'I—er—um—shouldn't have done that,' she said huskily, and loved it when, slowly, Lukas smiled.

'Oh, I can't agree with you there,' he murmured, and, taking charge, he pulled her into his arms. The next she knew he was kissing her as she had never been kissed before.

Nor did he stop at one kiss; he seemed as hungry for her mouth as she was for his. Locked in his warm embrace, Jermaine welcomed his kisses, a fire igniting in her, bursting into flame as his strong arms held her, binding her to him.

'Beautiful, beautiful Jermaine,' he breathed against her mouth, kissing her again, gathering her yet closer to him.

She felt his warmth, his heat, and as he pressed close to her, she, her heart going crazy, pressed closer to him. She heard a groan of wanting escape him, and felt she would faint from the utter rapture of it when, with his mouth on hers, drawing her very soul from her, his caressing hands sought and found the swollen globes of her breasts.

She wasn't sure that a groan of wanting didn't escape her too, for Lukas broke his kiss to smile tenderly down at her. 'All right?' he asked.

Wonderfully all right, she wanted to tell him. But as the flame of unsuspected passion continued to spiral upward in her, and she found herself in a never-before-known land of urgent desire, of wanting, with no thought of holding back, she could only suppose it must be some latent and totally-not-required strand of modesty that caused her to answer, 'I'm not very sure we should be doing this.'

Those grey eyes were as steady as ever as Lukas looked into her fervent violet ones, that had darkened to a much deeper colour as her desire for him had rocked her. Then she saw his mouth pick up at the corners.

'Why?' he asked gently, teasingly.

Again she recalled his 'scared' comment, and she didn't *want* him to think she was scared of him, or of making love with him, and so she told him honestly, 'Because I—um—think I like it.'

He laughed then, and it was a wonderful sound. 'You're simply gorgeous,' he said softly. But instead of renewing his onslaught to her mouth, to her senses, when he must know the advantage was all his, he kissed her tenderly and, taking his arms from her, took a small step away. 'And absolutely right, of course.'

'I am?' She hoped she didn't sound as disappointed as she felt.

'It's nearly lunchtime—we could be interrupted at any moment,' he reminded her.

'I—see,' she said slowly, and as she did begin to see, and went hot all over as she visualised Tina perhaps coming in to tell them that the meal was ready, Jermaine moved back from him. Ridiculously, when she considered how not long since she had been clinging to Lukas like a second skin, she was suddenly overcome by a dreadful shyness.

She turned desperately away, warm colour rushing to her face, and was glad to espy her jacket—completely forgotten about until then—still hanging over the back of the chair. She grabbed it up and quickly put it on.

'I'll—er—see you later,' she threw in his general direction. But made the mistake of looking at him.

'Don't rush off,' he said, and, coming close again, caused her insides to jump some more when he stroked tender fingers down the shy blush of her cheek and asked, 'What are you doing for Christmas?'

She was mesmerised by him and tried hard to concentrate. What *was* she doing for Christmas? 'I'm spending it with my parents,' she replied, barely able to remember that part of her telephone conversation with her mother yesterday where she had doubly confirmed that she would be there.

'All of it?' Lukas asked.

'All of it,' she answered, her head swimming as she tried to decipher what all this was about.

'Can I come too?' he asked.

She knew then that he was joking! A man of his charm, his sophistication, would have something better to do than spend a homey Christmas with her and her parents. 'What?' she questioned, pretending to be aghast. 'And let your fan club down?' Jermaine was certain, Edwina aside, that his festive season engagement diary would be full to overflowing.

He grinned. Then, to her amazement, urged, 'Spend your Christmas here?'

Her heart started to pound. Was he serious? Of course he wasn't. Couldn't be, she decided, and fearing to make an utter fool of herself by allowing herself to take him seriously, insisted, 'My parents are expecting me.'

'You always do what your parents expect?' he asked, humour playing around his superb mouth, and she felt light-hearted suddenly.

Though she kept a straight face as she assured him, 'Always.'

'You'll come home Boxing Day?'

'Home?' She wasn't sure she understood his question.

'Home—here. To Highfield,' Lukas answered.

Oh, how she loved him. She had to look away from him. She wanted to swallow on the knot of emotion that caught in her throat—he *had* been serious. She felt then that she would have given anything to tell Lukas yes, yes, a thousand times yes. By the sound of it all her prayers would be answered and she *would* be able to see Lukas again when he returned from his business trip. But the reality of it was that her parents would be very much upset, and hurt, if she and Edwina broke their promise to spend Christmas with them.

So, from somewhere, Jermaine managed to summon up a smile, and, much though it hurt her, 'I can't,' she told Lukas. 'I gave them my promise.'

CHAPTER SEVEN

THE days stretched long and achingly for Jermaine after her departure from Highfield. She had not managed to have a moment alone with Lukas once she had left his study—Edwina had seemed to be always everywhere.

Jermaine spent hours reliving those minutes she had been in his arms. She again felt the rapture of being held by him and of being kissed by him.

He had been in no hurry for her to leave, she recalled dreamily, and felt warmed through and through to remember, again and again, that Lukas had asked her to spend Christmas with him at Highfield. Ash would be there too, of course, but surely Lukas wouldn't have asked her to Christmas at Highfield on any mere passing whim?

To invite someone into your home over that special festive time had to mean that they were a tiny bit special too, didn't it?

Oh, come off it, argued her more realistic self. You're not even the tiniest scrap special to him. Have you forgotten so completely that he regards you as a bit of a challenge? Good heavens, get your head together do. For pity's sake, you don't have to look further back than Sunday, when *you* kissed *him.* You responded fully when he kissed you back; my, how you responded! Lukas must have thought, No challenge; a walk-over! And *that* was why he invited you to spend Christmas in his home, purely and simply because he thought you were *willing!*

Well, she wasn't willing—well, that was what she

tried to tell herself. Although, as she recalled just how eager she had been for his kisses, in all honesty she couldn't have said that she was *un*willing.

Pride insisted on reminding her that she had demurred a little when she'd told him that she wasn't very sure they should be doing this. But only for her pride to take a hammering when she recollected how he'd agreed a very short while afterwards that she was absolutely right.

Perhaps, then, that meant that he'd decided she was not so much as 'a bit' of a challenge after all. Then why had he asked her to spend Christmas in his home?

At that point Jermaine realised she had come full circle. That did not stop her from thinking continually about Lukas. But she had never been in love before. Though as she did not want to listen to her common sense, her realism, as a few days passed, so she had to accept that she was not the remotest bit special to Lukas. Had she been, then surely he would have managed to pick up the phone—wherever he was? When he'd been in Sweden he'd found a moment to ring Edwina, Jermaine recalled.

No, no, no, she was not going to think of Edwina in relation to Lukas. She couldn't, Jermaine fretted. There were enough emotions tearing at her nerves now, without adding jealousy.

She had never felt so low, but, since she was the only one who was going to know it, Jermaine adopted a cheerfulness she was far from feeling. The evening of the company's Christmas dinner came—with Nick Norris eager to take her home.

'I'm driving Stuart home,' she was glad to be able to answer.

'You mean I have to wait until the New Year to get to spend any time with you?' he complained. But, brightening, he persisted, 'Fancy partnering me at a New Year's Eve party?'

She didn't. 'Some other time,' she told him, and tried to feel good that somebody wanted to date her anyhow.

She went out for an Indian meal with Stuart on Friday, was home by ten, and spent the weekend half wishing she had been able to break her promise to her parents and go to Highfield for Christmas instead. Even while she hated herself for that half wish, Jermaine couldn't help but fully wish she had been in a position to accept Lukas's Christmas offer. She ached to see Lukas again, wanted to see him again—oh, so desperately.

Jermaine spent her lunchtimes on Monday and Tuesday doing her last bits of Christmas shopping, and went home to her parents on Christmas Eve, laden with a large suitcase plus many carrier bags, where she was warmly welcomed—and, metaphorically, dropped from a great height when, greetings over, she asked what time Edwina was expected.

'She's not coming,' Grace Hargreaves replied flatly.

'Not…?'

'They so badly wanted her to stay, it seemed criminal to keep her to her promise,' Edwin Hargreaves defended. 'Especially as Edwina has been through such a rough time with her back.'

'They?' Jermaine asked, fearing the worst but striving to keep her expression even, as looking to her father, she waited for him to deliver the body-blow.

'The Tavinors, of course!' her father replied. 'Edwina rang this afternoon and was quite excited that Lukas Tavinor himself had just been in touch, asking her to join him and Ash. Having met them both, I'm happy that they'll take care of her—I told her to go, with my blessing. She's not fully recovered yet, you know.'

Jermaine was aware that her father was defending in advance any criticism of his elder daughter's actions, but Jermaine was too heartsick to think of telling him that Edwina was more than capable of taking care of herself.

As the evening progressed it became apparent, when the subject of Edwina frequently came up, that her father was of the opinion that it was only because Lukas Tavinor was head of the household that he had personally phoned Edwina to ask her to stay. However, in Edwin Hargreaves's view, it was really his brother Ash who had extended the invitation.

Oh, how Jermaine would have loved to have believed that. But she knew differently. Hadn't Ash himself told her he'd made one colossal mistake where Edwina was concerned, and had allowed lust to rule his head? From that Jermaine could only imagine Ash meant that Edwina was now out of his system. It therefore figured that it wasn't Ash who wanted Edwina at Highfield over Christmas—but Lukas.

Inconstant swine! Inconstant? Just because he asked you first? For heaven's sake. Jermaine brought herself up short. Anyone would think Lukas had declared undying love to her, when all he'd done was to ask her to spend Christmas with him and, when she'd refused, asked her sister instead. Well, wasn't that inconstant? No, it wasn't. What it was was telling her that she might refuse his invitation but that there were dozens of others who would accept. Indeed, someone already had. Someone ready and more than willing to drop her other plans and dash to Highfield.

Christmas Day passed with an exchange of gifts and Jermaine helping with the preparation for the evening meal. Needing a break from being forever cheerful, she took herself off for a long walk during the afternoon.

She discovered on her return that her father had been unable to wait any longer for Edwina to ring, as he'd expected, and that he'd telephoned Highfield himself. Jermaine was glad she had not been there. Her father might well have asked her to get him the Highfield number, and she didn't know, should Lukas have answered the phone, whether or not she would have wanted to speak to him.

Jermaine wasn't sleeping well. That night was no exception. Had Edwina been in Lukas's study? Had he kissed her the way he'd kissed…? Jermaine blanked off her mind, but was still wide awake, sitting up in the window seat in her room, at one o'clock on Boxing Day morning, when it began to snow.

She watched for some while as huge flakes quickly covered the ground. How silent everywhere was, how beautiful the night. She wished she were with Lukas. Pathetic. She sighed and got into bed. Put the man out of your mind, do.

But he was even more difficult to put out of her mind when later, around eleven that morning, when she had just hunted out some old snow boots with a view to taking herself off for another solitary walk, Jermaine, shrugging into a jacket, heard the sound of a vehicle crunching over the snow-covered drive.

'Who's this?' she heard her mother ask, plainly not recognising the vehicle as belonging to any of their friends.

Jermaine went and joined her, and, taking a glance out of the window, saw a Range Rover standing there. When none other than Lukas Tavinor stepped out of it, she thought—as a symphony started up in her head—that she'd had him so much on her mind her brain had conjured him up; that because she so wanted to see him she was imagining it was him.

But Lukas was no figment of her imagination. 'Isn't he Lukas, Ash's brother?' her mother exclaimed. As Grace Hargreaves worriedly pondered, 'Do you think something's happened to Edwina?' Jermaine had to try to rapidly get herself together.

'I shouldn't think so for a minute,' she answered, glad her father was out at the village shop, hunting up some reading matter. He'd panic like crazy if he thought Edwina had had 'another' accident.

The doorbell sounded and Jermaine, who would by far have preferred her mother to answer it while she composed herself a little more, went to the door. If something awful *had* befallen Edwina, and Lukas was coming to tell them in person rather than break bad news over the phone, then Jermaine saw it was up to her to answer the door.

A blast of cold air hit her as she pulled back the door—she barely noticed it.

Oh, how wonderful it was to see him. Her heart felt so full that for long, long seconds time seemed suspended and she just stared at him.

Lukas too seemed stuck for words as he looked back at her, though she very soon realised her imagination was going off at a tangent. For, as casually as you like, he was suddenly saying, 'I was in the area...' And with a smile that turned her knees to water, he continued, 'I thought I might stop by and cadge a cup of coffee.'

The sun came out on the whole miserable time she'd had since she had last seen him. A smile started deep inside her. 'I was just going out for a walk,' she blurted out—and could have kicked herself. Now she'd just deprived herself of fifteen minutes, perhaps half an hour, of his company.

'You're going on your own?' he enquired.

'I love the snow,' she said, and wondered what was happening to her brain. That was no sort of an answer.

'No diabolical Stuart walking with you?'

She laughed. Oh, joy, oh, bliss, just to see Lukas. 'Everything all right?' Her mother appearing at her shoulder brought Jermaine abruptly down to earth. All too plainly there was nothing the matter with Edwina, and her mother should be told so at once.

Jermaine opened her mouth to tell her that Lukas had merely stopped by for a cup of coffee when, to Jermaine's delight, he said, 'Good morning, Mrs Hargreaves. I've come to borrow your lovely daughter for a walk, if you've no objection.'

Grace Hargreaves was all smiles, and, to Jermaine's total embarrassment, she obviously believed Lukas had driven the many miles on such a bad-weather day merely to take her youngest daughter for a walk. But, before Jermaine could find her voice and say that Lukas just happened to be in the area, her mother was inviting, 'Perhaps you'd like to stay to lunch when you come back? After yesterday's feasting we're only having a cold meal today, but you're more than welcome.'

'Thank you,' he promptly accepted, and Jermaine forgot everything, save that she had just been assured of a couple of hours, or more, of Lukas's company.

'See you later,' she said to her mother.

Buttoning up her jacket as she went, Jermaine tried desperately hard as Lukas fell into step with her for some kind of normality. 'You've Edwina staying with you, I believe,' she said nicely as they approached some of her father's outbuildings.

'She's having a lie-in this morning,' Lukas replied.

Because she had a late night last night? Jermaine wondered, and, as sudden jealousy raged at that thought, she found she had stepped inside one of the outbuildings—as if to get away from Lukas himself.

'Looking for something?' he enquired, following her in, observing that she appeared to be staring into space.

Oh, heavens! Jermaine abruptly collected herself and knew she would just about die if Lukas gathered so much as an inkling of the savage green-eyed emotion that racked her when she thought of him with her sister.

'There's a sledge in here somewhere,' some guardian angel remembered for her. Jermaine looked at him then, saw him affable, friendly—and sophisticated. 'But of course you wouldn't...'

'I would,' he promptly assured her.

She stared at him. 'You wouldn't?'

'Would,' he said.

She laughed, and knew then, even though she might regret it later, that she was going to enjoy this time with him. She loved him so, and had missed him more than she had dreamt it was possible to miss anyone.

The sledge, when they found it, was rusty and cobwebby, but otherwise sound. 'Lead on, Miss Hargreaves,' Lukas commanded, taking hold of the rope and pulling the sledge behind him. 'Presumably you know the best sledging spots.'

'You know you're going to get soaked?'

'I don't care,' he said, and looked so terrifically wonderful that Jermaine wanted quite dreadfully to kiss him.

She looked away and desperately fought to banish any such impossible impulses, while seeking to find any safe topic that would get her away from this moment of weakness. 'So, what did Santa bring you for Christmas?' she asked lightly.

Lukas was silent for a few moments. 'Not what I wanted,' he answered at length.

'Shame,' she jibed. 'You couldn't have been a very good boy.'

'That's the trouble,' Lukas complained. 'I've been so good, you just wouldn't believe.'

'I wouldn't,' she laughed, feeling then that she wanted to give him a consoling hug, and was glad that they had arrived at the small trio of hills they'd been making for.

They didn't have the hills to themselves, but for Jermaine there was no one else there as she gave herself up to the sublime pleasure of just being with the man she loved. Up and down the hills they trekked, she squealing, Lukas laughing, as they bumped and tumbled—and never had she been more happy.

She wasn't feeling hungry, but guessed it must be nearing lunchtime when the assorted bunches of sledgers started to thin out, until there was just her and Lukas there.

Her conscience prodded her. 'We'd better go back.'

But she felt that Lukas was as reluctant as she when he suggested, 'Just one more.'

'Your trouble is you've never grown up,' taunted she to the man whom she full well knew carried a tremendous load of responsibility on his shoulders.

'I'm allowed to play sometimes,' he declared, dramatically and defiantly. She laughed, and she wanted to kiss him again, because he was just so—Lukas—but couldn't.

'Come on, then,' she sighed, equally dramatically. 'Just one more.'

Together they climbed up the hill for the last time and

sat close together—and moved off. Gathering speed as they travelled the short trip, Jermaine just knew that this time they were going to come to grief—she didn't care. Never had she enjoyed an outing so much. This time was precious to her, and would live in her memory for ever.

They were going too fast, the route having become icy with use, and they did come to grief; in fact there was no way in which Lukas could prevent it. They both came off the sledge, but as she lay looking at the bluest of skies on a sunny winter's day Jermaine just had to laugh from the pure and utter joy of it.

Then, all at once, something was blotting out the sun. Lukas was leaning over her and looking down at her— and still she laughed. Lukas continued to stare down at her, his eyes warm, and somehow tender.

She saw him swallow, and imagined he liked her quite a lot when he said softly, 'Look at you. Soaked. Your wonderful hair soaked, your make-up long gone. Know something?' he asked, and when she shook her head he told her, 'You look absolutely fantastic.'

Jermaine loved him. She loved him, loved him. 'Is my nose red?' she asked, her mouth still smiling.

He bent and kissed her nose. 'It's like ice,' he stated.

'You should see yours, mister,' she laughed, and he kissed her once more. Suddenly it was the best Christmas she'd ever had. 'I'll give you thirty minutes to pack that up,' she told him cheekily, and a kind of groan escaped him.

Then he was kissing her, and again kissing her, and holding her, and she was kissing and holding him in return. 'I've missed you,' he murmured against her mouth. But she couldn't believe he had said what she wanted him to say—that he'd missed her—so she kissed him.

Lukas looked into her lovely violet eyes as the kiss ended, and then tenderly he kissed her snow-chilled face. 'Come on, let's get you back home. You're frozen,' he declared, helping her to her feet.

Jermaine didn't feel in the least frozen, but supposed she had been too nicely brought up to confess about the fire he had caused to burst into flame within her.

They were silent but companionable on the short walk back to her family home, where her wonderful mother had asked Lukas to stay to lunch. She had about another hour of his company, Jermaine mused, and she was going to enjoy it. That life was going to be pretty bleak afterwards—well, she just wasn't going to think about when Lukas left today.

'I'm sorry if we're a little late,' Lukas apologised to her mother, as they stood in the hall shedding their top clothes.

'There's nothing to spoil,' Grace Hargreaves assured him. 'But you're both soaked!' she scolded, instantly forgiving Lukas his every sin when he smiled.

Jermaine looked across at Lukas to see how this giant in the world of big business was taking being scolded, and was delighted to see that he appeared to be quite enjoying her mother mothering him.

And mother him she did. While she sent Jermaine upstairs to have a hot shower, Jermaine heard her showing Lukas the downstairs facility, requesting his topcoat and suggesting he let her have his clothes for her to whip round in the tumbledrier.

Jermaine, while wanting to hurry to be back with Lukas, thawed herself out under the hot shower, and then washed her already shampooed-that-day hair. But by the time she had dried her hair and had decided, since he had been dressed casually, that she would dress casually too, she could wait no longer to see him again.

Swiftly, her long legs encased in a smart pair of trousers, Jermaine went down the stairs. She found Lukas and her parents in the drawing room, and saw at once that Lukas must have submitted to her mother's ministrations.

'All dry?' Jermaine commented, more because she felt suddenly shy to have this man in her family home, where it must appear that he was *her* visitor.

Lukas studied her. 'No ill effects?'

'You came off the sledge, naturally,' her father commented before she could reply, and continued, though it was totally untrue, even if he must have believed it to be true, 'Edwina always used to love sledging.'

After that, it seemed as if no other topic could be raised without Edwina's name being brought into the conversation by Edwin Hargreaves. They moved to the dining room to eat, but lunch was not a comfortable meal for Jermaine, and she was beginning to regret that Lukas had ever come or that her mother had invited him to share their meal. Jermaine was used to her father singing Edwina's praises, but Lukas wasn't. Might he not be weary of it?

Jermaine's new-found enemy jealousy suddenly started an attack; perhaps Lukas wasn't weary of it? He had, after all, invited Edwina into his home for Christmas. In fact in his home was where Edwina was right at this minute.

So what the dickens was Lukas doing here, with her?

Jermaine had come to no sort of conclusion before her father was suddenly embarrassing her to death by saying, very pointedly from where she was viewing it, 'Of course, Edwina's being extremely brave. She hasn't fully recovered from that injury to her back yet.'

'Backs can be the very devil,' Lukas agreed evenly.

'I'm not sure she's fit enough to even now be left on her own—without another female in the house,' Edwin Hargreaves hinted, and Jermaine wasn't sure whether she went ashen, or scarlet.

In the ensuing silence, she wanted the floor to open up and swallow her. She was aware of Lukas's eyes on her, but she wouldn't, couldn't, look at him after her father's very near outright suggestion that Lukas take her back to Highfield with him.

She sought desperately hard for some topic with which to change the conversation, but was so swamped with mortification that she couldn't think straight. Which meant she had to leave it to Lukas or her mother to change the conversation.

Only her mother was saying nothing, and when Lukas did speak, Jermaine was staggered that he didn't change the topic at all, but told her father, 'I did ask Jermaine to spend her Christmas at Highfield, but...'

'You did?' her father cut in, jovial all of a sudden as he turned to glance at his younger daughter.

'I promised you and M...' she began, but was cut off before she could finish.

'You must have known that neither your mother nor I would hold you to that sort of promise if you'd prefer to spend that time with your friends,' her father remarked, and Jermaine heartily wished she'd got the nerve to run from the room.

Were it not for drawing attention to the fact that inwardly she was dying of embarrassment here, she might very well have made a dash for it. But by no chance was she going to let Lukas know how utterly miserable this whole conversation was making her.

Though, quietly, he was suddenly saying, 'The offer is still there, Jermaine.'

She looked at him then, saw a sensitivity in his fine grey eyes—but didn't want his pity. 'I'm sorry,' she began to decline—only for her father to speak over the top of her.

'There you are,' he cut in cheerfully. 'Here's Lukas, pleased to have you stay. You'll be able to check if Edwina is all right when she says she's all right, and not just putting a brave face on it, and...'

'It's very kind of Lukas,' Jermaine interrupted, starting to feel desperate, 'but I couldn't possibly...'

'Of course you can,' her father triumphed. 'You're not going back to work until January the second, so...'

'I can't!' Ye gods, her father would have her spend the next seven nights at Highfield, when she was sure Lukas had only meant his invitation for one or two!

'You can, you know,' Lukas said softly, by her side. And, when she stared unhappily at him, he added, 'I'd very much like you to.'

Her heart did a crazy kind of flip—he sounded, looked, so sincere. 'That's settled, then,' Edwin Hargreaves announced.

Jermaine looked from Lukas to her father, and then to her mother, who appeared for once as if she might want to bury an axe in her husband's head, but was too polite to start one of her rare altercations with him in company.

'What do you want to do, sweetheart?' Mrs Hargreaves dared her husband's wrath by asking her younger daughter.

But when Jermaine, because the feeling of humiliation was weighing her down, was about to tell her mother that she didn't want to go anywhere, Lukas was lightly organising, 'We'll go in my vehicle—I don't want you having trouble driving your car if we're snowed in at Highfield.'

She hadn't thought as far as that. 'My car?' she questioned witlessly, while thinking she really should stir herself, even if she was unused to opposing her father.

'I'll bring you back to collect it,' Lukas assured her, as if that was what he thought her question was all about. And when she looked at him, he smiled his devastating smile and added, 'You'd better bring your overnight bag.'

By the time Jermaine had packed her case and was ready to go back down the stairs again, some of her mighty bewilderment was starting to clear. It was then that, while knowing her father would make the rest of her holiday quite awful if she told him she wasn't going to Highfield and her sister, Jermaine also knew that, while she couldn't possibly stay on in her old home, neither could she go to Highfield with Lukas.

'Ready?' Lukas asked when he saw her, taking her case from her and, with her father, going out to the Range Rover.

Jermaine turned to her mother. 'Bye, Mum,' she said, giving her a hug and a kiss.

But her mother didn't let her go. 'Are you all right about this, love?' she asked, going on, 'I saw you and Lukas coming back from sledging—and you looked so happy to be with him. But if you're not, and you don't want to go, you must stay—and I'll deal with your bullying father.'

What could she say? To agree that she felt bullied and browbeaten by her father would only cause disharmony in the home, and who wanted that kind of atmosphere at Christmas?

'Do you mind—about my going? About me breaking my promise?' was what she did answer, and her mother smiled.

'Much as I would want to, I always knew I couldn't keep you with me for ever.'

Jermaine went out to the four-wheel drive feeling very much cheered. They weren't a family who went in for saying how much they loved each other. But, from what her mother had just said, Jermaine knew, as she supposed she'd always known, that as her father idolised his elder daughter, her mother loved her younger daughter very much.

Though that did nothing to alter the fact that Jermaine had decided she was going to spend the rest of her Christmas in her own small flat. Which was why when, having said goodbye to her parents and Lukas having driven a mile down the road, Jermaine asked if he would mind driving to a nearby taxi rank and stopping to let her out.

He did not wait until then to stop, but pulled over at once and turned to look at her. 'Aren't we having fun any more?' he asked, his grey eyes steady on her serious face.

Her heart turned over at the gentleness in his expression. But while it warmed her through and through that Lukas seemed to be saying that he'd enjoyed their time in the snow together every bit as much as she, it just wouldn't do.

'I can't come with you,' she blurted out in a rush.

'What did I do?' he teased gently.

'You—didn't do anything.'

'What did I say?' he persisted. 'That makes you want to deprive me of your company?'

Deprive? Her intention faltered—but pride wasn't so easily defeated. 'You didn't say anything,' she answered honestly. 'But you know as well as I that until less than an hour ago you'd no intention of taking me back to Highfield with you. I can't come with you,' she repeated, feeling quite wretched.

'Even if I want you to?' he smiled coaxingly.

Oh, don't, Lukas! Her pride seemed to be a very wishy-washy thing. Again she hauled it back to attention. 'If my father...' she began, and halted, torn by loyalty not to bring her parent into this. But, since all this was of her father's making, she was unable to see how she could avoid doing so.

Lukas came in and helped her out. 'My dear, Jermaine,' he turned her bones to water by saying quietly, 'believe me, I want very much that you should come and stay at Highfield.'

'But...' she tried to insist, her brain a poor organ in the light of Lukas stating he wanted *very much* that she should stay at Highfield.

'And,' he went on, when she seemed a little stuck, 'if your father, in his concern over Edwina, hadn't suggested it, I would have.'

Jermaine stared at Lukas, wanting quite desperately to believe him. Would he have—or was he just saying that to soothe her wounded pride? 'You would have?' she asked slowly. With those steady grey eyes of his fixed on her and his 'my dear Jermaine' still dancing dreamily about in her head, she didn't seem capable of better argument than that.

'I would have,' he confirmed, and, smiling a gentle smile, he leaned to her and tenderly, without haste, he kissed her. Then, still unhurriedly, he pulled back and looked into her warm violet eyes. 'You'll come—to please me?' he asked softly.

Oh, yes, yes! urged everything in her. 'If—you're sure,' she answered huskily.

'I've never been more sure of anything,' Lukas murmured, and looked deeply into her eyes for long, long moments, 'Trust me?' he asked, and seemed unwilling to look away. It even seemed, Jermaine felt in a bemused kind of way, as if he had to force himself to turn the key in the ignition and to drive on.

Never had she ever felt such a fluttery mess of jumbled emotions that she didn't know where to start first in order to sort herself out. Lukas had called her 'my dear' and had sounded as if he meant it. Somehow she had an idea he was a man who was never too free with his endearments. He had said that he wanted her in his home; her—not Edwina—but *her*.

Jermaine was silent beside him as he steered the Range Rover in the direction of Highfield. Her every instinct seemed to be telling her, screaming at her, that it was her that Lukas wanted, regardless of Edwina being already established in his home—her, not her sister.

Never had Jermaine felt so full of love for him, so excited and yet, at the same time, apprehensive too. She didn't know if she should believe that there was anything more to his invitation than was on the surface. Didn't know if she dared to let herself believe that there might be. But Lukas needn't have called to see her while he was in the area that morning, need he? But he had. *And,* he'd said he would have asked her to come back to Highfield with him—without her father's massive hint.

Jermaine felt so shaky inside it would not have surprised her at all if she were not thinking straight. But, and she had probably got it crazily wrong, but dared she imagine that Lukas had come over specially to see her?

At that point she realised that the events of that day— Lukas turning up out of the blue, their fun together in the snow—had addled her brain.

What was irrefutable, however—while she sat beside Lukas, her insides still a nonsense—was that she was going to his home with him. She, who had been down in the depths that she might never see him again was going to his home with him and would stay overnight there. Oh, weren't the fates just too, too splendid? Not only was she seeing him now, right at this very minute, but she would see him again tomorrow too. What better Christmas could anyone in love have?

She turned her head to look at him just as Lukas turned to look at her. 'Happy?' he asked.

She was too full to speak. She nodded, and then smiled. He had asked her to trust him—and trust him she did.

CHAPTER EIGHT

BOTH Ash and Edwina came out on to the drive when they saw Lukas's vehicle pull up. But they did not stand close together, in fact were some yards apart, and Jermaine received a very clear impression that they were no longer at all friendly.

Ash came round to the passenger door immediately he saw her. 'Jermaine! What a lovely surprise!' he exclaimed, yet didn't seem at all surprised to see Lukas take her case from the vehicle.

Jermaine had not seen Lukas greet her sister, and, as the teeth of jealousy gave her a spiteful nip, she was glad she'd missed any too friendly greeting that might cause more green-eyed darts to bombard her.

Edwina smiled a pretty smile as Jermaine approached her, but Jermaine didn't miss the hardness in her sister's eyes as, still smiling prettily, she hissed, 'What the devil's going on?'

'How's your back?' Jermaine asked sweetly, and, receiving a withering look for her trouble, was glad that Lukas and Ash were by then too close for any other private conversation.

The four of them ambled into the house, but Jermaine guessed she would be hearing more from her sister before too long. Only then did she realise that she should have given thought to how Edwina would react to her arriving so unexpectedly. It went without saying, of course, that she wouldn't like it. But, Jermaine realised, she had been so taken up with her happiness at just being with Lukas that she just hadn't given a solitary thought to how her sister would react that Lukas had gone out on his own and had returned with a passenger—complete with suitcase.

'Tea?' Lukas suggested.

Suddenly, ridiculously, probably because the other two were there, Jermaine was swamped by an unexpected shyness. It was absurd, she freely admitted. But then, since Cupid had released that powerfully potent arrow, she had suffered various confidence-wrecking emotions which until then she had been a total stranger to.

'I think I'll take my case up and...'

'I'll take it for you,' Ash insisted.

Jermaine looked across to Lukas; he smiled, and her heart seemed to tilt. She managed to smile back, and then Edwina was intruding on the moment with a friendly offer of, 'I'll come and help you unpack, Jermaine.'

Feeling a touch startled, Jermaine switched her glance from Lukas to her pleasantly smiling sister. Edwina didn't intend to wait any longer to find out what the devil was going on, apparently.

Ash led the way to the same bedroom Jermaine had used before. It smelt clean and newly polished, and the bed, which she had stripped on leaving the last time, was made up with fresh linen. Jermaine smiled—Mrs Dobson obviously always liked to keep guest rooms aired and ready.

Ash did not stay long once he had deposited Jermaine's case, but as he departed so too did any semblance of pleasantness from Edwina. 'What's with the sweet smiles?' she demanded aggressively once the door was closed.

'Sweet smiles?' Jermaine echoed.

'You were damned near swooning at Lukas not two minutes ago!'

Swooning? Oh, heavens, surely not? What must Lukas think? 'Well, you'd know, with all the practice you've had!' Jermaine refused to let her sister squash her spirit.

Edwina, plainly observing that Jermaine had no intention of being pushed around, adopted another tack. 'How did you meet up with Lukas, anyway?' she demanded hostilely.

'He happened to call in...'

'On the parents!' That Edwina could hardly believe it was obvious.

'He was in the area and...'

'What for?'

'I don't know what for! I didn't ask!'

'You wouldn't!' Edwina scorned in disgust. But, not done yet, she carried on, 'You needn't have come back with him. I'll bet you asked. You fancy him, don't you. Well, hard luck, Jermaine. He wasn't giving you a thought last night when we...'

'You've brought this on yourself!' Jermaine cut in sharply. She just didn't want to hear what Edwina was saying. As ever, she would spoil everything for her if she could. 'And I didn't ask to come here with Lukas— Dad near enough did that.' Unfastening her case, Jermaine saw the gift she had brought her sister reposing there. She handed it to her. Edwina received the gift-wrapped bottle of her favourite perfume without thanks.

'Dad!' she exclaimed shortly. 'How? He...'

'He's still worried about your back. Even though only the evening before I'd mentioned Mrs Dobson being here, Dad seems to think you might be feeling uncomfortable without another woman around.' Unsmiling,

Jermaine looked at her sister. 'Which just shows how little he really knows you,' she added acidly.

She saw Edwina's eyes narrow, and guessed she would be paid back for that sooner or later, but as Edwina went angrily from the room Jermaine sank winded on to the bed. Edwina, with her 'he wasn't giving you a thought last night when we...' had already put the poison down.

What *had* Lukas and Edwina done last night? Stop it, Jermaine demanded of herself. You know Edwina. She always has been able to embroider the truth—even lie outright without so much as blinking. If whatever it was had been so wonderful, why had Lukas left Edwina on her own, or rather with Ash, today, while he conducted business out of the area?

Jermaine unpacked her case, trying to recapture the happiness of her time with Lukas in the snow—he hadn't been desperate to get back here to Edwina, Jermaine re-minded herself. But that happiness eluded her. When, prior to her conversation with Edwina, Jermaine had felt she might well go back down the stairs again once she'd got her belongings stowed, now, somehow, she had no heart to go down to the drawing room. Yet she felt a need to be doing something other than pacing her room. Restlessly Jermaine considered popping along to the kitchen to see Mrs Dobson, but decided against it. The housekeeper would be up to her ears in things domestic at this hour.

Had not darkness descended, Jermaine would have given in to the urge to go and visit that tranquil spot by the brook—perhaps some of that peace and tranquillity would rub off on to her.

But winter's darkness *had* descended, and, as if to wash away the feelings of disquiet Edwina had sown with her intimate reference to her and Lukas last night, Jermaine went and stood under the shower, prior to getting ready to go down to dinner.

When, an hour later, good manners, if nothing else, decreed she could not stay skulking in her room until tomorrow, she was very much wishing she had never let Lukas persuade her to come.

But as she left her room she recalled the manner of Lukas persuading her to come, and his gently teasing 'What did I do? What did I say that makes you want to deprive me of your company' and her mood began to lighten. 'My dear, Jermaine' he'd called her. Oh, Lukas.

She saw him! He was standing at the bottom of the stairs as if waiting for her. Jermaine fought hard not to break out into smiles just to see him; Edwina's poison was still at work. But Jermaine's instinct belatedly roused itself to scoff that she should never have taken any heed of Edwina's half-sentences—good heavens, she'd grown up listening to Edwina making up anything to suit her own ends.

'You didn't come down,' Lukas accused as Jermaine reached him.

Her heart fluttered, thoughts of Edwina with Lukas a million miles away—Lukas sounded as if he'd waited and waited.

'I—er—I'm here now,' Jermaine managed.

'So you are,' he smiled, and took her into his arms and kissed her. Reluctantly, it seemed, he let her go. 'Don't you just love Christmas and all the mistletoe?' he asked softly. Jermaine looked up and just had to laugh out loud, because while she could not deny it was Christmas, and the hall was decorated with plenty of holly, she could not see so much as the merest sprig of mistletoe.

She still had laughter about her mouth when, somehow holding her hand, Lukas strolled with her to the drawing room. Nor did he seem in any hurry to let go of her hand when they went in. Edwina was already downstairs, decorating one of the sofas, Jermaine saw.

She also saw Edwina's eyes immediately laser to their entwined hands, and didn't miss the tightening of Edwina's mouth the moment before she broke out into girlish smiles and teased, 'Making an entrance again, Jermaine?'

Oh, how could she? Jermaine wondered if she was the only one to notice the barb beneath the smiles. 'What would you like to drink, Edwina?' Lukas asked, letting go Jermaine's hand. *Milk might suit.* 'Jermaine?' Having asked the elder Hargreaves sister, he turned to the younger one.

So the evening got underway, with Ash moving to sit next to Edwina, where he chatted pleasantly to her until it was time to go into the dining room.

Thankfully, the meal progressed without Edwina making any more barbed remarks under a smiling cover. Though Jermaine didn't miss the hard look Edwina couldn't immediately hide when she was not the object of Lukas's attention but Jermaine was.

Again Jermaine's emotions went all out of gear. For it seemed to her that when she was alone with Lukas she was able to forget all else. That she was able to trust him and to just enjoy being with him. She didn't even need to wonder where their friendship was going, be it nowhere at all—it was enough to be with him. But with Edwina there—though not so much Ash, funnily enough—Jermaine felt stilted, awkward, as if she had to watch every word... As if any minute now Edwina would pounce and spoil everything. Was she imagining it because she wanted it to be so, Jermaine wondered, or was it true that, while being the perfect host, Lukas looked *her* way more and more frequently? Almost—as if he was hard put to it to take his eyes off her.

Imagination, scoffed her love-filled heart. Though she had noticed that Edwina was watching all points and, to anyone who knew her as well as Jermaine, seemed to have her nose put out of joint.

That evening they had coffee at the dinner table, but returned to the drawing room afterwards. 'Would you like a drink of something to finish off with?' Lukas asked Edwina, who went through a pantomime of being unsure what she would like and so went over to the drinks cabinet with Lukas in order to choose.

Ash was all at once taking the seat next to Jermaine. 'I don't seem to have had a moment to talk to you alone.'

'Have you enjoyed your Christmas?' she asked, smiling while her emotions see-sawed, because Edwina seemed captivated by something Lukas had just said to her.

'Can we be friends, Jermaine?' Ash, instead of answering her question, was asking one of his own.

Jermaine determinedly gave him her full attention. Ash seemed extremely serious suddenly. 'You sound as though it's important to you,' she commented lightly.

Ash stared solemnly at her. 'Actually, it is,' he answered. 'Though I wouldn't blame you if, after the way I treated you, you told me to get lost.'

Jermaine looked back into his sombre expression. 'Water under the bridge,' she smiled, and because he was Lukas's brother, and because she bore Ash no ill will, and would indeed like to be friends with him, she agreed sincerely, 'Friends.' She was about to extend her hand in friendship when Ash beamed a smile and kissed her—in friendship.

'Have lunch with me one day next week?' he suggested—but never received an answer, because suddenly Lukas was there, standing over them.

'What are you having to drink, Jermaine?' he cut in abruptly, in contrast to the pleasant way he'd been with her, all at once sounding quite aggressive.

If he asked like that, she'd die of thirst, rather. 'Nothing, thanks,' she answered politely, and could only think that Edwina had been putting more poison down—this time to Lukas. 'If no one minds,' she began, getting to her feet, 'I think I'll go to bed.'

'You're sure?' Ash was on his feet too. Lukas walked away.

'I'm sure,' she smiled, wished everyone a general 'Goodnight,' and found she had her sister for company.

'I'm without my hanky, I'll just come up and get one,' Edwina trilled, and went with Jermaine out into the hall. 'Enjoying yourself?' she asked as they started up the staircase, for once fairly bubbling with good humour.

Jermaine's suspicions were aroused. All evening she'd been getting nothing but surreptitious ill-humoured looks from her sister. Yet suddenly, with no one there to witness, she was giving her the benefit of her sunnier side?

'What happened to cheer you up?' Jermaine asked with sisterly candour.

'Isn't he wonderful?' Edwina sighed, and Jermaine knew at once that she shouldn't have asked.

'Presumably we're not talking about Ash, here?'

'Lukas has just asked me to stay at Highfield for as long as I like,' Edwina answered, barely able to contain herself, and, smiling a sly smile at Jermaine, she added, 'Wouldn't you call that progress?'

Thankfully, at that moment they reached the top of the stairs. Jermaine felt too choked to answer and left Edwina to go to collect the hanky she had come up for while she went three doors down to her own room.

Jermaine owned that she felt near to tears, but she wouldn't cry! Oh, how she wished she had never come. Sledging in the snow, laughing, kissing with Lukas that day—suddenly it all seemed light years away. His manner to her just now—cold and aggressive—had been a huge contrast.

She started to get angry—she wasn't having this! First he used his charm on her, and then switched to Edwina! Jermaine started to grow more and more incensed. Who did he think he was, playing ducks and drakes with her emotions? Not that he knew so much about her emotions, of course. Nor did she want him to. But he must have gleaned that she liked him a little at least—or why would she have accepted to come here today?

Jermaine found then that she could not sustain her anger against Lukas, and it departed as swiftly as it had arrived. But she felt restless again, and was taking her fourth shower of the day when she paused to wonder—had Edwina been speaking the truth? Or was this just some more of her poison?

It was a fact that her sister had seemed riveted by every word Lukas had been uttering to her over by the drinks cabinet. But then Edwina could bat her eyes for England if she wanted something. Could it be that, perhaps from some small word Lukas had said, Edwina had picked up her crewel needle and begun yet more fabricated embroidery?

Jermaine recalled the way Lukas had taken her in his arms and kissed her when she'd earlier left her room. She remembered also the moments during dinner, when he would look over to her, and had appeared to enjoy having her there.

She was nightdress-clad and in bed when she wondered if she could trust her instincts. Could she trust that feeling that—well, that Lukas sort of liked her—well, a lot—in the romantic way?

But that was when she also remembered how she had trusted his brother, Ash, and Jermaine came down to earth with a very hard landing. Oh, great! Realising that she must be the biggest chump going, and that the philandering Tavinor brothers were having a fine old time at her expense, Jermaine was all set to leap out of bed, get dressed and get out of there right that minute.

Someone tapping lightly on her door took the moment from her. She picked up her watch—it was comparatively early; not quite ten-thirty yet. She didn't think this Boxing Day night that anyone else was retiring yet, and in the next second she was out of bed. Rapidly tying in her robe as she went, she streaked over to answer the door. It wouldn't be Edwina. She wouldn't knock, but would come straight in. But if this was one of the Tavinor twosome, she was ready for him—the one who wanted to be her friend or the other one, who'd said he'd 'missed' her and called her 'my dear.'

Angrily she pulled back the door—and her ridiculous heart wobbled. 'Yes?' she demanded coldly—and for her sins had to stand there and endure his scrutiny.

'I knew I'd upset you,' Lukas said quietly.

'Pfuff!' she exhaled on a careless breath.

Lukas smiled deep into her stormy violet eyes. 'According to my old nanny, one should never go to sleep on an argument.'

'We didn't argue!' Jermaine reminded him pithily. She didn't want him to smile; it weakened her.

'Are you going to let me apologise?' he asked nicely, and she was weakened further. She wanted time alone with him, she so desperately wanted to be back the way they had been.

'Forget it,' she said stubbornly, and started to close the door.

'You kissed my brother!' Lukas reminded her urgently.

'When?' she answered, startled, the door still open.

'Not long since—in the drawing room.'

She stared at him. He'd been aggressive, cold to her—because of that kiss? Her heartbeat picked up speed. Somehow she managed to get herself back together. 'I didn't kiss him. He kissed me.'

'You're not going to have lunch with him, are you?' Lukas asked winningly, and a staggering thought suddenly stunned her.

'You're—not...' she hardly dared voice the word '...jealous?'

'Me?' Lukas scoffed. But when she was ready to run at the mortification she felt from what she'd just voiced, Lukas answered, self-deprecatingly, 'Just because my brother was sitting chatting to you, just because he was kissing you?'

He *was* jealous! Her heart started to thunder, and any anger she had felt melted into nothing. Oh, he couldn't be jealous—could he? She tried hard to keep both feet firmly on the ground. 'He—Ash—wants us to be friends,' Jermaine replied, having been through the agonies of jealousy herself, not wanting that pain for the man she loved.

'Ah!' said Lukas—just as though that explained everything.

But Jermaine was starting to backtrack on her notion

that Lukas might be at all jealous in any way—and began to feel awkward that she had actually suggested to his face that he might be.

'Goodnight, then,' she bade him, and would have closed the door, but again his words stopped her.

'Don't you want to see your Christmas present?' he asked, and while Jermaine stared witlessly at him Lukas bent to the side of the door that had been hidden from her view and picked up a square, flattish parcel. 'Happy Christmas, Jermaine,' he wished her softly, handing her the gold-wrapped parcel.

'Oh, Lukas!' she wailed. 'I didn't get you anything!'

'Don't be upset. My gift is supposed to make you happy,' he teased.

'May I open it?'

He nodded, a warm light in his grey eyes as he studied her face, but as a welter of emotions began to fluster her Jermaine had to turn from him. She didn't want him looking into her eyes, seeing her very soul. She walked back into her room, her fingers busy with the gold wrapping.

She removed the first wrapping to find that, whatever her gift was, it was protected by a firmer second wrapper. But once that had been done away with a gasp of utter astonishment broke from her. 'Lukas!' she cried, and spun round to stare at him open-mouthed. 'You...' she gasped, but was rendered speechless by the unexpectedness of his gift.

He had closed the door and had stepped a little way inside her room. 'You like it?' He smiled, her incredulous expression already telling him that 'like it' was an understatement.

Jermaine's violet gaze went from him and back to the painting he had given her. 'It's the *Boy With A Barrow!*'

she told him what he already knew. 'We saw it at that art gallery…' Her voice tailed off. 'I can't take it!' she exclaimed suddenly.

'You *don't* like it?'

'Oh, Lukas, you know that I love it. It's the most marvellous Christmas present ever,' she replied honestly, huskily. 'But it must have been expensive, and I can't…'

'Oh, my lovely girl, you can,' Lukas interrupted gently. 'May I not have the pleasure of seeing you enjoy your picture?' Her picture! Jermaine's eyes grew dreamy. That sounded so personal, somehow. As if—as if whenever Lukas had looked at the picture he had thought of it as her picture. 'I promise you it wasn't so very expensive,' Lukas went on to assure her when she still looked uncertain. And, for a killer punch, 'You must know, sweet Jermaine, that I couldn't possibly allow anyone else to have it.'

Her backbone went to water. 'Oh, Lukas!' she cried tremulously.

'You're not going to cry?' he asked, looking a shade worried and coming further into her room.

She laughed. 'I'm going to kiss you,' she said.

'Of the two, I can bear that better,' he grinned—and held his arms out to her.

Jermaine took one last look at the blue and pink, and the touch of red in the painting, then carefully put it down. With the whole of her being starting to tremble, she went into Lukas's outstretched arms.

His mouth against her own was the salve she needed for her earlier unhappiness. In the harbour of his arms all feeling of restlessness vanished. One kiss became two, and as Lukas held her firmly to him so she wanted more and more of him. He did not seem in any hurry to let her go.

Soon passion began to flare between them, going from warm, to hot, to fire, as Lukas traced kisses down the side of her throat and pressed her to him. She arched to him, and a murmur of wanting left him. She felt him, his body heat through the thinness of her robe, felt his hands low on her waist, at the curves of her behind as he pulled her into him.

'Lukas!' she gasped, delight such as she'd never experienced shooting through her body.

Lukas pulled back to look into the depths of her lovely violet eyes, his grey ones smouldering with his desire for her. 'We should stop?' he asked her throatily.

She swallowed hard. She didn't want to stop. She wanted more of his kisses, more of his touch. 'Do—we have to?' she asked.

'My darling!' he breathed, and as Jermaine's heart leapt, so she knew that she was ready, eager, to go wherever he led.

She smiled up at him, and as she leaned forward and kissed him so Lukas lifted her up and carried her to the bed, and gently laid her down upon it. She knew that he would join her. It was what she wanted.

She closed her eyes, her heart full. She felt the bed go down, and as Lukas came to lie beside her she opened them again and saw he had shrugged out of his jacket. He took her in his arms and they clung to each other. It was bliss, pure and simple, to be this close, to feel his body heat.

Again and again they kissed, and, as his hands caressed her so her hands seemed to roam of their own volition over his back and shoulders. Gently his seeking hands moved to her breasts, and she realised he must have heard her shaky breath.

'You're not frightened, sweetheart?' he asked.

'No,' she whispered. 'No,' she repeated, fearful he might not have heard the first time and might stop making love to her. 'Just a bit—um—shy, I think.'

Gently, tenderly, he laid his lips on hers. 'Sweet, Jermaine,' he breathed against her mouth, parting her lips with his own. Slowly, as if not to hurry her in this momentous happening for her, Lukas's hands went to the tie of her robe. 'May I?' He was still giving her all the time in the world to back away if she was in the least unsure.

'Yes,' she answered, and loved him, loved him, loved him, as gently he removed her robe.

Her nightdress had ridden up and Jermaine felt her face flame when she felt Lukas's hands underneath her nightdress, felt his warm touch on her bare upper thigh.

'L-Lukas!' she whispered tremulously.

His hand stilled, but there was nothing but tender understanding in his sensitive grey eyes. 'You're not quite so sure?' he asked, looking down into her lovely violet eyes, her love-flushed face.

'I am,' she assured him as quickly as she could, given that her throat felt dry. 'It's—it's just—it's all a bit—um—new, that's...'

'I know, sweetheart,' he said. 'It will be all right. Trust me.'

'Oh, I do,' she sighed, and kissed him lovingly, and had not the slightest demur to make when his stilled hand moved upwards under her nightdress, and, taking her breath with the delight of his touch, his warm, searching hand roamed her belly and upwards, to capture the swollen globe of her breast. 'Oh!' she sighed.

'You're not afraid?'

She wanted to tell him that because she loved him so

everything seemed so right. 'Not with you,' she said shyly.

'My darling!' Lukas breathed exultantly, and for long, delicious moments he kissed and caressed her. Apart from a natural shyness, Jermaine was in utter rapture when he carefully took from her her last covering. 'You are a delight, sweet love,' he murmured as he gazed into her eyes, a moment before he feasted his eyes on her pink-tipped breasts. 'Oh, my Jermaine,' he murmured throatily, and Jermaine knew yet more bliss when he trailed kisses down to her breast. While one hand held, caressed and moulded her right breast, he caressed her left breast with his mouth.

Jermaine knew further enchantment when, with one arm holding her close, his sensitive fingers at her breast teased the hardened peak, cupping her breast, while his tongue at her other breast made a nonsense of her as he tasted its sweet fullness.

Again they kissed, and held and kissed, and caressed and kissed—and suddenly, in her enchanted world, Jermaine all at once became aware that Lukas had removed his clothes and was lying completely naked next to her.

'Lukas!' she cried shakily, instinctively pulling back.

'You're shocked?' he asked.

'No, no. I...' She didn't know where she was, what to do, what to say. 'Help me,' she begged.

He pulled a little away from her. 'You want to make love with me, little darling?'

'Y-yes,' she answered on a thread of sound.

'But?' He seemed to sense there was a hint of hesitation there.

'But nothing,' she answered, and swallowed hard a moment before she begged, 'Kiss me, please kiss me.'

'Sweet love,' Lukas murmured, and bent to kiss her, their bodies close once more. Jermaine clutched hard on to him, the physical feel of him, his skin, next to her on-fire skin, causing her to need a second to adjust. Biology lessons had never prepared her for this moment of being so acutely aware of a man and his need.

'Lukas,' she breathed his name jerkily. But just then the crash of a door slamming somewhere, so out of place in this moment of deep and sensitive loving, caused her to jump in alarm. And all at once Lukas was making a decision which she didn't want him to make. He sat up fast, pulling away from her. While she hadn't a clue what was happening, he began to speedily don his undergarment and trousers—so speedily it was as if, if he didn't hurry, he might change his mind. 'What?' Jermaine questioned, sitting up too.

'This isn't right, for you, my love,' Lukas said, turning to look at her, his glance flicking down to her breasts and hastily away again.

'It isn't?'

She saw a muscle jerk in his jaw. 'I thought it was. I thought we…' He broke off, and then, obviously referring to the banging of the door that had made her jump, 'But there's too much traffic… We need to be totally alone somewhere, where I can…' He broke off again, his glance seeking hers. 'Do you l…care for me?' he asked, and suddenly his eyes were steady on hers.

Jermaine wanted to tell him that he was the whole world to her, but, sitting there as naked as the day she was born, she was suddenly overwhelmed by shyness.

She realised that Lukas had seen her shyness when, 'Come here,' he breathed, and took her gently into his arms and held her, her breasts pressed against his hair roughened naked chest. Then, gently, he put her from him. 'That wasn't such a great idea,' he admitted with a crooked kind of grin. And holding her firmly by her upper arms, he admitted, 'Being with you here, like this, is just too much, sweetheart. I'm having trouble thinking straight.' Determinedly he moved away from her, and, when all Jermaine wanted to do was to lie with him through the night, he said, 'If you care anything for me, my love, meet me tomorrow—away from this room…' He paused, then smiled. 'I'll wait for you on our bench. Do you know where I mean?'

'By the bridge, the brook?' she answered huskily.

'Nine sharp,' he said, then changed his mind. 'No, I can't wait that long. Eight-thirty?'

Jermaine desperately wanted to say 'eight,' but her heart was pounding wildly and—was Lukas saying *he cared* about her?—she wasn't thinking very straight herself. 'Half past eight,' she agreed.

'Oh, my darling,' he groaned, every bit as if he had gleaned from her agreement to meet him that care she did. 'I'm going,' he said firmly. 'While I still can.' He looked at her, and Jermaine folded her arms defensively in front of her bare breasts. 'You're absolutely exquisite,' he said softly, quickly kissed her—and was gone.

CHAPTER NINE

JERMAINE barely slept that night. Yet even awake she felt as if she was dreaming. 'Our bench' Lukas had said. Their bench. If she was dreaming, what a wonderful, wonderful dream it was.

Again and again she recalled his tenderness, the gentle endearments he had murmured while making love to her. Was she his sweet love, his darling, his sweetheart? Oh, she so wanted to be.

She tried hard for logic, tried hard not to believe what she wanted to believe. Admittedly, she didn't know very much about it, but weren't men apt to say anything in the heat of lovemaking?

But—she changed her mind—she didn't want to listen to logic. Besides, even desiring her as he undoubtedly had—and here her insides were all of a mish-mash as she recalled their mutual desire as they'd lain naked together—Lukas was more sincere than that. Somehow she instinctively seemed to know that, even while he desired her, he would never, even should his physical need try to rule him, say something he did not mean.

Which—her heart gave a flutter—must mean, if she trusted her instinct, that when Lukas said, 'If you care anything for me,' he in turn must care a little something for her. Oh, could she believe that? She so wanted to. Why else, if he didn't care for her, would Lukas want to meet her away from the house?

There was too much traffic in the house, he'd said. Which must mean that he wanted to be alone with her—

away from the house. Didn't that then mean that he wanted to talk to her? No way did he want them to meet away from the house so that they could make love. Jermaine smiled at the thought. Lukas was hardly likely to get amorous sitting on that bench with snow all around. So—what did he want to talk to her about?

Her brain refused to go any further, to speculate, to hope. She began to feel all of a tremble inside, and couldn't stay in bed any longer. By seven o'clock she had been up ages. She was showered, dressed, had light make-up applied, in fact she was all ready to go—and had an hour and a half to wait.

But by the time half past seven came around she was in a hopeless muddle of differing emotions. She couldn't sit; she couldn't stand still. She took to constantly looking at the painting Lukas had given her, but was in such a turmoil she could not concentrate on seeing more in the painting than she already had.

She loved her gift. It was so personal. She had no idea when he had bought it, but it had to have been before last night. Lukas had bought it especially for her—had meant it for her because he knew that she had been so taken with it. Did that mean that he cared a little for her? Or was she being totally stupid?

At eight o'clock she felt she could not take walking up and down her room, combing her hair, checking she looked all right, washing her hands and lingering over her painting for much longer.

It was ten past eight when, by then in too much of an agitated state to stay in her room another minute—yet not wanting to appear too eager if she had got everything impossibly wrong by going to that bench twenty minutes ahead of time—Jermaine had the vague idea of perhaps popping into the kitchen and whiling away some time with Mrs Dobson.

To Jermaine then it seemed about the only decision she was capable of making, and, remembering the way that door had slammed last night, she was desperate not to disturb the whole household. It would just about finish her if she had got everything totally muddled and wrong, and she alerted Lukas to the fact she couldn't wait to see him and was leaving her room so much ahead of time.

Silently, hardly breathing, Jermaine left her room, closing the door without a sound. She was fully aware that her sister never surfaced before nine, so was taken by surprise when, almost at Edwina's room, Jermaine spotted that the door stood wide open!

In two minds about retreating back to her own room—she had other things in her head besides doing battle with Edwina if she was on the prowl about something and was watching for her to pass—Jermaine almost did an about-turn. But she had already spent enough time pacing up and down, and perhaps Edwina wouldn't spot her.

Edwina did spot her though—she looked directly at her through half-closed eyes. But as a smirk of a smile tweaked Edwina's mouth, and she closed her eyes and her expression became dreamy, it was all too clear that she had other concerns than baiting her younger sister. But that did not stop Jermaine from feeling pole-axed. Because Edwina was not alone!

Feeling totally shattered, the colour draining from her face, Jermaine just couldn't believe what her eyes were telling her. For there, holding her sister aloft in his arms, was the man with whom Jermaine had an assignation in twenty minutes' time!

Staggered beyond bearing, Jermaine was incapable of moving, and so had to stand and watch while the man who less than twelve hours ago had picked her up and carried her over to her bed, now carried her dreamy-expressioned sister over to *her* bed!

Stunned, reeling, it was only the thought that she too must have worn pretty much the self-same expression that Edwina was wearing now that maliciously stabbed Jermaine into life.

Ten minutes after that and she was coming out of shock to realise she was back in her room and that, quite without being fully aware of what she had been doing, she had tossed her belongings into her case and was ready to leave.

Her eyes lit on her painting, the one she had so idiotically allowed herself to believe Lukas had purchased for her because he had some liking for her. The pain that hit her then was almost physical. She looked away from the painting, looked out through the window, absently seeing that Ash had just brought his car round to the front of the house from the garages at the rear.

He had got out and was using some de-icing device when Jermaine suddenly came out of her only half-aware state and was all at once galvanised into action.

When Jermaine left her room, she left behind her picture. She didn't want to think. To think hurt too much. But she knew without thinking that she could not take with her the picture that had meant so much to her and so little to him.

The door to Edwina's room was now closed. Jermaine sprinted past it, only just holding down a sob. Was he still in there with her? Were they laughing together at the thought that the stupid virgin would shortly be out there, sitting waiting on a bench in the snow, while the man Jermaine would be waiting for was very patently *busy* elsewhere?

Unable to bear the nightmare flashes in her head, of Lukas lying with Edwina in the same way he had lain with her last night, Jermaine hung onto a thread of sanity and raced out of there. It was that or go storming into that room to have a few short, sharp words with the venomous snake Lukas Tavinor.

Ash was in the driving seat about to pull away when Jermaine hared out through the front door. She was suddenly too incensed to be aware if the case she hauled with her weighed two pounds or two hundred.

'Jermaine!' Ash exclaimed, getting out of the vehicle when he saw her white and anguished face. 'What...?'

'Would you take me to the nearest railway station?' she cut in without more ado.

'But, sweetheart...'

My stars, they were both at it! 'I'll walk!' she snapped.

Ash moved. He moved fast and grabbed her case from her. 'Get in,' he said, and, going round to the passenger door, he opened it for her. 'What...?' he began again.

'If you really want to be my friend—as you last night wanted to be—you'll drive on without questioning me!' she told him tautly—and didn't breathe freely again until after Ash had started up the vehicle and had driven half a mile away from Highfield.

She was aware then that Ash had been glancing at her from time to time, but it was about five minutes later when he glanced at her again and assured her, 'Believe me, Jermaine, I'm not trying to pry. I can tell you're upset. But may I know why you need to get to a railway station?'

She would have thought that was obvious. 'I'm going home,' she replied bluntly.

'To your parents?'

Oh, grief. If she went back there, her father would go

on and on about her leaving Edwina on her own. The way she was feeling, Jermaine didn't think she would be able to refrain from telling him a few home truths about his elder pride and joy.

'To my home, my flat,' she answered, and found that Ash had been speaking the truth about being her friend when he insisted that he would drive her back to London.

'The trains may not have resumed a full service after the holiday yet,' he reasoned. But added after a moment or two's thought, 'Though I'll need to fill up with petrol first.'

Jermaine realised she was putting him to a great deal of trouble, but with Lukas and his treachery spinning around and around in her head she could only feel grateful to Ash for getting her away from Highfield and that cold-hearted monster.

It had gone nine when Ash finally found a petrol station that was open. 'I won't be long,' he said, opening the door after filling up and pointing to the office, where he was going to pay.

She followed his direction, but as weak tears suddenly, unexpectedly, pricked the back of her eyes, she looked away. Pride rushed to the fore, decreeing that no one should see exactly what Lukas Tavinor had done to her.

'Take as long as you like,' she said as brightly as she could, which wasn't all that bright in reality, and as Ash went to settle the account she stared out of the car window, unseeing of anything as the pain of Lukas and his duplicity started to get through the barrier she was trying to erect.

Ash could have been away two minutes, or twenty. Her head was so full of Lukas, of the way they had been with each other last night. For all she knew, he could have last night gone straight from her room to Edwina's.

Ash had started up the car when a shaken dry sob caught Jermaine out. She quickly turned it into a cough, but saw Ash glance swiftly at her. 'Jermaine, I...' he began, as if her cough hadn't fooled him at all.

'Don't, Ash,' she said tightly.

'All right, love,' he agreed, but went on, 'Er—do you mind if we don't go on the motorway?' Adding, before she could answer, 'The thing is, while naturally I'm only too pleased to take you anywhere you want to go, I was on my way to do an errand across country.'

Jermaine managed to find a smile. 'I'm truly grateful to you, Ash,' she replied, when what she really wanted to do was to get back to her flat with all speed, close the door, and perhaps keep it that way until it was time for her to return to work. 'Please do your errand first. I'm in no hurry,' she assured him.

The errand Ash had to do added about forty minutes to the journey. He pulled up outside a house out in the wilds somewhere. 'I won't be long,' he promised, and, true to his word, was soon back.

They were further delayed, though, because Ash didn't want to risk going too fast with the roads still snow laden in parts. To Jermaine's mind, Ash was being excessively cautious. But, she owned, he probably wasn't. It just seemed that way because of her urgent need to be somewhere by herself, where she could lick her wounds in private.

Her head was still besieged with everything that had taken place in the last twenty-four hours when they reached London. Why, oh, why had Lukas called at her parents' home yesterday? Why, when he was so obviously enamoured of Edwina, had he not ignored her father's broadest of hints that he take his younger daughter back to Highfield with him?

Memories of the wonderful time they had shared sledging in the snow tried to get a foothold. She pushed them angrily away. That time was as phoney as Tavinor was phoney.

All she'd been to him was a challenge, a challenge to his male ego; she saw that now. My stars, how could she have been so blind? Had she so soon forgotten his reaction, his 'get thee behind me, Satan' when she'd more or less told him she hadn't yet met the man who would make her want to make love with him?

He hadn't been able to resist the temptation to put her to the test, had he? He'd even put aside his preference for Edwina for a short while. Jermaine swallowed down another dry sob as she recalled how she had been his for the taking last night. He had known that too—test over.

Would he have made complete love to her, had not that door slamming brought him to an awareness that he had another, more experienced and therefore more exciting, willing woman three doors down...?

Jermaine abruptly snatched her mind back from where it was going. She didn't think she could take much more without breaking down, and if that happened she wanted to be somewhere on her own.

Thankfully, a minute later and Ash was pulling up outside where she lived. 'Thanks, Ash,' she said, when on the pavement he extracted her case. 'I'll ring you about that lunch,' she added, out of a need to part from him cheerfully.

'I'll carry your case in for you,' he answered.

'There's no need.' She was talking to his back, and there was nothing she could do but follow him and extract her keys from her bag.

She unlocked the outer door. But when she stretched out her hand for her case, Ash opened the door and went in first. Oddly, instead of making for the stairs once he was inside, he glanced about and, though he knew the way to her flat from the days when they'd used to see each other, he did no more than place her case down on the hall floor.

But, since nothing would surprise her any more—or so she'd thought—Jermaine didn't take much heed, until she suddenly heard him say, 'Been here long?' She turned to see whom he was addressing—and what little colour she had drained completely from her face.

'Thanks, Ash,' Lukas answered. *Lukas!*

Totally and utterly stunned, Jermaine stared at Lukas, vaguely realising that one of the other occupants of the building—most likely having recognised him from a previous visit—must have let him in. But that wasn't important. Because as she stared at Lukas she started to sense that something was going on between him and his brother—Ash didn't seem at all surprised to see Lukas there.

She switched her gaze from Lukas to Ash, 'You *phoned* him?' she accused, bringing out the only logical thought in any of this—while more logic questioned why on earth Ash would do anything of the sort. 'You rang him on your mobile from that garage!' she exclaimed, even as she wondered why, anyway, would Lukas, in response to that call, beat all records to get here before them?

'Make yourself scarce, Ash,' Lukas suggested evenly to him before he could answer her.

'You'll be all right, Jermaine,' Ash looked at her to promise.

'I won't hurt her,' Lukas assured him—and Jermaine came hurtling out of her trance, suddenly outraged.

'That's right, you won't!' she yelled. 'You're both leaving!'

Ash looked doubtful. Lukas settled the matter by ignoring the fact that Jermaine had a murderous kind of glint in her eyes and escorting his brother to the door.

'Be in touch—soon,' Ash requested.

'I will,' Lukas assured him quietly, let his brother out from the building and then, turning slowly around, he looked Jermaine steadily in the eye. 'Now,' he challenged harshly, refusing to let her look away, 'what have you got to say for yourself?'

CHAPTER TEN

WHAT had she got to say for herself? Of all the confounded nerve! Fuming, her eyes flashing fire, Jermaine glared at him. She had expected, before this, that she would feel nothing for Lukas—that her feelings for him would die an instant death the moment she learned of his double-dealing with her sister. It had always happened before. But this time it had not. When she would by far prefer not to, Jermaine found that she still loved the perfidious rat.

'What do you mean what have I got to say for myself?' she flew, enraged. Love him she might, but at this very moment she felt very much like burying something large and sharp in his head.

His steady gaze did not waver, but when, just then, one of her neighbours began to emerge from further down the hall, Lukas enquired, his tone tough and uncompromising, 'Do your want to go the full twelve rounds out here?'

She didn't. She was hurting, and she felt humiliated enough without having half the apartment block knowing all about it. 'Close the door on your way out!' she tossed at him hostilely, and made for the stairs.

She had forgotten her case, but she was too proud to go back down for it while he was still in the building. Evidence that he was still in the building—and she was looking nowhere but straight in front—was there in the fact that, to show her what he thought of her hostile

514

dismissal, Lukas kept pace with her as she stormed up every stair. He was carrying her large case too.

It came in handy for him when, reaching her door, she unlocked it intending to go in, do a swift about-turn and shut the door on him. It didn't work out that way, because as she went to shut the door—she discovered that her suitcase was wedged in the doorway.

Jermaine threw Lukas a speaking look and turned her back on him. It did not surprise her that he followed her, uninvited, into her home. She heard the door close as she walked into her sitting room. She was not feeling any more friendly to him when, reaching the middle of her carpet, she spun round to face him.

'Well?' she snapped. The nerve of him! The utter, villainous nerve of him!

Her fury, it seemed, was not lost on him. He even seemed a bit put out himself, she realised, as he grated, 'I don't know what the hell you're so wild about!' The audacity of it! 'I was the one who was stood up!'

'Stood up?' she echoed—she didn't believe this! He thought he could fool around with her *and* her sister and...

'We had a date, you and me,' he snarled forthrightly—should she require any reminding.

Ooh, was he asking for it—right between the eyes. 'As I remember it, there was a proviso on that arrangement!' she flared. 'It went something along the lines of "If you care anything for me".' Didn't she know the words off by heart? Hadn't she relived them, been enraptured by them all through that long night as she'd waited for dawn to come? But—suddenly she was aware that Lukas seemed badly shaken.

'You're saying you care nothing for me?' he asked tautly.

'There—I always knew you were intelligent,' she lobbed back sarcastically. She wanted him to go. Her anger was on the wane and she was starting to hurt again.

Lukas stared at her unspeaking for some tense moments, then he took a deep and controlling breath. And then, very clearly, he clipped, 'I don't believe you.'

Anger, born of panic that he might see just how deeply she did care for him, became her ally again. 'I don't give a button what you believe!' she hurled back at him fiercely.

'You'd have me think you were the way you were with me last night—and didn't care for me?' Trust him to bring that up! 'You'd have me believe you didn't care for me whatsoever, yet would have given me what you've given no man?'

'Charming!' she derided.

'You deny it?'

She wished she could. He knew her too well, it seemed. She turned away, presenting him with her back. 'Why have you come?' she asked dully—and started to feel more churned up inside than ever when she realised he must have taken a couple of steps closer to her. For his voice was directly behind her when he answered.

'I've come, basically, because I find it too difficult, too hard, to contemplate that you have no feelings for me at all. I've come because...'

'Don't,' she stopped him. 'Don't, Lukas.' She drew a shaky breath that was a half-sob, and supposed he must have heard it, for the next she knew he had taken an urgent hold of her shoulders. She shrugged him angrily away. 'I *saw* you!' she cried on a flare of anger, her emotions riding high.

'Saw me?' Lukas questioned, taking his hands from

her at the distress he picked up in her voice. 'What do you mean, saw me?'

'I'm used to being the "also ran" when men see Edwina as the better option,' Jermaine answered, striving mightily to keep herself together. 'I just foolishly thought—thought—oh, never mind!' she snapped. For heavens' sake, she'd nearly told him that she'd thought he might prefer her, rather than her sister. Almost told him that she'd thought he was different from the others—indicating that he was special. Good heavens— Jermaine went hot all over—she'd nearly told him that she'd thought that there was something special between her and him—the two of them!

She took a step from him, but before she could go any further Lukas caught a hold of her, and this time when she went to shrug him off he refused to let her go. What was more, it appeared he had grown tired of not being able to read her face, her eyes. For, regardless of her resistance, he began to slowly turn her until at last she was facing him. When she stubbornly refused to look at him he, as obstinately, if gently, placed a hand beneath her chin and brought her head up.

His grey eyes searched into her wounded violet eyes for some seconds, then, very quietly, he said, 'But I do mind, Jermaine.'

'Tough!' she retaliated, but it was a weak effort. She wanted to oppose him, all the way she wanted to oppose him, only it didn't seem so easy now that he was here, in this very room, with her, his eyes holding hers. She supposed she might still be suffering from the shock of seeing him so unexpectedly.

'So you saw me,' Lukas took up, ignoring her opposition and seeming determined to get sorted that for which he must have sped all the way along the motorway to get sorted. 'And this has to have something to do with your sister, or you wouldn't have mentioned her...' He broke off, his brow suddenly shooting back as clearly something he hadn't thought of struck him. 'Oh, my love,' he mourned. 'You saw me in Edwina's bedroom this morning!'

'Too true, I did,' Jermaine answered coldly. How *dare* he call her his love?

'Why didn't you come in and...?'

'That depraved I'm not!' Jermaine erupted volcanically, giving him a violent shove—to no avail. For it seemed, with his hands clamped to her upper arms, that he had not the smallest intention of letting her go. What was more, it looked as though he was starting to get angry himself. The sauce of it!

'What the hell do you think I am that...?' he began to rage—but she wasn't having that!

'Don't you come the holier than thou with me!' she cut in furiously. 'You'd already asked Edwina to stay at Highfield for as long as she liked, and the next thing I know,' she charged on, feeling more and more outraged by the second, 'is that you're in her room, carrying her to her bed, the same way you were in *my* room last night...' Hot colour surged to her cheeks. '...last night carrying me to *my* bed!' Lukas tried to get a word in, but Jermaine was in too much of an uproar by then to let him utter so much as a syllable. 'And we both know what happened then—what would have happened,' she tore into him, 'had not that door slammed somewhere and brought you to the realisation that there was a more experienced, more exciting female a few doors down who...'

'How dare you think that of me?' Lukas interrupted her on a bellow of sound—about the only way he could get a word in—and Jermaine had never seen him so explosively angry. His hands were biting into her arms as 'Hell's teeth!' he raged. 'I *knew* you were different, *knew* you were…' He broke off and, as if striving to put a rein on his fury, took a deep breath—and only then, while still holding her there in front of him, did he release some of the pressure on her arms. Then he took another long-drawn, controlling breath and, looking straight into her eyes, he more calmly stated, 'The only reason I tore myself away from you last night was because making love for the first time will be very special for you.' Her face flamed, and a hint of a smile touched his otherwise serious expression. 'I wanted you to know…' He stopped, then went on, 'I didn't want to rush you—knew I wanted to be alone with you, without interruption. Then that door crashed and gave me pause to realise that if you and your sister are like my brother and me, Edwina could waltz into your bedroom at any time—without bothering to knock. My home seemed crowded suddenly. I…'

At that juncture Jermaine came to an abrupt awareness that his talk of their lovemaking had made her all weak and spineless, causing her to be in danger of believing his every treacherous word. 'No wonder it was crowded—you'd invited too many people to stay!' she flew.

Lukas didn't care for being interrupted either; she saw that from the tightening of his fabulous mouth. But, when she was sure he would cast her to the devil and go rushing back to Edwina, he surprised her by staying exactly where he was and admitting, 'Yes, I did ask your sister to stay a few days longer at Highfield…' He broke off again when Jermaine struggled to be free, but held her firm and doggedly went on, 'But only for the same reason I extended the Christmas invitation to her in the first place. I...'

'I don't need to hear all the gory details.' Jermaine chopped him off disdainfully.

He didn't like that either, she saw, as his jaw jutted, but still he refused to let her go. 'You're going to hear anyway,' he told her bluntly. 'My oath, never have I met such a woman!' he muttered.

'You can say goodbye any time you like!'

'Shut up and listen.' She objected to being told to shut up, but before she could acquaint him, vitriolically, with her objections, he was going on, 'Believe me, and I don't mean to be unkind, but I'd had more than enough of your sister before...'

'It looked like it!'

Lukas tossed her a killing look, but, as determined to have his say as Jermaine was determined not to shut up, it seemed, he pressed on, 'The only reason I tolerated her at all was because, having assured Ash that my home was his home while he searched for the right property to buy, I didn't want to alienate him by showing her the door. Their relationship looked serious in those first few days—for all I knew, he was planning on making her my sister-in-law. I think a lot of him,' he understated. 'I could put up with her if I had to.'

'Oh, the hardships you have to bear!'

He ignored her comment as if she hadn't spoken, but Jermaine didn't miss the glint in his eyes. Manfully, he controlled what he was feeling, albeit that he had to take a steadying breath. But he promptly proceeded to startle her when he went on, 'I've put up with that woman when I've known from almost the beginning that there was absolutely nothing wrong with her back. I've...'

'You knew she was faking?' Jermaine gasped, shock

causing the words to rush from her. 'I mean…' Jermaine tried to recover, feeling guilty at having admitted her sister was a fraud.

Lukas's expression softened. 'You're so loyal to her, my love, but I knew you'd rumbled her from almost the start. That, of course, was the real reason why you refused to come and look after her.'

'I'd—er—phoned her on her mobile,' Jermaine found herself confessing.

'So you knew, before you even saw her, that she didn't require you in attendance?' Jermaine thought she had been disloyal enough, and did not answer. He continued, 'I think it was around then that my once clear and logical thinking started to get a little cloudy.'

'It—did?' Jermaine found herself questioning. She didn't want to ask questions. She wanted him to go—didn't she? But, equally, she wanted not to love him. Always before when she had known herself betrayed she had lost interest in a moment. So why wasn't it happening now?

'It did,' Lukas confirmed, and Jermaine felt all wobbly inside and in need of some severe stiffening of her backbone when, still holding her, Lukas moved her over to her sofa and sat down with her. She wanted to say something sarcastic—such as, Feeling tired?—but as Lukas had stayed here this long when she felt certain he had already endured enough of her acid, further barbs seemed to have temporarily deserted her. 'It was logical, to my mind,' he took up, when he could see that for once she wasn't going to interrupt, 'when Edwina refused to see a doctor or have a nurse—not that she needed either—that one of her relatives should come to Highfield to fetch and carry for her.'

'You weren't having Mrs Dobson doing it,' Jermaine put in.

Lukas smiled. 'We're on the same wavelength at last,' he said softly. But he was determined, it seemed, to tell it how it was.

'You ordered me to come and look after my sister.'

'And you let me know what you thought about that!' He paused. 'I own, sweet Jermaine, that I'm not used to women treating me like that.'

'You didn't care for it?' Why was she smiling back at him? This man was a treacherous toad!

'Why should I? Why, too, should I be irked every time I thought of you? How dared this woman talk to me like that—this woman with a beautiful voice who didn't care who the devil I was if she felt like going for my jugular. You actually told me to go and play with my train set,' he reminded her. 'Can you not see that after that, while of course I wasn't at all interested in you, I decided to come and see you? I left this apartment that night having met a most stunning-looking woman, but a woman whose attitude had annoyed me intensely. Was it any wonder I was unable to put you out of my mind?'

Her heart did a crazy kind of somersault—Lukas thought her stunning-looking! But Jermaine forced herself to remember his duplicity with her sister only that morning. Although somehow her trust in him was starting to kick in, and something, some instinct, was telling her to hear him out—she could trip him up later.

'Was that why you went to tell my parents about Edwina?'

He had the grace to look a smidgen abashed, but revealed, 'I was chatting to Ash when I got back to Highfield about some business I had near Oxford the next day. He told me Edwina's parents lived in that area.' Lukas hesitated, then added, 'Ash also said how your father doted on Edwina.'

'It's not news,' Jermaine inserted, realising that Lukas's hesitation must stem from his sensitivity that she might be upset by that fact.

Lukas gave her hands, which he was still holding, a gentle squeeze, and went on, 'I then asked Ash if your father didn't treat you the same as your sister, to which he laughed and said your mother loved you. When I asked, did you love your mother? Ash said your mother had recently had flu and that he'd gained the impression that you'd do anything for her.'

'So you asked him for my parents' address?'

His lips twitched. She loved him. She rather thought she always would. 'Only very casually,' Lukas answered. 'But I didn't have any definite plans to call on them. Only if my business finished early and I was in the right area.'

Jermaine felt her lips twitching too. 'And, hey presto…'

'I had the added information that your mother might still be feeling a shade tired after her flu and, yes, hey presto—it worked like a charm,' he admitted. 'My only problem from then on, sweet Jermaine,' he added softly, 'having been unable to ask your sister to leave without risking a split with my brother, was that when it became apparent that Ash was quickly getting over his infatuation with her I began to fear that *he* would be the one to tell her to go.'

Something in Jermaine began to ice over. 'Because you were starting to grow infatuated with Edwina yourself,' she stated coldly.

'*No!*' Lukas denied vehemently. 'Never in a million

years! You daft woman, haven't you seen yet that it's *you* I care about?'

Suddenly her emotions were all haywire again, any ice in her veins going into a rapid thaw. 'M-me?' she stammered. 'You care—about me?'

Lukas stared at her. 'Quite desperately,' he replied quietly.

'Oh,' she whispered, and was too dazed to say anything else.

She wished he would smile, but his expression, as his eyes searched hers, was deadly serious. 'Why otherwise would I be here?' he asked.

Jermaine stared back at him, and all at once she wished he hadn't asked that question. He was here because she had bolted from Highfield. And why had she bolted from his home? Because she had seen him carrying her sister to her bed. The same way he had carried her to her bed last night!

Even while part of her was urging her to give him the benefit of the doubt, Jermaine was attempting to get to her feet. 'No,' Lukas denied her, holding her, anchoring her down. 'You...'

'So tell me about Edwina,' Jermaine cut in. This had happened too many times in the past for her to be able to freely give him the benefit of the doubt. She had been hurt in the past, but never anywhere near as badly as now. Before, it hadn't mattered so much. Now, it did. Lukas meant everything to her. 'Tell me about the love scene I witnessed this morning!' she exploded, barely aware of what she was saying. 'Tell...'

'*Love scene!* Utter rot!' Lukas scorned. 'Hells' bells...' He checked, steadied himself, looking nowhere but into Jermaine's lovely violet eyes. 'I hardly slept. Last night,' he confessed, 'I barely slept at all. Bed became torturous. I was going to see you again, but not until half past eight. I don't know how I got through those sleepless hours—what if I'd got it all wrong? You were different from any other woman I'd known; I knew that. What if, because I wasn't used to anyone like you, I'd misread what I'd imagined were positive signs? What if, because of your innocence, you were giving off the wrong signals?' Lukas halted, then further owned, 'My room became a cage. I left it—quietly, I thought. But Edwina must have heard me, because when, after prowling outside for a while, I came back in and up the stairs, her bedroom door was wide open and she was in a state about some over-large spider on the rampage.'

'She called you in to *catch a spider?*'

'I very much doubt now that there was any such bold arachnid. But at the time I'd got you so much on my mind I thought it best to deal with it quickly—I wanted to be first at our bench. Anyhow, when Edwina fainted, I...'

'Edwina fainted?'

'I thought she had. She appeared to go limp from the shock of seeing the eight-legged animal. It was instinctive to catch her before she hit the carpet. What...?'

Remembering the way her sister had looked directly at her a moment before she'd closed her eyes, Jermaine spoke her thoughts out loud, relief, joy trying to break free. 'Edwina didn't faint.' Lukas hadn't been duplicitous.

'You—sound sure?'

'She does a good faint,' Jermaine answered.

'She's done it before?' Lukas asked, but could see that Jermaine's loyalty was being stretched to the limits, so didn't press her for an answer, but said instead, 'I thought her grip was a bit fierce for somebody who'd passed out. When she wouldn't let go of me after I'd put her on her bed I began to suspect there might be a little play-acting going on there.' He paused, and then revealed, 'She certainly came round pretty quickly when I said I'd get Mrs Dobson to sit with her until she felt better.'

Jermaine had to smile. 'Edwina wouldn't think much of that.'

'I don't think she did, but I'd got other plans. I'd waited for hours to see you, and I couldn't take waiting much longer. No way was I going to call you to hold her hand. To be honest, my dear, if you were going to hold anybody's hand, I wanted it to be mine.'

'Oh,' Jermaine whispered shakily.

Lukas raised her right hand to his lips. 'You believe me, love?' he asked earnestly. 'You believe me that I am not, and never have been, remotely interested in her? Believe my being in her room this morning happened the way I've just said?'

Jermaine knew her sister, knew quite well what she was capable of. It was just that in her adult life she had grown used to male friends deserting when Edwina beckoned.

But Jermaine realised that, as Lukas seemed to think she was different, so she could trust that Lukas was different. She didn't doubt that he knew a lot about women—and began to take in that he had seen through Edwina straight away and had been unimpressed by her. Then it was that Jermaine knew that believe him she did.

But because she was so much in love with him, she owned, it had made her devastatingly vulnerable where Lukas was concerned. Because of past happenings Jermaine still felt on distressingly shaky ground—it seemed impossible that when others had forsaken her for Edwina's charms Lukas was totally immune to them.

'You—um—asked Edwina to stay?' Jermaine reminded him quietly.

For an answer Lukas leaned forward and gently kissed the side of her face. 'It was you I wanted in my home,' he told her softly, and confessed, 'Where at one time I couldn't wait for her to leave, the more I grew attracted to you, the more I realised that if Edwina left you'd leave too. That, in fact, if she wasn't there, you wouldn't come to Highfield at all.'

'You wanted me there?'

'So much. One date with you wasn't enough. One hour with you, two, three, were too quickly passing. I wanted a day with you, two days with you.'

Oh, Lukas. Her heart was pounding. Oh, she did believe him; she did! 'You invited me to stay for Christmas,' she whispered dreamily. 'You invited me to spend Christmas with you.'

'Of course I did. I'd discovered a serious need to see you more and more. Yet I was going away. Lord knew when I would see you again. If you spent Christmas at Highfield, I stood every chance of seeing you on Christmas Eve, the first day of my return.'

Suddenly Jermaine was smiling. 'And when I refused you invited Edwina to stay, thinking—no, not thinking, plotting—that if you came to my parents' home when you were "in the area" on Boxing Day, Edwina might be a lever...'

'In my persuasion to get you to come back with me,' Lukas finished for her, and, looking deeply into her eyes, 'You believe me, Jermaine?' he asked.

She looked back at him, her insides all of a tremble at the warmth and sincerity in his grey eyes. 'I believe you,' she said simply, and felt her bones go weak when the most wonderful smile lit his face.

She thought for a moment that he was going to take her in his arms, but he checked, and instead said, 'Then now, my dear, dear, Jermaine, may we have that discussion which I'd hoped to have several hours ago back at Highfield?'

Jermaine swallowed. 'The—um—one…?'

'The one that began with the two of us meeting, if you cared anything for me,' he encouraged. 'You had intended to be there—at our bench?'

Jermaine smiled a shy smile. 'I couldn't sleep either. I was early leaving my room.'

'Darling,' he breathed, and did then gather her in his arms. 'I love you so much,' he murmured. 'I was at the bench well before eight-thirty. At nine o'clock I bleakly returned to the house, not wanting to believe what I had to believe—that you cared nothing for me.'

'You waited in the cold for over half an hour!' she exclaimed.

'I couldn't believe you wouldn't come hurrying around the corner. Still didn't believe it when I got back to the house. I went up to your room; your case had gone, your belongings had gone—everything except that painting I gave you. It seemed to me then that you had quite clearly given me your answer. But, just as I was starting to despair, Ash rang and said he had you with him and that he had never seen you so upset.'

'You told him to delay getting me back here so as to give you time to get here first?'

'Too true. I told him to drive miles out of his way, call at any house as if he had business there if he had to. I'm sorry, my love,' Lukas said softly, 'but I wasn't ready to admit defeat. I just couldn't, or wouldn't, believe I'd got it so wrong. Arrogant it may be, but, after last night, I just couldn't accept what seemed to be staring me in the face. I chased after you, torn between fury that any woman could make me feel the turned-inside-out way I was feeling—and anxiety in case I lost you.'

Lost her! Her heart was thundering. 'D-did you—um—know you said you—loved me?' she asked huskily.

Lukas, unsmiling, stared into her shy eyes. 'You're embarrassed by my feelings for you?' he asked stiffly.

'Oh, no! No,' she assured him swiftly.

But still he would not smile. 'Then may I take it that, contrary to what you would have had me believe a few hours ago, you do care a little?' he asked tensely.

Jermaine looked solemnly back at him. 'Um—more than a little, actually,' she answered.

Lukas stared at her, unsmiling still, for perhaps about another two seconds. Then, 'Come here,' he ordered—and as he gathered her in his arms she willingly obeyed.

Perhaps five or maybe ten minutes passed while they clung to each other, the pain of parting eased, the anxiety they had endured soothed away. Then gently, tenderly, Lukas kissed her.

'I love you so much,' he breathed. 'Time spent away from you leaves such a void it's like a physical pain. I've felt so empty apart from you.' Jermaine could barely believe her ears, and yet it was all there—his love—in his eyes, his face, his hold. 'You wouldn't mind elucidating a bit on the fact that you care for me ''more than a little,'' I suppose?' he queried, and seemed to be sorely in need to hear more.

Although they were words she'd never spoken before, and she felt shy to utter them, it was because of his need to hear them, that she told Lukas, 'Well, to be honest, the plain truth is—I love you—um—very much.'

'Sweet love!' And with that joyous cry Lukas held her and kissed her, and kissed her and held her. For a short while he seemed content just to hold her close, to glory in being able to hold her this close to his heart as all barriers started to tumble down. 'When?' he asked.

Jermaine drew back. 'Not at first.' She smiled.

'Certainly not at first,' he agreed. 'I wasn't at all nice to you.'

'You were a pig!'

'You're gorgeous.' He grinned, and kissed her. 'When?' he repeated, and she laughed from the pure joy of being with him. Seeing her laugh, he just had to kiss her again.

'When?' *she* asked.

'Cheat,' he replied, but willingly told her, 'Soon after you came to stay that first time, I think.'

'Back then?'

He nodded. 'We were working, yet when always before I've tended to be thoroughly absorbed in my work, I found that Friday with you there in the study with me I was repeatedly losing my concentration. You're so incredibly beautiful, my love, I found I kept looking over to you time and time again.' He kissed the tip of her nose, and smiled as he went on, 'Experience has taught me that outer beauty can hide an inner ugliness, but, given that you'd given me some lip, I just knew that you were beautiful throughout. When I started to get peeved that there seemed to be something going on between you and Ash, I had to face up to it—I was just a tiny bit attracted to you.'

Jermaine's eyes were shining with her love for Lukas as she looked at him. 'Anything between Ash and me was over before I met you,' she said gently.

'I know. I've known for some time.' He hesitated, and

then confessed, 'That didn't stop me from being tormented by jealousy again last night when he kissed you.'

'You *were* jealous!' she exclaimed.

'Not for the first time,' he agreed. 'If it wasn't Ash gnawing at my gut, it was your friend Stuart.'

'Stuart!' She had to laugh. 'Stuart's a friend, a work colleague,' she explained. 'We're pals, nothing more.'

'I'm relieved to hear it,' Lukas answered. 'Do you kiss all your work colleagues?' he wanted to know.

'As a matter of fact, I—don't,' she laughed. But sobered to quickly assure him, 'You've absolutely no need to be jealous of Stuart—or Ash either,' she thought she should mention.

'I realise that now. In fact, I knew last night about Ash, when you said that he wanted the two of you to be friends.'

'You did?'

'Ash and I settled matters when I decided I'd have to have a talk with him about you. Only seeing him kiss you last night, as you so rightly guessed, had that green-eyed monster jealousy letting me know what for.'

Jermaine stretched up and kissed him, but pulled back to exclaim, 'You decided to have a talk with him about me?'

'It had to come,' Lukas said. 'It was the last Saturday when you were at Highfield. Ash hadn't known you were coming and said he hoped you weren't dashing back to London. You replied that you were staying to type up the report on my Swedish trip.' At that juncture Lukas stopped, and then asked, 'Are you going to hate me if I tell you what Ash already knew—but you didn't?'

'I hope not,' she answered warily. And pressed cautiously, 'What did Ash know that I didn't?'

'He knew that I'd taken my PA with me to Sweden.

Phyllis Gladstone's name is a byword for efficiency. He knew as soon as you mentioned that I'd asked you to type the report on my Swedish trip I was up to something.'

Jermaine owned herself lost. 'Up to something?'

'Oh, dear,' Lukas murmured. 'Confession time is at hand.' Though first he gently kissed her, then pulled back to reveal, 'Don't hate me, sweet love, but Ash instantly knew that Phyllis Gladstone would have had that report already typed and ready for action before we'd even left Sweden.'

Jermaine's mouth dropped open. 'You...? She...? It was already typed?' she questioned incredulously. 'But—but why did you need it typing again?'

'I didn't. What I did need was some time alone with you.'

'You mean...?' Her stunned brain came rapidly awake. 'You're saying you—invented that work...?'

'So I could have your company all to myself without your sister batting her eyes at my wallet, or my brother trying to make off with you.'

'Good heavens!' Jermaine gasped. His lips moved upwards, and she loved him all over again. So she kissed him, was kissed in return, and totally forgot for the moment what they had been talking about. But, suddenly remembering, she recalled, 'You went—that afternoon—you went with Ash to view his new property.'

'I went with Ash because the time to have things out with him could no longer wait.'

'H-have things out with him?' she echoed, faintly staggered that things seemed to have been going on of which she knew nothing.

'My darling girl,' Lukas said softly. 'I'd taken you to an art gallery the evening before, and, watching various emotions cross your lovely face, hearing you laugh your lovely laugh, I started to fall head over heels in love with you. By the time I'd brought you back here, while knowing I had to go away on Monday until Christmas Eve, I was so much in love with you I just couldn't face going away and not seeing you again.'

Her mouth fell open. 'That was when—that night we were having dinner—you'd just swopped your meal with mine because I thought yours looked better, and you laughed—and I fell in love with you,' she confessed.

'Oh, love,' he breathed, and gathered her closer, kissing her hair. 'Would you have come to Highfield the next day, had I not invented Mrs Dobson needing help?'

Jermaine laughed. 'Of course,' she admitted. But, as she suddenly realised what he was saying, 'You already knew Mrs Dobson had all the help she needed?' she accused.

'Guilty as charged,' he agreed with a smile. Though that smile was totally absent when, going back to his discussion with his brother that Saturday, he explained, 'By the time Ash and I set off, ostensibly to do some house-viewing, all I knew was that I loved you so much that if Ash loved you too this would be one time when I would not be able to assist him all the way.'

'Ash doesn't love me,' Jermaine put in quietly.

'I knew that as soon as he admitted the truth of his behaviour. I'd no idea until he told me that he'd been going out with you *and* succumbing to your sister's charms at the same time.'

'Didn't I say?'

'You know you didn't,' Lukas answered tenderly. 'I can't see you putting the dirt down about either Edwina or Ash. But my anger with him that he could have treated you so was tempered by the fact that, if he could treat you like that, then he certainly didn't love you the heart-and-soul way that I love you.'

'Oh, Lukas,' Jermaine whispered, and received a wonderfully tender kiss in return.

'So, having established that Ash is extremely fond of you, I had his blessing to tell you of my love for you and...'

'You told Ash that you loved me?' she asked surprised.

Lukas nodded. 'He'd guessed—with regard to the *lack* of necessity of you and I spending time alone in my study—that something was going on.' He paused, and then revealed, 'Ash wished me well. You don't hold his behaviour against him? he asked.

'No,' she said simply. 'He was a little gem helping me today. And,' she added as an afterthought, 'phoning you behind my back to let you know what was going on.'

The both smiled. Smiled and kissed, and kissed some more, holding each other tightly as though wanting nothing to come between them ever again. 'You'll never know the relief it is not to have that jealous demon perched on my shoulder,' Lukas confessed, planting a delicious kiss on the corner of her mouth.

'Er—I've had my jealous moments too,' Jermaine felt honour-bound to confess.

'You have?' he queried delightedly.

'You needn't look so pleased,' she laughed. Lukas loved her. Wasn't that just too wonderful? 'Beverley Marshall,' she announced. 'I thought Beverley was a "she".'

'You felt jealousy before you knew? Back then?' he asked incredulously.

'I wasn't calling it that at the time,' she owned. 'But

I thought you were out with some female named Beverley when one night at Highfield I was at dinner but you weren't.'

'It was a Saturday,' Lukas instantly recalled. 'I'd kissed you and, for my sins, was feeling slightly adrift. I didn't like the feeling—I've always been the one in charge,' he inserted self-deprecatingly. 'I decided I needed to get away from you for a while.' Jermaine was still staring at him wide eyed, when he prodded, 'But tell me more.'

'You mean who else was I jealous of besides Beverley? There was Edwina, of course,' she admitted slowly.

His expression grew serious. 'I was never remotely interested in her,' he assured her gravely.'

'I know—now,' Jermaine said quickly. 'It was just that, well, when you phoned her from Sweden...'

'I didn't phone her, I rang Ash,' Lukas cut in. 'Edwina happened to answer the phone.'

Hearing him say that caused Jermaine to wonder why she hadn't worked that out for herself. Edwina was a past master at hints, evasions and downright untruths. 'I'm sorry,' Jermaine apologised, 'You'd think by now that I'd know better...' She broke off. But when, from loyalty to her sister, she would have left it there, she suddenly realised that from now on Lukas was the most important person in her life, and that because that was so she wanted none of her sister's past barbs and upsets to come between her and the man Jermaine loved. 'I've been...'

'You've been, my darling?' Lukas encouraged.

'A fool, mainly,' she admitted. 'Getting all stewed up that you kissed me that Friday when you returned from Sweden but then went home to Edwina. When, since she was a guest in your home, where else would she be? Even if it was late when you arrived back at Highfield...'

'And found Edwina lying in wait, as it were. Sorry, sweetheart, I know she's your sister, but you're the one I'm going to marry, and I'm not having you upset...' He broke off at the stunned look on Jermaine's face. 'What?' he questioned urgently. 'What...?'

'Do you know what you've just said?' she gasped.

'Explaining about having to be nice to your sister because she is just that—your sister? I'm sorry, my love, but I can spot a money-grabber from a mile off. I don't want to hurt you, sweet love, but I want nothing to cloud what we have. I want you to know exactly how it was— is—with me. How I've been love-sick to see you. How I wanted quite desperately to phone you while I was away the last time, only to discover that—having never been in love before—my self-confidence had taken such a hammering I was scared to ring in case the call went all wrong, and I'd be left stuck overseas feeling even worse and more love-sick than ever.'

'Oh!' Jermaine gasped on a whisper of sound. Dared she believe she was hearing what she was hearing; had she heard what she thought she had heard?

'My dear love,' he went on tenderly, 'I was hoping with all I had that you'd come back to Highfield with me yesterday—Mrs Dobson has been on red alert to have your room ready ever since I knew where my heart lay.'

Jermaine's eyes were saucer wide. 'Oh!' she gasped faintly again.

'Christmas Day was the worst of my life,' he went on to reveal. 'I wanted you with me, and, since that hadn't happened, I wanted no other company. Edwina was my guest, but I found there was only so much of her wittering I could take. So I prevailed on Ash to keep her company while I shut myself in my study and planned various courses of action if you refused to come back with me the next day.'

'Oh, Lukas,' Jermaine sighed.

'Jermaine,' he murmured, and kissed her, and confessed, 'And when, glory of glories, you did come back with me, I started to get all chewed up that if Edwina left you wouldn't see any reason to stay on at Highfield either.'

'So you asked her to stay as long as she liked,' Jermaine put in, her heart racing.

'I don't think I put it quite like that, but since it was *you* I wanted in my home I might well have gone over the top a bit in my bid to get closer to you—to have you with me for ever.'

For ever! Her heart did not merely race, it jumped and sped, and her throat went dry. 'Er...' she tried.

'What?' Lukas pressed when she seemed stuck for words. 'You know you can tell me anything, ask me anything—we are as one now.'

Oh, my heavens! *As one!* 'I—er—well, did you say what I thought you said?'

'Tell me,' he said urgently. 'If I've said something wrong, I'll mend...'

'You said something about marrying me, and...' His stunned expression caused her to break off, and she went scarlet. 'I'm sorry,' she said quickly. 'I misheard.' She went to stand up, but Lukas had no intention of letting her go.

'There's nothing wrong with your hearing,' he swiftly let her know.

'You're shocked?'

'True,' he agreed, holding her fast when again she tried to get away. 'But only because I've just realised that, as proposals go, I didn't do that very well. Forgive me, my darling,' he urged. 'There's been such a welter of anxiety within me, a need to clear away all misunderstandings—a need, basically, to get you to be willing to see me as a suitor—that I've missed the most important part.' Tenderly, then, Lukas looked into her wide violet eyes. 'I love you so much, Jermaine,' he told her quietly. 'And you've said that you love me. So am I hoping for too much, do you think, by asking you to marry me?'

She had never felt so fluttery inside. 'No,' she answered, unable to bear his tense expression as he waited. But, suddenly unsure if that should have been a yes, 'I mean, no, you aren't asking too much,' she added quickly.

But Lukas did not smile. 'Then, will you, Jermaine Hargreaves, marry me?' he asked.

She smiled, because she loved him. 'I'd be honoured,' she answered, and was pulled against his thundering heart for long, long seconds. Then, tenderly, he kissed her

'Thank you, my darling,' he breathed, and for an age just sat feasting his eyes on her, until, holding her close and still looking deeply into her eyes. 'I feel I want to shout the news that you've agreed to marry me from the rooftops. May I start by ringing Ash and telling him, my love, that Santa did bring me what I most wanted, after all?'

Look forward to all these
★ ★ wonderful books this ★
Christmas ★

BETTY NEELS
MARGARET WAY
JESSICA STEELE
All I want for
Christmas

Precious Gifts
Marion Lennox   Josie Metcalfe
Kate Hardy

Together for
Christmas
Leanette Kent & Sherryl Woods

Jasmine Cresswell   Kate Hoffmann
Tara Taylor Quinn

The
CHRISTMAS
VISIT
Margaret Moore
Gail Ranstrom
Terri Brisbin

SILHOUETTE
SNOWY
NIGHTS

HEATHER GRAHAM   LINDSAY McKENNA
MARILYN PAPPANO   ANNETTE BROADRICK

XMAS/LIST

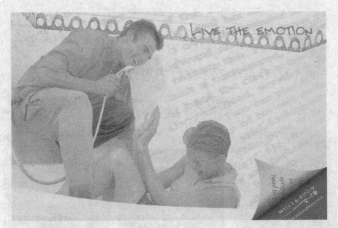

Modern
romance™
...international affairs – seduction and passion guaranteed

Medical
romance™
...pulse-raising romance – heart-racing medical drama

Tender
romance™
...sparkling, emotional, feel-good romance

Blaze™
...scorching hot sexy reads

Historical
romance™
...rich, vivid and passionate

28 new titles every month.

Live the emotion

MILLS & BOON®

MB5 RS

Modern
romance™

...international affairs – seduction and passion guaranteed

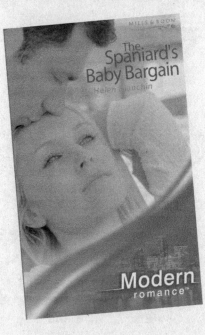

8 brand-new titles each month

Available on subscription every month from the Reader Service™

GEN/01/RS3

Medical
romance™

**...pulse-raising romance –
heart-racing medical drama**

6 brand-new titles each month

*Available on subscription every month from
the Reader Service™*

GEN/03/RS3